The Primrose Path

The Primrose Path

Susan Giles

Matador
5 Weir Road
Kibworth Beauchamp
Leicester LE8 0LQ, UK
Tel: (+44) 116 279 2299
Fax: (+44) 116 279 2277
Email: books@troubador.co.uk
Web: www.troubador.co.uk/matador

ISBN 978 1848764 965

British Library Cataloguing in Publication Data.
A catalogue record for this book is available from the British Library.

Typeset in 11pt Bembo by Troubador Publishing Ltd, Leicester, UK

Matador is an imprint of Troubador Publishing Ltd

Printed in Great Britain by the MPG Books Group, Bodmin and King's Lynn

For mother

Chapter One

The teacher decided to play for time, to withhold her response to the headmaster's allegation for a moment or two longer. She stole a glance around her classroom, the classroom that had been her domain for the past 15 years. The desks were now unattended, uncluttered, cleared of the accoutrements of learning – pens, pencils, exercise books; all had been put away. Shelves were tidy, cupboards closed; even the wastepaper baskets had been emptied. Now all that remained, once she had dealt with Geoffrey Harding, was to place the chairs on the desks ready for the cleaners to come in. An hour ago the room had been alive with boisterous ten-year-olds, joyful that school was over, thrilled that the summer holiday had finally come round. She wouldn't see them again for six weeks.

Her gaze came to rest on her desk and the pile of greetings cards neatly stacked there. Her class had brought them in for her. They always did that, every end of term… and on her birthday. Later she would take the cards home, where they would be displayed for a few days – before being discarded, put out with the newspapers for recycling. So many things were recycled nowadays: paper, glass, aluminium… teachers. Eloise James had a feeling her turn was coming soon. Maybe not in her professional capacity, but time was running out in another department nonetheless. Not that she could do anything about it. It had happened before, and no doubt it would happen again. That was the nature of recycling.

She turned back to face Geoffrey Harding. 'No, I'm not... not really.'

'Yes you are,' he said forcefully, ignoring her qualification. 'Admit it. You're chained to the past.' He stood tall, erect, his hands plunged taut in his jacket pockets, gazing down at her with mocking eyes... challenging eyes. It was his headmaster's posture, confident, assured, and sometimes – like now – boyishly arrogant. But Eloise had grown accustomed to it. She knew it was mostly show – a male display tactic – his preamble to mounting an argument. 'You're emotionally tethered,' he went on, 'like a puppy dog – a little puppy dog at the beck and call of a ghost.'

For a moment, she thought of making a yapping noise, or a whining one. But he was too serious, too intense for that – and she had no intention of pouring fuel on his fire. He could do that very well himself. 'I don't believe in ghosts,' she said.

'You don't have to, Eloise. It's enough that they believe in you.' He peered down at her. 'When you're engaged in one of your *episodes*, you switch off from the real world. You don't want to go anywhere, do anything. You lose interest in everything, apart from your past.'

She faced him, held his steady stare, which, she noted with amusement, as well as being accusing also contained more than a modicum of impatience. He wasn't used to facing contradictions from his staff in the classroom, even from her. 'So I lose interest in my job, in the kids, is that what you are implying?'

His eyes became scornful. 'You know very well that I am not referring to that – so don't try to avoid the issue.'

'I'm not,' she said evenly. 'But, anyhow, you're exaggerating my *detachment*.' Her emphasis was an ironic one, as was her choice of word, but Geoffrey appeared to miss her point, and his stare remained unchanged. She shrugged. 'But I think you will find that most women of my age come with a past.'

'Of course,' he said, moving closer. 'I am not denying that. But where theirs is an historical fact, dead and buried, your past is in the here and now, very much alive and kicking… kicking too damned hard.'

Eloise shrugged dismissively. She didn't want this quarrel to develop into a full-blown row. Not another one. What was the point? He always thought he was right; and he was… to a degree. 'I think you are exaggerating,' she repeated coolly, edging closer to her desk.

Geoffrey heaved a sigh and folded his arms across his chest. 'In all my days I have never known anybody quite so evasive as you, Eloise,' he said, shaking his head wearily. 'I wish you could be more honest with yourself – then perhaps you could beat this thing.' Eloise remained silent, trying to find a legitimate way to avoid his piercing stare. She knew that he felt hard done by, that he felt she was being disingenuous in her claims. But his frustration seemed so disproportionate to the scale of the disagreement… And she had tried. 'And you think that I exaggerate,' he continued. 'But I do not. You're contrary… Inconsistent. Your left hand doesn't know what your right hand is doing.' He paused. 'You could play a solo game of paper-scissors-stone without fear of cheating.'

Eloise stood her ground. 'You say that my performance here is unaffected. And I run a home… I shop… I cook. I do everything expected of a working housewife.' She fell silent, thinking. But of course, these were not Geoffrey's areas of complaint. His grievance was a more personal one. 'And if I have failed to please in another discipline,' she went on spiritedly, 'then I am sure that my past has absolutely no bearing on it whatsoever.'

Her words appeared to make up his mind for him. 'All right, then, I say yea, you say nay.' He paused, eying her speculatively. 'Let's see if the yeas have it.' And with that, giving her no time to react, he caught hold of her upper arms, pulled her forward and placed his mouth fixedly on hers, instantly moving his head in pursuit of her attempt to avoid the kiss.

He was a big man, powerfully built, a former rugby blue for his college – and he kept himself fit. Yet even though she was petite, less than half his weight, and a good head shorter, she nonetheless managed to break partially free. 'You've had a drink,' she said, trying to free her arms from his grasp. She tasted her lips. 'You've been drinking whisky.'

'Just one,' he said. 'It's my tradition. Every end of term, when I see the last pair of heels skip out the gate, I always have a drink – you know that. It's got nothing to do with this.' He tightened his grip on her arms. 'But enough talk, I intend to prove my point; I intend to have my way.'

'I don't want to, Geoffrey,' she said, trying anew to free her arms, and breathless from the exertion. 'Not here.' With an effort, she succeeded in getting her hands between their bodies, onto his chest, and attempted to push him away. 'Somebody might come in.' It was better that he thought it place rather than person. And of course it was: she loved him – but she was damned if she were going to allow him to bend her over her desk, like an animal.

He didn't answer and shuffled her backwards into a

corner of the classroom, by the door that let onto the corridor, there to hold her into the right angle formed by the two walls. 'No one's going to do that,' he said. 'The kids certainly won't return, everybody has gone home, and the cleaners always start in the first-year building. We've got plenty of time to ourselves, plenty of time for a little extra curricular activity, a spot of end-of-term fun.' He looked down at her, subduing her struggles with professional ease. One of his hobbies was jujitsu, and he was a black belt in it. 'And if you're really worried, look, I'll make us nice and secure.' He extended a hand, and, maintaining her imprisonment with his other arm, put the catch on the door. 'There you are,' he said. 'Nobody will disturb us now.' Then, leaning his bulk against her chest, he reached down and started to ruckle up her skirt.

'For God's sake, Geoffrey,' she said as calmly as she could manage. 'Remember where you are, and control yourself.' She tried to kick his leg, but he avoided the blow and lifted her off the floor, guffawing as he did so. He seemed to think it a joke. Well, it wasn't. She kicked out again, but now she had no leverage, and her kick spent itself ineffectively, flailing in mid-air like a lopsided pendulum. 'Put me down,' she said. But even to her, her words sounded comical, appeared merely to emphasise her physical vulnerability. 'If you don't, I'll scream.'

He set her back onto the floor. 'Don't be infantile, Eloise,' he said, reaching for her skirt once more. 'You may work with infants but that's no reason to act like one.'

'I am not,' she said, managing to catch his stare. 'You are the one doing that.' She glared at him. 'And I want you to stop. Now.' Then she trod with all her available weight on his foot.

But her manoeuvre had no obvious effect, and he pinioned her arms against her sides, holding her as if she were no more than a rag doll. 'I'm going to do it, Eloise.' He paused to quell another of her struggles. 'Be in no doubt of that. I'm going to do it – and there's nothing you can do to stop me.'

It occurred to her then that he might have temporarily lost his mind, that the prospect of the long summer break had kicked off some kind of psychological insouciance. Or that he had watched too many smutty films. She knew that he had downloaded some from the Internet. Eloise tried to turn sideways, left, right, any which way to escape his capture. But he had her immobile. Then she felt him reaching for her skirt again, felt him bunch the material into his hands. 'Geoffrey… Please let me go.'

'After I've had my way, my dear.'

There was a chill in his voice, a ring of certainty, and she grasped his wrists in her hands, locked her forearms at the elbow, and fought to match his strength. With her arms braced like this, she realised that she could exert more resistance than she had previously thought possible: there was now more likelihood of her being lifted off the floor than of anything else. Eloise felt that she had his measure. But no sooner had that thought come to her than she felt her elbows begin to bend. It was like trying to resist a pneumatic machine. She tried again to kick at him, but now he had her wedged tightly into the corner, and there was no space for her to effect a back swing. Her kick carried no force. She told him again to stop, to let her go – but he ignored her, and she felt her hemline continue to rise.

Facing up to the inevitability of her situation, Eloise experienced a sudden fatigue take hold of her mind, experienced the quiescence of resignation, and mentally prepared herself for Geoffrey's assault. But surely, he wouldn't force her here, not here in her own classroom? If he did that, she would never be able to teach in the room again.

'You'll enjoy it, Eloise,' he said, overcoming her weakening resistance. 'And later we'll laugh about it, about the risqué riskiness of it... About how I made you come in class.'

At once further disquieted, Eloise decided on another tactic. 'I can hear somebody outside in the corridor, Geoffrey.'

'I can't,' he said, ignoring her open-eyed expression. Then he drew her skirt higher, exposing her thighs. 'C'mon, Eloise, I told you that nobody would disturb us.' He chortled as he subdued her renewed struggles. 'Come along, don't disappoint your headmaster.' His voice seemed theatrical, staged for the occasion, as if he were acting out a sexual fantasy. And he might well have been: for she knew he was given to such things, that his imagination had a make-believe drift. 'C'mon, Eloise,' he ran on excitedly, 'show me you're a woman, a mature woman who can put her past behind her.' Then, laughing anew, he hooked his thumbs into the waistband of her underwear.

In her mind's eye, Eloise saw the classroom populated by her pupils; she saw each young face turned towards the corner, a miasma of curious eyes fixed on what the headmaster was doing to Miss. 'I said not here, Geoffrey.' She wrestled with him, struggled desperately with his wrists, attempting to push them down, and with them the hem of her skirt. But he was too strong. She shot a glance at the window in the opposite wall, half expecting to see it filled, cartoon-like, with tiers of leering faces, each caricature hell-bent on witnessing her sexual downfall. 'Wait until we get home. Please... Geoffrey.'

Her attempt at appeasement appeared to work, for she felt his grip on her relax. 'Please, Geoffrey,' she encouraged. 'It will be better at home.' She felt his grip relax a little more, and started to ease away. But then, all at once, she felt his grip tighten, and she heard him say:

'Oh, I know you. Tonight it will be different. Tonight it'll be, *not now Geoffrey. I'm tired… I've got a headache, Geoffrey.*' He slid his hands onto her bottom, lifting, kneading her flesh. 'I vote we do it now.'

Eloise experienced her heart perform a somersault. In the front row of desks, the precocious Jamie Bryant turned to his pal Robert Johnson. 'I know what they're doing, Bobby. I've seen my dad do that with my mum. They're doing sexual intercourse.' Using all her strength, she tried to push Geoffrey away. 'No, I won't,' she said breathlessly, pushing at his chest. She lowered her eyes. 'No, I won't. I promise.'

He let go of her, and released her from the corner. 'You were convinced that I was going to do it, weren't you?' he said, taking a step back, and grinning roguishly as he studied her expression. 'Yes, you were. I can see it in your eyes. You look scared to death.' He paused, nodding his head. 'But I've proved my point, Eloise. I've proved my point, and you have lost the argument.'

'No,' she said, smoothing her skirt down over her knees. She walked round him, keeping her distance, maintaining eye contact in case he should come at her again, and stood behind her desk, trembling a little. He meant to do it. It might have started out as something different, a joke, a device to test his assertion, but he would have done it, if she hadn't resisted him… if she hadn't made the promise. 'I never know with you,' she said, clutching the edge of her desk. 'You can be unpredictable at times… Hot-headed even.' She held his stare, his mocking stare, watched his eyes roaming her face. 'And you can be assertive, physically persuasive, when you want your own way, when you want something badly enough.'

'Oh, c'mon, Eloise,' he said, suddenly animated. 'Have I ever coerced you into doing anything?' His look became disdainful, and he approached her desk. 'Have I ever *inflicted* sex on you?'

Under his attack, she lowered her gaze. 'No,' she replied, shaking her head.

'Damned right I haven't.' He paused, his eyes smouldering. 'That's not my style. That's…' Suddenly his face broke into a grin, and, stepping backwards, he bowed dramatically, with a flourish: he was at once a classical actor taking a curtain call, Sir Francis Drake calling on his queen. 'Nevertheless,' he continued grandiosely, his grin growing wider, 'tonight I fully intend to take up me lady's generous offer.'

A roller-coaster motion – that was what it was – a big dipper of undulating sinusoidal curves, falling and rising, falling and rising, down and up, down and up, seeming to pause at the zenith, only to plunge back down again once the crest had been breasted. And with it came that familiar nausea, memories from long ago, when she had been sick while travelling in her parents' car. Removing her hand from her side, she inched it towards the bedside lamp. With that switched off… But she couldn't quite reach it. She tried again, stretching with extended fingers, like an anxious backstroke swimmer feeling for the pool's edge. But it was not to be done, and the shadow on the wall went on repeating its remorseless rhythm.

Eloise turned a little towards the lamp, tried in tiny timed shuffles to edge closer to it. But still it couldn't be done – and it was impossible to work her way any nearer. And even if she could, she realised then, her hand would always be in the wrong orientation to operate the switch. Eloise closed her eyes... Then opened them again. She looked away... Then returned her gaze. It wasn't pleasant. She didn't want to look. But it was like when someone has a spot on his nose, or a fleck of food on his mouth, and your eyes keep being drawn back to it no matter how hard you try to resist. The lamp had a 100W bulb. That was too powerful. There had been a power cut last week... When those workmen had severed a cable with their digging equipment. They should have known it was there... It should have been marked on their plans. Luckily, nobody had been killed. But if there was another interruption now, that would – but then you never knew how long they would last. Some had gone on for... And those financial accounts for the twinning committee would need finishing tomorrow, otherwise they would be chasing her for them... Oh, yes, and on Monday dig some vegetables... take them across to the refuge... And there was her sight test to book too...

Geoffrey raised himself onto straight arms. 'Christ, Eloise, making love to you is like making love to a cadaver.' He released a protracted sigh of vexation. 'You're just as cold and just as unresponsive.'

Eloise came back from her chores. Geoffrey's pyjama top was unbuttoned, the sides hanging loose like the flaps of a tent, and she could see that his nipples were erect, like little top hats – stiff. That made it worse somehow – as if this visual signal of his ardour were a taunt to her own indifference. 'Sorry,' she replied, closing her eyes. 'I don't–'

'Yeah, I know,' he interrupted impatiently. 'Those chains are reeling you in again, aren't they?'

'It's not that,' she said quickly, eager to rebuff his allegation. 'It's not that.' But she knew he was right. For despite her rebuttals this afternoon, called now to honour her promise, she could not honestly deny the truth of his accusation. It had all come to the forefront of her mind again, in a sense like a dream, but not exactly so. It was more real than that, controlling… Jealous. It was almost as if she were being manipulated by a psychic puppeteer. But that was probably putting it too strongly. She could still think, reason. She still had free will. The problem was, when this thing came upon her, she had no motivation to exercise it.

And doctors were no good. Not one had been able to save a single relationship. They always told you you were depressed, and then prescribed medicines that either made you artificially cheerful or turned you into a zombie – or got you hooked. But she knew that it wasn't depression, not in a strict medical sense anyway. Whenever a mood came upon her, she was quite contented… Had no real desire to be cured. And why would she – for she was reliving that time? It was a classic Catch-22 situation: treatments that addressed the symptoms were no use. She needed something that would treat the cause. And that was impossible.

'It's me then, is it?' he said irritably, still holding himself above her and staring down. 'It's my fault – my poor technique… not enough foreplay. Well, excuse me but I thought you were ready.' He paused, clearly upset. 'I can put on some lubrication, if you're having difficulties.'

'There's no need to be crude, Geoffrey.' She could see the frustration in his eyes – the hurt there too. She loved him. She wanted to please him, and she knew that some times she did. It was just that– 'Geoffrey!' She called his name in protest at the sudden angry thrust that he had aimed into her body.

'Yes, that's the only way I can get a response,' he said scornfully, 'the only way I can get any reaction from you, when you're wallowing in one of your self-pitying moods.' He thrust again; it was a bitter, spiteful lunge, one of pent-up frustration, and she winced.

'Please, Geoffrey… it's not nice.' They exchanged glances. 'I want you to stop.'

He rolled off her and lay on his side, facing her. There was a restless, almost wild, look in his eyes, and his breathing was shallow, rasping; she knew that he was unfinished. 'I want you so much,' He placed an unsteady hand on her breast. 'I want you so bloody much, but I need you to want me too – it's infuriating the hell out of me, Eloise.'

She turned her head towards him. 'I love you, Geoffrey,' she said, placing her hand on the back of his hand. She held his gaze as her brain searched for more words of reassurance. 'I love you,' she repeated. 'You know I do.'

'Do I?' He squeezed her breast, then tugged on the nipple, pinching it sharply between his thumb and forefinger, as he endeavoured to elicit another response. 'I have only your word for it,' he added sarcastically, ignoring her cry of pain.

'That's not true.' She coughed to chase away a sudden emotional spasm from her voice. 'Apart from our jobs, we share so much of our lives; we have so much in common – we do things together. Look at our shared interests: we've got the amateur dramatic society, we swim, we go to the rugby, we travel… We've been over to Canada twice for holidays with Charlotte and her family. We have had some really great times.' She paused briefly. 'And we have or own separate interests, too, which is a good thing in any relationship… You said that yourself.' Eloise lowered her eyes to her hands, which were fidgeting with the duvet. She knew she could have expanded her argument, but it would not have helped, for she also knew she had not addressed his key concern. 'And sex has been good,' she added.

'Past tense,' he said bitterly. 'But you forgot to mention the present that you gave me for my birthday… Oh, and the one for Christmas too.' He paused and scoffed ironically. 'Yes, sorry, you do love me.'

'Now you are being silly,' she said. She placed a hand on his shoulder. 'I do love you, Geoffrey, whatever you choose to believe. Since we've been together, I have been happy.' She ran her hand along his shoulder and onto his neck, then began to massage the taut rib of muscle. 'You have made me happy; but I cannot always be how you want me to be.'

'I'm not demanding slavish devotion, Eloise,' he said. 'You know that. But when you're like this, you shut me out; you become insensate… an emotional automaton. And it can go on for weeks. I try to be patient with you.' She started to speak, but he hushed her into silence. Then, after a few moments, he went on evenly: 'And it's not a question of how *I* want you to be. It's a matter of how *any* woman should be with the man she loves.' He held himself against her hip. 'But of course you can't be with the man you love, can you?'

'I am with the man I love. I'm with you.'

'Physically,' he said. 'Mentally, you're light years away.' He paused. 'No, it's farther than that. Your mind is in another dimension entirely: it's back there in the past, with your ghost lover.' He fell silent again, his expression reflecting both his anger and his frustration. Studying his face, Eloise experienced her heart sink in her chest; she wanted to help him but she didn't know how. If only he could be more understanding. Then she saw his expression change, saw him shake his head, and then she heard him say: 'God, I bet you two went at it like rabbits.'

She looked at him with spirited eyes. 'I wish you wouldn't use language like that, Geoffrey,' she said, angrily. 'It's offensive… And cheap.' She held his stare. 'But, for your information, Paul and I never made love.'

At her words, he propped himself onto an elbow, staring intently at her face, his brow furrowed, his lips pensive. It was as if he were seeing a different person to the one he had come to bed with. 'That's not true.' he said. 'You're joking; you're having me on… Aren't you?'

'No,' she replied evenly, turning away. 'We never made love.' She turned back to him, holding his stare with eyes that were quivering with emotion. 'We didn't need to,' she added.

He continued to scrutinize her face, his gaze searching every emotional hiding place – his eyes focused on her with the resolving power of a microscope. At length, he said: 'I don't believe you.'

Under his examination, she began to experience a sense of unease, a sense of invasive anxiety. It was like being interrogated by someone who knew the answers, or thought that he did – like being counselled by a psychiatrist who had already made his diagnosis from your GP's referral notes. Eloise dropped her gaze. Geoffrey was waiting for a reply, but she decided against giving him one.

'I don't believe you,' he said again stubbornly.

His repeated assertion broke the spell, snapped her out of her silence. 'I'm not lying,' she retorted angrily. 'Paul and I never made love.'

He held her affronted stare. 'No, I didn't mean that. I believe that. It's what you said about not needing to.' A telling look passed across his face. 'But I think you did. I think you did, Eloise – and I think you know it.' He paused, his expression a bundle of triumph. 'The *great* love affair was not consummated… You didn't do it. That's what this is all about, isn't it? It's the catalyst for your woes. You didn't fuck.' He shook his head as if stunned by his conclusion. 'You did not fuck. And that's what is continually dragging you back. It's the thing that has destroyed all your previous relationships.'

She glanced at the wall. 'Of course not,' she said, wishing she could turn off the light, but knowing that he wouldn't let her. But it was so typically a male response; that side of a relationship was so important to them. A psychiatrist had jumped to the same conclusion years ago. She had only visited him once. She turned back to Geoffrey, breathing evenly so as to control her emotion. 'I don't think that I loved any of them… really,' she continued hesitantly. 'I think that I was just lonely, afraid that I would end up an old maid, with no family of my own. I wanted to have a daughter… To be like my mother was with me. And I suppose that I made some poor choices of partners; some relationships fell apart before they had been properly put together. None lasted long enough to commit to starting a family.' She sniffed. 'No, I was just lonely, afraid of growing old with no one of my own.'

He squeezed her arm. 'You didn't address my point, Eloise,' he said, in a tone of reproachful sarcasm. 'Just more evasion tactics.' He pulled the bedclothes over her chest. It seemed to Eloise a gesture of resignation, as if he were giving up on a failed contract, or closing a chapter of his life. 'But that's where I fit in, isn't it?' he continued. 'I'm the latest companion, the latest companion to assuage your loneliness. And, of course, as you yourself said, you didn't love any of us.'

Eloise turned her head on the pillow, sought his stare… And saw that it was one of despondency, of resignation. She knew she had to reassure him of her love, to convince him that she cared, otherwise she was going to lose him. 'I love you, Geoffrey,' she began slowly. 'I suppose that I did love the others, in a way… Or thought that I did, at first. But we were different, you and I. Ours wasn't a rushed-into affair… I suppose none of the others were either, not exactly – I'm not like that.' She paused, holding his stare, gathering her thoughts, trying to find the words that would best convey her feelings, that would make him realise that he had not been used. 'We knew each other for months before you asked me out,' she went on. 'We were sure of our feelings. And we were older… When we met at the school as colleagues… When you came there to work.' Despite the urgency, the gravity of her objective, Eloise felt her thought train drift then to Geoffrey's appointment. The local education authority had classified St Mark's Junior as a 'failing' school. But she knew that it hadn't been that bad – at least not as flawed as the assessment had made it sound. Certainly their examination results hadn't been brilliant, and they had been near the bottom of the government's league tables. But league tables weren't everything. There were so many influences operating in a school that could have a negative effect of them – influences not directly linked to the standard of teaching. In her class alone, there were seven children who could honestly be described as being slow learners. And of course the social mix of the catchment area should have been taken into consideration too. Besides, there was more to education than exam passes. But that was where the government's emphasis had been… Targets… Results – and they had been judged on them. Yet all the staff had worked hard, and grades had been improving – and it had been a little bit of a surprise when Geoffrey had been sent in to "sort things out".

She hadn't taken to him at first. It hadn't been because of any personality issues: it had had more to do with the manner of his appointment. She wasn't normally biased in that way but she'd liked the old headmaster, not for any particular reason other than he left you alone to get on with things. Granted he had been a bit set in his ways, a bit old-fashioned, but to pension him off like that, to put him out to grass after nearly forty years in teaching hadn't seemed quite right. And so, as far as she was concerned, Geoffrey's arrival hadn't been an auspicious one.

Eloise continued to hold his gaze. 'We worked together,' she went on, 'and I came to admire all that you were achieving… How the kids responded to you… The parents too.' She paused, remembering how adults and children alike had responded to his enthusiasm, to his personality. 'Your starting a parent forum was a great idea. I don't know why we hadn't thought of it ourselves… I guess it took a fresh pair of eyes. But it wasn't just your achievements, it was how you accomplished them: you listened to us, answered our questions, discussed our concerns, praised what we were doing, what we had already done. And you convinced us that a few minor changes were all that was required to turn around our academic fortunes.' Eloise smiled wryly. 'But I wish you had warned us beforehand that your few minor changes would involve our taking on a major workload.' She recalled all the out-of-school hours she had put in – and still put in – managing the parent forum. 'And we did improve,' she added. 'We even received a commendation from the local authority in their last assessment. It was a journey for all of us.' She paused, reaching for Geoffrey's hand. 'And somewhere along the way, I fell in love.'

He gazed at her, a level stare, questioning. Eloise couldn't gauge what he was thinking. It didn't seem that he was going to respond to her. Perhaps he wanted her to continue listing his achievements. There were more. But she didn't intend to list every last one of them. She wasn't going to mention his work on improving the school's sports facilities, or expanding the sports programme, if that was what he was waiting for. She had all but written his curriculum vitae already. After a while, she said: 'You know it's true.'

All at once, Geoffrey grinned impishly, the smile touching the whole of his face. 'Remember how we used to joke that Tony Blair had brought us together?' he asked, idly stroking her arm.

'Balls,' she said.

His head jerked in her direction. 'Pardon?'

'Balls,' she repeated. 'It was Ed Balls. He was the schools' minister then.'

Geoffrey nodded slowly. 'Oh, yes, you're right,' he said. 'Nice chap.' He paused, gazing at her. 'I've got a lot to thank him for.'

A tear overflowed her eyelid and ran down her check. She swiped at it with an impatient hand. Her little speech had patched up their row. 'I do love you, Geoffrey, I really do,' she said.

He kissed her neck. 'I apologise for what I said – I was angry.' He paused to brush a stray hair from her cheek. 'I love you, Eloise; and we can beat this thing. I'll be here to help. We can beat it together... If you want to.' He kissed her. 'You do want to, don't you?'

For a little while she gazed at him, absorbing his eagerness, the expectancy of his expression. Yes, of course she did, but she had tried before. And previous partners had tried to help, professionals too – but all attempts had ended the same way. 'I love you,' she said.

He kissed her again. 'That's lovely,' he said. 'But you have to say it. Please say it for me.'

She nodded. 'Yes, I want to,' she said.

'Thank you.' He grinned and guided her hand under the bedclothes and placed it on himself. 'Let's seal our pact,' he added, starting her hand off.

Eloise fought off the impulse to pull her hand away. That would ruin everything. And she did love him. She tightened her hold. He was a bit like the grand old Duke of York in the nursery rhyme: neither at the top of the hill, nor at the bottom of it. But she knew in which direction he wanted her to lead him.

A little while later, Eloise lay on her back staring at the ceiling and listening to Geoffrey's contented breathing, each exhale sounding like a little sigh of pleasure. She glanced across the room. The shadow had gone and the wall was clear again, a pastel shade of rose. It was almost like looking at it through rose-coloured spectacles.

Chapter Two

Bracing herself for the effort, Eloise turned the garden fork over, lifted the plant by its stalk, and shook the loose earth from the potatoes. That was another good crop. A few more like that one and there would be plenty to take to the refuge. She always took vegetables over there, anything that was in season. They were always grateful. The refuge was for women who had fled from domestic violence and had nowhere else to go. It was a registered charity but it received nothing from the government, and its sources of income were limited to the usual charitable exercises: donations, collections of unwanted clothes, jumble sales – those sorts of things. Eloise turned over another fork of earth. Even better this time. The horse manure had been a good investment – and the soil was always better in these mature gardens. She had once owned a brand-new "starter" home, and the soil there had been littered with the builder's debris, from off-cuts of plastic pipes to broken roof tiles. Years into her tenure, and she had still been unearthing the stuff. Her present house was a Victorian terrace, and the garden would have had plenty of use over the years, plenty of digging and fertilisation. She stood up straight and stretched – plenty of aching backs too.

Nudging her spectacles higher on to the bridge of her nose, she focused her gaze on the brambles that were growing along the wall at the bottom of the garden. The blossom was over, and you could see there would be plenty of blackberries there later for making jam. And look at the raspberries; the fruit was almost ready for picking. Her gaze came back up the garden a little way. It had been a good decision to prop that netting over the strawberries, otherwise the birds would have had the lot by now. But this wouldn't get anything done. She started to load a wicker basket with the potatoes, brushing off any remnants of soil as she went.

Then, through the open window, Eloise heard the telephone start to ring. She glanced at her watch. Who could be calling this early in the morning? Well, they could wait. She continued to load the basket; but the telephone went on ringing – a strident call for attention. Pity she hadn't opted for that answer phone service. She'd had one once. But with those things, the telephone always seemed to cut out just as you got to it. And if you had to reply to a message, then that cost you. It might be Geoffrey.

Methodically pulling off her garden gloves as she went, she trudged up the path towards the backdoor. She hoped it wasn't Geoffrey: she was too busy for long-drawn-out conversations right now. But, yes, it might be him: he had said that he would ring in a day or two, to see how she was getting on. Then the telephone stopped ringing. Swearing under her breath, she turned and walked back down the garden path.

There was enough space at the bottom of the garden for an apple tree. Her neighbours, on the right hand side, had one – a Brambly. It would be fun to grow one from seed, like she had with the silver birch. She had collected the seeds one autumn, then kept them in the fridge over the winter in order to mimic natural conditions. It had worked, and now there was a thriving sapling plumb in the middle of the front lawn. There wasn't all that much space round there though, and it would need cutting back eventually. Eloise glanced at the Brambly next door. Maybe an eating apple would be better, a native like a Cox's Orange Pippin. But for pollination purposes you had to plant at least two trees – and they had to be different varieties too. But would there be room for two trees? A russet might be worth trying; they had a sand-papery skin, but a nice taste, perhaps an Ashmead's Kernel, or a… Then the telephone started to ring once more.

Eloise retraced her footsteps, kicked off her boots by the kitchen door, then went through the archway to the living room. Go on then, she dared, eyeing the telephone as she crossed the room, stop ringing, now that you've got me in here. But it didn't and, a little breathless, she lifted the receiver. 'Hello–'

'Eloise! It's Charlotte. Thank goodness you're there.' There was a pause, before Eloise heard Charlotte continue hesitantly: 'Um… are you all right? I mean… I was just wondering if… '

Eloise pressed the silent telephone to her ear, puzzled by her friend's greeting, by the abrupt change in tone – from urgency to indecision. It was as if Charlotte were the bearer of bad news… And loath to pass it on. 'I'm fine, Charlie,' she replied. She tightened her grip on the telephone. 'Is everything all right? David – the family?'

Charlotte laughed nervously. 'Yes. But I just wanted to ask how you are – to say hello. You know me, I like to keep in touch.'

'Charlotte, it's half past two in the morning where you are.'

'Yes, I know,' Charlotte said. 'I realise that… but I had to ring – I really had to. When I woke just now, I had the strangest feeling… Oh, I know you will laugh… but it felt like you weren't there any longer.'

'You mean, like I had passed on?' Eloise said, sliding the phone along the coffee table so that she could reach it from her sofa. Charlie was usually good at giving an explanation, imparting news, clipped speech, straight to the point. It was part of her job. But she was making a hash of this, of whatever she had to say.

'No, it wasn't like that, Ellie – just that you were not there. I can't explain it any better than that… It was a weird feeling – but quite real, tangible. You know, like having a premonition of something you later find out to have actually happened… It felt like you were unreachable, that I wouldn't be able to phone you.'

Eloise sat down. It was likely to be a long conversation – and she had news of her own. 'Well, I am most definitely here; and you have phoned me.'

'You are OK then, Eloise?'

'Yes, I said so, didn't I?' Eloise closed her eyes against the headache that had crept up on her without warning. She would have to take a tablet later. 'And my health is fine, Charlotte,' she said reassuringly.

'Good. But it's just… well, because of the day. I know you've got Geoffrey now but–'

'I hadn't realised it was the anniversary of Paul's death,' Eloise interrupted. 'But, anyhow, look, I…We…' She fell silent, knowing there was no way to avoid telling her friend that another one had gone. Charlotte would have cottoned on soon anyway. She was clever in that way: intuitive… Unlike herself.

'Eloise, something is wrong,' Charlotte broke back in. 'I know you. Something's happened over there.'

'Geoffrey has left me,' Eloise said, as casually as she could manage.

'Oh, Ellie, I am sorry. But… But are you all right? I mean, when did he leave?'

'Last week,' Eloise replied. 'On Saturday… The day after term ended. But I'm fine.' She paused briefly, before adding airily: 'In fact – as the saying goes – I'm quite enjoying my freedom.'

'Oh, Ellie, you should have phoned… But I thought this time… After all, you've been together for–'

'Two years… Almost,' Eloise interrupted. She scoffed, and grinned wryly. 'A record for me.'

'And when you two were over here last, I thought you were so "together": when we went to the theatre, at restaurants, here… all the time. I even said to David that we'd be flying over for the wedding soon. He said yes and that we had best buy some baby things to bring with us.' Charlotte huffed. 'Well, you know what he's like,' she added apologetically.

'I'm a bit past that,' Eloise retorted lightly, squinting over the top of her glasses at an object she knew to be her piano.

'Are you sure that it's over?' Charlotte asked, after a brief pause. 'I mean… As I said, when you were over here last… It was uncanny but it was like you and Paul all over again. The way you and Geoffrey were together, your closeness, oh, little things, your holding hands, how you looked at each other, how you talked, a couple in love–' Charlotte halted abruptly at the little catch of breath that had come to her down the telephone.

Eloise dabbed at the tear that was teetering on the brink of her lower eyelid. She gazed forlornly at the damp patch on the tissue. This wouldn't have happened with any of the others… She put on her glasses and took a deep breath. 'We had a row on Saturday… Well, to be honest, it sort of carried over from the day before. We… We both said some pretty unkind things to each other – him especially.' She gave her friend an abridged account of what had occurred, ending: 'And he said that the ghost in my past was preventing me from making a proper commitment to him… Or words to that effect.'

Charlotte coughed. 'Well… Please don't be upset, Eloise – and allowing that you and Geoffrey have been pretty much on the button – whatever else you two said to each other, he's right on that one, isn't he?'

Eloise clutched the phone tighter. 'What do you mean?' she asked defensively. It wasn't always wise to admit your faults. It did you no good. After all, look what had happened with Geoffrey. She had bared all, and he had still left her. Besides, she didn't want to be drawn into an argument with Charlotte: her friend was good at lecturing.

'Nothing,' Charlotte said levelly, 'other than I think that memories can sometimes prevent people from moving on. Memories are set in one's mind, unchanging. They don't have faults, they can't make mistakes, say the wrong things. How can anyone possibly compete with that?'

'That's tantamount to saying it's my fault – that I'm to blame,' Eloise accused. 'Some friend you are.'

'Ellie, I've known you all my life, ever since we were kids at that school you now teach at.' Charlotte paused. 'And I'm sorry, but from what you've just told me, I think it is your fault… Mostly. You do dwell on the past… And your record goes against you, doesn't it?'

'You're right,' Eloise said tartly. 'He's right. And what's more, before he left, I told him so.' If Charlotte wanted a row, then she could have one.

'You're hopeless.' Charlotte said tersely. Eloise heard her friend's groan come down the line, and turned her attention to the living-room curtains. They were a Laura Ashley design; fawn scrolls on a vermilion background. Geoffrey had put them up. He was very good at that sort of thing. But that was the thing she missed most whenever she was left alone: a man's DIY skills… and of course if anything went wrong with the car. But then, when she was all right again, when her depression had lifted, she missed the other thing that a man was good for. 'But why do you have to be so stubborn about it?' Charlotte was going on. 'Oh, I know you've seen doctors and… and things, but it seems to me you don't really want to put the past behind you. You don't try. Sometimes I think you actually enjoy feeling sorry for yourself.'

'What else can I do?' Eloise asked resignedly, staring through the open window. They were all against her; nobody understood – or wanted to. She had tried. But it wasn't easy, as anybody who had ever suffered depression would confirm. 'Actually, I do try,' she said. 'And I did, last Friday. After our row, when he had calmed down, we discussed things… Everything, including my *dwelling* on the past – as you put it – and he agreed to help me.' She paused, pondering, gazing vacantly at the telephone, fidgeting with the lead. She didn't know whether to tell Charlotte the rest: she could guess what her friend's likely reaction would be. But then a sudden flight of conceit – or was it bravado? – prompted her to run on: 'And on Saturday, he started to help me; he…' She paused, realising her mistake.

'Go on,' Charlotte encouraged.

Eloise decided to press on: Charlie would understand. 'He said the first thing to do was to remove everything that could remind me of the past, and of those times… And… And the first thing was Pal–'

'Oh, God, Eloise,' Charlotte cut in, 'you haven't still got that bloody teddy bear, have you?'

'He took him from the dressing table, and was about to throw him in the rubbish bin… and then we started to row again.'

'Ellie, Ellie, surely you two didn't row over a teddy bear, over a cuddly toy…' Eloise rode out the pause, before hearing her friend go on: 'Yes, you did… But if you feel so strongly about keeping it, then why don't you just put it away somewhere? That's what adults do with childhood keepsakes. I've got things… dolls, cards, knick-knacks in a trunk in the attic right now. Why can't you do the same?'

'I have stuff put away too. But Pal is different. And he is not just a childhood keepsake – and you know it.' Eloise fell silent. 'But anyway, Geoffrey was being unreasonable: that wouldn't have been good enough for him.'

'It sounds to me as if you didn't give him the chance to decide for himself…' Eloise heard her friend's sigh. 'But you were lucky that Geoffrey just argued with you: some men would have throttled you.'

'What else can I do?' Eloise asked again.

'Grow up, Eloise. Oh, and I'll tell you what else, phone Geoffrey and…' But before Charlotte had chance to conclude her advice, the telephone connection became irregular, faltering, causing the pitch of her voice to rise and fall, to overlap eerily, as if the conversation were being conducted in an echo chamber.

'I think we're losing the link or something,' Eloise shouted. 'I'll call you later.'

'Put the bear away, Ellie,' Charlotte shouted in return. Then the line went dead.

Eloise stared at the telephone. Charlotte was wrong. There was no harm in keeping things from the past, things that reminded you of happier times. Golly, one of the teachers at school had dozens of cuddle toys scattered around her flat, and no one suggested that she was childish. But Eloise had always been treated differently: if anyone else did something that was a little unusual, they were merely unconventional, a bit eccentric. But if she did something similar, then she was nutty, insane, in need of psychiatric help. It had occurred to her once that this difference in how she was regarded might have something to do with her habit of trying to explain herself – her reasons, her motives – to other people all the time. It wasn't like making excuses, justifications: it was simply giving explanations to people... out of a sense of needing to let them know. But in doing so you gave people the opportunity to be judgemental, to criticise – you revealed too much about yourself, your character. And maybe this was seen as a sign of weakness, as though you were always trying to please, as though you were afraid of upsetting people – and then you were taken advantage of. People were like that. Nevertheless, it had come as a surprise when Charlotte had taken Geoffrey's side.

Eloise tried to return Charlotte's call, but there was no ring tone. Just as well: if she had got through, in her present mood, she might have lost her friend as well as Geoffrey. She rang a local Exeter number. That worked fine. Eloise placed the telephone back on its mount. So much for modern technology: earlier this morning her Internet connection had failed; now the satellite connection to Winnipeg was lost too.

She went to the kitchen and opened a bottle of wine, then fetched a glass from the cabinet and filled it. She needed cheering up. Through the window, she saw her wicker basket partly loaded with potatoes. She would finish that later. The headache had got worse; a dull throbbing now gnawed at her temples. Eloise took two painkillers, and then took her glass of wine through to the living room. Even though she'd never had one before, it felt like she was developing a migraine. There were several flashing lights in her peripheral vision – and that was how they were said to start.

The wine tasted good, a Château de Camarsac, 2006. Geoffrey had got her started on drinking wine, not much, just a glass now and then. It helped her relax, especially after school. She wondered if Geoffrey would telephone. He had stormed out, angry, upset... Completely lost his temper with her. She poured another glass of wine. The headache wasn't getting any better. But that was the trouble: the painkillers they sold nowadays were useless. You used to be able to buy proper codeine tablets, the ones in the brown bottles – non-proprietary. They would have got rid of this headache, migraine or not. Then Eloise saw that she had brought the tablets with her from the kitchen. She took another one, then swallowed it with a gulp of wine. You weren't suppose to do that... But it wouldn't matter – just one.

Charlotte could have been more supportive though, more sympathetic, especially as she'd known that Geoffrey had just walked out. And it was wrong of her friend to suggest that Eloise hadn't tried to overcome her bouts of depression. She had tried hard over the years; seen a lot of doctors, popped a lot of pills. She finished her drink, then poured another glass, noting the tremble of her hand. Blooming headache. Eloise took another tablet.

Geoffrey had promised that he would help, had convinced her that he could. She stood up, intending to fetch a box of tissues from the sideboard, but lost her balance and sat down again. She wiped her eyes with her sleeve; sipped her drink, stared at the bloody liquid, swirled it round the glass, thinking, letting her mind drift… But nobody else was to blame for her problems. It was her own fault, entirely: she was abnormal, dysfunctional. Charlotte was right about that. She couldn't even hold down a relationship for more than five minutes. She had made a mess of her life… Thrown away all her opportunities… And there had been plenty of those. She should have done better than a junior school. Marriage… There would be no daughter now – no family. And look at Charlotte: university lecturer, author of several academic books on the romance poets; married to a doctor, with children… Absently, caught up in her negative thoughts, she placed another tablet on her tongue, swallowed it with more wine, felt it progress down her throat. God, how many had she taken? Four? Five? If she took any more, they would find her dead – a cold corpse. But that wouldn't matter… It wouldn't make any difference to Geoffrey. She topped up her glass.

She glanced at her piano, set her glass back onto the coffee table, then lifted her spectacles, thinking, gazing at the musical instrument: it was only an electric one but it had the full seven octaves – and the tone was good too. After years of promising herself, she had belatedly started taking lessons, and was doing all right – she was due to take the Grade One examination at the end of the month. She would need to step up her practice soon, practise her scales… Keep her fingernails short. That was important, otherwise you tended to go at it with straight fingers; and the examiners wouldn't like that. Playing in front of people wasn't going to be easy though; and she was bound to be nervous. Still, at least she knew the pieces she had to play... And then the piano started to rotate, to circle round and round, performing slow vertical pirouettes without leaving the floor. Other objects were doing it too. In fact they all were, even the Jack Vettrianos on the wall... And the migraine lights. She was tipsy of course... Plus those tablets... A feeling of...

It was fortunate that Eloise knew she going to be sick some moments before the actual event, otherwise she would have ruined the carpet, a practically new Axminster shag-pile beige with a cut leaf pattern. It was a present from Geoffrey. But there was no downstairs lavatory; the bathroom was too far away, and so the kitchen sink would have to do – and it did.

After a while Eloise made herself a mug of almost-black coffee. She couldn't drink it totally black; she always needed a splash of milk, or else it was too bitter – no sugar though. A dry biscuit would be nice, it would settle her stomach, absorb any nasty dregs of her foolhardiness.

Sitting on a kitchen stool, holding her coffee mug in both hands, Eloise gazed out the window. She would fetch in those potatoes in a minute, when her head had cleared, then take them over to the refuge. She felt a lot better now, now that she'd freshened herself up. But what a fool she'd been, taking those tablets like that, kidding herself that she was trying to cure the headache. She had known what she was doing, feeling sorry for herself, blaming everyone... Even poor old Charlie, who was much more sensible than herself. But of course the wine had made her mood worse, contributed to her depression... Had brought her down. Good thing that she had been sick, for that had brought up the tablets. Eloise grimaced. Her propensity for being easily sick had probably saved her life.

The headache was fading, and there were no more flashing lights – so one or two of the tablets must have stayed down, got into her system. But she felt warm now, flushed, as though she had a temperature. Perhaps the headache was a precursor to a summer chill… Or influenza. And the house seemed suddenly humid, suddenly oppressive, claustrophobic, as if the building had shrunk around her – the walls closing in, the ceiling pressing down. Eloise felt a need to escape, to be outside, to get some fresh air into her lungs… to walk, to think. Rougemont Park was nice at this time in the morning – never many people. But she might see Geoffrey there. He had moved in temporarily with his brother and sister-in-law, and they had a flat on the other side of the park, in the city centre. Geoffrey liked Rougemont Park – so there was a possibility. And if she did meet him there, might he not suppose that she had gone there with just that in mind. The last thing she wanted was for him to think she had engineered a meeting. Maybe it would be better to walk the other way, towards the river.

She fetched a bag from the cupboard under the stairs, then let herself out into the road at the front of the house. The light was dazzling today. Maybe the migraine, if indeed that was what the headache was, had made her eyes sensitive to it. It might be worth going back to fetch her sunglasses. No, it would be all right: she wouldn't stay out for long – and anyway her eyes would soon adjust to the light. Shielding them with a hand, she started off up the road.

'Are you all right, dear?' The question interrupted Eloise's reverie and she turned unsteadily to her elderly neighbour, Margaret Male, who was leaning over a nearby garden gate. 'I was watching you come down your path and noticed you wandering a bit,' she continued. 'Do you feel OK?'

Eloise laughed. 'Yes, Margaret – I'm fine. Slight headache, that's all.' She laughed again, rubbing her forehead through her fringe. 'Too much wine at the twinning committee last night, I expect.'

'You don't look so perky, me dear,' Margaret Male continued. 'Why, you're looking quite pale.' She swung open the gate. 'Now you come on inside, and I'll make us a nice pot of tea.'

Eloise steadied herself on the gatepost. 'Thanks. But I think what's really needed is a walk.' She paused, noting the old lady's crestfallen expression. 'I'll call in on my way home... About half an hour?'

'I'll have the kettle on.'

Eloise smiled. 'It's always on,' she said, turning to continue her walk.

'And there's nothing wrong in that.' Margaret Male placed a hand on Eloise's shoulder. 'Do you want me to come with you?'

Eloise shook her head. 'No, I'm fine, Margaret – really.'

'I will if you want me to.'

'I'll see you in a bit,' Eloise said jovially, starting off again.

Five minutes later, having decided on her initial destination, Eloise turned off the busy thoroughfare by the Central Railway Station into Rougemont Park. The flower-beds were doing exceptionally well this summer, brilliant floral contrasts – pinks, chrysanthemums, marigolds, peonies – all paraded against a backdrop of emerald green. She started up the hill towards the war memorial. Look at those climbing roses on the terraces; you could smell their scent from over here. Clearly, everything was thriving in the good weather – just like the produce in her garden.

At the war memorial Eloise took the path that curled down between the lawns towards the adjacent railway station. It would be cooler there. Fewer flowers though, just trees and shrubs, jungle greenery: magnolias, hydrangeas, rhododendrons – that kind of thing. She had a rhododendron bush in her front garden, between the gate and Margaret's fence. But it was getting too big now and required some serious pruning. She had thought of replacing it with a lilac.

Just then a train rattled into the station. Keen to get a better view of it, Eloise crossed the strip of grass between the path and the row of iron railings that bordered the western perimeter of the park. She had always liked trains – train journeys. But didn't everyone? Gliding through the countryside, the ever-changing scenery, stopping at wayside stations, going on holiday, visiting friends, going to the seaside – but most of all, the romance. *Brief Encounter.* Trevor Howard and Celia Johnson, parting at the railway station… The steam… The passing expresses. Just for a second, she thought she saw Trevor Howard beckon her from the platform. She blinked and adjusted her spectacles. No, it wasn't him. Now that would have been something to tell Margaret when she went back.

Unless it was a long journey, she didn't really go anywhere by rail now; the car was more convenient. But she and Paul had often travelled by train: on the branch line to Exmouth, or the other way to Barnstaple. And they had often gone on the main line to Dawlish and Paignton; and once they had gone across the Tamar River, over Brunel's bridge, into Cornwall. That had been terrific, with all the little boats bobbing colourfully in the water far below. Of course, then, before Privatisation, you could just turn up at a station and buy a ticket without having to worry about different tariffs and different companies. What's more, if a train was on the timetable, then you were sure that it would turn up. You couldn't be so sure of that nowadays.

Eloise peered through the iron railings. The train wasn't a local one, from Exmouth. It was a Voyager, an express, with a locomotive at each end – and so would have come all the way down from London, Waterloo. She watched the passengers disembarking, going their separate ways, some heading for the northern exit, others opting for the one that let out onto Queen Street. They all seemed in a hurry, almost racing each other along the platform, sprinting – like bargain hunters at a sale.

Then she realised the headache, which had all but gone, had returned. She supposed the effect of the tablets she'd taken earlier – or might have taken earlier – had worn off. Perhaps it would be best to curtail the walk and return sooner than planned to Margaret's for that cup of tea – take another tablet… Better not do that though, just in case.

Eloise turned to face back up the path, paused momentarily to steady a sudden whirligig in her vision, then took a step forward. Underfoot, the soft turf, although cushioning her tread, did little to cushion her headache. Perhaps she should have let Margaret accompany her after all. Hindsight. And now she had vertigo.

Golly, but she felt queer, light-headed – a little drunk. Maybe her nausea, being sick, had not fetched up the tablets after all. Possibly most had remained in her stomach. Mixed with the alcohol… they might have… But surely that red, slurry-like paste that had drained so disgustingly into the waste disposal unit had been the remnants of them? Could that have been something else… wine-stained porridge? And now her dizziness was getting worse. So this was what it was like to die from an overdose.

In an effort to steady herself, Eloise placed her back against the railings and dug her sandals into the soft humus of the lawn. Her shoulder bag slid from her arm. She held its strap for a moment, then lost it. The bag tumbled in a surreal topsy-turvy dance to rest against the railings a yard or two down from where she was standing.

Battling for her balance she dug her heels deeper into the turf, forced her back into fixed contact with the iron railings, and gazed up at the canopy of a nearby tree, its branches sparkling now like the lit boughs of a Christmas decoration. Sunshine broke through in luminous shafts; beams spotted the ground around her. Her skin started to prickle. Actually, dying was quite pleasant: a kaleidoscope pattern that now became a whoosh of accelerating air.

Eloise was barely aware of her back sliding down the iron railings, hardly felt her cushioned touchdown as gravity sat her torso neatly on the grass, making her appear for all the world like a summer stroller who had sat down for a rest and then fallen asleep.

Chapter Three

Eloise awoke with a jolt and her heart leapt. What had happened? She felt like she had been nodding off at a twinning committee meeting and had been pulled back from the brink. She was sitting on a lawn with her back propped against some iron railings; it wasn't especially comfortable – her bottom felt numb. Not a little bemused, she straightened her glasses. And then she remembered: the dizziness, the headache, the tablets, the wine, the nausea, coming to the park – all of it came back in a rush of jumbled memories. She must have passed out – fainted. But that had never happened before, not in her entire life. So was that caused by the overdose… If indeed she had taken one? She felt OK now – the headache had gone. Eloise gazed around, at the manicured lawns, the resplendent flower-beds… the people wandering idly along the pathways of the park. There was something not quite right about all this, something wasn't making sense – but she couldn't figure out what it was. She still wasn't quite with it.

After a little while, having further recovered her equilibrium, holding the railings for support, she pulled herself upright, stretched, rubbed her bottom… No, nobody was looking. There was her bag, over by that acacia. She retrieved it and slung it over her shoulder, then took out her powder compact. Her hair looked unkempt but apart from that she seemed all right: it didn't appear as if she had suffered any harm from mixing those tablets with the wine. She tousled her hair with her fingers, shaking her head so that her fringe fell into place. That was the beauty of a short style: it didn't require much maintenance. Now, what was the time? Damn! Her wristwatch had gone. Eloise remembered putting it on this morning, recalled checking the time when she'd come out. No, it wasn't in her bag. She started to sift through the longer grass by the railings, where she had fainted. It was practically new – a birthday present from Charlotte.

'Have you lost something, madam?'

Eloise glanced up from her search, at the man who had asked the question. He was about six feet and burly, with blond hair – a bit like Geoffrey, but not so good looking. She saw that he was wearing navy-blue dungarees and a navy-blue jacket, with a white shirt and maroon striped tie underneath. A peaked cap with an enamel badge completed his ensemble. At first she thought he was a railway worker who had seen her searching for something and had come to help. Then she noticed that he was holding a trowel and that the badge carried the logo 'D.C.C. Parks Department'.

'Yes,' she said. 'Yes, my watch.' She ran her eyes over the man's attire again. Devon County Council had certainly splashed out on its park attendants' work clothes. No wonder the council charge was so steep.

The man crossed to where Eloise was still searching. 'Don't look so worried,' he said, 'we will soon find it.' He crouched down. 'Now, what does it look like?'

'It's rectangular with a leather strap.'

'Rectangular with a leather strap,' he repeated, nodding thoughtfully and sweeping his eyes over the turf.

'And it's digital… LCD numerals.'

The man stopped searching and glanced at Eloise. 'Digital, LCD,' he said. 'What type is that?'

'Liquid crystal display… Oh, and it gives the date, too.'

The gardener returned to his search. 'It's a foreign one, is it, madam?'

'Yes.' Eloise replied. 'My friend in Canada bought it for me.'

Five minutes later and with no sign of the watch being found, the park attendant turned to Eloise. 'I don't think we're going to find it,' he said. 'The best thing to do, madam, especially if the watch has sentimental value, is to report its loss to the police station. Then, if someone finds it and hands it in, they will contact you.' Fat chance of that, Eloise thought. The man looked her up and down, his gaze appraising, slightly suspicious, as though he thought her story of the lost watch a cover for something else, something more sinister, more clandestine. 'Now, do you know where the police station is?' he asked.

Eloise nodded. 'Yes – it's in the Heavitree Road.'

'New to Exeter, are we?' the gardener asked. He glanced in the direction of the park gates. 'It's in Waterbeer Street, madam.'

Waterbeer Street, indeed! He was the one new to Exeter. She knew very well the police station was located in the Heavitree Road. 'Do you know what the time is?' she asked.

The workman shook his head. 'I don't own a watch,' he said. 'But it must be about eleven o'clock.' And with that, he turned and started off along the path that ran parallel to the railway station.

'Thank you,' Eloise called.

She stared after the park attendant, now disappearing between two rows of rhododendron bushes. He had been helpful, unusually so. But something had changed. She hadn't noticed before, searching for the watch, concentrating on that. But now… The migraine was gone. It was more than that though. Something was different about here. The ambience of the park had altered. She gazed up the hill, along the walkways, through the trees… She should keep looking for her watch though – after all, it was a present. But there had been no sign of it just now.

A train entered the station behind her then. Eloise turned around, peering through the railings, as the train eased to a halt at the southbound platform. It wasn't like the streamlined one that she'd seen earlier: just an old diesel locomotive – probably a local service connection.

Idly, still concerned about the loss of her wristwatch, she gazed at the passengers alighting from the train, watched them wandering towards the exits. They certainly looked a bit old-fashioned, dated, unlike those from the London train, who had been dressed in the latest styles. Self-consciously, she glanced at her own clothes: sandals and a floral-print V-neck frock, and the white plastic belt that she'd got at the jumble sale. Eloise suddenly felt embarrassed. Actually, the frock had come from a charity shop – anyone would think her a pauper. Well, she had been gardening before she came out.

It was a pity that Charlotte wasn't here – the fashion conscious one. She would have been able to pinpoint these styles. Like that teenager over there with the circular skirt: that was dated. Who would wear that nowadays, especially on such a hot day as this? But on reflection, she could actually remember her friend wearing one like it – years ago though – keeping the shape full by wearing layers of stiff petticoats underneath. But that was Charlie all over, suffering just to be 'with it'.

Memories.

And that time by the river on a school photographic trip, when Charlotte had fallen in: all she'd been worried about was that she might have ruined her dress. Not a jot concerned about the physical danger she was in – not that she was in any though: the water was only inches deep there.

It would be best not to mention anything to Charlotte about losing her birthday present. Charlie would be sure to go on about her being scatterbrained… or worry about her 'supposedly' increasing forgetfulness. But she wasn't becoming forgetful: it was just that she couldn't remember things so well now.

Putting aside her concern over the missing watch, Eloise dusted several newly mown grass clippings from her frock. Yes, it might have come from a charity shop but it was good quality – and it was clean. But the watch would turn up… Perhaps she hadn't put it on this morning.

She felt good though, even better than when she had come to just now. The post-malady feeling had galvanised her energy. The cup of tea with Margaret could wait a while longer. A walk into the shopping centre and Cathedral Green would be nice. Perhaps buy a book. She set off towards the park gates along the path that exited on to Queen Street.

And if the watch didn't turn up, well, she could always buy another one… another one just like it – and Charlotte would never be any the wiser.

All at once, she halted in her tracks, staring down at the shiny object that had just caught her attention. Crouching down, she brushed aside several grains of loose earth and retrieved the silvery disc from the flower border. She held it up for examination. It was an old half-crown. Eloise hadn't seen one of those in years. The flower border looked freshly dug, so it must have been turned up then. It looked quite new though, for something that had been buried for years. But weren't they made from silver? That might explain why it wasn't tarnished. Or was it only gold that didn't do that? Geoffrey would have known. Oh, well… Taking a handkerchief from her bag, she rubbed the coin between her fingers and thumb; then, smiling to herself, she slipped it into the purse in the lining of her bag.

There used to be eight half-crowns to the pound… 12½ pence in today's money. Not much now – but a whole week's pocket money when she was a girl. Eloise took the coin out of the purse, glanced at the date, then put it back again. She would show it to Margaret when she got home. It would interest her. Margaret collected old coins, had kept some from when they had been legal tender – and she had also found one or two in here herself.

Pleased with her find Eloise sauntered down the path and exited the park on to Queen Street, the street that led to the city centre. But here she paused. Like the park, it too had changed. She adjusted her spectacles, then gazed curiously up and down the street. Although, it wasn't so much that it had changed but that it was different…

Maybe she had lost her watch somewhere along here – before going into the park. It might be a good idea to retrace her footsteps, back towards home, look for it before too many people had had chance to find it. On the other hand, anything dropped along here would surely have been picked up by now. She set off again, heading for the shopping centre.

Then she stopped. But hang on; things were different; had changed. Eloise stood stock-still and peered around. This was Queen Street... but not the one she knew. Gone were the glass bus shelter, and the crescent where taxis normally waited. No florist shop. Vanished too was the music shop and its electronic keyboards. No traffic-calming points in the street. No Exeter College building. All had disappeared, to be replaced by the old-time thoroughfare… And old-fashioned cars. It was like being on the film set of a period movie. All that worrying in the park about her lost watch had blinded her, had distracted her from the obvious. But out here on the street… The people's styles… She'd noticed that in the park, too, and should have twigged before. God, was she losing her mind?

Eloise ventured several paces along the pavement, and then stopped again. The Rougemont Hotel looked OK… Well, sort of OK but there, farther along the street towards the city centre, was the old Higher Market. That had been closed for years. And there was the corner of Paul Street, with all its old shops still intact. And where were the Guildhall and Harlequin shopping arcades? They had been here yesterday: she had walked through them; she remembered doing so. Eloise swallowed. This was serious: something extremely untoward was happening today. She wasn't losing her mind – she had already lost it.

Suddenly alarmed by the prospect, Eloise retreated into the park, found a seat, and sat down – a refuge in her sea of confusion. There was no record of madness in the family… that she knew of. She took off her glasses and began absently to polish the lenses with a handkerchief. But what was going on? Was this Exeter? Vaguely… She replaced her glasses on her nose and glanced towards the street, half afraid that some other puzzle would present itself. It used to be something like this… When she was a girl. Perhaps this was a dream. Eloise pinched her arm. No. She shot a glance towards the street again, perplexed, confounded by the childhood memories that confronted her. Exeter used to be like this.

Eloise decided to remain where she was for a while, on the park bench, gather her thoughts, and try to work it through – after all, there was bound to be an explanation. But suppose she really had lost her mind, had gone insane, what should she do? The park attendant had told her where the police station was. Actually, he had been partly correct: it had been in Waterbeer Street, until its move to the new site in the 1970s. So she could go there, tell them… But she was thinking, being rational… She surely hadn't gone mad. She continued to examine her surroundings, gazed at the people in their outmoded fashions, thinking, pondering things that her brain told her could not be. Thinking…

All at once, Eloise had the answer: she was dead. That hadn't been a faint back there in the park: the tablets mixed with the wine had been a fatal overdose. She had died; she had died and this was… this was Heaven. Under cover of hooded brows, Eloise squinted in all directions, examining the strollers with a renewed interest. None of them had wings or haloes. But anyway she was an atheist and wouldn't come to Heaven – so it could not be that. Yes, but… if you had led a decent life, had done nobody any harm, had given to charities, had helped people where you could, would the fact that you were a non-believer necessarily preclude you from an afterlife? Not necessarily, not if God was a judicious deity, a just creator… had His wits about Him. Eloise had often thought that she would stand a better chance of going to Heaven, if it turned out that there was one, than would one of those Catholic priests who abused children. She nudged her spectacles, and then gazed around. Heaven? But she was breathing; she could feel; she could smell the flowers;

and that was the sun up there in the sky… the earth beneath her feet. Surely these were all verifications of life – confirmations of her being alive?

Just then Eloise noticed a couple approaching the park bench. They appeared to be normal: a couple enjoying a stroll in the sunshine. They had a little dog with them, a Jack Russell. She made up her mind. 'Excuse me,' she said, swallowing dryly, and looking up at the lady. 'Excuse me, but…' She let her gaze wander. 'But is this Heaven?'

The lady's eyes followed Eloise's gaze. 'Some people say that it is, my dear,' she said, smiling down at Eloise.

Eloise watched the couple walking towards the park gates, observed the amused glance pass between them, then heard their shared chuckle. Sensing a fresh supply of saliva on her tongue, she returned to her thoughts.

She was alive; and she hadn't gone mad. Unwittingly, she took off her glasses, then put them back on again, fell once more to surveying her surroundings. Exeter used to be like this. Yes, it did… Yes, it did once… in the past, when she was a girl. A tiny titbit of a thought tugged at her brain, began to gnaw intelligently at her grey matter. Yes. This was Exeter… but not today. Eloise experienced a sudden quickening of her pulse. Time… Could that be the answer? No, it couldn't – don't be ridiculous. Yes, it could… It was no more ridiculous than supposing she had died and gone to Heaven, or thinking that she had gone insane. And Eloise had eliminated those two proposals. So it had to be the other one – there really could be no other explanation. Well there might be, and she would consider its probability should it present itself to her. But for the time being, this one would do. Time… Eloise stumbled, trying to articulate the thought… Time travel – she had travelled back in time. But that was impossible; the stuff of science fiction books. She looked around again, at the fashions, at the buildings and, through the park gates, at the passing motorcars; she had though. As incredible as it might seem, she had time-travelled. That faint, or whatever it'd been, had taken her to another dimension. Eloise got up off the park bench and moved round in a little circle of confirmation, a turn of wonder, awestruck, taking it all in, absorbing the scenery. How many times had she walked through here as a teenager? She had often hoped for something like this to happen. Hoped for it, yes, but she had never actually expected it to.

In a little while, she left the park and started off up the thoroughfare towards the shopping centre. Other than seeing some of the old shops, she hadn't yet thought what she might do when she got there. It was all a bit much to grasp in one go. She could visit the Cathedral… See some of the old sights… Walk down to the quay… Sit by the river. She and Paul used to go for walks along the riverbank. She could do that… Then a question occurred to her. Why had she come back like this? Why her? There was nothing special about her. She was ordinary. If this sort of thing could really happen, why not have someone go back and prevent Hitler's parents from meeting? Or send someone to Dallas 1963… She was just ordinary Eloise James. Then another thought presented itself, a more practicable one this time. How was she going to get home, return to the present? It was all very well to be here, but it would be nice to know there was a way back.

But funnily enough – and you would think that she would be – but she didn't feel threatened by what had happened. She glanced at a passing motor scooter; the rider had no crash helmet. Apprehensive that she might be stuck here… Perhaps. But being here didn't frighten her. Maybe it had something to do with her mood, and with the taking of those tablets… The overdose. Nothing any worse than that could happen to her. She just didn't care. Goodness, look at those girls with backcombed hair. She'd been confused at first – she still was, she supposed – but she wasn't fazed by any of it. Eloise carried on up the street towards the city centre. Yes, she was OK with all of this. Indeed, if it came to that, she felt safer walking along here now than she had done yesterday, doing the same thing.

When she arrived at the junction with Paul Street, she paused to survey the area. There was Hansfords shop down there, on the corner of Goldsmith Street, advertising that it sold cakes and pastries. Also showing were those old tin signs for Players Cigarettes and Old Holborn Tobacco. Would Brussels allow such disparate items to be sold together in a small shop like that one? Probably not. And the EU decided everything nowadays – so this had to be the past. On the pavement outside the shop, a variety of fruits and vegetables were on display in open wooden crates. And those bananas looked bent – too crooked for the common market. She noticed too that the local paper was on sale.

'The *Express and Echo*, please,' Eloise said, dipping her hand into the purse in her bag. Then she realised that, like her watch, her money was lost, too. Only her recent find was there. Maybe somebody had stolen the items when she'd fainted? But surely they wouldn't have taken just the money – stayed around to empty it from the purse. Surely they would have taken the bag too.

'That'll be thrupence, dear.'

Eloise fished in her bag, took out the half-crown and, smiling encouragingly – hopefully – handed it across the counter.

'Two shillings and thrupence change,' the shop assistant said. She plucked a paper from the pile on the counter. 'And don't forget this,' she added, smiling at Eloise's confusion.

Outside on the pavement in the cloudless sunshine, Eloise gazed at the change from the newspaper purchase: a two-shilling coin and a three-penny-piece, the ones with the multi-faceted edges. The half-crown coin may have gone, but this little coin would interest Margaret all the same.

She held the newspaper up before her – great unwieldy broadsheet – and found the item she was seeking. She nodded slowly, thoughtfully. Indeed, taking everything into account, the fashions, the shops, the cars, that would be about right – she would have guessed at that. Eloise read the date again and promptly sat down on the step of Hansfords shop, staring down the street. That cyclist should take more care: there was a crossroads at the bottom of the hill. And it was odd but from around here she always remembered being able to see the river and the railway line beyond. Eloise glanced over her shoulder, back in to the shop. Time was like that though: it could play tricks with one's memory.

'Excuse me, love.' The voice interrupted Eloise's reverie, and she looked up. 'Do you mind if I pass by into the shop?'

Eloise rose to her feet and moved to one side. 'Sorry.'

The shopper paused. 'You all right?' He nodded towards Eloise's newspaper. 'Bad news?'

Eloise managed a wan smile. 'I don't think so,' she replied.

The shopper grinned. 'You look like you've seen a ghost,' he said, turning towards the shop door.

Eloise watched him climb the step. He'd been nice; considerate.

She began to walk up Goldsmith Street, towards the city

centre, stuffing the paper into her bag as she went. The day seemed hotter now, more humid. She could feel beads of perspiration moving on her temples. Pausing momentarily, she dabbed at them with her handkerchief, then moved off once more, at a jaunty pace. She knew where she was going now.

Eloise was all but knocked down by a speeding Ford Anglia as she crossed Waterbeer Street, had to skip the final feet to the pavement in fact. She swore under her breath. The police station was just down there. She should go in and report the driver… And the missing watch and money. They might recover it by the time she got home.

In a little while, near where the Marks and Spencers store would be built in a decade's time, Eloise came out on to the High Street. That shop on the opposite side of the street, Hinton Lake's, was where she and Paul used to buy their photographic equipment. She crossed to it and peered in the window. Oh my. There was a Tenax automatic camera, just like the one she'd had: £29-10-6d, with a leather carrying case at £4-10-8d extra – over thirty-four pounds altogether. That was expensive... probably about two weeks of her father's engineering wages. How she'd saved up to buy one of those: pocket money, running errands, chores… She had even washed her father's car twice in one day, that's how badly she'd wanted one. Then he'd refused to pay her twice. Her mother had come up trumps in the end though, had found the money from somewhere – they hadn't been rich.

Eloise continued to stare at the two price tags. When she had been a girl, they had had to multiply sums like those together. Addition and subtraction calculations were OK, but multiplication of pounds, shillings and pence – three different denominations – was an entirely different matter. You had to bring it all to the lowest common denominator, do the calculation, and then convert it back into pounds, shillings and pence again… or something like that. And sometimes there were halfpennies and farthings thrown into the equation too – and that really could send your brain into overload. Of course it was so much easier nowadays with decimal currency. She could just imagine the kids in her class tackling those old-fashioned figures… Without calculators.

Shaking her head, Eloise walked on past the shop and turned right into St Martin's Lane. Here, to give right of way to a man wheeling a barrel of beer along the middle of the path, she slowed her pace and stepped to one side. Surprisingly little had changed here. Apart from how beer was stored, the old *Ship Inn* probably hadn't changed at all. In fact, it looked the same today as it had the last time she and Geoffrey came in for a drink. And as for St Martin's Church, well that had been consecrated in 1065 – an easy date to remember, of course.

In a moment, Eloise stood on the cobbles of the Cathedral Yard, a lump in her throat, and studied the sixteenth-century building that was the Moka Café. This was it, their favourite destination whenever she and Paul had visited the city centre – the place where she had failed to be on that final Saturday afternoon all those years ago. She opened the newspaper again, checked the date. Today. But there had been a good reason for her not being here. It hadn't been her fault; she had done all she could to make it. She stared at the door of the café, watched a couple go inside, watched the door close behind them. Today. And so was that why she was here, to…to save Paul – to prevent the car accident? If everything else that had occurred today was not an illusion, not a lie, then that seemed an obvious assumption. But that would mean changing the past, not just for Paul and herself but for a myriad of other people too – and that was surely impossible. But she was here nonetheless. Shielding her eyes against the reflected glare of the sun, she gazed up at the Dutch-style gable, the third floor that had been added to the building in the nineteenth century. She'd never liked that addition: it clashed with the older architecture – made it a mishmash of styles. It made the building look confused.

The Moka was closed forever the following year, a casualty of the invasion of the American-style coffee bars, with their milkshakes and jukeboxes and "frothy" coffees. Lots of people had come in on its final day, Charlotte, other friends – gathering souvenirs. She still had the coffee mug that Charlie had brought back for her… and the engraved spoon. But Eloise hadn't felt able to come. It had been too soon. Their last time together had been here, and then he had driven her home. Neither of them had seen her father hiding behind the curtains of the open window, watching, listening – hatching his plan.

She had later regretted not coming in though, to say goodbye, to draw closed the metaphorical curtain. It might have helped her to forget, helped her move on. She continued to stare at the café. It looked a bit run down, its casement windows needing a clean – and those beams would benefit from a coat of paint… Or whatever it was they put on them. But that had always been part of its charm, its attraction: a bit worse for wear on the outside, but a touch of culture on the inside. Even though she hadn't been to either place then, for her it had been Paris of the 1920s, Berlin of the 1930s – Fitzgerald and Pound, Auden and Isherwood.

The Moka Café – Paul and Eloise. Eloise smacked the back of her hand, admonished herself. **You were always the dreamer** – but wasn't that half her trouble? She glanced at the leaded-glass panes in the entrance door. There was plenty of change left over from the half-crown, so she could go in now.

After a short delay, Eloise secured the table in the bay window on the right hand side of the room. There had been other tables vacant but this one had been worth waiting for. It had been their favourite, permitting as it did an unobstructed view of the western side of the Cathedral and, even more important, the comings and goings of the Royal Hotel. They had seen Rolls Royces pull-up there, and even, on occasion, pop stars of the day scampering inside in order to avoid the over-zealous attention of fans. They'd seen Del Shannon and Billy Fury from this very window. Memories. And what about the time Charlie had almost been crushed by the crowd while trying to get that autograph at the Rolling Stones concert? Eloise sipped her coffee. Gosh, Charlotte had been lucky that day.

The concert had been held in the grounds of Longleat House in Wiltshire, and Charlotte's father had driven the two thirteen-year-old fans over from Exeter. She could picture the scene now…

The band playing on the steps of the Elizabethan house, lots of people, loads of noise, and a dazzle of colour – a scrumptious sunny Sunday afternoon in August. Charlie in her bell-bottom jeans and skimpy T-shirt, with her bra stuffed full of cotton wool to make it look as if she had a bust… and Lord Bath in the doorway of the house, trying to look "with it" by sporting a Beatle-style wig – for which he would be ridiculed the next day when pictures of him wearing it appeared in the national newspapers.

To prevent fans from getting too close to their heroes, a metal barrier had been erected around the top of the steps; and, a little way back from these, in the courtyard of the house, a linked-wire fence provided additional security. Everything had been well thought through. But nobody had anticipated the enthusiasm of Charlotte – or of those who would follow her lead.

The performance was nearing its end, and the audience were pushing forward, especially the teenage girls. She and Charlotte had managed to work their way to the middle of the area adjacent to the makeshift stage, tight against the linked-wire fence. They had a splendid view from there; just yards from where Mick Jagger was strutting his stuff, and sending some of the girls into a tizzy with his gyrations. It was already quite a crush near the front. Charlotte's father had wisely remained behind the main crowd. It wasn't really his kind of music: he had only come as chauffeur. The Stones were playing their hit *The Last Time* when, astonishingly, Eloise had seen Charlotte hoist herself over the fence, dash across the narrow open area between the fence and the steps, and, hopping about in her exuberance, wave her autograph book at Brian Jones. Charlotte preferred him to Mick Jagger – most girls did.

Charlie hadn't given any sign of her intention, hadn't uttered a word to her. She had just gone for it. She had claimed later – when her father had scolded her – that it was a spur of the moment decision… but she'd had her autograph book ready. Of course, Eloise had shouted to Charlotte to come back, but her friend had either not heard the call or had decided to ignore it. But knowing Charlie, it was almost certainly the latter.

If Charlotte had managed to obtain her autograph there and then, and had climbed back over the fence, things might have been OK. But other female fans had witnessed her caper and, as if deciding *en masse* that they too wanted a piece of the action, had also started to breech the fence. Sensibly, Eloise had stayed where she was; but even so she'd felt herself being squeezed tighter and tighter against the fence as the crush had gathered momentum. The thought had crossed her mind that if the fence gave way she would be knocked over and trodden on, crushed, by those pushing from behind – they all seemed so much bigger than her. It had been quite scary, pinned there, trapped, with a growing sense of claustrophobia – and of course wondering also about the robustness of the fence.

Soon the area between the fence and the steps had become packed with jostling girls – some were screaming; the hubbub had all but cancelled out the band's music. But she had still been able to make out Charlotte, in the vanguard, still waving her autograph book at Brian Jones, who had stopped playing and seemed unsure of what to do next. In fact, the entire band had seemed stunned by what was happening, although they must have experienced similar scenes before. But maybe they hadn't expected this in rural Wiltshire.

Some girls immediately behind Charlotte had fainted due to the stampede and were clearly in danger of being trampled underfoot. Eloise hadn't known what to do. To be honest, there wasn't much she could have done. She was pressed tight against the fence, and hadn't had the strength to free herself from those around her. It had been difficult to breath, and she'd started to become more and more alarmed. But then, suddenly, before real panic had set in, Charlotte's father had appeared from nowhere, caught hold of her arms, and pulled her clear of the throng. It had felt like being rescued from a straitjacket. Leaving her then in a gentler eddy, he had plunged back into the crowd, and had begun to push his way towards his daughter. But his help would not be needed; for at that moment, Eloise had seen a stagehand reach down over the metal barrier and haul Charlotte up on to the steps.

Other girls were also being lifted out of harm's way. But Charlotte had been the first one on to the steps, and could now be seen, as unflappable as ever, asking Brian Jones for his autograph. And she got it, too. But that wasn't the end of it. Oh, no, for then the guitarist had taken her in his arms and kissed her. OK, it wasn't much more than a quick peck really – but it was Brian Jones.

Golly but how Charlie had embellished that story down the years. Even in its first telling, she had snogged Brian Jones. And it hadn't been long before the guitarist had actually asked her to marry him, had whispered his proposal in her ear, apparently – Charlotte had always been precocious. Although on the car journey home she hadn't been quite so forward – not after the dressing down she'd received from her father, anyway. You didn't often see Charlie subdued… That hadn't lasted long though. But it had been a good afternoon out, one to remember.

Smiling to herself, Eloise pushed her spectacles along the bridge of her nose and glanced out the window of the Moka Café, to the adjacent Royal Hotel. Some of the Exeter gigs were held in the ABC Cinema at the top of the High Street. She would walk up there later and see what was on. They, she and Paul – and Charlotte – had seen some good shows there, she had many good recollections of it. The Beatles had played there.

And The Theatre Royal was only a stone's throw away – on the other side of the street – what good times they'd all enjoyed there. One Year, Norman Vaughn had brought his summer show up from Torquay for a week… and Charlotte had got all snooty and wouldn't come to see it, because she considered it "light weight" – yet she'd had no qualms about going to any of those pop concerts. But Eloise and Paul had gone, and had thoroughly enjoyed it.

Memories.

Eloise glanced at the clock on the wall behind the counter. Paul wouldn't be here for a while; that gave her plenty of time to compose herself, to plan her strategy. For she couldn't just declare who she was, take him by the hand, and lead him to safety. That wouldn't work. Gosh. But this time travel thing was weird: he was coming here to meet her, and he would, except that she would be years older. Of course, there was no way that he would recognise her. She didn't look her age though. Charlie and others had told her that. But she would have to reveal herself somehow. Perhaps tell him something that only she would know… Something from her school days would be best. Like telling him what she had done after her illegal drive up the hill at Lyme Regis. He would have to believe her. Her thoughts drifted then to how they had first met – she the naïve schoolgirl, anxious, concerned about the forthcoming exams, he the new teacher, edgy, clearly keen to make his first day a success. She smiled and closed her eyes – she could picture the scene now.

Chapter Four

Eloise turned to her best friend Charlotte, who occupied the desk next to her own. 'Once Mr Bridgestock has been introduced, I hope there will be time left for study this morning,' she said. It was the start of the autumn term, and she was one year into her GCE advanced level studies. She didn't want another teacher, not now. No, it was more than that; she couldn't cope with the thought of it. Someone new to get to know, someone who didn't know she had problems with spelling and worried about her grammar… And, on top of that, she needed top grades to get into her chosen university.

She was hoping to go to St Hilda's College, Oxford, to study English literature. Her mother had once won a scholarship to study there – which was a pretty difficult thing to do, coming from an ordinary grammar school. Mary had been unable to take it up though. The outbreak of the Second World War had put paid to that. By the time that was over, she had met and married Percy… And it was too late. Her mother would have done well at St Hilda's, but as for herself, it was going to be difficult just getting there.

English was her best subject, but something had gone awry this year. She hadn't lost interest; it was nothing like that… Not really. Ordinary level had been a doddle, but 'A' level hadn't really clicked for her. And it wasn't the new books, the new texts – she liked them all… Well, she didn't

like that Hemingway thing, with all its machismo rubbish…
Grace under fire… But something was missing – and now a
new teacher to get used to. Of course, Charlotte would be all
right with the new teacher: it all came so easily for her. But
if only her favourite teacher Miss Marshall had not passed on
so suddenly.

'I expect he will be an anticlimax,' Charlotte replied,
absently, examining her fingernails. 'Not a bit like the
rumours anyway.' Charlotte was planning to go to the same
university as Eloise but unlike her friend, her immediate
interest lay in matters other than learning.

'I hope he *is* an anticlimax,' Eloise said, watching her
friend. 'In the sense you mean, that is.'

Charlotte smiled knowingly. 'Oh come on, Miss James,
you listened to the rumours too.' She paused and winked at
her friend. 'You know, *à la* Mr Lawrence's *The Virgin and the
Gypsy*, mysterious, jet-black hair, even darker eyes, swarthy
from a life spent roaming-'

'But I did not instigate them,' Eloise broke in. 'And
neither did I participate in spreading them.'

'There's no smoke without fire,' Charlotte countered.
Her eyes twinkled, and she wrinkled her nose. 'Romantic…
Perhaps a little too much so – a breaker of maidens' hearts…'

'Oh, stop it, Charlie,' Eloise said. 'He is an English
teacher.' She glanced towards the door. 'Anyway, he'll be
here in a minute. Then we shall see.'

'Indeed we shall,' Charlotte said. She sighed. 'But as I
said just now, I expect he will be an anticlimax.'

Remaining silent, Eloise allowed her gaze to roam around
the classroom, to the oak panelling, the double-hung sash
windows, the ornate niches, and the Palladian door, with its
Doric columns and triangular arch – classical Georgian. Her

gaze swept past the rickety blackboard and easel, the bruised head desk, and settled on a battered globe, so ancient that it still showed a British Empire on which the sun never set – fifties Georgian. That globe would look more at home in her mother's antique shop than it did in this classroom.

Yes, it would… These old desks, too. But even though some of the school's equipment was worn, a mite dilapidated, a bit past it, Eloise knew that St Leonard's School for Girls had a good reputation for its teaching. Her mother had told her that more of its pupils went on to study at Oxford or Cambridge than did students from the city's largest grammar school – and it was only a fraction the size of that. Some girls sent here had passed their eleven plus examination – Charlotte was one of them. And class sizes were low, too; there were only twelve girls in this one. If she had gone to the secondary modern, she would have been one of over thirty pupils. Not only that, but the secondary modern was a mixed school, boys and girls. Eloise wouldn't have liked that.

And she knew that her parents had had to make financial sacrifices to send her here. Percy had spent longer days at the factory, where he worked as an engineer. Holidays, if not entirely curtailed, had certainly been culled. Her mother had taken the lease on tiny premises just off the Fore Street in Exeter and had opened them as a shop selling antiques. Eloise suspected that this small business venture was where the bulk of her school fees came from. Her mother had once been a buyer for a dealer in antiquities, and contacts made then, she knew, had provided many a bargain for the enterprise. Even so, it was obvious that the costs of sending her to a private school must have stretched the family's budget no end.

Eloise raised her eyes from the globe and glanced towards

the door… But could the new teacher really take the place of Miss Marshall, whose way of teaching had suited her needs so well? She'd had Miss Marshall from the start, through 'O' level, right up until the end of last term. They'd got on so well – and mother had liked her, too. She'd been like one of the family, like a wise old aunt.

Charlotte noted her friend's abstracted gaze. 'It will be all right, Ellie,' she said. 'At this level and this far into the study period, he need only be a guide, someone to mark our essays… He is bound to be well qualified – you know what the school is like for getting the best teachers.'

Eloise nodded absently. The new teacher would know the curriculum, which books, which poems, they were using. And the fact that he was a man, well so too was their geography teacher… And he was super. And at that moment in her reverie, the door swung open and the headmistress, Miss Staidler, led him into the room.

The first thing Eloise noted, was that he was about the same height as Miss Staidler, five feet nine inches… Perhaps an inch taller. He wasn't swarthy as rumour had it; his complexion was quite pale, but his hair was dark – almost black, in fact – and parted on the left. He had deep-set dark eyes under bony brow ridges that, she thought, gave him a slight Neanderthal look. She glanced at Charlotte. 'How old do you think he is?' she asked.

'Twenty-seven,' Charlotte replied with confident authority.

'No, he is older than that, I think,' Eloise said. She set her glasses higher on the bridge of her nose. The older he was the better, for it would mean that he had more teaching experience, more experience of preparing students for examinations… And it wasn't really all that long now…

Well, nine months. But worrying about it wouldn't help.

She returned to her appraisal of the new teacher. His expression, although perhaps now reflecting a slight nervousness, or a minor apprehension, sent out the impression of a permanent smile – his lips not turned up at the corners but, rather, defined by a pleasing physiognomy, a wide mouth; proportioned bone structure, a strong jawbone. He was not unlike the actor Alan Ladd, whom Eloise liked, partly because he reminded her of her father, but mostly because he always played the nice characters in his films.

'He's in awe of her,' Charlotte whispered to Eloise.

Afraid that any conversation would be overheard by Miss Staidler, Eloise turned to her friend and shushed her disapproval.

Charlotte smiled. 'He is. Look. He's standing a little behind her, staring at his feet – he's intimidated by her.'

'Shush,' Eloise repeated.

Miss Staidler rapped the lectern with her knuckles. 'This is Mr Paul Bridgestock, girls.' Much to Eloise's relief, the headmistress's stare settled on Charlotte, who was gazing back with that confident smile of hers, the one that always won people over. 'As you are aware, Mr Bridgestock has deemed himself sufficiently accomplished to take up Miss Marshall's former role.' She paused, baring her teeth. 'And that is no little undertaking... and certainly not an enviable one, for we all know – everyone of us – how dedicated, how devoted, how patient our dear Miss Marshall was. I am sure that all here will concur when I say that Miss Marshall will be sadly missed.' The eulogy for the late teacher went on for several more minutes. Paul Bridgestock was not mentioned again, before Miss Staidler spun on her heel and marched from the classroom, leaving the new teacher to his new class.

Paul Bridgestock gazed around the assembled class of girls. He coughed. 'Miss Marshall was an exceptional teacher Miss Staidler tells me and, taking into account the standard of your work, I have no reason to doubt her estimation.'

He had examined their work then. Eloise was pleased with that piece of news. But in how much depth? A cursory glance at their marks, or a full assessment of their essays? She gazed at his brow ridges, partly concealed by bushy eyebrows, which she now noted met in the middle above his eyes. Eloise was eager to get on with things: only three terms to the examinations. That was not long… But she should have read more of the set books during the holidays, given herself a head start. She adjusted her glasses, and focused on the new teacher.

'I am not a hard taskmaster,' he was saying, 'but in only nine months' time the finals will be upon us…' Eloise felt herself nodding in agreement. 'And that is a short enough span given the amount of material left to cover. Nevertheless, and notwithstanding the absence of Miss Marshall, if we all work to the full extent of our abilities, I am confident of a welcome outcome.' He paused and placed both hands on the lectern, leaning forward towards his class. 'You will find that my practice is not solely to talk while you listen,' he continued. 'On the contrary, we will share our ideas, discuss them – we will explore our subject together. We may indeed have a lot to get through, and time may well be pressing but…' Then Eloise noted his complexion had reddened ever so slightly.

Someone behind her tittered, and the blush deepened.

The new teacher moved back behind his desk and, brushing aside a lock of hair that had fallen across his forehead, turned towards the blackboard. Eloise watched him, waited to see how he would handle the situation. It was an odd occurrence; she hoped there would not be too many of them. Paul Bridgestock faced the device, immobile for several moments, breathing deeply, before carefully and determinedly erasing several spent markings. Moments later, when he turned around to face his class again, his embarrassment was over. He cleared his throat. 'Nevertheless, as brief as our time may be,' he said, 'I think that perhaps we should first introduce ourselves.'

Eloise nodded her head. Despite her concerns about her abilities to obtain the requisite academic grades, the new teacher's speech had left her with a feeling of optimism. She agreed with his summary of the situation without Miss Marshall, and wouldn't have cared if he had actually declared himself to be a hard taskmaster – to be frank, that was probably what she required. Furthermore, as long as it didn't delay their studies, she was not put off by his diffidence and, while such a trait might perhaps not suit their chemistry mistress, she felt that for the teaching of literature a sensitive nature was not a disqualifying factor. She wished though that he had not been quite so in awe of Miss Staidler, whom Eloise thought ruled all her staff by domination. Miss Marshall had shared a house with her, but she had not seemed to mind the other's dominance.

Paul Bridgestock introduced himself to all his pupils individually, making comments here and there on the quality and content of their essays, and Eloise soon realised that he had obtained more than a superficial acquaintance with their work. His earlier remark about their accomplishments under Miss Marshall had clearly not been made in mere deference to their former teacher: no indeed, he must have spent considerable time and effort in preparation for this moment. And then it was her turn.

Eloise looked up and caught his eye. 'Yes,' she said brightly, sitting up straighter in her chair. It suddenly occurred to her then that he had deliberately left her to last. There was something in the way that he had called her name, a modulation of tone, a hint of expectation – or something like it – that made her think that he had been looking forward to this moment. She wondered if he would mention her essay on Philip Larkin's poem *At Grass*. She had taken an unconventional stance on that one, and thought it one of her best.

Paul Bridgestock coughed. 'And so you are Miss James,' he said, smiling. His expression told Eloise that she'd been right: he had saved her until last – but why would he do that? 'I note,' he went on, still smiling, 'that you are at odds with the general consensus of opinion over *Lady Chatterly*. You argue the novel banned because of its treatment of class rather than because of its love element.'

How could that have got in there? Eloise was suddenly aware of the gas lamp that had, or so it seemed to her, started to hiss like a harassed gander. She felt her face beginning to redden. That wasn't a set essay, merely a review that she had written as a joke – for a laugh.

The new teacher coughed again, his gaze softening as he surveyed his pupil's increasing embarrassment. 'Nonetheless,' he said, placing his notes on his desk, 'for what it is worth, I am entirely in agreement with you. Lawrence's treatment of class, his suggestion that a Lady of the Realm could be attracted to a common gamekeeper, was far more influential in the prohibition of his book than was his description of… of atypical love.'

Eloise tried to smile but her lips seemed frozen in a permanent grimace of shame. 'It wasn't a real essay,' she said stiffly, 'just a bit of fun. The other ones are though… real ones, that is.'

Paul Bridgestock glanced at the pile of essays on his desk, then returned his gaze to his pupil. 'Well, real or not, its premise is a good deal better than much of the nonsense that appeared in the newspapers at the time.' He paused, leafing through the pages of Eloise's essay, where, from her desk, she could see several comments written in red ink. 'But you should be more attentive to your sentence constructions… There are several instances of spelling errors, too.' He fell silent again, thinking. Then, after a little while, returning his gaze to Eloise, he concluded: 'But leaving that aside, you clearly have been very thorough with your research.'

Someone to Eloise's left giggled and, feeling the warmth of her earlier blush returning, she covered her cheeks with her hands.

The new teacher looked round the classroom, his expression indicating that he now realised he had just said the wrong thing. He rubbed his chin thoughtfully, then went on: 'And I see, Miss James, that you have also taken an unconventional position on *At Grass*. Well, in spite of your persuasive arguments, I have to say that I disagree with you over that one. All leading critical opinion has it that the poem addresses the state of human superannuation.' He paused, thinking, then continued: 'That its subject is a lament for the passing of the British Empire, is an extremely marginalized one, supported solely by those pursuing a particular political agenda.' He paused again, assessing his pupil. Then, with a new smile playing on his lips, he added: 'And dare I suggest, Miss James, that this time your research may not have been quite so thorough?'

At this remark, most of the class began to titter; even

Charlotte's expression had developed into a huge smile, a smile clearly indicating her eagerness to hear her friend's response.

Eloise held the new teacher's gaze. 'You may be correct,' she said, shrugging her shoulders dismissively. 'But, on the other hand – like so many other naïve reviewers before you – you may *just* have been misled by the sour ideology of bourgeoisie imperialism.' She turned to Charlotte.

'I don't think that I shall be able to work with him,' she whispered.

'No doubt we shall have many an interesting discussion on the topic in the months to come,' Paul Bridgestock said, smiling to himself.

'I hope so,' Eloise said under her breath.

The new teacher then went on to inform them that he originated from the Isle of Man, where his retired parents still lived, and that he entered teaching following a brief career in journalism working for BBC Radio in the North East of England. He had written a small volume of poetry but, with a wry smile, informed them that he always seemed to be out of kilter with contemporary taste whenever he attempted its publication.

The English literature lesson then got underway.

Charlotte turned to Eloise. 'Boring,' she said, screwing up her face. 'And I thought he was going to be our very own gypsy… or at least a Mellors.' She paused. 'I told you he would be an anticlimax, didn't I? Dullsville.'

Eloise lifted the lid of her desk and rummaged inside. 'At least we will not have any distractions,' she said, picking up a pencil.

Chapter Five

Of course, it wasn't the actual wintry conditions that she so disliked; she could dress appropriately for those. The lack of real sunlight was the biggest problem – coming to school in the half-light of morning and going home in the twilight of afternoon. Lack of natural light had always left her feeling lethargic, listless… She had often thought that it would be nice to hibernate for the winter, like hedgehogs do. And it was harder to concentrate in winter – motivation came more slowly, too. Yes, it did… She knew that her seasonal malady had already begun. And, to make matters worse, the clocks "went back" this weekend – the end of daylight saving time. Winter was on its way.

Once she'd been in her bedroom doing her homework. It was a dull day, really dark; late March, or perhaps early April – she couldn't remember now. She had been struggling to see, was going to switch the light on. But then, all at once, the sun had broken through the clouds. What a difference: the room had been flooded with light, an inspiring brilliance, and the warmth was just as instant. What a pity the sun hadn't stayed out.

'Are you still with us, Miss James?'

Eloise continued to gaze abstractedly out the classroom window, her chin cradled in upturned palms, her elbows forming a triangle with the desktop. And look how gloomy those clouds were, depressed, blanket-like, as though the sky was being pushed down by a giant hand. And why did the same temperature in autumn always feel colder than it did in spring?

'Miss James!'

'Ellie.' Eloise felt the touch on her arm, the gentle shake, and jumped out of her reverie. For an instant, she knew how a rabbit must feel when caught in the glare of headlights.

'Ellie,' Charlotte repeated. 'It's Mr Bridgestock.'

Eloise turned her head from the window, and focused her stare on the teacher at the front of the class. 'Yes?'

'If you are not too preoccupied with matters beyond the scope of this classroom, Miss James, then I would like to discuss your essay.'

'Yes… I am sorry. I was just…' Eloise became aware that some of the class were giggling. She was certain to get a reprimand. Mr Bridgestock had once told them that he wasn't a hard taskmaster – and that was right. But, since then, he had shown them on more than one occasion that he expected their attention during lessons. He was quite strict in that respect. Pamela Palmer had received a real ticking off for talking in class; although, to be fair, she had been warned about it earlier… And there were other issues with her, too.

Mr Bridgestock smiled. He looked even more like Alan Ladd when he did that, Eloise thought. 'Well,' he began, 'in view of the fact that you appear to have returned to us from whence you wandered, do I have your permission to proceed?'

Eloise tried to return the teacher's smile, but, from how it felt, she guessed that it came out looking more like a grimace. So she nodded instead.

'Thank you, Miss James.' Mr Bridgestock plucked an exercise book from his desk, and held it towards his class. 'I wish to commend this essay to you all.' Golly. Eloise was surprised. It was dashed down in a single session. 'I have singled it out for attention,' the teacher continued, 'not because of its – shall we say, grammatical niceties – but rather for the invention of its plot and, even though it is not always sustained, for the evocative power of its prose.' Miss Marshall had praised those elements of her writing, too. She had told her not to worry too much about the other things, anyone could learn grammar, punctuation – when to use a semi-colon instead of a full stop. But imagination, being able to invent, that was different, she'd said: you couldn't learn that.

The subject of her essay was the Hindenburg airship disaster of 1937. Following a successful crossing of the Atlantic from Germany, the airship, filled with hydrogen gas, had burst into flames while attempting to land at the Lakehurst Naval Station in New Jersey. Thirty-seven of its passengers and crew had lost their lives in the ensuing inferno, with many more suffering horrendous burns.

Paul Bridgestock had obtained a tape recording of the famous radio commentary made by the tearful reporter Herbert Morrison and had played it to his class. Eloise had listened to the tape and, moved by Morrison's emotional phrases, "It's burst into flames… Oh, my, this is terrible…" and "Oh, the humanity and all the passengers" had composed her response.

Mr Bridgestock opened Eloise's exercise book and scanned several pages. 'As you are all aware, there were numerous theories put forward at the time to account for the catastrophe: a bomb planted on board; a lightening strike; the dirigible colliding with the docking tower.' Eloise noticed a flicker of a smile touch his lips. 'Even one that had local farmers shooting at it because it had frightened their livestock.' He walked round his desk and stood facing his class. 'All credible hypotheses,' he announced. 'However, Miss James has come up with an alternative proposition. She imagines the catastrophe as being the consequence of a communist plot, a scheme designed to undermine the manifest superiority of Germany's technology over that of the Soviet Union's. He paused to glance at the exercise book. 'And also as a measure to weaken the increasing Nazi threat to international permanence… You will recall that we are discussing an event that occurred not so very long before the outbreak of World War II.

'Now, for the mechanics of the exploit, Miss James has a copper wire stretching from the steel base of the docking tower, across the compound of the landing area, and under the perimeter fence of the naval station.' He glanced at the open pages of the book. 'From there it continues into a copse of trees, where, craftily concealed, is an electrical generator. The wire is connected to the terminals of this piece of equipment… Bear with me, this is quite complicated… Ah, yes… At the appropriate moment, it is the conspirators' intention to electrify the wire, thus also to electrify the steel structure of the docking tower, which, they have calculated, will then produce an electrical short circuit between the tower and the metal frame of the airship.' He paused again to take another glance at the exercise book. 'Heat will be generated – and the highly flammable hydrogen gas in the dirigible's envelope will ignite.'

The teacher rested himself against the front of his desk. 'I do not claim to be an expert and I am unsure if any of this electrification would indeed produce the effects described.' He shot a glance at Eloise. 'However, be that as it may, let us concede the technical issues to poetic licence, consider…

'"Comrade Vladimir noted the preordained signal and,

with a trembling hand, threw the lever forward. The charge, wielding the sizzle and flash of lit dynamite, was on its way, unleashed, speeding towards its target with the lethal force of a death ray.

"'With baited breath, the collaborators watched… and waited…

"'Nothing happened. The tower did not take on an iridescent glow. The sky did not erupt in fiery Armageddon. And the airship sustained above them, a defiant out-post of fascism, the swastika on its side a badge of contempt, an emblem mocking the feeble efforts of Stalin's assassins.

"'They had failed.

"'The collaborators continued to watch… To wait… Still nothing happened.

"'They had failed.

"'But then, just when all seemed lost, deadly desire doomed, the cohorts felt an easterly zephyr begin to blow against their upturned faces. They waited, prayer-like, crouched in the undergrowth beside the purring generator, as the easterly inched the ship's underbelly inexorably towards the safety of the docking tower.

"'In the radio room, Herbert Morrison spoke into his microphone: It's practically standing still now… They've dropped ropes down out of the ship's nose… It's burst into flames… Oh, my, this is terrible…

"'And the rest is history.'"

Mr Bridgestock closed the exercise book with an exaggerated slap, then came between the desks to where Eloise was sitting. 'Well done, Miss James,' he said, passing her the book with a warm smile. 'Congratulations. And you will see that I have awarded you a high mark.' He walked back to the front of the class, then turned and caught Eloise's gaze. 'But please do not become complacent, Miss James, there is still room for improvement to be made in your work… '

'Teacher's pet. Eloise, you're teacher's pet.'

Eloise glanced over her shoulder, to see Pamela Palmer following her along the corridor. The English lesson was over, and the class was on its way to the refectory for lunch. She had no intention of responding to the teasing. Experience had taught her that it was always wisest to avoid such juvenile behaviour.

'Teacher's pet,' Pamela Palmer continued. 'Don't try and deny it, Eloise. We all know you're Mr Bridgestock's favourite.'

Eloise heard one or two of the other girls start to giggle… Pamela Palmer's cronies. Then she felt the other girl's hand on her shoulder. 'Teacher's pet.' That did it. Despite her resolution, and Charlotte's linked arm now urging her away from the teasing, Eloise swung round to face Pamela Palmer.

'I have no idea what you mean,' she said evenly, holding the other girl's stare. 'But if you are referring to what Mr Bridgestock said about my essay, then you should remember that he criticised it, too.'

'That is what I mean,' Pamela Palmer returned, stridently. She folded her arms across her chest. 'He said that he gave you a high mark, and we all know how sloppy your writing is… You're the worst speller in the class.'

Eloise sighed. 'Pamela,' she began, as calmly as she could manage, 'he gave me seven out of ten – that's all.'

'Yes, and he only gave me a six… Mine was better than yours.'

'But you haven't read mine, have you?' Eloise pointed out the obvious flaw in the teaser's assertion. 'So how do you know?'

'I just know… I just know from what Sir read out – and, besides, I'm better at grammar and punctuation than you are.'

Eloise smiled. She knew the argument was won. 'The exercise wasn't about those things, Pamela,' she said, patiently. 'If you remember, Mr Bridgestock said that it was an exercise in writing narrative, something with which to develop our creative skills.' She paused, still holding the other girl's stare. 'It wasn't part of the 'A' level curriculum. If it had been, he would have marked me lower.'

But Pamela was not to be so easily appeased. 'He told me off for talking in class, and look what you got away with today,' she whined, '– goggling out of the window. Why, he just made a joke of it… Teacher's pet.'

'It wasn't disobedience like it is with you,' Eloise retorted, feeling her colour rising. 'It was merely–'

'Day dreaming,' Pamela Palmer interrupted. 'Not paying attention. And that's as bad as anything that I've done wrong. You get away with it, while I get told off – and I get lower marks.'

'Pam, sometimes we all talk in class when we shouldn't. But whenever you are reprimanded for it, you argue with him, you show him no respect…' Eloise paused to straighten her spectacles. 'Sometimes you are downright rude.' She started to move away, but then turned back again. 'And you are usually late in the mornings, as well,' she added.

'I've noticed the way you look at him, Eloise.' Pamela Palmer rolled her eyes extravagantly. 'And the other evening at the camera club. "Oh, Mr Bridgestock, I've got one of those, too".'

Shortly after his arrival at the school the new teacher had started up a camera club, which had chimed well with Eloise, as photography was a favourite pastime of hers. Mr Bridgestock had explained that the activities of the club would be to go on field trips to scenic spots around the county, and also to meet one evening a week at the school, where they would learn how to develop and print photographs from their films. As well as herself, a half-dozen other pupils had also joined the club – including Pamela Palmer.

'I didn't say "Oh, Mr Bridgestock" like that.' Eloise mimicked the other girl's mannerism. 'I merely remarked that I owned a camera like the one he had brought to the club.'

'That's what I mean–'

'Girls, girls,' Charlotte broke in, clearly seeing that the argument was going nowhere. 'This isn't a kindergarten.'

'Oh, that's right,' Pamela Palmer said, rounding on Charlotte, 'stand up for your little friend, as usual.'

'I don't need anyone to take my side,' Eloise countered, nudging Charlotte aside. 'But just for the record, Pamela, you're wrong. You're wrong on all counts.'

By this time most of the other girls had lost interest in the argument and had left for the refectory, and Pamela Palmer now started to do the same. 'He likes you and he doesn't like me,' she whined, side-stepping past Eloise. 'That's why you got a higher grade.' She glanced back over her shoulder. 'I suppose you'll be bringing him in an apple tomorrow.'

Chapter Six

Eloise followed Miss Staidler down the tiled passageway. She had no idea why, moments before, in the middle of a geography lesson, she had been summoned to attend a meeting in the headmistress's study. It had nothing to do with her mother's recent illness, the teacher had immediately assured her of that. But, knowing Miss Staidler as she did, she guessed that it would not be to receive a commendation for her work either. On the other hand, she had not under performed, had done nothing amiss that she knew of. So, then, whatever could the summons mean?

It was the first week back at school following the Easter break. It was also the start of Paul Bridgestock's third term as English master – two full terms already completed. During those two sessions, there had been highs and lows in Eloise's studies, though thankfully more of the former than of the latter. She had worked hard, especially at the more practical elements of English – but as important as Mr Bridgestock said they were, he still encouraged the creative side, too. She had taken to his philosophy of "exploring our subject together", had been drawn into the debates that it had generated. She had come to like the new teacher's methods. So much so in fact, that she hadn't been unduly concerned when reasoned argument had persuaded her to capitulate her earlier position on Philip Larkin's poem.

But, for all that, she still sometimes missed Miss Marshall's familiar ways. The teacher's death had been so unexpected. The result was that she had found herself labouring over disciplines that had hitherto seemed simpler. Attempting to unravel the structure of T. S. Eliot's poem *The Wasteland* had brought her her lowest mark of the year – and she'd spent hours over that damned poem. "April is the cruellest month…" How could anyone who loved the springtime be expected to tackle a poem that began like that? And so many different narrators… Obscure literary references… Eloise had struggled – and, to be fair to Mr Bridgestock, doubtless would have done so under her former teacher. But Miss Marshall had had a knack of teasing out the mysteries of poetry – even from the most arcane works – and would surely have saved April from being her "cruellest" month.

But it was earlier in the year when Eloise had suffered her cruellest blow. For during the particularly cold winter of that year, her mother had suffered a stroke. A week spent in hospital undergoing tests had diagnosed the stroke as being only a minor one. But the anxiety caused by her mother's illness had affected her schoolwork. For most of the important winter term – the final complete period before revision took over – serious study had been shelved as her responsibilities had shifted from narrative to nursing. And it wasn't just a case of doing well in English, for she was also taking geography and French.

But Mr Bridgestock had come to her rescue. He had suggested that she defer sitting the examinations until November, which would give her time to recover lost ground. Both Miss Staidler and Eloise's parents had agreed. Eloise was aware that November was when examinations failed in June were usually retaken, and although she would not in fact be doing exactly that, had accepted the offer. The extra months would make all the difference. And as she and Charlotte planned to take a year out before starting at university, taking the examinations some five months after her friend had taken hers would not affect their plans.

Eloise continued down the corridor, her heels occasionally click-clicking as she skipped to keep apace with the striding figure in front. All the way down here – past the chemistry laboratory, past the drama studio, the kitchens, the refectory – the headmistress had remain silent, and so Eloise was still unaware of the reason for her unexpected summons. She knew it would not be about her standard of work… And it did not concern her mother's illness…

Then they were at the door of Miss Staidler's study… and at that moment Eloise had it. Her mother had made a good recovery from the stroke, "a remarkable rehabilitation", the doctor had said. So they wanted her to sit the examinations in June… Barely two months away. They were going to tell her that she had to return to the original schedule. But that was unfair. She had reset her study timetable for November. Beginning to feel the onset of panic, she watched the headmistress open the heavy door and disappear into her study.

She too prepared to cross the boundary… The Rubicon, as some girls called it. Certainly that was an appropriate description for today's business. But of course, Mr Bridgestock was bound to be here as well, to back up Miss Staidler. Well, as her mother had often told her, "worrying would do no good". Adopting a nonchalant air, she straightened her glasses and went into the room.

She found herself in the small study, austerely furnished, apart that was from the antique French chaise longue. Rumour had it that Miss Staidler had courted Miss Marshall on that. The sash window set into the farther wall, looked out over the narrow footpath that ran behind the school. Some of the more daring girls would sneak round there and pull faces at the headmistress through the window. Golly, if Miss Staidler ever turned around and caught them at it… Adjacent to the path, an unkempt hedge of hawthorns joined forces with a row of mature elms in an effort to reduce most of the available north light to a dingy minimum.

Eloise saw that Miss Staidler had already taken up position behind her desk, by the window, facing into the room. Her face was set as though chiselled in marble, her lips tautened into a thin line – like an adjudicator at a court marshal. Sitting beside the desk, also facing into the room was Mr Bridgestock. He flashed her a wan smile. He didn't look at all like Alan Ladd now. So she was right, then: the exams. He seemed nervous – and so he should be. Also present, was her mother, seated stiffly, facing Miss Staidler, her back to the door. Her mother hadn't even acknowledged her entry into the room, hadn't even glanced at her own daughter. Yes, definitely about re-scheduling the examinations. All in cahoots, even her own mother.

'Please be seated, Eloise,' the headmistress said, indicating the vacant chair facing her desk.

Eloise walked the few paces to the chair, shuffled it a little closer to her mother, and then sat down. 'There was no need for you to come in today, mother,' she said. 'You should be at home convalescing.' She paused to glance at the headmistress. 'I am quite capable of discussing examination dates myself.'

'Please do not fuss, Eloise,' Mary James told her daughter. She too glanced at Miss Staidler. 'And we are not here to discuss examination dates.'

'Oh…' Something had clearly annoyed her mother. Looking down at her hands, Eloise said: 'But I could have managed June… I think.'

The headmistress coughed and shuffled some papers noisily. 'If we are all ready, let us be done with this business.' She directed her gaze to Eloise. 'I have already discussed the matter with your mother and your teacher, Eloise…' There was an unmistakable emphasis in the way that Miss Staidler had spoken the words "and your teacher" that indicated to Eloise that Mr Bridgestock was not in attendance solely because of his being her tutor. After all, he was only one of four. '…Nonetheless,' Miss Staidler continued, 'I wished to have all concerned brought together in order that there can be no possibility of misunderstanding and-'

'Believe me, I shall ensure that that does not happen,' Mary James interrupted.

Eloise glanced nervously at her mother. Yes, indeed, mum was "ready to go" over something.

'Quite so,' Miss Staidler replied. 'To the point, then.' She turned to Eloise. 'Your photography excursions, Eloise, I have been informed that many of them have involved just yourself and Mr Bridgestock… Alone.'

So that was it: the camera club trips – the ones that she and Paul had gone on by themselves. Eloise furrowed her brow. Miss Staidler thought… Although, Charlotte mentioned it – how it might appear to others. They'd laughed, made a joke of it: Mellors and Lady Chatterley – Bridgestock and Lady James. "Don't let him persuade you to photograph any daisies," Charlotte had teased, alluding to the scene in the book where the gamekeeper Mellors uses the flower to titivate the private parts of his mistress Lady Chatterley. Eloise glanced at Paul Bridgestock, to see that he was looking down at his hands, which he held nervously in his lap. If she hadn't known otherwise, she would have judged him guilty. She turned back to the headmistress. 'Yes,' she said brightly. 'Often we are the only ones able to go.'

Miss Staidler nodded. 'Indeed. But have you not considered how such a state of affairs might be construed–'

'*Mis*construed by those with no moral code, those whose only concern is to see wrong where none exists,' her mother interrupted. She stared at the headmistress, flushed, her bosom heaving. Nevertheless, bringing her outburst under control, she continued: 'However, is it not the school's responsibility to ensure that measures are in place to prevent ambiguity arising from such activities?'

At this observation, Paul Bridgestock began to speak, but only to find himself immediately shushed into silence by his headmistress.

'Of course it is, Mrs James,' the headmistress said flatly. She flashed a grimace at the silenced teacher. 'And I have addressed our lapse.' She paused. 'Nevertheless, where there exists a potential for misunderstanding to occur, we all have a part to play; it is the responsibility of all of us to ensure that the reputation of the school is not compromised.'

'My only concern is that my daughter's reputation is not compromised,' Mary said. She turned to Eloise. 'Eloise is merely a child.'

'Lolita was younger than I am, mother,' Eloise said, smiling. All this was silly. But just wait till she told Charlotte.

'Please try to be serious, Eloise,' her mother snapped. 'The situation does not warrant flippancy.' She turned back to Miss Staidler. 'As I said, Eloise is merely a child.'

The headmistress settled her gaze on Mary James. 'Eloise is seventeen – will soon be eighteen.' She paused, allowing the gist of her remark to be digested by the parent. 'But, be that as it may,' she continued, 'I am satisfied that nothing untoward has occurred between your daughter and her teacher.'

'I am absolutely certain of it,' Mary replied vehemently.

There was no need for her mother to be that certain. Eloise was a little bit miffed, a little bit disappointed. She may not be as attractive as Charlotte… Mousy old hair, and her nose was too big – but she had her good points… Besides, she and Mr Bridge – Paul – could have… Yes, but they hadn't, had they? No, but they could have. The opportunity had been there. Like that time in the darkroom, here at school, when his arm had brushed against her breast. Her eyes hadn't been totally accustomed to the darkness, but she could have sworn something had registered in his expression. Perhaps, if she had been prettier… Eloise turned to her mother. 'So am I, mummy,' she said.

Ignoring Eloise's intervention, Miss Staidler peered across her desk at Mary, and, despite the parent's assertion, a faint smile softened her lips. 'It is not sufficient that a situation such as we have here *is* innocent, Mrs James. On the contrary, that situation must also be *seen* to be innocent. That is equally important. Unfortunately, there are those – as you yourself rightly indicated earlier – who do wish to misconstrue, those who revel in spreading rumour for rumour's sake. We have to ensure that that does not happen.'

Mary James nodded and picked up her daughter's hand.

The headmistress smiled again. 'We have to ensure that it doesn't happen, Mary, both for the sake of your daughter's good name and also for that of the school's reputation.'

Paul Bridgestock shuffled his feet nervously on the bare floorboards. 'I fear that this is entirely my fault,' he began timidly, addressing himself directly to Mary James. 'As you are aware, this is my first permanent teaching post and clearly I have been naïve in allowing a situation to arise whereby your daughter has been compromised. Therefore, with regard to all future photographic trips – if indeed they are permitted to continue…'

Eloise looked down at her hands. It would be awful if the camera club were disbanded. They had such fun, went to swell places… And she often used the facilities to develop her own photographs. No, it mustn't happen. She glanced at the club leader.

'If the camera club is allowed to carry on,' he was saying, 'then I shall ensure that a chaperon is always present, that we are always a group.' He paused. 'Mrs James, please accept my apology for any distress that my thoughtlessness may have caused you and your husband.'

Mary smiled at Mr Bridgestock. It was a signal absolving the teacher of any lasting blame, Eloise instinctively knew – more importantly, she could see that he read it that way too.

'Yes, yes, of course, Mr Bridgestock, we all understand,' Miss Staidler said, dismissively. Clearly pleased at her handling of the matter, she grimaced at the other two present, 'Unfortunately, despite His infinite wisdom, the good Lord failed to give the male of the species the same degree of common sense as that He afforded us.' She sighed. 'In fact, and without fear of contradiction, I hold that men are for the most part quite nonsensical.'

At this final remark, Eloise experienced a giggle beginning to rise in her throat, and was forced to twist round in her chair in order to prevent the headmistress from seeing it manifest itself in her expression. She saw that Miss Staidler's dictum appeared to have lifted Mr Bridgestock's spirits too… And her mother's.

Suddenly appearing to catch the changed mood in the room, Miss Staidler rapped the desk with her knuckles. 'I would like to make it absolutely clear,' she began resolutely, 'that my paramount purpose here this morning has been to protect the school's reputation.' She paused, glancing from one stony face to the next. 'Let no one be in any doubt about that.'

Eloise stood up, kissed her mother on the cheek, then left the room and started off up the corridor to return to her geography lesson, where Charlie would be waiting eager to hear her news. But that would of course need to be embellished... Perhaps Miss Staidler had revealed the leader of the camera club to be a modern-day Don Juan whose practice was to photograph his conquests – of whom there would be many. Or possibly their teacher had confessed – under duress, naturally – to having a penchant for cultivating daisies. Smiling, Eloise bustled along the corridor. She hoped, though, that their photographic excursions would not be suspended; for that would be silly over such a trivial misunderstanding.

To her relief, later that day, she learned that Miss Staidler had decided to allow the activities of the camera club to continue. It was welcome news. The headmistress had made one stipulation however: in future, all field trips would be required to have two members present above and beyond that of Mr Bridgestock in his role of club leader. It would be a nuisance, having to find someone else to go with them – although she knew that Charlotte would always make up the numbers when no one else was available.

Charlotte wasn't interested in photography. They were pretty much together on most things, but taking pictures wasn't one of them. Eloise had tried to raise her friend's interest in the hobby, had even allowed her to use her own precious Tenax camera – but to no avail. But Charlie was her best friend, and wouldn't let her down. The camera club field trips were safe. The show would go on.

In what seemed like no time at all, it was June, and the start of the examination period, a protracted one that year; one which would take them through to the end of term. For Eloise it was a time of mixed emotions. On the one hand, she wanted to be taking her 'A' Levels, along with Charlotte, to get them over and done with. On the other, she realised that the study time lost earlier in the year had left her inadequately prepared to do so. She had missed every single one of the discussions on Shakespeare's *Richard II* and George Orwell's *Animal Farm* – and one of those was bound to come up in the examination. Several days of potential frustration loomed, floating in limbo while her peers got on with things. In the event, what with her own continuing studies, together with assisting Charlotte's last-minute preparations, the time simply flew by. The examinations were over, finished – done and dusted.

Charlotte had fared well in them; Eloise knew from the fact of her friend's attempts to play down her performance, which was a great relief for she knew that Charlie, in spite of her renowned coolness under pressure, also had a tendency to allow her mind to wander from the task in hand at the most crucial of moments. To a certain extent, Charlotte was too laid back. Still, it appeared that she had acquitted herself well – and that was one concern less to deal with. Now all she herself had to do was prepare for November… But that was a long way off. First there were the summer holidays.

Chapter Seven

Paul Bridgestock stood on the riverbank, shielding his eyes against the reflected glare of the afternoon sun. 'Please be careful… Both of you,' he shouted. 'The river may be deeper than you think.'

With the hem of her frock held above her knees, Eloise led Charlotte through the stream towards the shingle island. She paused to glance over her shoulder. 'Don't worry so, Mr Bridgestock. We're almost there now.'

'It's quite safe,' Charlotte said. She squeezed her friend's hand and, smiling mischievously, added: 'And once we are there, you will be able to take photographs of the school's sirens basking on the shingle.'

'Charlie! He will hear you.'

'What was that about sirens?' Paul Bridgestock shouted.

Eloise paused momentarily in the current. 'Charlotte said that it's quite safe,' she called, raising her voice above the ripple of the river. 'And not to worry, because, if we fall in, we will wail like sirens to attract your attention.'

Paul Bridgestock moved closer to the water's edge. 'I am not worried,' he said. 'It's just that I don't fancy getting wet wading out to rescue you both.'

It was the start of the school summer holiday and two members of the camera club and chaperon were on a field trip along the River Exe, about a mile north of the city. When travelling past here by train the previous week, Eloise had spotted a kingfisher hunting and had enthused to Charlotte of the locality's unique photographic potential. 'The place is ideal,' she had declared. 'A kink in the river's course has created a small inlet, causing the current almost to stall. And beyond that, just steps from the riverbank, is a raised bed of shingle – a splendid spot to set up the equipment and await the inevitable.'

But Charlotte had not been so convinced, declaring: 'Just because you saw one bird fishing there, it doesn't necessary follow that it's their regular haunt. We might be there for hours, just sitting around waiting.'

'No, the pool is ideal,' Eloise had insisted. 'And anyway, just bring along a book and sit in the sun reading.'

'There is a reference to the Fisher King in *The Wasteland*,' Charlotte had mused. 'I'll bring that and see if it inspires you.'

And so a deal had been struck.

Eloise trudged determinedly up the slope on to the shingle island. Cool. They had made it. She nudged her glasses up the bridge of her nose, then turned and helped Charlotte up out of the water. Once Charlie had settled, she would set up her camera and focus on the inlet, which was just a matter of yards downstream.

Charlotte sat down and shuffled her toes into the sun-warmed shingle. 'Gosh, Eloise, it may be summer but the water is freezing.' She fished a handkerchief from her bag, then dabbed at the water droplets on her legs. 'Brrr,' she said extravagantly. 'This isn't the way to get me interested in photography.' She glanced at her friend. 'And I hope that after all this palaver you get the pictures you want.'

Eloise gazed at the ribbon of silver-speckled ripples they had just crossed, back to the riverbank – shallow above the current – to where Paul had erected his tripod and camera. 'Can you view all of the deeper pool from there?' she shouted.

'Shush!' Charlotte said, grinning widely. 'Even hungry kingfishers won't fish with all this noise going on.'

Paul Bridgestock looked towards Eloise and raised a silent thumb.

Eloise returned the gesture.

Charlotte drew idle fingers through the shingle. 'I expect we will get some swell pictures, Ellie,' she said. She fished in her bag and took out a packet of cigarettes, lit one and drew deeply. She released the smoke with a sigh. 'In fact, I am certain we shall.'

Presently, following a check on the light conditions with her light meter, Eloise trained her camera on the sweep of river where, over time, the eddying current had chiselled out the inlet. She adjusted its focus, bringing every salient detail into sharp contrast. A mirage of midges swam above the gentle meander. They would attract the fish, which, in their turn, would attract the kingfisher. Perhaps there would be more than one. The situation here was perfect: the sun high in the sky and directly behind them; the light clear; sharp. Indeed, if they remained here quietly and undisturbed, they should be lucky. She checked her camera's shutter speed setting. Yes, that would be fine. And she had a "fast" film loaded for the action shots. She glanced towards Mr Bridgestock. He seemed ready, his camera prepared. Perfect. So all they had to do was–

'Oh, help. Help! Please help me.'

The plaintive cries interrupted Eloise's revelry, and she turned in their direction. No, it couldn't be. Sitting bolt upright in the middle of the stream, between the shingle island and the farther riverbank, was Charlotte. She must have attempted to wade to the other bank but had slipped and fallen in. Eloise hadn't noticed that her friend had set off exploring alone, and could now only stand and stare, watching in absorbed fascination the skirt of Charlotte's frock billowing in the current… like a freshly flung fishing net. But Charlie was in no danger: it wasn't deep out there.

'Help! Please. Will someone please help me?' The plaintive cries came again.

'I thought you said the water was cold,' Eloise called, placing her camera carefully on the shingle, as she prepared to go to the aid of her friend.

Charlotte cast a hurt glance back across the river. 'It's not funny, Eloise. I am stuck here.' Then, as if to substantiate the truth of her remark, she placed her hands on the riverbed and attempted without success to raise herself from the water. 'I can't get up,' she added, despondently.

Eloise started across the shingle bank. 'I'm coming, Charlie,' she cried, splashing into the stream. And at that moment there came a further watery commotion as Mr Bridgestock came past her heading for his stricken pupil. Eloise followed in his wake.

Taking an arm apiece, they pulled Charlotte to her feet, then guided her back past the shingle island to the safety of the riverbank and lowered her onto the sun-baked grass.

The teacher took off his jacket and wrapped it around Charlotte's shoulders, drawing it tight to preserve her body heat. Eager to help, Eloise joined in and began to rub her friend's upper arms.

Charlotte shivered into the coat. 'Gosh but the water was cold; the shock as I sat down was quite fearsome.' Her gaze trembled between her two assistants. 'It was worse than the swimming pool.' She shivered again, but more theatrically this time. Then, grinning up at Paul, she added: 'But the worst thing was when I found that I was stuck and unable to get up; then I had a vision of a tidal surge sweeping up the river and drowning me.'

Eloise rolled her eyes. 'It's not the River Severn, Charlotte.'

'That's as may be,' Charlotte replied, 'but when you are trapped and your best friend ignores your plight, all kinds of fearful notions become plausible – piranhas, electric eels… Even awakening Kraken.'

Paul Bridgestock coughed. 'The water is cold because it's come all the way down from Exmoor,' he said. 'And because it's so fast-flowing, it never really warms up – even on a hot day like today.'

'And the chill is exaggerated by its contact with contrastingly warm, suntanned skin,' Eloise said authoritatively. 'Granted it's a startling shock, but one soon gets used to it nevertheless.'

'Really?' Charlotte said. 'So I'll soon get used to this wet frock clinging to me.' She paused to pluck a piece of duckweed from the garment. 'And it's ruined, too,' she concluded, sadly.

Eloise knelt by Charlotte and fanned the folds of her friend's soiled skirt wide on the grass. 'The sun will dry it in no time.' She pressed Charlotte's hand. 'And it is cotton, so one wash and it will be as good as new.'

'It was new,' Charlotte said, glumly – 'and a Christian Dior original.'

Eloise smoothed the material of the garment. 'Really?'

Charlotte scoffed. 'Don't be silly. If it had been, I would have been back in the river by now… drowning myself.' She glanced at Eloise. 'But I have spoilt your photography trip,' she said. She lifted the damp skirt from her legs, the better to aid its drying. 'My stupid attempt to wade all the way across the river has ruined everything. The noise, the splashing about… No kingfishers will venture within a mile of here now.'

'In retrospect, I don't think they would have anyway,' Eloise said. 'My idea to place ourselves over there was a misjudged one. It is simply too near to where they feed.'

Paul Bridgestock wandered back from the water's edge then, where he had retreated during the dress-drying manoeuvres. 'Hindsight is a marvellous–' And at that moment there came the sound of a splash from the inlet pool, causing him to abandon his hackneyed observation. 'Was that what I think it–' And he was silenced for a second time as, a moment later, a rainbow of colour in the shape of a kingfisher rose from the river, together with its catch flapping frenetically in its beak.

'Look at that,' Eloise said.

'Well, I'll be…' Paul said.

Eloise reached for her camera. Paul reached for his too. But by then the kingfisher was long gone.

'Did you see the droplets of water cascading from its feathers as it emerged from the pool?' Charlotte asked. She touched her still-damp frock. 'Wish I could dry as quickly as that.' She paused, thinking. Then, gazing overhead, she added in hopeful tones: 'Perhaps another one will come along in a moment… Or maybe that one will come back again.'

'Possibly,' Paul Bridgestock replied, 'although I rather doubt it. It's caught its family's supper – and that's its chores completed for the day.' He started to dismantle his photographic equipment, detaching camera from tripod, zoom lens from camera – and began to pack the items into his holdall. All at once he stopped and straightened again. 'That café over there,' he said, pointing across the river towards the main road, 'that looks inviting.' He winked at Charlotte. 'We will have to retreat to the bridge to cross the river – can't risk your getting wet again.' He picked up his holdall. 'C'mon, the lemonades are on me.'

Sitting in the café overlooking the river, Eloise sipped her lemonade. It was a shame they'd missed their chance with the kingfisher. But she had been right about the location. They would have to come here again. It was a pity about poor Charlie's mishap though. Next time they would have to… Suddenly grinning as the image of her friend stranded bolt upright in the river reappeared in her mind, she said: 'In my opinion, Charlie, your falling into the river was merely a calculated attempt to get yourself photographed.' She placed her glass on the table. 'Is that your opinion, too, Mr Bridgestock?'

'Indeed it is,' Paul said. His eyes settled sternly on Charlotte. 'A clear case of playing the siren taken to the extreme.'

Charlotte almost dropped the packet of cigarettes she had been taking from her bag. 'Oh, you didn't,' she said, expression aghast. 'You didn't actually take…' Her question petered out as she noticed the concerted grins of her two companions. 'You rotters!' She lit a cigarette and drew deeply. After a second or two, she exhaled. 'But I simply could not get up. I think that somehow I became wedged between two rocks. You know, sort of stumbled against the first, lost my balance, and then fell between that and the second one.'

Paul Bridgestock ran his fingers through his hair. 'My

theory is that it was a preconceived ruse,' he said, 'a joint effort by the pair of you designed to play on my sympathy in order to extract lemonade and crisps.'

'And it went off like clockwork,' Charlotte said.

'Except that we didn't get any photographs of the kingfisher,' Eloise mused. She removed her glasses and started to polish the lenses. 'And that fish that it caught, flapping, desperate to break free… Wow, it would have been a terrific image.'

'Blame Eliot,' Charlotte said, dryly. 'His poem was a *waste* of time.' She paused. 'But never mind, Ellie: there will be a next time. We were unlucky today but…' She paused again, turning to gaze out the window, where the noisy arrival of several motorcycles had claimed her attention. After a moment's thought, changing the subject, she said: 'I would like to ride pillion on one of those, sweeping round corners like they do.' She lifted her hair out straight behind her and swayed from side to side. 'Wearing no crash helmet – and the wind rushing through one's hair… just like on the fairground rides.'

Eloise finished cleaning her glasses and replaced them on her nose. 'They are too dangerous,' she said. 'I would prefer a ride on a scooter. You know, like the one we saw in the car park when we came in.' She nodded towards the window. 'They don't lean over as much as motorcycles do when they go around corners.' She extended her arms and raised the palms of her hands. 'And they have those screen things that protect you from the wind and rain.'

'They are not as safe as motorcycles,' Paul Bridgestock said. 'Their small wheels make them extremely unstable, especially on uneven road surfaces.'

'And they don't lean over so much on corners,' Charlotte

chipped in, 'simply because they don't go as fast as motorcycles.'

'Then that makes them safer,' Eloise said.

The teacher coughed. 'Both of you have valid points,' he said. He grinned. 'But give me my old jalopy any day. Protection from the elements; and its four wheels make it unerring on corners.'

'Look at that!' Charlotte suddenly exclaimed. She tapped her cigarette against the rim of the ashtray, then returned her gaze to the window. 'Just look at what that boy is doing.'

Eloise and Paul followed Charlotte's stare, through the window to the car park, to where the scooter of Eloise's dreams was parked. The motorcyclists had surrounded it and one boy was calmly twisting one of its mirrors around the handlebars. Another member of the group then started hooking the scooter's horn.

'That's awful,' Eloise said. 'They shouldn't treat other people's property like that… It's against the law.'

She saw there were about a dozen motorcyclists in the gang, lads in leather jackets and denim jeans, leather gauntlets and leather boots. Their crash helmets were painted with all sorts of designs and motifs, a Prussian eagle, a spider, a chequered strip, a Pegasus – one helmet even had a swastika on it. 'They look to be a pretty rum crew,' she said, under her breath.

Charlotte stubbed out her cigarette. 'I'm going out there,' she said determinedly. She stood up. 'I am going to–'

'Please don't attempt to intervene, Charlotte,' the teacher interrupted. He too stood up and, placing a hand on her shoulder, persuaded her to sit down again. 'It is not our responsibility to become involved,' he added, retaking his seat.

'Mr Bridgestock is right, Charlie,' Eloise said. 'There is nothing we can do.' She glanced out the window again. 'They don't look the type to worry about hitting a girl.'

Just then someone in the alcove seat next to theirs rose quickly and made off for the door. Eloise saw that he was a boy of about eighteen or nineteen, slim – almost skinny – and not very tall. He was smartly dressed in a brown suit and white turtle-necked shirt. If the scooter belonged to him, and he intended going outside to tackle the motorcycle gang, then he was surely about to get himself hurt. She watched as, at the door, he stopped to put on a parka jacket from the coat rack there. That wouldn't afford him much protection.

Charlotte turned to her friends. She had also seen the boy heading for the door. 'We have to do something,' she said.

'It will be all right,' Paul Bridgestock said. 'I noticed the proprietor making a telephone call a moment ago. Clearly, he has witnessed what is going on outside and has telephoned for the police.' He rose to his feet. 'Nevertheless, I will check.' His stare settled on Charlotte. 'Now, Charlotte, please stay where you are. We men will take care of this.' He started to walk away, but then turned back to Eloise. 'Eloise, please ensure that Charlotte stays here with you.' And with that he was gone.

Eloise nodded and gripped Charlotte's hand, fearful that her friend's previous impulsiveness might return, might re-ignite and cause her to go dashing off after Mr Bridgestock. But Charlotte appeared to have calmed down, and Eloise returned her attention to the proceedings outside in the car park, just in time to see the motorcyclist snap the wing mirror completely from the handlebars of the scooter.

Charlotte had witnessed the event too, and swung round to face Eloise. 'I am not going to sit here and watch them damage other people's property,' she declared, starting to get up once more.

But Eloise held her friend's hand, refusing to let go, and pulled her back onto the bench seat. 'Stay here, Charlie. Look. Mr Bridgestock and the café owner are going out together.'

"And so they jolly well should,' Charlotte declared, indignantly.

Eloise watched the teacher and the café owner striding across the car park, towards where the scooter owner was remonstrating with one of the motorcyclists. She thought that Mr Bridgestock and the proprietor looked particularly resolute, moving purposefully, expressions set... Marching along. The owner of the café appeared to be giving Mr Bridgestock some form of instruction. He probably had experience of dealing with this sort of thing. The two men would surely settle the argument, before it had chance to escalate and came to blows.

Then Mr Bridgestock and the proprietor arrived at the scene. Suddenly nervous, Eloise glanced at Charlotte, seeking reassurance, but her friend's focus had switched to the lighting of a cigarette. She quickly returned her attention to the window. There were more motorcyclists than she had first thought. But the two adults would sort the situation out. After all, they had authority. Mr Bridgestock was a teacher… The café owner was quite a burly fellow… They were outnumbered though. No, it would be all right.

Her assumption appeared to be correct; for she saw the proprietor step straight into the melee, pull the scooterist free from his detractors, and then start to escort him back across the car park towards the café. The boy was safe. Although, that left Mr Bridgestock completely alone, alone to face the entire gang, who seemed – or so it appeared to her – angry at having had their prey so abruptly snatched from them. Without diverting her stare from the window, she said: 'It looks like it might develop into a nasty situation, Charlie. Mr Bridgestock is all by himself now.'

'The café owner will go out again,' Charlotte assured, 'as soon as he has brought the boy back here.'

'By then it might be too late,' Eloise said.

But the situation outside the window appeared to be under control, for the teacher could clearly be seen reasoning with the motorcyclists, attempting to calm them down, while, at the same time, trying to draw them away from the scooter. And, Eloise thought, Charlotte was right: the proprietor was bound to return to help Mr Bridgestock, once he had the boy safely inside the café.

Then it happened. One of the gang, who had surreptitiously circled round behind the teacher, now removed his crash helmet and, using it as a weapon, brought it down squarely between Mr Bridgestock's shoulder blades. Eloise watched as the teacher wheeled around and, still apparently unnerved, attempted to disarm his attacker. However, while he was doing so – his attention distracted from the gang – another motorcyclist lashed out with his boot, catching him directly behind his right knee. Eloise gasped as she saw the teacher's expression contort in pain – and then again as she witnessed him buckle and fall forwards onto his hands and knees.

Hardly aware of anything other than that she was going outside to help Paul, Eloise was up on her feet and heading for the door. She had no idea what she might do when she got out there – if indeed she could do anything useful at all. She had acted on instinct. She hadn't heard Charlotte calling her back. If she had heard her friend or, better still, if Charlotte had tried to hold her back, then she might have come to her senses. But neither thing had occurred, and now she was almost at the door.

Eloise tore headlong through the door, now unclosed by the returning café owner and rescued boy, the latter being forced to jump aside to avoid being bowled over by the human tornado.

Disregarding the proprietor's cry of "come back", Eloise traversed the car park, her stare fixed firmly on the motorcyclist, whom she saw had Paul's head locked in some form of wrestling manoeuvre. The rest of the gang had linked their hands together to form a ring encircling the two combatants and were egging on their man with cheers of encouragement, while disparaging Paul with cries of "weakling" and "sissy".

Eloise ducked beneath the clasped hands of the human ring, into the arena where the brute was wheeling Paul round and around…

Ellie, are you all right? Ellie… Ellie… Ellie, please say something. Eloise, don't try to move. Everything's going to be all right. Discarnate voices floating in the ether of her dream – coming and going, rising and falling, a discordant harmony of conflicting intonations. What day was it? *Eloieeese…* Was it a school day? *Eloieeese…* Or was it the weekend? *Eloise, try…* If it was a school day, then she would have to get up soon. Eloise unclosed her eyes, only to close them again against the painful effort of doing so.

'Ellie, are you all right?'

What was Charlotte doing here? Eloise demanded of her awakening self. What day? And a headache.

'Eloise, don't attempt to get up. Just lie still a moment longer.'

Whatever was Mr Bridgestock doing here – here in her bedroom? But this didn't feel like her bedroom. School..? Yes, that was it: school… Miss Staidler's study. Then she must have had an accident, fallen down… knocked her head. Grimacing against the throb of the headache, Eloise tried again to open her eyes.

'Stay still, Eloise.' Mr Bridgestock's face swam in and out of focus, a reflection in disturbed water, rippled, undulating like a submerged photograph. 'Lie still a little longer, until you feel more able.'

'Ellie, please say something,' Charlotte's face said.

'Where are my glasses?' Eloise asked. 'I need my glasses…'

'They're broken, Ellie.' Charlotte's face reappeared. 'You broke them when you went outside.'

In the playground… Eloise's eyes fluttered between the far-away expressions of Charlotte and Mr Bridgestock. 'Where is Miss Staidler?' She grimaced again; then glanced from one blurred image to the other. Spectacles weren't cheap: mother would be annoyed. 'Did I hit my head when I fell?' she asked, instinctively starting to pull herself upright.

'Don't try to get up,' Mr Bridgestock's voice said. She felt his hand on her shoulder. 'Lie quietly for a while. We have telephoned for an ambulance, and it will be here in a moment.'

Ambulance? She wasn't going to die, was she? 'Where's mum?' She felt the sudden onset of a panic attack arrive with a thump. 'I want mum; I want mum here. Is she coming, too?' Then she felt Charlotte's hand in hers.

'They're all coming, Ellie: Your parents and mine.'

So she was going to die, then.

'You're going to be all right, Ellie,' Charlotte reassured, squeezing her friend's hand. 'Nothing serious has happened, and you're going to be fine… Just a minor mishap: and it's nothing to be concerned about. You've bumped your head, and you have a bit of a bruise on your forehead, that's all.'

Mishap? Bump? What kind of…? Eloise lifted a hand to her forehead, wincing as her uncoordinated fingers collided with the swelling. She pulled her hand away, dropped it beside her. But… How…? This wasn't Miss Staidler's study. Then, in her mind's eye, she saw the gang of motorcyclists, saw Paul being whirled round and around… Saw herself running across the car park… towards… Eloise closed her eyes tight, tried to blot out the returning memory.

'Ellie… Ellie, are you all right?'

After a while Eloise opened her eyes again. 'Help me up, Charlotte,' she said. 'Please. I want to sit up.'

'I don't think you should, Eloise,' Mr Bridgestock said. 'Please wait until the ambulance arrives.'

'This is the café, isn't it?' Eloise said, simply. She started to sit up. 'I don't think that I need to wait until it gets here.'

And at that moment, the door opened and two ambulance men came into the room.

Tentatively, gingerly, Eloise explored the bump on her forehead, then, even more carefully, eased her head in Mr Bridgestock's direction. 'And so you gave me this?' she said.

The medical examination was over, and, despite being diagnosed with slight concussion, she had been allowed to stay in the café to await the arrival of her parents. But whether this was due to her fitness or simply because Charlotte's father was a surgeon, she wasn't sure. She had also been given an analgesic, and with the headache eased was feeling much better.

Paul Bridgestock, who had also been pronounced fit, touched what appeared to be a similar bump to hers on his forehead. 'Yes, I am afraid so. I was being propelled around… And you came into it all… just at the wrong moment.' He paused. 'I am sorry.'

'Are you all right though?' Eloise enquired. 'I know you weren't knocked out like I was, but you were kicked in the leg?'

Paul Bridgestock nodded. 'My leg is fine,' he said. 'One of the tendons is a touch sore… But I'll mend. He grinned and patted his forehead lightly. 'And this absorbs most knocks.'

In her mind's eye, Eloise saw the bony brow ridges: no wonder she was knocked out.

'When I saw you collapse,' Charlotte said, 'I came outside.' She fell silent. 'But it was finished then… really. When those ruffians saw that you were hurt, they fled pretty sharpish.'

'The proprietor has registration numbers of the motorcycles,' Paul said. 'And so the police will soon apprehend the riders.' He paused. 'Charlotte was extremely brave, Eloise. Had she not come outside when she did, then the outcome might have been much worse.' He glanced at Charlotte again. 'When she said it was finished, she was speaking modestly. Indeed, she looked very determined as she came across the car park.'

'Will someone please fetch me a drink of water?' Eloise said.

'I will,' Paul Bridgestock said, turning towards the door.

Eloise pressed Charlotte's hand. 'And so you saved the day, Charlie,' she said.

'I don't know why he said that, Eloise. As I said, it was practically over by the time I got there. To be honest, I think that he was just trying to make me feel better.' Charlotte looked down at their clasped hands. 'You know, that I let you go out all alone.'

'You were the sensible one,' Eloise said, wistfully. 'How I wish now that I hadn't gone out there.' She shivered as once more she saw herself leap up from the table and make a beeline for the door. 'Besides, you couldn't have stopped me: I bolted off like a runaway train.'

Charlotte lit a cigarette. 'But why did you go, Ellie?' she asked – 'And right into the thick of it, too.' She looked down at her friend sitting on the sofa. 'After all, there was nothing you could have done.'

Eloise shrugged her shoulders, then immediately winced. 'I don't know,' she said. 'But, anyway, you were ready to go out earlier, as well.'

'Yes, I know I was,' Charlotte replied, studying the glowing tip of her cigarette. 'But I wouldn't have got involved in the actual fight, like you did. I would only have reasoned with them.' She shook her head. 'It was so impetuous, Eloise; not a bit like you. And look what you got for your trouble.' She paused to stroke her friend's bruised forehead. 'A bigger bump than Mr Bridgestock's… and his is on the other side to yours.' Charlotte paused again, thinking, then concluded: 'Twins, friends in the fray… Crusading cousins.'

The ghost of a smile touched Eloise's lips.

And at that moment the café owner came into the room

to inform them that the police had arrived, together with two sets of parents.

The ghost vanished.

Eloise planted her feet firmly on the ground and pushed herself upright on the sofa. 'I am absolutely fine now, mother,' she said, impatiently. She took a deep breath in an attempt to quell the lightheaded sensation caused by the effort of sitting up straight. 'I was merely dazed for a moment; they brought me in here to recover. And so I have done.'

An hour had passed since the arrival at the café of police and parents. For Eloise it had been sixty tedious minutes of answering questions and giving statements, and all the time being treated like an effete invalid by her mother – all extremely tiresome. But at least the police had completed their tasks and had left to file their reports. So it wouldn't be long before they went home.

Mary James shook her head. 'You were knocked unconscious, Eloise.' She paused to pull aside her daughter's fringe. 'It is quite an egg,' she said, moving her head from side to side the better to inspect the bump. 'And there's bruising, too. It reminds me of the time you fell off your tricycle.' She paused. 'We took you to hospital then.'

Eloise adjusted the spare pair of spectacles that her mother had brought to the café with her. 'I was only little then,' she said. 'Anyhow, the ambulance men said I was fine, and Charlotte's father doesn't think there is anything to worry about… And he's a surgeon.'

Percy James, who had also been engaged in examining Eloise's forehead, rounded on Paul Bridgestock. 'And if that turns out to be the case, then that is just as well,' he said, folding his arms in a gesture of implied threat.

The teacher shifted uneasily, one foot to the other. 'When I went outside to try to alleviate the situation, sir,' he said, 'it didn't occur to me that Miss James would attempt to assist in so physical a manner.'

'Then it was my daughter's fault,' Percy James said, brusquely. 'Is that what you are implying, Mr Bridgestock?'

'No! No, sir,' Paul began hastily. 'I am not say– ' But he never got the chance to conclude his defence, for Eloise cut him short:

'Of course it was my fault, daddy. Paul… Mr Bridgestock didn't ask for my help. I went of my own accord.'

Percy James' stare softened. 'Well, it's a good thing that Eloise hasn't been badly hurt,' he said. He nodded his head. 'Indeed, it is a jolly good thing.'

Charlotte's father, Christopher Chapplewood, cleared his throat, then turned to Percy James. 'There is no evidence that the concussion will be lasting, Percy.' His gaze settled on Mary James. 'In my experience, Mary, the young rebound with amazing alacrity from such knocks.' He fell silent for a moment, thinking. 'Nevertheless,' he continued, 'to err on the side of caution, it would be prudent to have Dr Shepherd conduct a full examination in the morning.'

'I agree,' Mary James said. 'It will be for the best'.

'Well that's OK then,' Eloise said, flatly.

Mary James turned to her daughter. 'The thing that baffles me about all of this, Eloise, is just why you went rushing off outside like that. You are usually a sensible girl.' She fell silent, shaking her head. 'I cannot understand it.'

Eloise glanced across to the far side of the room, to where Charlotte appeared to be receiving an admonishment from Mrs Chapplewood. Her stare fell to her hands, which were now clasped tightly in her lap. 'Neither can I, mother,' she said.

Chapter Eight

'I just called by to see how the recovery is going,' Paul Bridgestock said, jovially. He walked across the room to where Eloise was sitting on the sofa, reached down and squeezed her hand. 'It was quite a knock you took last week… But your mother tells me you're doing fine.'

'Fighting fit,' Eloise replied, grinning as she fought to suppress the memory of her encounter with the motorcyclists… And Mr Bridgestock's head. It was surely one of nature's little ironies that arranged to have the initial loss of memory replaced by easy recall later – when you didn't want to remember. She lifted her fringe. 'Look. The bump's gone down… And the bruise is almost gone, too.' She glanced at her mother, who had shown the teacher into the living room. 'There was absolutely no need for concern. Charlie's father was right: the young recovery with amazing alacrity.'

Mary James smiled at her daughter. 'Christopher's prognosis did indeed turn out to be correct.' She turned back to their guest. 'And we followed his advice, and I took Eloise to see Dr Shepherd.'

Well, that was right, Eloise thought – but she could have gone to see the doctor alone. She glanced at her mother. 'And he agreed with Mr Chapplewood,' she said, sharply. Eloise didn't care for unnecessary fussing, for being treated like a child – especially in front of others.

'And he also indicated, dear, that we were correct in being cautious.'

Eloise settled her glasses on her nose, then turned to her teacher. 'And how about you,' she began, studying his raised brow ridges – 'no aftershocks from coming into contact with the formidable James skull?'

Paul Bridgestock shook his head. 'No,' he replied, laughing. He swept his hair back from his eyes, then tapped his forehead. 'It was an unequal contest.'

'But your leg was hurt, wasn't it?' Mary enquired.

The teacher became serious. 'I limped for a day or so,' he said, 'but once the inflammation in the tendon subsided, everything was fine.' He paused. 'And it won't affect my batting,' he added beaming.

Eloise knew that he had played cricket for his university and that he now played for a local side. He was their opening batsman and styled himself on the England player Brian Close, whom Mr Bridgestock said was a cavalier player and wasn't afraid to take a few risky swings. He'd also had a trial for the county team, and was still awaiting news of that. But he had said that he didn't expect to get accepted, because he wasn't a local boy; he had heard that the selectors were biased in that respect.

Percy James came into the room then, and, following a perfunctory handshake with Paul Bridgestock, went to his armchair where he immediately set about the lighting of his pipe. Eloise noted that her father had brought a technical journal with him into the room. Her mother had always scolded her father for doing that, when guests called. Still, as long as he didn't read it when Mr Bridgestock was here, it would be all right. At length, with the bowl of his pipe glowing red, Percy James cast a sideways glance at the teacher.

'I don't intend to apportion blame for what occurred last week,' he said, indicating to Eloise with his pipe. 'That will get us nowhere… And things could have been worse. Even so, leaving aside my daughter's health, the thing that concerns me most is the disruption caused to her studies.' He paused to draw on his pipe. 'They have been put further behind. Indeed, this past week, Eloise has shown little inclination for any of her subjects.'

That wasn't true. Eloise started to protest, but only to find herself hushed by her mother.

'There is no doubt but that she has made some improvement in English,' Percy James continued in a more conciliatory tone of voice. 'However, this business could, in my view, unsettle her efforts and potentially put her back several weeks.' He paused to glance at Eloise. 'If this lapse were allowed to continue, her success in the examinations could be seriously jeopardised.'

'They aren't until November,' Eloise put in swiftly. 'That leaves me more than enough time to be ready.'

'Time can slip by before you know it, Eloise,' Mary cautioned. 'And don't forget the books and texts you missed earlier in the year. There's an awful lot to catch up on yet.'

'I know that Eloise could have taken geography and French in June with the other pupils,' Paul began thoughtfully. 'It was merely the consideration of her obtaining the best possible grades that determined our decision to postpone those until November… But of course in doing so, we have unfortunately added more pressure to the other disciplines.' He paused, focusing on Percy James. 'Nevertheless, as you indicated, sir, Eloise has progressed well of late, and consequently I see no reason for not being optimistic.'

'Unfortunately Eloise has a tendency to be easily sidetracked from her work at times, especially at home,' Percy said to the teacher, 'she does of course lack the power of concentration that we men have.'

'Percy!' Mary rounded on her husband. 'There is no difference between the sexes.' She glanced at Eloise. 'Besides, it is summer, and Eloise is always more alert then.'

Eloise couldn't understand why her parents were so concerned. She had obtained copies of the examination questions that Charlotte had taken last month and, as well as catching up on the set texts, her plan was to use those as practice papers. So there really was no need to worry. It was almost as if her mother and father were trying to manipulate the situation to their advantage, as if they were attempting to lure Mr Bridgestock into committing himself to something.

'Yes, it may well be summer,' her father said, 'but if I know anything about it, Eloise will be out with Charlotte. Other… less academic, interests will hold sway.'

'Of course I'll be going out,' Eloise said, forcefully. 'But there is plenty of time for everything. And, anyhow, Charlie is on holiday for the next two weeks.' She turned towards her teacher. 'Besides, too much study is bad for you, isn't it, Mr Bridgestock?'

Paul Bridgestock fidgeted uneasily in his chair. 'Yes… Yes, too much,' he began, falteringly. 'Nevertheless, it is vital that a correct balance be struck… Of course, we have the schedule in place. As you know, Eloise will spend some time back at school from September onward… and the holiday period was planned to be less intensive anyhow – independent study.' His gaze, which had been alternating between Eloise's parents, settled on her father. 'I had been thinking, sir,' he went on, thoughtfully, 'of proposing, for the duration of the unsupervised period, that I set some practice essays, together with some exercises in English, for Eloise. I could call round once a week for an hour – possibly two – and go through these with her.' He fell silent, his gaze once more swinging between Mary and Percy James.

'But won't you be going home to visit your parents this summer?' Mary asked.

'Yes, for a few days – now and then – Mrs James,' Paul replied. He thumbed his cheek. 'But I can work around those trips.'

Percy rested his pipe in his ashtray. 'In my opinion, it sounds an excellent arrangement.' He turned to his wife. 'What do you think, Mary?'

'Providing that Eloise is not required to entirely forego her holiday, then I think that it would certainly be of benefit to her.' She glanced at Eloise. 'Do you not agree, dear?'

'Slave drivers,' Eloise replied with no little feeling. She nudged her spectacles onto the bridge of her nose. It would help, though, to have Mr Bridgestock as her private tutor. And she wanted more than anything to go to St Hilda's with Charlotte. She smiled to herself. Not only that, but with the camera club leader calling on her, it should be possible to arrange some photographic excursions in his car. Yes, they could go to the Exe estuary to photograph the sea birds. They could go to Exmoor. 'Yes, I agree,' she added.

The teacher turned to her and smiled. 'I promise to mark leniently,' he joked.

Eloise then noticed knowing looks pass between her parents. She had been right. She frowned and shook her head. They had been angling for something; and now, having achieved it – or something like it – Mr Bridgestock was going to be invited to stay for afternoon tea.

She was right again; for her mother did just that.

'Well, that's awfully… awfully kind.' Paul appeared taken aback by the invitation. 'Yes… Well…'

Eloise returned to the living room. The meal was over and her mother had sent her on ahead of the completion of the chores with specific instructions to prevent her father from boring their guest with technical talk. 'Don't let him talk work,' her mother had said. It was legend that, given half a chance, Percy would usurp any conversation and use it to discuss his favourite subject. And as she sat down, with her returning presence having gone unacknowledged, she guessed that she had arrived too late.

'You see, the problem is that this soft, granular copper has to be plated first, before the tougher electro-plated copper. We can't use that at this stage because there is nothing between the outside layers of the boards to form a circuit – nothing conductive, that is. Later in the process, after certain other operations have been done, we can of course use the electro-plated copper. Now, unfortunately, one of these other operations involves the use of a copper etch.'

Her father was well into his patter. She had heard this particular problem being discussed before. She still didn't understand it though. Except that the hard electro-plated copper required an electric current for it to work, and the other soft type didn't. That was a crucial difference, apparently. She glanced at Mr Bridgestock. To be fair to him, he appeared to be interested in her father's work problem; he appeared to be nodding at the right times. But he was probably just being polite – or nodding off to sleep.

'Now, with this initial copper being so relatively soft,

unless everything is set up spot-on during the other processes, it is darned easy to etch too much of it away – and that leads to untold problems later when we do the electro-plating.' Percy paused, shaking his head. 'My goodness, son, the amount of rejected work that it causes is frightening. It costs the company a small fortune… Thousands of pounds each year.'

Just then Mary came back into the room and, clearly noting the tenor of the male conversation, cast a disapproving glance at her daughter. But Eloise knew that it wasn't her fault: she'd got here too late. She noted that her mother's return, like her own, had also gone unacknowledged by the two men. That was a bit much – although Mr Bridgestock had glanced at her mother, as if he had been about to say something. Perhaps he had been rendered speechless by Percy's diatribe.

'And you see there's no way,' her father was saying, 'that we can avoid plating the soft, granular copper first. It's imperative, absolutely essential to the other operations.'

'But if you could lay down the electro-plated copper first, then there would be no problem… Is that correct?' Paul Bridgestock asked.

Percy James sighed. 'Not a single one, son. But that's not possible: it contravenes all the laws of electro-plating chemistry.'

Her father's final words appeared to have delivered the death nail to any solution to his problem, and Eloise was just about to jump in and rescue Mr Bridgestock from the introduction of any further technical issues – which was an extremely likely thing to occur with her father – when she heard the teacher say:

'Would it not be possible, immediately after putting on

this soft granular copper, to apply just a minute amount of the electro-plate, do the other operations, and then return to the normal operational sequence?'

All of a sudden it seemed that it was her father's turn to be struck dumb. Eloise studied his expression; the set of his jaw, the pursing of his lips, the slight flush that had come to his cheeks, the surprised look in his eyes. All these things were surely signs of a dawning realisation. Mr Bridgestock's suggestion had sounded like double Dutch to her, but her father had certainly heard it spoken in English. She had always wondered what a Eureka! moment looked like.

Percy got up from his chair. 'By Jupiter, son,' he exclaimed. 'I think that's it – the answer.' He crossed to where the teacher was sitting and shook his hand vigorously. 'It will require some additional work... But not much... And, anyhow, that will be offset a hundred fold in savings made on fewer rejects.'

Eloise studied the two men, both now grinning like schoolboys planning a prank. She guessed they would have looked very much alike at such an age. Pity there were no films of Alan Ladd as a child actor.

Paul Bridgestock rose then and announced that he had "better be on his way". Eloise watched as he shook her father's hand once more. But Percy now seemed preoccupied; was muttering something about the small cost of an extra container. But abstracted or not, he appeared to be pretty pleased with the outcome of the afternoon. Mr Bridgestock had more than acquitted himself of any blame from the motorcyclist affair.

She saw Paul take her mother's hand, heard him thank her for tea. Then he turned to her.

'I am thinking of going to Exmouth tomorrow,' he said,

brightly, holding her gaze. 'The weather forecast looks OK, and I am going to try my hand at some night-time photography at the funfair.' He paused. 'You know, contrast the bright lights of the fair-ground against the ambient darkness – catch some stars in the background, too, if possible.'

'Sounds like fun,' Eloise said.

'What I am really looking forward to,' Paul Bridgestock ran on, 'is to shoot a stationary object against the whirl of a ride at a slow shutter speed… to emphasise the feeling of movement.'

'One fifth of a second would be about right,' Eloise mused.

'That's what I thought, too,' the teacher said, nodding to himself. 'I reckon at one fifth the lights would come out "streamed" on the photograph… but of course it would depend on the speed of the ride – it will be a matter of trial and error.' He fell silent, thinking. 'It's not really a camera club outing as such,' he went on, 'But would you care to come, too?' He paused again, and then turned to Mary James. 'With your parents' permission, of course.'

'I don't think Eloise's health is–'

'Yes it is,' Eloise interrupted, anticipating the gist of her mother's objection. 'I am absolutely fine now – and I've never done that type of photography before…' She fell into reverie. 'We could try other things, too… I've got plenty of "fast" film, which would be ideal for freezing movement at a fast shutter speed… Can I go, mum? Please say yes.'

'It is only a week since we were concussed, Eloise,' Mary pointed out. She paused, taking note of Eloise's nods of encouragement. 'However, if your father agrees.' She glanced at her husband. 'What do you think, Percy?'

But Percy James was still preoccupied with other matters, and merely responded with a perfunctory nod at the mention of his name.

Eloise turned to her mother, her eyes urging the older woman to ask Percy again. But before Mary could do so, Paul said:

'There is a problem I'm afraid – and it has only just occurred to me but, as it's the school holiday, there will be nobody available to accompany us.'

Eloise felt her hopes, buoyed by her mother's tacit approval, suddenly dashed – Miss Staidler's imposed rule on camera club field trips had thwarted them. 'I shan't be able to go, then.' She turned to Paul Bridgestock. 'Sorry.'

'Never mind,' he replied, smiling kindly. 'Perhaps when Charlotte returns from holiday, we can arrange something.'

But Eloise knew that the fair would be over by then – it was only a travelling fair, not a permanent one – and she was bitterly disappointed. She took off her glasses and began to polish the lenses. She'd been enthused by her teacher's proposal, and now she couldn't go. Then she heard her mother say:

'Although it doesn't sound like a camera club outing to me. Didn't you indicate as much just now, Mr Bridgestock? No, indeed, it seems more like two photography enthusiasts going to the fair to try out some novel techniques. Wouldn't you agree, Percy?'

At the second mention of his name, Percy James surfaced from his thoughts, to stare quizzically at his wife. He obviously hadn't heard the question, let alone the discussion.

Mary repeated the question to her husband. Eloise watched and, after what seemed an age, her still preoccupied father nodded his assent.

Eloise was going to the fair.

'I'll call round and pick you up at seven-thirty,' Paul Bridgestock said to Eloise. 'That will allow us plenty of time to get there and park.'

Long before the waltzer ride finished, Eloise knew she was going to be ill. From experience, she knew that, once begun, there was only one way these feelings concluded. It had been one ride too many, and now she was going to pay the price. The undulating motion of the spinning attraction was bad enough – like repeatedly plunging over a humpback bridge in a car – but add to that the extra gyration of the whirling chair they were trapped in, then it was all too much, especially coming on top of all the other rides they had tried… The jungle ride, the galloping horses, the Ferris wheel, the dodgems… Oh, no… But if she could just hang on until the ride was over…

The photography session had gone off well, with all the planned activities being accomplished – but of course, they had still to see the results. Then, with the technical stuff behind them, Mr Bridgestock had suggested they take some fun shots. For her part, setting the full moon in the background, she had taken a close-up of him holding a small stick so that it appeared as if the moon were a lollipop. And he had taken a similar one of her, making her appear taller than the helter-skelter. It was simply a matter of getting the perspective wrong. She couldn't wait to see the pictures. Then, after that, they had stowed their cameras in the car and returned to the fairground for some fun.

Was the ride beginning to slow down at last? It seemed an awfully long time since it had started. The flashing lights weren't helping how she felt either. And there was a lot of noise, too: the pop song being played loudly and the laughter and shouts from other riders enjoying themselves. And it had been unwise to eat all those things. She could see that now. She should have stopped after the toffee apple and candyfloss. Eating the hotdog and ice cream had been greedy; over-indulgence, fun taken too far.

Giving no word of warning to Mr Bridgestock, and using circumferential motion as an aid, Eloise came off the ride, pelted down the wooden steps, dodged round two girls in cowboy hats, and darted between the waltzers and the jungle ride. She had made it. Nobody would see her here; no one would be offended by her illness – and there, in the relative tranquillity afforded by the two adjacent attractions, she was sick; copiously so. She knew that she would not feel better straightaway. It was like the nausea of seasickness: you needed to have been sick and off the boat for a while before that happened. The body's equilibrium took a while to be restored to normal.

She straightened her glasses on her nose, then took a handkerchief from her bag and wiped her mouth. She felt stupid, ashamed. She had acted silly, like a kid on her first adult trip to the fair; had overdone her enthusiasm. How she wished she could turn back the clock, start the evening over again. But the damage was done. Whatever would Mr Bridgestock say?

Just then the teacher came down between the backs of the two rides, to where Eloise was hastily popping a peppermint into her mouth. 'Have you been sick?' he asked, studying her face. 'When you dashed off so precipitously, I guessed that perhaps you felt unwell.'

Eloise wiped away a tear that had been caused by her retching. Well, he hadn't been unkind, hadn't chided her...

Not yet. 'Yes,' she said. 'But that ride was a bit of a wow.' She paused. 'And the assistant spinning the cars,' she added, 'I am sure that he concentrated on us.'

Paul Bridgestock nodded. 'Yes, they always focus on the vulnerable riders, those who look apprehensive… Seeking a reaction.'

'He certainly got one,' Eloise said. She grinned sheepishly. 'I am sorry though. Knowing what I'm like on rides, I should have had more sense.'

Paul Bridgestock squeezed her hand. 'It's easy to be wise after the event,' he said. He squeezed her hand again. 'C'mon – this way.'

He led her back to the main area of the funfair. Eloise saw that people were still bustling colourfully between the rides, laughing, joking, enjoying themselves. She wouldn't try any more rides this evening though… Or eat anything else.

The teacher sat her down on the steps of a ride, in the lee of the descending balustrade, cut-off from the surging throng of people. Then he too sat down. 'I am a little concerned about your sickness,' he said, turning to her. 'It may be connected to the concussion you suffered last week… A delayed reaction triggered by all of this.' He indicated to the surrounding hubbub of the fairground. 'I believe that that sort of thing can happen.'

Eloise shook her head. 'No, last week has got nothing to do with it,' she declared, emphatically. 'I always have to be careful, have to limit my time on the rides… You ask Charlotte; she knows what I'm like. I have to be so careful.' She paused to shrug her shoulders. 'And tonight I wasn't. I just got carried away with the fun. I simply overdid it, that's all.'

'Are you sure?' Paul Bridgestock asked, holding her gaze, his eyes asking the question as meaningfully as his voice. 'It really could be a delayed reaction.' He started to get up. 'I had better take you home... inform your parents–'

'No, honestly,' Eloise interrupted. 'I'm feeling much, much better now.' She didn't want her parents to find out, to learn of her childish behaviour, going on one ride after the other. Her mother would be disappointed with her daughter's lack of sophistication. 'It's just the motion of the rides, plus all that I've eaten. I even have to be careful when travelling by car on long journeys. Mum always brings tablets for me – just in case.' Her tension eased as she felt the teacher settle back onto the step. 'I'm all right in the front seat of a car,' she ran on, eager to convince. 'You know, watching the road... And in the back too, as long as I can still look out of the windscreen. I sort of pretend that I'm driving, mentally steering the car round the bends and through the junctions. I concentrate on doing that – and it usually works.' She grinned at his unchanging expression. 'I must be the youngest driver ever,' she added.

Paul Bridgestock smiled at her joke, then glanced at his watch. 'Anyway,' he said, 'I had best get you home before my car turns into a pumpkin.'

'And you won't tell my parents about what happened?'

The teacher became thoughtful. 'I really feel that I should, Eloise... After all, I am responsible. Your mother and father have put their trust in me... And if this actually does turn out to be connected–'

'It won't,' Eloise interrupted. 'Definitely.'

A little pause in the conversation then ensued. Eloise studied her teacher's face. She could tell that he was still thinking, hadn't made his mind up yet. But surely he would realise that it was just motion sickness. She had convinced him, hadn't she? Her mother really mustn't find out… Future outings might be banned. Then she heard him say:

'All right, Eloise.' He fell silent, and for a moment she thought that he had changed his mind – after all, looking at the situation from his point of view, it would be right to be circumspect. But then she heard him continue: 'All right… But only on condition that, if in the next day or so you feel unwell again – like this – you promise to tell your mother about tonight.'

'I promise,' Eloise replied, passionately.

'Everything, mind you, not just a watered down version of what happened.' He looked her up and down. 'Some times, Eloise, you can be too wanting for your own good.'

What did he mean by that – too wanting? Did he mean too persuasive, wanting her own way… Selfish? She'd only been honest. She had only been trying to explain; there had been no subterfuge behind her explanation. Other people never understood her reasons, her motives. That was a problem she had always encountered – and she always put other people first, above her own wishes. Everyone else always seemed to understand each other… That little knack they all had of knowing, the knack that she didn't seem to have. She was all right with the self-evident, but the subtle undertones, the faint nuances of conversations, had always eluded her – the things that were unsaid, just known. She repeated her promise, without asking her question.

Paul Bridgestock rose from the steps then. Eloise stood up too. She thought of all the pictures they had taken – more for the collection. She took a final glance around… A lot of people were still on that ride. Then, together, they started for the exit, walking past the line of sideshows, coconut shies, darts and hoopla games – and stalls selling foodstuffs. Just look at that girl over there eating a bag of mussels and whelks, popping them into her mouth one after the other with a cocktail stick. Eloise didn't want anymore of that sort of thing, thank you. But it had been a swell evening, really great. Pity that Charlotte was on holiday and hadn't been able to come. Charlie would have enjoyed it. She would have ridden those rides, every last one… Would have goaded that assistant on the waltzers until his arms ached. Charlie would have done it.

All of a sudden, Paul Bridgestock drew up and, turning to her, asked her to wait for him there. She watched as he went over to a nearby rifle range. He wasn't going to have a go himself, was he? She knew that it was an extremely difficult thing to do. You had to hit moving cutout ducks that were attached to a wire at the rear of the stall… They moved pretty fast, too. She remembered her father once having a go. He hadn't hit a single one – and he had served in the army and had used guns before. Her father had told them, her mother and her, that the game was fixed because the wire was set up to move unevenly, that every time he trained the sights of the rifle on a duck it jerked forward, making him miss. Eloise smiled. She didn't know about that, but her mother had told Percy that he should have aimed a little ahead of the target, and then he wouldn't have missed. That had made her father moody, and he had hardly spoken for the rest of the evening.

Eloise watched as the smiling stallholder passed an airgun across the counter to Mr Bridgestock; saw the teacher load the first pellet. She moved a little closer, to get a better view. Then Mr Bridgestock held the weapon to his shoulder, took aim, and fired. It was that quick: one, two, three – no hesitation. And, amazingly, one of the little cutout ducks fell sideways from the moving wire. Mr Bridgestock had hit it with his first shot. And then, just as astonishingly, her teacher did it again. A second duck had been hit. Yes, but he had to do that three more times to win.

Someone nudged Eloise's arm then. 'Pretty good shot, ain't he?' a voice said. 'Is he your boyfriend?'

She turned around, to see a youth grinning at her. He was a tall, gangly boy with buckteeth and spiky hair. He was wearing a leather jacket, and reminded her of one of the motorcycle gang from the café. She didn't like the look of him. 'No, of course not,' she replied, feeling inexplicably embarrassed by the question. 'He is my teacher.' And that sounded silly, and she felt even more embarrassed.

'Cor,' the youth said, nudging her arm again. 'Look. He's hit another one – that makes three in a row.' He scoffed. 'He won't get all five though, not many do…' He paused to look her over, his eyes finally settling on her chest. 'Say, if he's not your boyfriend, can I take you home?'

'No,' Eloise replied, flatly. That sounded a little too harsh. 'No,' she replied again, smiling as she returned her attention to the rifle range.

She saw that a small gathering had assembled in front of the stall. News travelled fast. She watched as Mr Bridgestock levelled the rifle once more, took aim, and fired. A fourth ducked keeled over. All stages of the manoeuvre were as smooth as the click of her mother's knitting needles. Even though she couldn't see Mr Bridgestock's face, she knew that he looked just like Alan Ladd in one of his Westerns.

'You sure you won't let me take you home?'

Eloise turned back to the youth once more. 'Yes, I am sure,' she said, flatly.

And at that moment a cheer rose up from the crowd by the rifle range. Eloise swung back towards it. Alan Ladd had shot his fifth "Baddie".

She felt another nudge on her arm. 'I've got a car,' the boy said. 'It's getting chilly now. You'll be nice and warm in there.'

Eloise glanced at him. 'It's OK,' she replied. 'We've got a stagecoach.'

At the rifle range the crowd was parting to allow Mr Bridgestock to pass through. Some of the people there were patting him on his back. 'Quite a feat, mate,' she heard someone shout. Someone else had picked up a rifle and was obviously going to try his luck. Eloise hoped that he won, too.

Mr Bridgestock was coming back, beaming as he walked towards her. She saw that he was holding something behind his back. He came up to her. 'Beginner's luck,' he said, grinning wider. She gazed up at him, her eyes quizzical. 'An airgun's velocity is quite slow,' he explained. 'If you aim a fraction ahead of the target, you can't miss.' He pulled his arm from behind his back. 'For you,' he said, handing her a teddy bear. He watched, still grinning, as she held it in her arm. 'C'mon, he said, suddenly. 'Your parents will think that I've kidnapped you.'

Chapter Nine

Eloise dismounted from her bicycle, the hill was too steep for further cycling. She turned to Charlotte, who had also gotten off her bicycle to walk. 'I don't recall the lane as being quite this steep, Charlie.'

'Don't forget you caught the bus when you came here with your mother, Eloise.' Charlotte grinned. 'So there wouldn't have been any pedalling involved.' She paused to glance around the rural setting. 'But, anyhow, are you absolutely sure this was the route you took then?'

Eloise also surveyed the country setting, the winding lane now seeming – in the wake of her friend's reminder of her previous excursion – too narrow for motorcars, let alone omnibuses. 'Well, I'm fairly sure that we left the city on this road… and the farm that we passed back there looked familiar.'

'They all look the same to me,' Charlotte said dismissively. She brushed aside a stray strand of hair that the eddying breeze had blown across her eyes. 'Anyhow, if you are correct, we should come to a stile somewhere along here. On the right hand side, you said, didn't you?'

Eloise puffed and nodded. 'Yes. And if we find that, then we should also find what we have come here looking for.'

'I hope so, Eloise, because all this cycling is exhausting me.'

Eloise guided the front wheel of her bicycle around a

pothole, then glanced at her friend. 'It will be nearly all downhill on the way home. We will be able to free-wheel and– there it is!' she exclaimed, pointing excitedly up the hill. 'The stile.'

'Stylish,' Charlotte acknowledged, happily. 'No more pushing our bikes up this mountain.'

'We are almost at the top, anyway, Charlie,' Eloise replied, hoping to encourage her friend.

They propped their bicycles against a convenient tree in the hedgerow adjacent to the stile. Eloise lifted her spectacles and gazed at it. "There was a crooked man who walked a crooked mile and found a crooked sixpence upon a crooked stile". It was bound to be the right one. She turned to Charlotte. 'They will be safe here,' she reassured, having noted her friend's sudden quizzical look. 'They're on the grass verge – and I doubt many people come this way. Besides, who would want to steal our old bone-shakers?' The afternoon was going splendidly to plan. They would find it this time.

'If you say so, Eloise,' Charlotte replied. She retrieved her bag from the basket on the handlebars of her bicycle, rummaged inside and fetched out a packet of cigarettes. 'I've been waiting for this for the past ten miles,' she said, breathlessly. She lit a cigarette, drew deeply, then released the smoke in a protracted sigh. 'Too much pedalling can make a girl seriously unfit.'

Eloise laughed. 'Ever since you saw that film where Humphrey Bogart lights Lauren Bacall's cigarette in that silly way, you have been addicted to their daft depiction of sophistication.'

'It's more than that, Eloise,' Charlotte snapped, clearly hurt by her friend's accusation.

'Indeed, it may be – *now*,' Eloise countered. But that was one of the drawbacks with smoking; you always seemed to want more. OK they gave you a decent feeling, relaxed you – but it didn't last long. Then you wanted another one. She hadn't smoked for long herself; had soon given it up. Besides, it made your clothes and hair smell. She swung round to face the stile. 'Anyway, let's move on.'

'It's all pleasure,' Charlotte mumbled to herself.

Infused with a gathering optimism for a successful outcome to their day, Eloise clambered over the wooden structure, then turned round and helped her friend over too. If she remembered correctly, they had less than a mile to walk to their goal. She was certain they would locate it this time. Memories were coming back – it was better than *déjà vu.*

'I wish that I'd worn jeans, like you did,' Charlotte moaned, brushing fibres of wood debris from her dress. 'That stile is rotten.' She glanced at her watch. 'Anyhow, which direction do we take?'

Eloise surveyed the open meadow they had found themselves in. 'It's this way,' she replied, confidently. She indicated to a copse of trees at the crest of the hill. 'We follow the footpath along by the hedge towards those trees, then through there, along a bit farther, curving left, and then it should be downhill into the valley.'

"Of death rode the six-hundred," Charlotte spouted, quickly. She paused to draw on her cigarette, then, prancing forward theatrically, continued: 'C'mon, then, I'll lead the way.'

'No! No, you mustn't,' Eloise called. She scooted around her friend. 'I have to do that.' It was too great an expedition to have the second in command arrive first. Could Oates have planted the flag ahead of Scott? Eloise swallowed dryly. But that was an inappropriate analogy for their own endeavour: neither explorer had planted… Not to worry, it would be all right. And, if she were the leader, would Charlotte be prepared to make the ultimate sacrifice? Eloise fixed her stare on the crest of the hill, set her bearings. She herself would. But it wouldn't be necessary. Every thing would be all right.

Beyond the copse of trees, the footpath brought them out into another meadow, where a herd of black and white cows studied their approach with wary eyes. Eloise adopted a suspicious stare, also. Even a Friesian could see they weren't kindly farm hands. But, on the other hand, even a moo-cow could tell they were not unkindly butchers either.

'They're not likely to charge us, are they?' Charlotte asked. 'I'm not as fleet of foot as you – so if they do chase us, it will be me who gets caught in the rear.'

'They are only cows, Charlie. Anyhow, I remember reading somewhere that an aspect of their vision process makes them see everything bigger than it actually is – magnifies it – so we probably appear like giants to them. We are quite safe.' Eloise grinned. 'Just keep your eyes peeled for their cowpats.'

Charlotte cast an automatic glance at her sandals, reflexively clenching her toes away from the front of the exposed footwear.

Continuing to claim the vanguard of their mission, Eloise strode purposefully along the footpath, noting with satisfaction the commencement of a downward trend to the meadow, which would surely descend into the valley. But would it turn out to be the correct one? After all, there were many such… Yes, of course it would – this time.

And at that moment in her reverie, there came the unmistakeable sound of a train's klaxon. It was far off and came to them borne on the wind but it was there nevertheless. That settled it for Eloise. She'd heard a similar sound years before, when her mother had brought her here. All elements of the enigma were falling into place. She drew to a halt and trilled a reflective response to the train, then turned to her friend. 'I am absolutely certain that we have found it,' she blurted, happily.

Charlotte gave her a gentle nudge forward. 'Lead on, then, Gunga Din,' she said, grinning.

Eloise obliged, allowing gravity to set her in motion again, down the tumbling footpath. Charlotte followed on behind, stepping precisely in the grassy depressions left behind by her leader.

Then, all at once, seemingly in the blinking of an eye, they were over the brow of the hill, the slope steepening with each step taken. And there, come in view, was the farther side of the valley, not quite as lofted as this side, but further proof of their correct location nonetheless. 'We are on the primrose path,' Eloise sang, happily. She stole a glance over her shoulder. 'We will spy them in a minute, Charlie. You just wait and see.'

At the good tidings, Charlotte skipped forward to overhaul her eager companion, only to stop dead in her own enthusiasm, gawking at the scene spread out before her. 'You remember what you said earlier about free-wheeling home,' she said, staring down the precipitous incline, 'well, without wishing to sound like a kill-joy, before we do so we will have to climb back up this hill.'

'We will soar up here on the wings of triumph,' Eloise replied.

'I doubt the thermals are quite that uplifting,' Charlotte said, laughing. 'However, if you insist on going all the way to the bottom, then I suppose–'

'There they are,' Eloise suddenly exclaimed, coming to an angled poise in the meadow. She pointed down the hill, towards the valley basin. 'I give you the stream, the bank, and the primroses.' She turned to Charlotte. 'I said this would be the time, didn't I?'

'You say that every time you persuade me to accompany you on this… on this floral pilgrimage,' Charlotte retorted. She was still contemplating the route of their return journey, and clearly not relishing the prospect. Nevertheless, despite her undisguised lack of enthusiasm, grinning, she placed her arm around her friend's shoulder. 'Well done, Ellie,' she said. She gave the shoulder an affectionate squeeze. 'Well done. But I always knew you would be successful one day.'

Eloise shook her head. 'I never really believed…' she said thoughtfully. 'Not truly thought that…' She clasped Charlotte's hand. 'Until now.'

And then, together, arm in arm, the two friends set off down the primrose path, heading in high spirits for the stream and its bank of golden yellow primroses. 'We're off to see the wizard, the wonderful wizard of Oz,' they trala'd. 'If ever there was a wizard there was, the wonderful wizard of Oz there was…'

They hadn't gone far, however, before Eloise noted with no little dismay that, contrary to what she knew to be true, they were not in fact making any progress down the primrose path. She stopped singing. It was almost as if they were on a treadmill, tramping the same bit of ground over and over again. Or was it that the footpath was getting longer, stretching out like a ribbon of elastic, and thus making their destination recede in opposition to their downward trek? And furthermore, even though she could visualise Charlotte and herself descending the hill, it actually felt as if they were going the other way, climbing the hill, leaden boots in leaden soil.

Sensing something was going awry with the culmination of her beautiful plan, she turned to Charlotte, whose arm was linked to hers, only to discover that her friend was no longer there. A panicked glance back down the valley showed her that Charlie was not alone in vanishing, for the stream had gone… And the bank of primroses. All below was now petrified earth. And then, before her very eyes, defying all logic, the valley basin became cloven into two bottomless fissures. Charybdis and Scylla – and she could not avoid either. There could only be one outcome: she was going to die. And then, as if to confirm her conviction, the hillside transmogrified itself into a giant muddy slide. 'Charlie!' But her friend had already gone. 'Mum!' But her mother wasn't there. She was all alone.

She was all alone as the hillside tilted some more… And some more… Mum! Then, gasping in alarmed protest, she folded onto her backside and began to slide down the fairground attraction, began to helter-skelter towards the centre of the earth. Mother!

Eloise opened her eyes and peered around the twilight darkness, focusing on the shadowy yet familiar objects that made up her bedroom. She was at once aware of the pounding, unruly rhythm of her heart, the hypertensive beat that surely presaged the onset of a heart attack. She was safe though: there was no bottomless pit opening to swallow her. Yet even though she knew she was safe – her mother in the adjacent room – she was still too scared to move: the nightmare could easily restart. And so she lay there, concentrating on wakeful things, listening as her heartbeat slowly yet surely lessened.

She'd had nightmares before, worse than this one, where there had been a monster at the foot of the bed, about to "get" her. Then, with the thing there, rising up with its hideous mouth agape, she had woken up. She had propped herself onto an elbow, gazing at the foot of the bed – and it was all right: there was nothing there. But she hadn't really woken up: she had still been asleep, dreaming that she was awake – it was all part of the nightmare. But she'd been convinced that she was awake. And then the monster had reappeared, its hideous mouth even more agape, set to devour her limb by limb, and she'd nearly died of fright. Of course, then she'd woken up properly… And it was different. But you never knew the difference when you were dreaming. Those types of nightmares were really scary.

In a little while, safely distanced from sleep's returning grasp, and with her pulse returned to normal, she rolled on to her back, to discover that body movements caused by the nightmare had coiled her nightdress into a damp swaddling of tangled material that had, or so it seemed, mummified her body. With an effort – for she felt like an effete – she raised her bottom clear of the mattress and unwound the sticky garment. She relaxed once more. It had been a dream, just a dream.

Eventually, she propped herself up onto her elbows and reached for her glasses on the bedside table. She hadn't found the primrose path. She gazed half-heartedly at her dawning reflection in the dressing-table mirror. No, she hadn't found it. Even in a dream, it had eluded her.

Chapter Ten

One day near the end of the summer holiday, Paul Bridgestock arrived at Eloise's home to collect her in his Morris Minor motorcar. It was an early version of the model but not rusted and quite serviceable, if a little lacking in comfort. An afternoon's photographic trip was planned, but when they had spoken earlier, Paul had teasingly refused to reveal its location.

Eloise knew it would be the last outing of the holiday. Paul would be back at school in a week, and she would have to resume formal study. Paul's home tutorials would end. She'd enjoyed those – had made progress, especially with spelling – and he had given her permission to address him by his Christian name. But they'd had a good summer, photography field trips had been numerous – Exmoor, Dartmoor, the coast, and a lot around the historic sites of Exeter. It had been a great time – and for the last outing of the season, Paul had promised her that they would go somewhere really special. But she wished that he would tell her where it was.

'C'mon, Eloise,' he called up the stairs, to where Eloise was getting ready in her room. 'If we don't get a move on, the things that we're after will have all become extinct.'

'Just two minutes,' she called back.

'Make it just one.'

'I'm sure that whatever it is you are so secretive about

won't mind waiting sixty seconds,' she countered.

Less than a minute later, Eloise walked in to the living room. 'I'm ready,' she announced. She folded her arms across her chest. 'But it would be nice to know where we're going... If only to know which type of film to bring.'

'C'mon, then,' Paul said, rising from his chair. 'And don't worry about the film – that's already taken care of.'

Eloise looked towards her mother, her eyes searching for a clue. But Mary James merely smiled, then reached for a magazine.

'You two are in collusion,' Eloise said, swinging round and starting for the front door.

Outside in the road, Eloise helped Paul stow their photographic equipment and the picnic tea that her mother had made for them in the car's boot. She walked round to the passenger seat. 'Where are you taking me then?'

'You'll see.' He swept a wave of dark hair back from his eyes, and then started the motor. 'It's somewhere we have never been to before,' he added, steering the car away from the kerb.'

'I'll soon guess,' she said, lifting her clip-on sunglasses out of her line of vision.

'No you won't.'

Eloise stretched her legs out straight, noting that below the hem of her denim shorts they were, following the summer of outdoor activities, tanned to a golden hue. She glanced at Paul, who was now concentrating on getting the car across the Heavitree Road. 'Yes, I will,' she said, smiling confidently. 'I'll guess before we have travelled even a mile'.

'I'll bet you half a crown," Paul said. His eyes twinkled and he glanced across the car. 'Of course, if you want to bet more...'

'A half-crown will do,' Eloise said. 'I don't wish to–Budleigh Salterton,' she exclaimed, as Paul took that road out from the city.

But Paul did not answer, and Eloise could see that he intended to reveal nothing – and minutes later they drove past the Budleigh Salterton turning and continued along the Sidmouth road.

'Sidmouth,' she said, nodding to back up her conclusion.

'We have been there before.'

'Seaton, then?'

'We have also been there before.'

'Lyme Regis,' she said triumphantly. 'I should have guessed earlier. We can get some smashing pictures of the town, if we walk out along the Cobb.'

'We could,' Paul said.

The tone of his voice told Eloise that Lyme Regis was not their intended destination. 'You're kidnapping me,' she exclaimed in mock horror. 'That's it. You are kidnapping me and mean to demand a ransom from my poor parents.' She turned towards him. 'Well let me inform you, sire, they will refuse to pay. The only way you will get your dues is to barter me on the white slave market.'

Paul's gaze met hers. 'You are reading too much fiction, Eloise.'

'That's good coming from my English teacher.'

'Well romantic fiction, then.' He glanced at her again, smiling. 'You should read more Woolf and less Lawrence.'

Eloise returned the smile. 'At least he got to play in the sand – and it doesn't look like I am going to today'

'You know very well which Lawrence I mean.'

'Maybe this will be a *Sentimental Journey* after all then,' Eloise said, making her expression stern for Paul's benefit.

Paul laughed. 'You are incorrigible, Eloise.'

'The fault's all yours, for taking me on this mysterious mystery tour,' she replied, gazing at the passing scenery.

'I think my half-crown is safe,' Paul said, gravely.

As she had guessed earlier, Lyme Regis was not their intended destination, for Paul drove past the turning for the town and continued along the main road. They weren't going to Weymouth, were they? That was an awful long way to go just for the afternoon. Now, what places of interest were there between here and Weymouth? And just then, a still-puzzled Eloise heard the little semaphore-signalling arm on the right hand side of the car click into operation, and Paul guided the vehicle on to another road.

'Charmouth…' she said, thoughtfully, swinging her sunglasses into place against the sun's rays, which now, with the car's change of direction, shone directly into her eyes. 'Now, let's see, what is there at Charmouth?'

'Can't you remember?' Paul glanced towards her. 'It's got something to do with school.'

'Fossils!' Eloise said. 'Cool. We are going fossil hunting.'

'And we shall take some photographs, too.'

During the term before the summer break, Mr Barnes, the geography teacher and a keen collector of fossils, had brought several from his collection into school for his class to examine. Eloise had been fascinated by the fossilisation of fish and marine plants that had lived millions of years before and had told Paul about them. He had promised to bring her here to try their luck at finding some. She had forgotten about it, but he had not.

'Do you think we might find a dinosaur?' Eloise joked, glancing across the car. 'I mean, Mr Barnes would love one of those.'

'If we do,' he said, grinning as he steered the Morris Minor into the car park, 'we will need a lorry to get it home.'

Needless to say, their search failed to uncover a dinosaur. But they had a successful hunt nevertheless, finding several ammonites, the spiral shellfish variety that they both recognised, and one that Eloise described as resembling a miniature walrus, but which neither one of them had seen before. Certainly, there had been nothing like it amongst those brought into school by Mr Barnes. Never mind though, they would take it back for him to identify. The only problem was that it was embedded in a sizeable piece of rock that would clearly be difficult in recovering to the car. But they resolved to do so all the same.

At first, determined to play her part in effecting the recovery, Eloise tried to assist with the lifting but, after making a joke that Paul had given her the heaviest half, she abandoned the task and begged the help of two holidaymakers.

Dusting her hands on her shorts, Eloise watched the group lug the stone from the beach beneath the cliffs to the little wooden bridge that spanned the River Char. Golly but it looked heavy. Paul was strong but beads of perspiration had appeared on his face, and the slimmer of the two holidaymakers looked as if his legs might buckle under the weight. She hoped that none of them suffered injury from the effort. She hoped too that the bridge would take the weight. No need to worry though, for it looked substantial enough: it would be all right.

In a little while, Paul and his helpers had crossed the bridge to the car park, there to deposit the stone behind the Morris Minor.

Paul fished in his trousers pocket for the keys. 'Unlock the boot, Eloise,' he said, handing them to her, 'and we will lift it in.'

With the men standing by, hot under the afternoon sun and clearly grateful for the respite from their effort, she opened the car's boot and peered inside. It was a touch cluttered. Would there be room for Wallace the walrus? Stooping into the space, she removed the picnic hamper, cameras and tripods – these items would be OK on the rear seat – then she cleared several spanners and other tools to make as much free space as possible. Yes, he should fit in here. She straightened and stood to one side, to allow room for the lift. 'There you are,' she said, placing her hands on her hips. 'It's all yours.' She felt a little helpless, not being as strong as the men, but anyway there was barely enough room for the manoeuvre even without her assistance.

The three raised the rock again, shuffled forward until their legs made contact with the car's bumper; then, on Paul's order, they lowered it gently into the boot, shifting it a little to spread the load equally between the rear wheels of the vehicle. Eloise gave a skip of joy. Cool. Nothing damaged. Even so, as careful as the operation had been, she noted that the rear of the little car had sagged several inches under the load. Not to worry, perhaps Mr Barnes had a way of cutting the fossil from the stone, and then he could have it for his collection.

Together with the two lads who had assisted them with the lifting, they had their picnic on a grassy slope of hillside overlooking the beach, adjacent to the wooden footbridge. Eloise's mother had packed plenty of sandwiches and cakes, so there was enough for everyone. Then, with the sun still wanting of the western running cliffs, they started for home, having decided to call in at Lyme Regis on the way for some photography.

They parked the car and walked along the harbour front to the Cobb, to where some good pictures promised. The tide was backed up against the harbour wall, so high that it seemed to Eloise that a dipped toe or another spoonful of water would overflow the ocean. She set up a tripod and took several shots of the town, looking now in the late afternoon sunshine at its most picturesque. A man in a striped top and denim jeans watched her from a skiff that was moored at the quayside. She took some pictures of him too, and he held up a string of mackerel for good measure, as though his catch were a great sporting trophy – Ernest Hemingway holding aloft a freshly caught marlin.

Eloise was persuaded by Paul to walk out to the end of the Cobb – to where the next stop was France. And here she posed for some pictures, trying not to look pensive as she gazed out across the channel. She wasn't the best swimmer in the world and this narrow strip of man-made breakwater, bounded by fathoms of ocean on either side, wasn't the ideal location for looking one's coolest. Glancing back, she saw that the shore looked miles away too. Just then, a seal popped its head above the surface of the water and fixed her with its big brown eyes. She took a very quick picture, then, bustling Paul before her, started to walk back. It was all very well for seals; they were natural swimmers.

In a little while they collected the car from the small car park adjacent to the sea front at the bottom of the hill, and then started the journey home, pleased with their afternoon's excursion. However, their spirits were about to be dampened, for as they drove up out of the town, the little car went slower and slower with the increasing incline of the hill.

Paul engaged first gear, and for a while the little vehicle appeared to be getting the better of the contest. But it was destined only to be momentary, for the ascent was extremely steep and, just beyond the town boundary, a sharp bend in the road decided in favour of the hill, forcing Paul to pull over to the side of the road.

He applied the hand brake. 'She's not going to make it,' he said, glancing at Eloise. 'I'm afraid that she's underpowered for the incline.'

Eloise knew of the hill's reputation and the difficulty that drivers of older cars – especially those with small engines – had when negotiating it, which of course was made worse if the cars were over-laden with passengers or heavy loads. Indeed, on occasion, her father's car, when they were all in it, had struggled to get up the hill – and that had a medium size engine… Although it was quite old too. The problem, apart from the steepness of the hill, was that you couldn't get a good run at it; at least, that was what her father had said. 'What are we going to do?' she asked.

Paul considered her question for a moment. 'She would make it without that heavy rock in the boot. We might have to leave that behind.'

'But it is such an extraordinary fossil,' Eloise said, disappointed at the prospect of having to abandon their find. She glanced over her shoulder, to the boot of the car. 'And I expect that it's a rare one, too,' she added.

Paul was silent for a while, his gaze searching the interior of the car, as if he thought the answer to their problem might lie here. Eventually, apparently finding nothing that might assist their dilemma, he turned to Eloise. 'Don't misunderstand me,' he began, tentatively, 'but if you got out and pushed… That, together with the reduced weight in the car, might just make the difference.'

To anyone unacquainted with the locality, the suggestion would have sounded absurd, but Eloise knew that countless drivers and their passengers had resorted to it over the years. In fact, there was an even more precipitous ascent in Somerset called Porlock Hill, where it reputedly happened daily. 'I'll do it,' she said.

For what seemed an age to her impatient enthusiasm, Paul mulled over the offer. Finally, he turned to her. 'On second thoughts,' he said, 'I don't think it would succeed. Firstly, we wouldn't save sufficient weight to make the difference required and, secondly, I don't think you would be strong enough either.'

'Let me try anyway,' she said, more miffed at his rejection than her voiced showed.

'It would be too dangerous. Just imagine if the car rolled back, here, on the steepest bit. Why, you might be run over and killed.'

Eloise turned away to look out the window. 'Then I'll drive and you push,' she said.

'But you can't drive.' Paul shook his head. 'You don't even have a driving licence.'

'But you have let me drive before... You said that I was very good.'

'Yes, I have; and yes, you were very good. But that was on a track, not on the public highway.'

Eloise smiled as she saw the old cart track that ran from the beach of the rocky cove up to the main road. They had gone to Lynton in North Devon to photograph the wreck of a cargo ship that had lost its steering and run aground in a storm the previous winter. She had begged Paul to allow her to drive the car back up the track, and, following some basic tuition, during which she had successfully driven up and down the beach, she had done just that, much to the delight of her instructor.

Eloise turned from the window. 'I can do it; I know I can. And we would save more weight – and *you* would be strong enough.'

'Eloise, it is not a question of whether you are capable of driving, or of saving sufficient weight, or even of my being strong enough.' He paused, staring at her, as if seeing a different person to the one he had called upon earlier in the day. 'The fact is we would be breaking the law.'

'Oh.'

Paul held her gaze. 'Eloise, what do you suppose your parents would think of a teacher who permitted their daughter to drive on the public highway while she lacked any of the prerequisites to do so?'

'But they won't know, will they?' Eloise said, quickly. 'Nobody will know.' She rolled her eyes. 'And I can drive,' she persisted. 'The track where you let me do so was as steep as this… and it was rutted and stony, too… and that makes it more difficult than this road.'

'It's much too dangerous, Eloise. And if you do have an accident, your parents will know… as will the police.'

Eloise stared out the windscreen, up the hill. 'It's really only a matter of a few yards… A few seconds behind the steering wheel.' She glanced at Paul. 'Besides, mum has driven father's car on the road. And she hasn't got a licence. Neither has she had driving lessons.'

Paul's eyes searched hers, his own quizzical – but he remained silent.

'They were having a discussion,' Eloise continued. 'Father was arguing that the sexes have different inborn abilities. You know, women better at domestic things, men more adept at scientific stuff… girls better at the arts and humanities; boys better at maths and science – that sort of thing. Mother said that any differences were due to social conditioning; that it was because girls were encouraged to play with dolls and do knitting, while boys played football and had things like electric trains and meccano sets for birthdays and Christmas.

'Then father said men were better drivers than women, because driving was a technical thing. Mother said there was no difference, that anyone, male or female, could drive a car – and that she would prove it to him.' Eloise paused, grinning at Paul. 'You should have seen dad's face when mum picked up the car keys and went outside.'

'She actually drove the car… on the road?'

'Yes,' Eloise replied, nodding her head, eagerly. 'She told me later that it hadn't been her intention to do so, that she had planned just to go down the drive and back, which is only a few yards – but that seeing Percy's expression so aghast, she hadn't been able to stop herself.' Eloise touched her spectacles. 'In actual fact, she drove right up the road, did one of those three-point turn things, and then came back and reversed up the drive.'

'But she must have had some instruction… I mean, how did she know how to use the gears and the pedals?'

'She said that she'd watched Percy do it for years.' Eloise tried to keep a straight face. 'And that if a man could do it, then so could any woman… blindfolded.'

Paul started laughing.

Eloise glanced down at her hands. 'I'm not asking to be blindfolded,' she said. She tapped her clip-on sunglasses. 'These are handicap enough for me.'

Paul stopped laughing. 'The car would make it... I think. We would have to be-'

'You had better not stand directly behind it though,' she interrupted, sensing victory. 'Push from the side.'

Paul looked around, as if to see whether anyone was watching them. 'We'll give it one quick try – just one,' he said, sternly, holding Eloise's gaze. 'And if that fails, that's it, we leave the rock behind.' He then went on to outline the driving procedure that he wanted her to follow, ending: 'And if anything goes wrong, if the car starts to roll back – if it stalls – depress the clutch, and put on the foot brake and the hand brake together. Then I'll come and take over.'

'Got it,' Eloise said, confidently, but already wondering if she might not have taken on a challenge too far, might not have been too hasty in persuading Paul to let her drive. She reset her spectacles on her nose – surveyed the terrain. It was a narrow road; they had just made it round the corner when Paul had stopped the car. To be honest, from here, it looked as if they'd done the steepest bit. Everything would be all right.

Paul shook his head in a gesture of resignation. 'All right, then; let's change positions.'

In a minute or two Eloise sat in the driver's seat of the Morris Minor, her knuckles showing opaquely through the taut skin as she gripped the steering wheel. She stared straight ahead, up the hill, which now appeared to be considerably steeper than it had looked from the passenger seat. 'I keep the engine revving high and let the clutch out as I release the hand brake?'

'I cannot believe I am allowing this,' Paul said, leaning in the open window. He placed his hand on Eloise's shoulder. 'Yes, that's right. But remember what I said, if anything goes wrong, push the clutch in and put on both brakes at the same time. Then leave the rest to me.' And with that he took up his pushing position, at the rear offside corner of the car.

Eloise pressed her foot on the clutch pedal and engaged first gear. The car could do it. She glanced in the rear view mirror. 'I'm ready,' she called to Paul's reflection.

Paul slapped the car's boot. 'Go on, Eloise. Keep the revs high.'

As if driving by numbers she commenced the pre-determined routine, her left foot releasing the clutch as, simultaneously, her right foot depressed the accelerator pedal. Then, as the car's bonnet shuddered in response to the application of power to its rear wheels, she began to release the hand brake. Nothing happened. The vehicle remained stalled, there on the hill, immobile, as if held by some giant invisible hand, or glued like a fly to flypaper, its engine protesting noisily, sounding like a swarm of enraged hornets. Eloise glanced down at her feet. The clutch pedal was nearly all the way out. Something should have happened by now. So was this the time for their emergency procedure? And at that moment, as she prepared to abort the hill climb, with Paul braced behind it, the little car began to inch forward up the hill, slowly at first but, as the clutch began to bite, its momentum increased until Paul had to run to keep apace with it.

Paul stopped, panting from the effort he had put in. 'Don't try to change gear,' he called. 'Keep in first and stop where the incline levels off a little.'

Eloise did not have to drive far, perhaps fifty yards, certainly no more than sixty, before the slope lessened and it was safe to stop. Another driver going down the hill towards Lyme Regis, noting the pair, Eloise in the car and Paul now running up the hill again, stuck a raised thumb out of his window and gave a cheer. Eloise wondered if he would have been so congratulatory, so approving, had he been aware of all the circumstances of the scene. Still, too late to worry now, for they had done it. They had done it.

Paul arrived at the car then, puffing a little and his cheeks flushed from the exercise. 'Well done, Eloise.' He grinned, shaking his head as if in disbelief at her accomplishment. 'Well done. That was a cute piece of driving.'

Eloise ensured that the hand brake was well and truly engaged, then stepped out of the car to face him. She was just as much out of breath as he was, although from a different reason. But they had done it. She started to laugh, feeling both the elation of success and the relief of knowing that a policeman had not happened by to witness the whole thing. Paul was laughing too. Then, instinctively, without thinking, she threw her arms round his neck and kissed him, rising on to tiptoes as she brought her lips to his, and all the time thinking what a great guy he was and what cool times they had together.

It was the first time she had kissed anyone in passion, and although the kiss was not the starry-eyed thing of romance, she found that she quite liked the experience – the feeling of closeness, the feeling of Paul's lips on hers. Cool. See you later alligator – in a while crocodile. She clung to him, pressing her lips to his, kissing him all grown up. She was even reluctant to break the embrace. In the end, it was Paul who did that.

He held her at arm's length. 'Hey,' he said, laughing. 'It's only Lyme Regis. You haven't driven up Mount Everest, you know.'

She could not reply at first for her heart was a whirligig,

a lopsided gyroscope waltzing round her chest in a desperate bid to catch up with itself. She gulped, trying to recover her equilibrium. 'That was fantastic. Pat Moss, beat that.' She looked up at Paul, nodding her head. 'That was fantastic.'

Paul took her arm and led her round to the other side of the car, then opened the passenger door. 'C'mon, it's time we started back...' He paused and glanced at the car's boot. 'With our Mr Wallace the walrus.'

That night Eloise lay awake, finding that sleep would not easily come, her unquiet mind stubbornly refusing to do anything other than replay the day's events. The fossil hunt had been cool, paddling in the surf, turning over pebbles on the seashore, and never knowing what you might find. Of course, most of the time you were unlucky, disappointed, but now and then you were rewarded with an impression in the pebble of a creature that had lived millions of years before. The driving up the hill had been terrific, not least because of the element of danger involved but also, she had to admit, because of their flouting the law in doing so. But it was neither of these things that was preventing her from dropping off to sleep: it was the memory of the kiss that was doing that.

Try as she might, she could not block it from her thoughts, could not prevent the memory from recurring, from bobbing to the surface of her mind like a cork in water. Not only that, but every time it bobbed to the surface, a host of butterflies swarmed in her stomach, each time taking her a little further from sleep. In the end, she gave in to her wilful mind and considered the kiss. She had enjoyed it; that could not be denied. She had surprised herself in doing it though. But it had been a spur-of-the-moment thing, spontaneous –

an impromptu act of demonstrating her joy. Instead of simply saying, 'we did it' – although she had done that too – her exhilaration had manifested itself in the act of kissing him. There was nothing wrong in that. She closed her eyes tight shut against the moonlight that was now illuminating the room too brightly for sleep.

But the kiss… Golly, once it had started, she hadn't wanted it to end. Paul had had to do that. She would have fainted first, she almost had. Did everyone feel like that on their first kiss? She would have to ask Charlotte. She would know – after all, she had a boyfriend.

What had Paul thought about it though, her kissing him like that? It must have surprised him. But he had made a joke of it… something about her having not driven up Mount Everest… although he had definitely become a bit quieter later, on the way home. But perhaps he had been reflecting on the likely repercussions of her parents finding out about the illegal drive… Or was he upset that she had kissed him like that? After all, it must have seemed a bit forward of her… as if she were taking things for granted. But, anyhow, he probably only thought of her as being one of his pupils, as being only one of the girls in his class. She heard the grandmother clock in the hallway downstairs strike two then. It was a sticky night: she doubted that she would ever fall asleep.

But kissing was different to other pleasures, to other sensations. It wasn't for instance like eating strawberry ice cream, or listening to Billy Fury… though those things were good too – but in a different way. Yet it had the same effect. It made you feel good, gave you pleasure, made you want more – not that you always felt like that about strawberry ice cream though. But with the kiss there was the actual physical contact with someone else. In this case, someone whose company you enjoyed, had cool fun with, someone you respected, trusted, loved... Loved? Eloise rolled onto her side. Love. She considered the concept for a moment. She loved her parents; she loved Charlotte... But this was different. She'd known Paul for almost a year. They had been together a lot in that time, done a lot of things together, especially recently. They had shared interests too, in literature, in music, in photography, in exploring the countryside. All those things did not add up to loving someone though: they just made you compatible in a platonic way, were the stuff of friendships – that was all. Yet friendships could become... Could lead to... But what about the kiss, then? She closed her eyes and tasted her lips, where Paul's lips had pressed. Just because you enjoyed kissing someone, it didn't mean that you loved him... Did it?

Paul was older than her – twelve years older. She had never thought about that before. It had never been a thing to consider; it had never been important. But if it hadn't been important before but *was* important now, was that because something had changed... because she loved him? She rolled over onto her other side. And if it did mean that she loved him – and was important now – did it also mean that he was too old for her? But there was quite an age difference between her mother and her father. She did a calculation on her fingers... the same, in fact.

But did Paul think the same about her though? Was he at home now, thinking about her in the same way that she was thinking about him? She turned onto her back, her eyes following the moonlight shadows that wavered on the ceiling. No. Men were not supposed to be like that: not romantic. But Paul wasn't like other men. He was sensitive, considerate.

Besides, he was a poet. And he often revealed a passionate nature when reading romance poetry. On the other hand, perhaps her unseemly show of emotion had offended him, had already led him to question her modesty. Perhaps he would not take her out again. She closed her eyes tight against the thought. They had such fun times together. No, it would be all right – he knew her well enough. She still wasn't feeling sleepy.

She reached out and lifted her teddy bear from the bedside table. Alan Ladd had won it for her. She cradled it in her arm. The kiss had been cool though... for a novice. Her arms round his neck, then her lips smack bang on his lips. Wow! It was a wonder that old fossil in the boot of the car hadn't come back to life. Reliving the moment, Eloise giggled and cuddled her teddy bear beneath the bedclothes. Her first real kiss... Holding on to him... Their bodies together... Their lips together... Cool. Oh, golly...

Chapter Eleven

Eloise rose hurriedly from her desk, where she'd been writing an essay on Virginia Woolf's novel *Mrs Dalloway*. 'Tell him I'll be down in a moment,' she shouted through the closed bedroom door. Saturday evening! What a time to call to collect her essay. He wasn't supposed to be here until tomorrow. And the essay wasn't finished: it still required a final run-through, a final–

Catching a glimpse of herself in the dressing-table mirror, Eloise's thought train came off the rails. God... She stood stock still gazing at her reflection: old denim jeans that looked like she'd been gardening in them; scruffy pink T-shirt – the one that had been washed so many times that the material was almost threadbare; hair not combed since this morning; no makeup – but she seldom wore it anyway... Her face was too shiny though. She couldn't go down looking like this.

Paul had not visited or taken her out since their trip to Lyme Regis the previous week. She had thought the reason might have been because of her kissing him; that he thought her too forward – impetuous – and was now trying to cool their friendship. And of course there was the driving incident to consider. Perhaps he wasn't happy about how she'd persuaded him to agree to that. Although when he dropped her off last week, he had said that preparatory work for the coming school term would demand most of his time – and

he had given her plenty of school work to carry on with…
Too much. So maybe his absence from her life had nothing
to do with those things after all. But, on the other hand, it
might do, because to have someone thrust herself on you like
that…

She grabbed a comb and pulled it through her hair – at
least that was short, didn't take long to put right… Bit of
powder on her nose. Now, what to wear? She opened the
wardrobe doors, pulling them back in one synchronised
movement. That blouse would look better than… And that
skirt… Although a dress might be more appropriate – after all
it was Saturday evening… He was bound to be impeccable.

'Eloise, please don't keep Paul waiting.' Her mother's
voice came to her up the stairs. 'I'm afraid that he hasn't got
long.'

'Yes, mother… Coming…'

Eloise stepped back from the wardrobe, the better to
view her wares, bumped into a stool, held her balance for a
second… Then for a second longer… And another, before
toppling backwards – arms flailing like a distressed windmill
– towards the floor to land with a thump on her backside.
'Bugger!'

'Eloise, are you all right?'

Eloise scrambled to her feet, straightening her glasses as
she did so. 'Yes, mother.'

She looked at her reflection again. Scruffy. Never mind.
That would show him she didn't care, didn't care what he
thought of her – clothes or conduct. She picked up her essay,
left the room and started down the stairs – only to remember
that she wasn't wearing a bra.

Mary James watched her daughter coming down the
staircase, her eyes widening more with every step descended.

'Paul is waiting in the living room, dear,' she said. 'He's come to collect a composition you have written, is that right?'

'If that's what he says, mother, then it must be right, mustn't it?

Apart from the fossil hunt and the photography, Eloise had not told her mother about anything else that had occurred at Lyme Regis. She wanted to tell her mother about how she had kissed Paul, to discuss her feelings, but felt that, as a reason for doing so, she would have to include her exploit of driving the car. And how would her mother react to that? Badly, she guessed. It was an impossible situation. To confide one thing – to seek mum's advice – inevitably meant owning up to the other, and receiving mum's wrath. So, in the end, she had said nothing.

But did her mum know? Had she guessed that something else – apart from the others things – had happened last week? Eloise suspected that perhaps she might. One or two meaningful looks had come her way when she'd been telling her mother about the day's outing. Had she been too enthusiastic when describing something? Or had she been too guarded when talking about something else? Her mother was very good at that sort of thing: intuition, picking up on the unsaid; simply "knowing"… Those looks could signify something. On the other hand, they could be totally unrelated to what she'd told her mother; they could even have been imagined… Images inspired by Eloise's guilty imagination.

Clutching the essay on *Mrs Dalloway* to her chest, Eloise unclosed the living-room door and slid into the room. She could feel a tell-tale warmth suffusing her cheeks and knew that she must be blushing. What a fool. Ever since getting home from Lyme Regis last week, she had worried about this first meeting, and now, what with everything else, she had worried herself into this childish embarrassment.

She watched as Paul rose from the table and started to cross the room towards her, towards where she was standing, rooted to the carpet by the door, back pressed flat against it, as if she thought that by pressing hard enough she might disappear through it to the sanctuary of the hallway. Retaining her essay in its strategic position, she turned her mind to her tutor. Cool white shirt, school tie, grey flannel trousers, navy blue blazer, with the heraldic eagle embroidered in gold silk on the breast pocket... and the cow-lick of dark hair loose across his forehead. Tailored. Smart. Correct. Cool... Everything that she was not.

'Hello, Eloise,' he said, looking her up and down. 'You look like you've been working.' Then, without further ado, he kissed her on both cheeks.

Cool. She gazed up at the dark brown eyes, sparkling now beneath the bushy brows. Yes, she wasn't sure if she liked those pronounced bony eyebrow ridges –Neanderthal bumps. A lot of men were like that. She would have preferred a more regular line to his brow. 'Hello,' she said.

Paul smiled and lowered his eyes. 'Is that the critique on *Mrs Dalloway*?'

Eloise felt herself blushing again. 'Yes,' she said, glancing down at her near see-through T-shirt, hidden behind the sheaf of papers. He must wonder why she hadn't handed him the essay. 'I'll put it down over here,' she said, moving quickly towards the table. 'You will be able to read it better here… Although, I'm afraid that it's barely ready.'

Paul followed her to the table. 'I apologise for being a day early,' he said. 'But with term starting on Monday, I am afraid that my schedule is a touch tight… In fact, I have only popped across to take it home for later appraisal.'

'There you are,' Eloise said, tipping the essay onto the table and folding her arms in one seamless movement. She smiled sheepishly up at him. 'I'm afraid that it is a bit rushed: I have spent most of the day translating Voltaire.'

She watched Paul scoop up the essay and place it into his document case. Well, he hadn't mentioned her illegal drive, or the kiss, so everything must still be in good order, their friendship still intact. But at that moment the door opened and her mother entered the room. In her hands was a cardigan.

'You said you were feeling a little chilly just now, dear, and so I fetched you this.' She handed the garment to Eloise. 'Although you look warm enough to me now,' she added, smiling at her daughter, whose earlier abashment had still not completely left her cheeks.

Turning away from Paul, Eloise put on the cardigan and watched as her mother walked towards the door, glowering as the older woman stole a smiling glance back over her shoulder.

'Did you introduce Mr Wallace to Mr Barnes?' Eloise asked, turning back to Paul. She saw that he had just finished zipping up his document case – and appeared to have missed the point of the arriving cardigan. 'And did he have any ideas on Mr Wallace's antecedents?'

Paul told her that he had indeed delivered the fossil to the geography teacher, who, while being unable to identify it from his own books, was sure that a friend of his who worked at the Natural History Museum in London would be able to assist with that task. 'Once he's cut it from the rock, he intends to deliver it to the museum,' Paul concluded.

'Perhaps we have discovered a new species,' Eloise said, now feeling more relaxed and at her ease.

Paul grinned. 'If we have, then we shall have to name it after you… Now how would it go?'

'*Eloisa Poisson d'avil*,' she replied promptly, glancing down at her hands.

'We did not find it in April,' he said. 'And you are certainly not an April fool.'

'A September fool though,' she replied quickly. Then, before he had chance to respond, she ran on: 'I'd like to apologise. I'd like to apologise for persuading you to let me drive the car and… And for kissing you… I really am sorry.' There, she'd done it, got it off her chest. Now he could say what he liked, do what he liked… She didn't care.

Paul placed his hands on her shoulders, and she saw that his expression was stern. 'Eloise,' he began, 'sometimes we do things that we shouldn't do…things that we later regret doing. But what's done is done. We can't change it now.' He paused, holding her gaze. 'I think we both got carried away with the thought of bringing our find home… Let's both agree to learn by our mistakes.' He fell silent again, and she saw his eyes change. 'Besides, between you and me…' He winked at her. 'I quite enjoyed it… But of course that's not to suggest that we do it again,' he added quickly.

Golly, she'd gotten away with it. In fact, he'd actually made a joke about it. But that was probably only because he knew that her mother had once done something similar. Yes, maybe… And he had winked at her. She had never seen him do that before. It was as if he were indicating that they shared a guilty secret, that they were in league together. Eloise liked the idea of that: two rogues sworn to eternal secrecy by the heinousness of their crime. Her mother always said that it was unladylike to wink, otherwise she would return the gesture, would seal their unholy allegiance. But what about the kiss though? Driving the car had been illegal – she had broken the law – but for some reason, and she couldn't work out why, she saw her kissing Paul as being the more serious of her two misdemeanours. Perhaps it was that, knowing Paul had such a strict moral code, she saw breaking that as a more serious thing. But what would he say about it? Then she saw his eyes twinkle, felt his hands relax on her shoulders, and heard him say:

'And as for your exuberance, Eloise, well I don't know of any man who would complain because a beautiful young woman had kissed him.'

Eloise gazed up at his mouth, the lips slightly parted in a smile. What if she were to – she wanted to… To see what it felt like again… Their lips pressed together, her arms encircling his neck. She paused, reining in her train of thought. But he was making fun of her of course; mocking her. Beautiful young woman! She was anything but – mousy hair, big nose, uneven teeth, glasses. Frowning, she lowered her eyes from his lips.

'Hey,' he said, catching her changed mood. 'There's no need to be modest. I meant what I said: you're a very pretty girl.' He smiled kindly. 'And I'll go further. You are my star scholar… My most hard-working student.' Now she knew for sure that he was mocking her. She stared at her battered old granny slippers. And she probably wasn't sophisticated enough for him either, parochial, dowdy…

She looked up and gave him a wan smile. Yes, she was too unsophisticated for him… And he had called her his star scholar. "My most hard-working student." So that was how it was; that was how he thought of her: as his pupil, as a girl in his class – nothing more than that.

Then, before she had chance to shake off her thoughts, he was moving past her into the hall… and she was showing him out – the front door open… 'Goodbye… I'll see you on Monday.' And he was gone.

She turned around and started off down the hallway towards the stairs, just as her mother emerged from the kitchen, smiling.

'I'll take my cardigan back later, Eloise,' Mary James said casually as the two women paused in the corridor. Her eyes turned mischievous, falling to her daughter's bust, and she added: 'But as a rule I think that it is generally wisest to hold back one's choicest goods until the shopper is ready to buy.'

Eloise took off the cardigan. 'Oh, really, mother, sometimes you can be so frightfully infantile.' She handed the garment to her mother and started to stride towards the stairs. 'Beside, I am merely one of his students – a girl in his class, *that* is all.'

Chapter Twelve

For the tenth time in as many minutes, Eloise toyed with the buff-coloured envelope, shuffling it from hand to hand; it was as if she were a cardsharp intent on confusing her unsuspecting victim.

'Don't be silly, Eloise,' Mary James said, in motherly exasperation. 'I am sure that everything will be fine.'

It was the week before Christmas, six weeks since Eloise had taken her postponed 'A' level examinations, and she had been on tenterhooks for days, knowing the results were due to arrive through the letterbox at any time. Indeed, she had been unable to think about them without getting nervous – without getting butterflies. But now they were here, the envelope containing them in her hands, the grades just beneath that thin veneer of paper; the delay was over. She was no longer waiting on someone else. Waiting. She could end that any time she chose.

She leaned back in the leather sofa and stretched her legs out straight, toasting her stockinged feet before the coal fire that burned brightly in the cast iron grate. Earlier she had put up the Christmas decorations, and she was now taking a break before helping her mother prepare lunch. She twirled the envelope in her fingers, watching her name appear and re-appear as she did so. 'In a moment, mother.' She made as if to toss the envelope onto the fire, smiling at her mother's horrified expression as she did so. 'In a moment.'

'I am sure you have acquitted yourself well enough,' her mother continued. 'I'm sure there is no need to worry – you have worked so hard'

Eloise took off her glasses. 'I am not worried, mother.' And she wasn't: over the two-week period of the examinations, the sitting of her key subjects had all fallen on Wednesdays – and that was the day of her luckiest breakfast. She smiled to herself. They all thought her mad – even Charlie – because she had a different breakfast cereal for each day of the week. Monday was cornflakes, Tuesday was puffed wheat, and Wednesday was porridge – and that was her luckiest one – and naturally the other days had their allotted cereals too. It was one of her routines. Her mother went along with it, although she often complained that accommodating the seven boxes took up a whole cupboard in the kitchen.

Percy James coughed and glanced up from his paper. 'Don't keep us waiting any longer, Eloise. There is a fine line between drama and melodrama, you know.'

'Oh, all right…' Eloise replaced her spectacles.

Then the doorbell rang.

'It's Paul, dear,' Mary James said, leading Paul Bridgestock into the living room. 'He has dropped by to enquire about the examination results.'

Eloise laid the envelope on the sofa beside her, then picked up her teddy bear. 'A.L. will bring me luck,' she said, sitting the cuddly toy in her lap. She glanced up at the teacher. 'Won't he, Paul?' she added.

Following the successful commencement of the autumn term, Paul had started taking her out again. They went to the theatre, to the cinema, to the roller skating rink and, during Saturday shopping trips into Exeter, to the Moka Café. It was the era of the American-style coffee bar, and many of her peers went to the newly opened Wimpy Bar in Paris Street, where, she knew, they drank "Tastee Freez" milk shakes and listened to the latest forty-fives on the jukebox. But she preferred the Moka, where its sophisticated, heady atmosphere let her imagination persuade her that all manner of romantic trysts were being forged. Idly stroking her teddy bear, she continued to gaze at Paul. Her gaze became wistful – how she wished he would forge one with her.

Paul glanced at the stony expressions of Eloise's parents, his own cheerful expression sinking visibly as he did so.

'It's all right, Paul,' Mary James said, noting his concern, 'Eloise hasn't opened them yet.'

Paul Bridgestock grinned with relief.

Mary James turned to her daughter. 'Go on, Eloise. Do not keep us in suspense any longer.'

But examination-result jitters now got the better of Eloise. 'I can't,' she said, gazing sheepishly at her mother. 'I really can't.' She offered the envelope to her father. 'You open it, daddy.'

'Oh, women,' Percy James sighed. He took the envelope from Eloise, then, ignoring the letter-opener offered to him by his wife, tore it open and pulled out the single sheet of paper that it contained.

'Well, Percy?' his wife enquired, long before he'd had chance to unfold the piece of paper, let alone had the opportunity to read anything.

Percy James perused the results sheet, his eyes scanning the subjects and their grades line by line. Then, casting a non-committal glance at the three expectant faces, he slowly and deliberately re-folded the sheet of paper, before, just as slowly and deliberately, returning it to the envelope.

Eloise who had been studying her father's expression throughout the performance, looking for a tale-tell signal that might reveal something, now turned questioning eyes to her mother.

'Well, Percy?' Mary James asked again.

Percy James surveyed his audience, speculatively, his face revealing nothing. He was, despite his earlier denouncement of melodrama, clearly enjoying the moment. However, his gaze at last rested on his daughter. 'It looks like you can accompany Charlotte to Oxford,' he said, allowing his face to break into a smile.

In spite of knowing the examinations had gone well, Eloise was still a teeny-weeny bit surprised to hear that she had pulled it off. After all, she wasn't like Charlotte who could sit down and write an examination essay as if she were merely at home writing a letter to a friend. On the contrary, she got nervous at such times – very nervous. There was so much as stake. When it came to sitting examinations, she felt the pressure of having to perform there and then, of having to regurgitate material she had learned over two years and present it coherently (and legibly) in two hours. Sometimes her adrenaline levels rose so high that her senses became heightened to the point where she could actually smell the print on the question paper, and then she would feel sick. Still, she had come through well enough. Her gaze went from her father to her mother, then back to her father again. She lifted A.L. from her lap. 'Yes, I thought that I might,' she said, shrugging her shoulders. Then, turning towards Paul, she added: 'Because I had a super teacher.'

Paul Bridgestock moved uneasily in his chair. 'It would be immodest of me to take the credit for your daughter's success,' he said, addressing himself to Eloise's parents. 'That surely goes to Eloise, who has worked exceptionally hard, and also of course, and in no little measure, to Miss Marshall, who did so much before my arrival.' Eloise noted then that he was blushing ever so slightly, which made her feel strangely elated – more so, to be honest, than the examination results themselves had done. 'Besides,' he continued, 'my area of interest was merely the English element of the curriculum.'

'Poppycock!' Percy James said, rather too loudly. 'I'll have none of it. Why, bless my soul, we all worked hard.'

General congratulations then followed. Percy and Mary James got into a tangle while simultaneously attempting to hug Eloise. Paul kissed both Mary James and Eloise on the cheek, the latter deed prompting Eloise to think ruefully that had she not turned her head so readily to accept the kiss, he would have got her smack-bang-wallop on the lips. Unable to turn back the clock, unable to reclaim her lost chance, she absently watched her father shake Paul's hand.

Percy James then went to the sideboard and fetched out a bottle of Port and four glasses. A toast was proposed to Eloise's success – past and future – which made her feel of a sudden a trifle ambivalent about the whole thing. She was eighteen, had already worked through thirteen years of education, and now there were a further four years at university, four years with examinations at the end of each one. More study, more nerves – more butterflies. But Charlotte would also be there, reading for the same degree. And it wouldn't be all work. They would make new friends as well. It would be a hoot. Much to the surprise of her mother and father, not to mention Paul, she tossed back her glass of Port in one gulp.

Smiling, Paul turned his gaze from Eloise to her father. 'By the way, sir,' he said, 'what were the actual grades?'

Percy James handed him the envelope, and Paul then read them out aloud:

'Geography: "B".'

That was fair.

'French: "A".'

Candide.

'English language: "A".'

Surprising: there was at least one dangling participle; and she'd never really mastered the conventions of lie and lay and laid and lain. There were so many meanings, and the tenses...

'English literature: "Distinction".'

What would her mother and father say if she went and kissed him just as she had on the hill at Lyme Regis?

Chapter Thirteen

Paul left to visit his parents in the Isle of Man just before Christmas and was not due to return until the twenty-ninth of the month – thus Eloise now spent more time with Charlotte. The two friends passed their time between the usual rounds of festive parties, social outings and shopping expeditions into Exeter, where of course they always called in at the Moka Café.

Charlotte extinguished her cigarette, then gazed across the table to Eloise. 'But, presumably, he doesn't know how you feel?'

Eloise had just informed her friend of her feelings for Paul – at least as far as she herself knew what those feelings might be. She knew she was attracted to him, liked him a lot – had grown close during their time together, both at school and, more recently, in a social context. She had read an article in a magazine that had suggested a heart could be measured on the imagined loss of one's beau. On that criterion, she reckoned she was in love. It was the first time she had told anybody of how she felt about Paul. She had always shied away from doing so – even with her best friend – not least because of Paul's position at the school but also because of what she saw as the large age difference between them.

She sipped her coffee. Charlie had not pooh-poohed the possibility of a genuine relationship with Paul, had not brought up the teacher-pupil thing – although, that was really a past tense item now – and, more importantly, she had not mentioned the age gap. 'No,' she said, 'we have never discussed it.' She paused, placing her cup meticulously in its saucer. 'But it's not gone that far though...' She hesitated, then added: 'To be honest, I don't suppose there is any material reason for him to know how I feel.'

'But clearly you would like there to be one. Well, you two have been together a lot these past months. You do a lot of different things together... go to a variety of places. Perhaps he does know. Perhaps he has picked up on something you have said... Or sensed how you reacted to something he said.'

Eloise felt her heart skip a beat. 'Do you really think so? I mean, we share so many interests... and he is considerate, caring – he notices things.' She paused and her eyes brightened, as she ran on: 'And mother and father like him, especially mum – they get on tremendously well together.'

Charlotte held Eloise's expectant stare. 'He must like you, Ellie, otherwise he wouldn't take you out, would he?'

Eloise had hoped for something a little more upbeat, something a little more positive from Charlotte. Her spirits sank. She removed her glasses and absently began to polish the lenses. 'Oh, I don't know,' she said, disconsolately, 'sometimes I think that he sees the age difference between us as being an obstacle to a real relationship.'

'Eloise, Paul doesn't strike me as being the kind of man who would worry about something like that, if he liked someone. And anyway, it isn't as though he's years and years older than you, is it?'

Eloise nodded thoughtfully. 'Twelve,' she mumbled, more to herself than to her friend.

'Paul is a little bit old-fashioned,' Charlotte went on,

'not demonstrative. But although he may not have shown it, as I said, he must think a lot of you… After all, he's not going out with anyone else, is he?'

Even though Charlotte's words were clearly meant to reassure, an icy hand had gripped Eloise's heart at the thought of Paul being with someone else. 'Not that I know of,' she said, replacing her glasses.

Charlotte was silent for a moment or two. 'He isn't married,' she mused. 'Maybe he isn't interested in girls… in that way.'

'His life has been busy, working and studying, and now teaching,' Eloise said, stirring her coffee absently. 'But we were talking once, and he said that he'd had a relationship, when he was living in the North East – but it didn't work out… or something.'

Charlotte pursed her lips in thought. 'Did he say what sort of relationship it was?' she asked at length.

Eloise shrugged her shoulders. 'A relationship… Just a relationship. I didn't ask him whether he'd slept with the girl, if that's what you mean.'

Charlotte nudged the ashtray a fraction along the table. 'No, I meant whether it was a *normal* relationship.'

Eloise eyed her friend suspiciously. 'What are you talking about?' she asked. 'He had a relationship, when he was in the North East, before he came down here. That's what he told me.'

'Did he say whether it was with a girl?' Charlotte asked.

'Well, it wouldn't have been with another man, would it?' Eloise replied, casting a cursory glance across the table and smiling.

'Why not?'

Eloise held Charlotte's steady gaze. Charlie was in one of her silly moods, teasing, inventing intrigue for its own sake, for the sake of a good gossip. But this was too serious: Eloise wouldn't play along with it. 'Paul is not like that,' she said emphatically. 'That's dirty… And it's illegal.' She picked up her cup of coffee. 'Paul wouldn't do that.'

Charlotte picked up her bag and dropped it into her lap, then dipped her hand inside and began to rummage around.

Eloise watched Charlotte place a packet of cigarettes on the table, waited for her friend's response. Charlotte's expression was difficult to read – inscrutable… And she was taking a long time with those cigarettes. Perhaps she was deciding whether to continue with her silly innuendo. Well, she wouldn't let her do so. It wasn't the sort of thing to joke about. Then she saw Charlotte's face break into a smile, and heard her say:

'I know he wouldn't, Eloise.' Charlotte nodded her head vigorously. 'Our Mr Bridgestock is the straightest man I know.'

'You shouldn't involve Paul in jokes of that nature,' Eloise admonished. 'It's not nice and it's unfair.'

'Sorry, Ellie.'

Eloise studied her friend. 'That's all right,' she said. 'It's just that…' She paused and sipped her coffee. Then, glancing up – almost shyly – she went on: 'Charlotte, I may not have given you any indication before today, but I really do think that I love Paul.'

'You think that you love him?'

'Yes, I think… No… I am certain that I do. We have great times together… Why, we are as close as sister and brother.'

'As close as sister and brother. That's an odd way of describing a friendship that you clearly hope will develop into something more…' Charlotte glanced around the coffee shop, then back to Eloise. 'Do you feel that you would like to spend the rest of your life with him, cherish him, look after him, care for him in sickness and in health?' She paused briefly, as if waiting for an answer to her question. But then, before Eloise had chance to provide one, she added: 'Would you like to have his babies?'

In spite of being in the Moka Café – and for all its atmosphere of adult chic – Eloise felt herself blushing. 'Really, Charlotte,' she said, 'I don't see what having babies has got to do with loving someone.'

'In my opinion, it's got plenty to do with it,' Charlotte said, tonelessly. 'It's a good measure to go by. If you love someone, then surely you would have that desire of wanting to sleep with him… Together, with all that goes with it.' She fell silent for a moment. 'I'm only trying to help, Ellie.'

Eloise shrugged her shoulders. 'Yes,' she said. 'Yes, I see… I see what you're getting at.' She paused, thinking. But yes, she would like to sleep with him, to sleep with him in that way… Perhaps that had been how she'd felt when she'd kissed him. She had felt odd at the time; more so as the kiss had gone on. She'd felt excited, exhilarated, but that had probably had more to do with driving the car up the hill than with anything else. But she had also experienced a kind of desire, a feeling of what later reflection had identified as "a sense of being disturbed". Quashing her thoughts, and with a further shrug of her shoulders, she concluded: 'Yes, I suppose you are correct.'

'I know that I am,' Charlotte said authoritatively. She gazed steadily at her friend. 'Don't get obsessed with searching for answers, Eloise, analysing everything. Oh, I know you're famous for it, but some things defy logic.' She picked up her packet of cigarettes. 'Anyhow, for what it's worth, you and Paul seem to be having enormous fun together. But as for that elusive thing called love… *Nous verrons ce que nous verrons.*'

'What will be will be,' Eloise said, thoughtfully. Charlie

was right: it was no good getting uptight… No good worrying about something over which she had no control. And she and Paul were OK together. She grinned at her friend. 'You're right, as usual,' she said, happily.

Charlotte reached across the table and placed her hand on her friend's arm. 'Anyhow,' she said, with a knowing smile, 'do you love him like you love your parents?' Her grip tightened ever so slightly and, winking, she went on: 'Do you love him like you love me?'

Yes, Charlie was definitely in one of her silly moods today, frivolous, playing the jester. But despite her own earnestness, her need for reassurance, Eloise decided to play along with the school joke. 'No, not like that, Miss Staidler,' she said. 'It's nothing like the real thing. It's different to…' Her expression fell as her serious mood suddenly resurfaced and, frowning at Charlotte's flippancy, she went on: 'Anyway it's different to how I feel about mum and dad and different again to how I feel about you.'

Charlotte lit a cigarette, leaned back in her chair, then let out an exaggerated sigh. 'In my opinion, Eloise, a girl needs to have had several friendships with the opposite sex before she can truly know her mind. Let's face it, whatever you're feeling now, you have nothing with which to gauge it against, have you?'

'I don't need anything… I do love him, Charlie.' Eloise paused. Then, with her expression a bundle of animation, she added: 'And yes, I would like to have his babies… as you so tastefully put it.'

Charlotte drew on her cigarette, then caught her friend's hand. 'Eloise, you will know if you love him when you kiss.'

'Oh, yes, and how will that be?'

'Well…' Charlotte fell silent for a moment, thinking.

'You remember in chemistry when Miss Staidler placed that piece of sodium metal in the bowl of water and it fizzled like crazy and whizzed around in all directions with sparks and smoke coming from it as it dissolved.... Well, your heart will feel something like that – only more so.'

'Is that all?' Eloise said, dismissively. But actually it wasn't so far off the mark. She held her friend's gaze. 'Anyhow, we have kissed.'

Charlotte balanced her cigarette on the rim of the ashtray. 'You sly old goose. But I thought that you might have.' She leaned forward, elbows resting on the table, eyebrows raised. 'Tell me more.'

Eloise then related the Lyme Regis episode, making light of the unlicensed car drive but emphasising the kiss as only she could, concluding: 'I have never felt that way in all my life before.'

Charlotte had remained a silent but nonetheless incredulous listener throughout her friend's discourse; but now, with the story told, she leaned back in her chair. 'You haven't told your mother about the driving, I presume.'

Eloise traced a thoughtful finger around the rim of her cup. 'I know that I should have...' She glanced up at Charlotte. 'But I just couldn't; mother and father would have been really angry. As you know, Paul was my private tutor at the time, and that would have ended… and besides, if I had said anything, they would almost certainly have stopped me seeing him.' She paused, expression aghast. But then, quickly recovering her composure, she added brightly: 'Yet at the time, it just seemed fun. You know – a lark.'

'Well, Miss James,' Charlotte began, 'I've known you all my life but I would never have suspected you capable of just driving like that, without a licence.' Her gaze narrowed. 'I am surprised that Paul allowed it though.'

'It wasn't his fault,' Eloise said, earnestly, anxious to absolve Paul from any blame. 'I wanted to bring the fossil home so desperately that I… I sort of persuaded him to let me drive.' Her stare became imploring. 'But never mind all that, what do you suppose he thought of my kissing him like that?'

Charlotte shrugged her shoulders. 'To be honest, Eloise, I think that he would have attributed it to your elation. You know, of actually pulling off the driving exploit – nothing more than that.' She paused, thinking. 'And to be fair, that is all it sounds to me, too.'

'It was initially,' Eloise exclaimed. 'Of course it was… At first. But I held the kiss too long for just that. Golly, I just let it go on and on. I didn't want it to end.' She paused, trying to come down from the memory. 'And I'm certain that I acted differently towards him afterwards.'

'Differently?' Charlotte said. 'In what way?'

'Well… Oh, I don't know…' Eloise's gaze rose from her coffee cup, where it had fallen following her outburst. 'I was nervous with him, reticent, ill at ease… Oh, you know, guarded.' She paused and nodded to herself. 'And I'm sure that I acted like that for a long time afterwards as well. Perhaps he read something into that.'

Charlotte smiled and shook her head. 'Eloise, put aside how you felt when you kissed him, and how you think you acted afterwards.' She nodded sagely, like a judge who, having heard all the arguments, finally reaches a decision. 'You will only know his heart when *he* kisses you.'

Eloise scoffed. 'Oh really, Charlotte. In which penny dreadful did you read that?'

Chapter Fourteen

Following his return from his Christmas break in the Isle of Man, Paul took Eloise tobogganing on the Haldon Hills just south of Exeter. It had been a last-minute decision. Snow had fallen a few days before and frozen overnight, making ideal conditions for the sport. But the very next day a thaw had set in and, with the snow fast melting, and fearing that it might be their only opportunity of the winter, they had decided to take a chance and go. After all, they reasoned, the conditions might still be all right on the higher slopes.

Paul waited until another couple had pushed off from the top, then placed their toboggan ready to go. 'I think it will be the last run,' he said, gazing down the hill. 'Look, farther down, on each side of the run where the snow is less compacted, it's almost all grass now.'

'Yes,' Eloise agreed. 'Right down the bottom there's no snow left at all.' She looked towards Exeter in the distance. In the sunshine it looked as if spring had come early to the city. She pulled her bobble-hat lower on her forehead, then adjusted the skew of her glasses. 'C'mon then,' she said, taking her place behind Paul on the toboggan. 'Let's go before spring overtakes us.'

'Right you are,' Paul laughed. 'Hold on tight.' And, with that, using the heels of his shoes as levers, he coaxed them over the brow of the slope.

Feeling the rush of air against her face, Eloise peered

over Paul's shoulder, her arms clasped firmly around his waist as they descended the meadow. Except for the actual path, all around them was green. The last few days had just been a cold snap. And Paul was right: this would be the last run; it was too warm, too green... Soon the spring flowers would come. Spring flowers... And then the memory of a much earlier, childhood trip came back to her.

She had wanted to pick some primroses to take into school but, as children often do when wanting something very much, had feared they would not find any. Perhaps this was because, as they lived in the city, wild primroses were not a familiar flower to her young mind, cultivated blooms being the stuff of gardens where she lived. Nevertheless, in this unhopeful mood, and with a child's awareness of by how much two shillings and six pence exceeded the funds in her moneybox, she had promised her mother "a half-crown piece" if they found any. Her mother had grown up in the country and knew a place where primroses grew in abundance.

Surreally the spring day revisited her imagination. They boarded the bus at the end of the road, Eloise sitting nearest the window in order that she might be the one to see the wild flowers first. Then, when the bus got there, she would be the first to get off – and the first to the primroses. But did mummy really know where they would find some?

Soon the vehicle had left the city behind and was purring along a country lane with high hedges, dotted with trees, passing by on each side. But she did not think they would find any primroses. After all, someone else was bound to have got there first and picked them all. That was a problem with people: they never left anything for anybody else. Once, her mother had taken her blackberry picking but when they got there all the berries had been picked. But mummy had brought a walking-stick with a crooked handle and had reached up and pulled the higher boughs within reach. And they had picked a whole basket full.

The bus was going up a hill, not a steep one at first but now becoming steeper, and the driver moved a lever and the engine sounded different, like it was going faster, but the bus was going slower. That was why other people would have got there first: because they would have come in cars, and everyone knew that cars did not have to slow down for hills.

Then the bus pulled over beside a farm, where milk churns sat on a wooden platform, silver and cold in the hot sunshine. The farmer's children would know where the primroses were and would have picked them all by now. It was past lunch after all.

They walked along the lane a-ways, and then climbed a stile into a field, along a footpath along by the hedge, then through a patch of trees, where it was cooler, across another field, through a gate, still on the path; then they started down a very green meadow towards the bottom of the valley. In the distance, there was the sound of a train whistle. If they had come by train, they would have been in time to pick some primroses. Then she heard the sound of children's voices. They would be the farmer's children – with all the primroses.

As they walked along, she held her mother's hand; and a black and white cow, munching grass, watched them pass by, its big brown eyes following them without blinking. Other cows were in the field too, all with their muzzles buried in the grass, munching and chewing and shaking their heads and swishing their tails to scare away the flies that buzzed around unable to make up their minds over which way to go.

There were a lot of cows. Perhaps they had eaten any primroses that were left behind by the farmer's children.

The meadow was becoming steeper – too steep for primroses to grow. They had to dig their heels into the path, which was really like a staircase, to slow themselves down. Her mother had said just now that they were nearly there, nearly there to where the primroses grew. She still could not see them though.

At the bottom of the meadow was a stream. You couldn't hear the water running from this far back though. Its banks were raised above the bottom of the meadow. That was to keep the water in, otherwise it would all drain away. It was the same of course on the other side of the stream. Then the meadow over there rose up almost as high as this side, to where you couldn't see over it, except sky. But she still could not see the primroses. That was because other people in cars, and on trains – and the farmer's children – had picked them all. And any that were left over would have been eaten by the cows.

Then she saw the primroses.

With a whoop of joy, she let go of her mother's hand and dashed off the path and commenced down the hillside, going at full tilt, skipping over the neatly stacked molehills as she went. Primroses. Masses of them, drowning the bank of the stream at the bottom of the meadow in a sea of beaming suns.

'Oh thank you, mummy,' she cried into the rushing air. 'Oh thank you, mummy.' There were the primroses. 'Here's your half-crown piece,' she called, throwing the imaginary coin over her shoulder.

Then her mother was beside her, running too, her long hair flying out at the back. Her mother was singing, she was singing, they were singing. Running, skipping, calling to each other in the green meadow. And there were the primroses.

And there were the primroses that mummy had promised her.

Between them, they gathered several bunches of primroses, for home, for daddy, and for school. Then they had a picnic, climbed back up the hill, and caught another bus home.

Near the bottom of the slope, the toboggan lost momentum, and the rushing air collapsed. Paul waited while Eloise climbed off the toboggan, and then he too stood up. 'I'm afraid that's it,' he said, gazing at the melting snow at the end of the shortened run. He turned to face Eloise. 'But never mind perhaps–' He paused, his expression falling. 'Eloise, what's the matter? Why are you crying?'

Eloise sniffed. For the past half dozen seasons, she had been cycling out into the countryside in an annual attempt to find the primrose path of her childhood. Of course it was silly, childish really, this searching for the primrose meadow, when all she had to do was ask her mother where it was. But it had grown into a springtime event for her, a quest that was fast becoming a tradition – had become one actually – and to ask her mother where it was would spoil the whole thing. She had to find it herself. She hadn't done so yet – but she knew that one day she would. She laughed and brushed clumsily at her cheeks with her mittens. 'It's just the air against my face, that's all.'

Paul watched her as, with her glasses balanced precariously on the end of her nose, she wiped her eyes with a handkerchief. 'Are you sure you are OK?'

Eloise gazed up at his expression, crinkled with concern.

'I wish...' she began, 'I wish certain times could last for always... Not exactly that, but that you could revisit them whenever you liked. You know, a bit like watching an old cine film of yourself, except that you could step inside it, step into your old shoes... Go back in time, see things how they used to be, things young... With everything to look forward to.' She turned her gaze towards distant Exeter, its outline reddened by the afternoon sun. 'Sometimes I even wish we could live our lives in reverse. You know, start out old and live backwards towards the good times.'

He took hold of her hands, his gaze as soft as an old spaniel's. 'Eloise, you have a wonderful future ahead of you. Why, you're only eighteen. You are going up to Oxford next year, with Charlotte.' He paused, squeezing her hands in his. 'You will have a great time there, believe me – there's so much to do.' He wiped away a tear that was about to run down her cheek. 'You should be looking forward,' he went on, 'looking forward to your good times.'

Only eighteen... Going to university... With Charlotte... Looking forward to the good times... To the good times without him. He hadn't mentioned his place in her future. He obviously didn't see their friendship in the same way that she did, then. She released herself and got to her feet. 'I wasn't really thinking about myself,' she replied. She picked up the toboggan's towrope. 'I suppose we had better be going home now.'

Percy and Mary James had invited Paul to dinner that evening to celebrate his guiding their daughter through the English element of her delayed 'A' level examinations. He was due to arrive at seven thirty and, as the moment of his arrival drew near, she was fully prepared for the visit. She had shrugged off the disappointment that his earlier review of her future had brought her – as Charlotte had said, "what will be will be." And she was eager, in view of the season and occasion, to see if she would receive a traditional greeting, and, to this end, had tied a sprig of mistletoe to the hallway light fitting. Her plan was to back under it as she opened the door – she had practised the manoeuvre. She would then feign annoyance as it brushed against her hair. Doing that would absolve her from any idea of subterfuge – and, more to the point, he could hardly miss that it was there. He would then have to kiss her. She would ensure that it was a long one... passionate, and she could test Charlie's theory. A startlingly good plan, she had to admit.

At seven-thirty prompt, the doorbell rang.

Eloise went to the door and opened it. There was Paul, chocolates and wine in his hands, and, gazing over his shoulder, she could see the little Morris Minor parked in the drive, its star-lit headlamps seeming to ask if it could be allowed into the house too. She had driven it up the hill at Lyme Regis, with Mr Wallace in the boot... And then she had kissed...

'You don't intend to keep me out here on the step all evening, do you?' Paul asked, shivering theatrically against the chill night air.

The vision of herself kissing Paul faded from Eloise's mind. 'No, of course not,' she said, standing to one side to let him in.

She took his overcoat. Her plan wasn't working, as it should: she had forgotten about his coat, hanging it up. And now, making it too late to recover her scheme, he was walking down the corridor towards the kitchen, to where he knew her mother would be preparing dinner.

Eloise glanced down at the leather-bound volume of Auden poems that he had given her for Christmas, then up to the mistletoe hanging so conspicuously above her head. Despite her rehearsal, she hadn't got the height of that correct: she was wearing different shoes now to those she'd been wearing when she'd concocted her plan – she hadn't thought of that. Well, at least he was wearing the cufflinks.

At the farther end of the corridor the kitchen door opened then and Paul emerged. Eloise saw that he was smiling. She guessed that he would have kissed her mother. He started towards her. Stopped. Gave her a perfunctory wave. Smiled. Started this way again... Hesitated, then turned right and disappeared into the living room, where he would find her father reading a technical journal and smoking his pipe. Although his greeting had been cordial, he had not shown the slightest inclination to touch her, let alone kiss her. And the afternoon had been such fun... Well, she'd had that silly sentimental moment at the bottom of the toboggan run – but it had been mostly a robust afternoon. How peculiar men were. Puzzled, she went to the kitchen to help her mother with the dinner.

'What's the matter, dear?' Mary James asked, opening the oven door to examine the joint of beef and sizzling roast potatoes. 'Isn't he wearing them? Well, never mind. I expect that he just forgot.'

Eloise put on an apron and leaned against the refrigerator. 'Oh, he is wearing them.'

Her mother raised the lid of a saucepan and tested a potato with a fork. 'Well then, there is no need to look so glum, is there?' She lifted another saucepan lid, where carrots simmered. 'You did say that you had a good time tobogganing this afternoon, didn't you?'

'Yes,' Eloise replied. She thought that he should have kissed her. After all, this was a celebration – and it was Christmas. Even if he hadn't seen the mistletoe, he should have kissed her on both cheeks, and given her a hug as well. If he had done that much, she might have found a way to get her lips on his… But he hadn't given her a chance. She scooted a forgotten Brussels sprout along the worktop with a flick of her finger. 'He told me that I was *only* eighteen and that my good times lie in the future.'

Her mother smiled. 'I doubt he meant that you were *only* eighteen, Eloise.' She reached past her daughter and dropped a fork onto the draining board. 'And he is right: many of your good times do lie in the future.'

Eloise sighed. 'But I will be at university… A long way away.'

'But you will be coming home between terms,' her mother said, busying herself with preparing dinner, and appearing to miss the gist of her daughter's remark. She fetched a Pyrex jug from a cupboard. 'And I expect your father will drive us up to visit some weekends.'

Eloise did not respond. It was one thing to be a hundred miles away when you had a steady boyfriend at home, but it was an entirely different matter when you were a hundred miles away and the man you loved was at home teaching another class of girls, taking them on photographic trips, to Exmoor, to the coast, to Lyme–

'Eloise.' Her mother's voice shattered her image of perdition. 'Please stop moping over silly irrelevancies and help me with the vegetables.'

Eloise scowled at her mother. She wasn't happy. The celebration dinner had gone off without a hitch – her mother the perfect hostess; even her father, never a loquacious man, had found a suitable joke or two to jolly along the occasion; and she herself had even managed to put aside the earlier disappointment of her foiled plan. But she wasn't happy – far from it. In actual fact, she was desperately displeased. And it had nothing to do with dinner, the success of which had played on her mind. The origin of her displeasure had occurred later, in the rubbers of partner whist they had played after dinner. Paul, being the fêted guest, had been given first choice of partners, and he had chosen her mother, when of course he should have chosen her. After all, they were supposed to be going out together. But if that had been all there was to it, it wouldn't have been so bad. She could have put up with that. But further increasing Eloise's ill humour, Mary James had spent the next hour flirting with him like a silly schoolgirl. And to make matters even worse, he had revelled in the attention, even going so far as to tell her mother that she was the prettiest partner he'd ever had. It had been one indignity after another. Eloise had attributed their pitiful behaviour to the wine they'd consumed and, for her own part, had remained aloof to the silly banter and even sillier innuendoes. Her father had appeared oblivious to the whole embarrassing spectacle, when clearly he should have shown his guest the door. And it had only added insult to injury when Paul and her mother had won the match by five rubbers to nil. Her whole evening had been ruined.

And now it was time for Paul to leave. Still sore from having to suffer his exhibition with her mother, Eloise toyed with the idea of saying good night to him from her armchair by the fire. That would show them that she was an adult and not to be treated like a child. However, when neither her father nor her mother revealed any inclination to escort their guest to the door, she got up to perform the chore herself. Doing so would give her the opportunity to show her displeasure, to make him aware that she was disappointed with his behaviour. She would play it cool, be standoffish. She would ensure that he got her message.

Careful to avoid eye contact, she took his coat from the rack and handed it to him. The mistletoe was still attached to the light fitting. She hoped that he didn't notice it. She didn't want him getting ideas – not now. Eloise watched him button up his coat, one thoughtful button after another. He looked rueful, his gaze downcast. He seemed reluctant to leave, as if he wanted to say something first. Maybe he now regretted his earlier peccadillo. Maybe he was going to apologise. Well, it was too late for that now.

'Good night, Mr Bridge—'

And at that moment, surprising her with the deftness of the manoeuvre, he turned around and caught her hands in his. 'Eloise…' His speech faltered. 'Eloise, I would like to say something…' His speech faltered again and, seemingly unable to continue, he slid her hands behind her back, holding them there as his gaze transfixed hers.

She had not yet realised his intention and could do no more than return his gaze, her eyes wide in astonishment, her lips parted as if she were caught in the middle of asking a question. She could feel the heat of his body, the hot sensation given off by his intimate touch. But what was he up to? Had he gone mad, lost his mind? He seemed unnaturally agitated… She started to pull her hands away. And it was at that moment that *he* kissed her.

Oh my! She experienced his mouth moving on hers, felt her hands pinioned behind her back, tightly clamped, held there immobile, as if her wrists were cuffed by silken bonds. The enforced posture had propelled her bosom forward and up, as though she had been laced into a tight corset. The satin material of her blouse was pulled taut, the buttons pulled tight, as if they might go ping, ping, ping, one after the other across the hallway. She felt bared – vulnerable. This was better than the time when she had kissed him, and she wasn't about to stop him... even if she could. And with that thought, it got even better.

Finally though, he released her, and, holding her shoulders, broke the embrace. 'Well,' he said, at length, 'it seems that you are not the only impetuous one.' He glanced down at his hands. 'I had meant only to talk to you, but... Ultimately, this seemed the best way to convey what I had to say.'

She stared up at him, trying to control her breathing, unable to think let alone to say anything. 'Oh!' She continued to stare at him, her usually so-analytical mind in a whirl, a maelstrom of autumn leaves, each a torn thought, her rationality defeated for once by the emotional response of her heart.

His expression fell. 'I'm sorry... I should not have... have done that. I should have spoken first. I apologise. Please forgive–'

'No, not at all,' she interrupted, at last besting the turmoil of her heart. 'I'm glad you kissed me.' She removed her spectacles. 'You can do it again if you want to.' Oh God, that sounded forward. He would think her a nymphomaniac if she wasn't careful. It was nice, being kissed by him. But she really shouldn't have put it that way. No matter how much she wanted him to kiss her again, she should not have invited him so bluntly. She lifted her face to his.

But he did not appear put off by her remark and, drawing her to him, placed his mouth on hers again, kissing her in such a way as to make her aware of the masculine dominance of the embrace; the overwhelming desire to surrender her femininity, to surrender her femininity right there in the hallway – and with her mother and father just along the corridor.

She had never been held like this by a man before, had never been kissed like this before. The kiss she had received while playing that silly game of postman's knock on her fifteenth birthday had been poor preparation. There was more to the physical side of love making than she'd ever thought possible. Taking the sum of her experiences into account: her previous feelings for Paul… Films, books, television… Talking about it with her mother, even discussing it with Charlotte, hadn't prepared her for this. All those things had been inadequate – totally inadequate. She had to gain control of herself, check her feelings, and stifle this unnatural desire before she made a complete fool of herself. How quick she was to passion. With her head spinning, her heart pounding, and her body yearning, she pulled away from the embrace.

Paul gazed down at her. 'It's been a long day,' he said smiling. 'It's late now, and you must be tired.' He paused squeezing her upper arms. 'Shall we go for a drive tomorrow? We could go to Exmouth and take a walk along the sea front, if the weather permits.' He held her expectant stare. 'And we have lots to talk about.'

'Yes,' she said, nodding. But how calm he looked – so composed and unruffled – compared to her. She knew that her face was flushed… right down to her neck. In fact, she felt hot everywhere. It had all occurred so fast. 'Yes, that would be smashing.' She steadied herself against the door. 'Cool.'

'You were such a long time that I assumed you had gone straight to bed,' Mary James said as her daughter came back into the living room.

Eloise kicked off her shoes and climbed into an armchair, bringing her stockinged feet up beneath her as she did so. She felt odd, light-headed, in a daze – probably, she quickly worked out, an effect brought about by her racing pulse, which she could feel pumping against her temples. She knew that her face was still flushed too. 'No,' she began, 'no, we were planning tomorrow, that's all.' She turned her attention to the moving images on the television screen. She was, despite her experience out in the hallway, still a little vexed with her mother. 'We may go to Exmouth, if the weather is OK,' she added.

Mary James studied her daughter, a knowing smile playing on her lips. 'You seem much happier now. Has anything happened to change your mood?'

Eloise stared at her mother through eyes that seemed suddenly unable to focus properly. She was only half aware of her mother's question and had not even noticed that her father had already gone to bed. And now she felt sick, queasy; it was almost as if she were on a dingy wallowing on an incoming swell. She'd drunk only a single glass of sherry – so it couldn't be that.

'Eloise, do you feel unwell?' Her mother's words floated eerily across the space between them, like discordant notes masking a familiar melody, and seeming to come from far away yet being near at hand together.

'Yes. I feel…' All of a sudden Eloise knew she had to get

to the bathroom quickly. If she didn't she would be sick here in the chair. She glanced at her mother and gulped, as if trying to prevent the inevitable or, at the very least, to gain some time. But then, realising that time was fast running out, she clamped a hand to her mouth and ran from the room, heading for the bathroom. Yet as swift as her reaction had been, it turned out to be a pretty close run affair; for no sooner had she entered the room and dipped her face into the lavatory bowl, than she was overtaken by a violent spasm of nervous nausea, then another, and another, and another; until her chest ached from retching.

Eventually, she turned to the sink and started to wash her face – and at that moment a knock came to the door and her mother entered the room. If her mother's expression had been stern, or even indifferent, she would have been all right. But it was neither thing. It was the look that she remembered from childhood, the look that had always been there when needed, the look that came whenever she was ill or had hurt herself. At once all lingering pangs of teenage pique vanished and she went into her mother's arms.

In a little while, Eloise pointed to the lavatory bowl. 'Did we have carrots for dinner?' she said, dabbing her face with a towel.

Mary James glanced in the direction of her daughter's pointing finger. 'Yes, we did,' she said. 'Although those aren't pieces of carrot, they are small pieces of stomach lining. But not to worry, that always happens whenever anyone is sick.' She squeezed her daughter's hand, her eyes examining the other's tearful expression. 'Are you feeling better now?' she asked.

'Fine,' Eloise said, turning towards the sink. 'I'm fine, now that I've been sick.' She swung round to face her mother again. She had to be told. 'Mum, I'm in love with Paul.'

Her mother smiled. 'Yes, I know,' she said. She paused, then smiled again. 'I've known for quite a while.'

Eloise stared at the older woman. 'Well, I wish you had told me,' she said. She winced and rubbed her breast bone. 'It would have saved me a lot of pain, if I'd known earlier.'

'If I had told you when I first knew, Eloise, you would not have believed me.'

'Well you could have said something,' Eloise said. But that was the problem with her mother: she always knew everything. She studied her mother's face. 'Has Paul said anything to you and daddy?' she asked, suddenly sensing that perhaps her mother was holding something back. She had been slow in recognising this evening's intrigue; she should have twigged earlier. But Paul should have said something to her. All at once she was angry again… Although, to be fair to him, Paul was quite old-fashioned, conventional, a square, so perhaps he had thought that her parents would object to any relationship, because he was that much older than her – and so he had asked their permission first. And obviously he had obtained it.

But what would he have done if her parents hadn't given it? And they might not have: her mother, especially, was cautious… protective. Would he then have said nothing to her, carried on with their friendship as it was? Or would he have ignored her parents' objections and spoken to her anyway? Yes, but he must have known that her mother and father would give him their permission to talk to her. He had been coming round here for months; they had been going out together for months. It must have been obvious to him. He had, then, spoken with her parents first solely out of respect for them. Yes, that was Paul. She had worked it out.

Mary James returned her daughter's stare. 'Yes, he has spoken to us,' she said, confirming her daughter's reasoning. 'He is a fine boy, considerate… He was concerned that he is a little older than you.' She shrugged. 'But that is a matter between yourselves. As far as your father and I are concerned, the matter is of no consequence. Indeed, as you well know, Percy is somewhat older than I am.' She paused, her face abstracted in thought, her eyes on her daughter. 'However, I decided against saying anything to you before because I thought it better that you worked through your feelings yourself.' She paused again. 'Despite what you think now, Eloise, at the time, if I had said anything, you would only have accused me of interfering.'

Eloise knew that her mother was right. She would have seen it as that – meddling. She folded her arms across her chest and glanced down at the tiled floor, thinking. But Paul should have said something to her first – old-fashioned or not, he really should have asked her. By doing things this way around, he made it appear as if they were all taking her for granted. But, anyway, she had never really been confused about her own desires… not since Lyme Regis anyhow. But it seemed they all had her life planned out for her… 'To be honest, mother,' she said, 'I think that he really may be too old for me.'

Mary James smiled, but remained silent.

After a while, Eloise flushed the lavatory. If love was like this, it was going to make her seriously ill. She turned back to her mother. 'As he says, mother, he is older than me. Although…' she paused, pretending to be thoughtful, 'I think that I may be catching him up.' She winced and rubbed her chest again. 'And my stupid breast bone aches, too.' Then she began to giggle, still complaining though, as the process of doing so made her sternum hurt the more.

Her mother also started to giggle, apparently finding the spectacle of her daughter's ambivalent plight quite amusing, and soon both women were in fits of laughter, tears rolling down their faces as mirth fed on comedy.

In the master bedroom Percy James slept peacefully, totally oblivious of the commotion created by his wife and his daughter in the room next door.

Chapter Fifteen

'No, I don't,' Charlotte said, shaking her head. She shot a furtively glance around the coffee house, then, apparently assured that no one was within earshot, leaned towards Eloise. 'No, I never feel like doing that.'

Eloise gazed across the table and nodded, pursing her lips as she considered her friend's answer. She had just asked Charlotte if she ever felt like going further and actually making love when she and her boyfriend kissed. 'Not even when it's a good long snog?' she persisted.

'I wouldn't allow it to go that far, Eloise.' Charlotte paused to gaze round the room again. 'You know what boys are like. Their instincts are more base than ours, and if you appear to give them any encouragement...' She fell silent, clearly leaving the pause to convey her meaning.

'But suppose you had the same sexual freedom that men have, you know, your reputation independent of your sexual behaviour, no one thinking you immoral, no one judging you... You had *sexual equality*.' Eloise paused, smiling to herself. 'You would be just "one of the girls", would you do it then?'

'Certainly not.' Charlotte lit a cigarette, then stared across the table, eyes focused on her friend. 'Would you?'

'Of course.' Eloise glanced towards the next table, where two boys appeared now to be trying to eavesdrop on the conversation. Well, let them hear what she had to say. 'Charlie,

I do not care how society judges us. It's a double standard anyway: for boys it's acceptable, even expected… *De rigueur*… But for us it's wrong – taboo.'

'That's not quite correct,' Charlotte said. 'If a couple are engaged, or even just going steady, and they sleep together, I don't think that damages the girl's reputation. It's only when she is promiscuous and sleeps around a lot when that happens.'

'Exactly,' Eloise replied. 'But for a boy doing the same thing it would be fine.' She paused, her eyes bright with passion. 'But certainly I would do it. In fact, every time Paul kisses me properly, I want him to make love to me.'

Charlotte studied her friend's face. 'But you haven't… Have you?'

'No. Paul won't.' She glanced down at her cup and sighed. 'He says that he loves me but that he respects me too much. He says that it's better for us to wait until after we're married.' She paused. 'He's quite a prude really.'

'That's not being prudish,' Charlotte said. 'He is only thinking of what's best for you in the longer term, for both of you… best for your relationship.' She paused to draw on her cigarette. 'Act in haste, repent at leisure. He's thinking ahead, Ellie; he's thinking of the future.'

Eloise nodded in reluctant agreement. 'I admit that what he says makes some sense in that respect, but I love him. I love him and I don't want to wait for years and years, until we're married.' She fell silent, thinking. But the little sense it did make was surely more than outweighed by the thrill of being in each other's arms, loving one another, making one another happy. After a moment or two of further reflection, nudging her glasses along the bridge of her nose, she added: 'Besides, I do not agree that being celibate is necessarily the best thing for our relationship.'

'Only you and Paul can decide that,' Charlotte replied. 'But in my opinion, I feel that it is better to wait.' She paused, studying her friend. 'And you should consider your parents' feelings too,' she went on. 'If you were to sleep with Paul now it would devastate them, especially your mum… And suppose you became pregnant?'

'Oh, Paul has said that as well,' Eloise said. She smiled wryly. '"What about your parents? What if you were to become pregnant? Blah, blah, blah…" But you don't have to do that nowadays: I could go on the Pill.'

Charlotte placed her hand on Eloise's hand. 'If you sleep together now – before you're married – you will regret it later.'

Eloise laughed. 'Oh, he says that too…' She cast an upward glance. 'Later, later, later, every thing is *later*.' Her expression tightened and she gazed earnestly at her friend. 'But who knows how many of us will be here to regret it later? The way the world is going, the cold war, we could all be fried in a nuclear war soon.'

'Oh, nobody will do anything,' Charlotte said dismissively. 'Nuclear weapons on both sides guarantees that. You and Paul have plenty of time.'

Eloise sipped her coffee. 'There are plenty of other ways in which we can be cheated of our happiness – illness… An accident of some kind, the proverbial tile falling off a roof.' She placed her cup back in its saucer. 'Besides, I don't want to wait, and neither does my body.'

Charlotte glanced at the nearby table, where the two boys sitting there were now openly appraising both herself and Eloise. Tugging at the hem of her skirt, she said: 'You should learn to control your urges, Eloise, otherwise you'll be thought of as being no better than one of them – and we all know where their interests lie.'

Eloise laughed. 'If only you could hear yourself, Charlie,' she said. 'You sound just like a cynical old spinster.'

'I'm being like this for your sake, Eloise,' Charlotte said. 'You're my friend and I don't want to see you hurt.' She drew on her cigarette, then released the smoke in a single exhale. 'Anyway, boys aren't like us. It's a biological thing with them. They have different drives; they think differently, act differently.' She paused, shooting another glance at the other table. 'It seems to me they don't even need to be in love to want to do it.'

Eloise did not answer at once. Maybe she was like that; maybe her libido was more masculine than feminine; more base. No, it wasn't. She loved Paul: it was nothing more sinister than that. She was quite normal. Having said that though, would her body respond in the same way to whoever kissed her, to Paul, to any man? She too glanced at the next table. Perhaps she should… That one with the cowlick was quite cute… No, best not to. But Charlotte was right: they were different, like that. If Eloise went over there now… Well, perhaps not herself, but someone pretty like Charlie, that boy would kiss her – and if she then went out with him, he would certainly want to do it. Eloise remained silent. She noted then that Charlotte was scowling at one of the boys, who was clearly trying to peer down the front of her blouse. She watched as her friend started to button up her cardigan. But how would Eloise respond if another woman kissed her, passionately, in a sexual way, like a man? Would she experience the same sensation – the same desire – as when Paul kissed her? Perhaps her libido was multi… multi… ambidextrous, or whatever the word was. She had kissed Charlotte, lots of times. When they were kids, growing up, they used to play-act, kissing each other, taking it in turns being the boy. She'd felt nothing much then. Yes, but she was grown up now, she was going out with Paul, had been kissed by him, had experience. 'Charlotte,' she said speculatively, 'come round here and kiss me. I want to try something out.'

'Try what out?' Charlotte asked, absently contemplating her cigarette. She gazed across the table. 'Anyway, I have kissed you – dozens of times.'

'No, not like that,' Eloise said. 'I want to conduct an experiment, a scientific experiment that involves your kissing me exactly like a man would kiss me.' Hearing a snigger, she paused and glanced at the table next to theirs, to see that the two boys were grinning at her, nodding their encouragement. She turned back to her friend. 'I want to see if I am different to everyone else.'

'Of course you're not,' Charlotte said. 'I've known you all my life: you are quite normal...' She smiled, then added: 'At least in that respect, anyhow.'

'But you don't know that side of me, Charlotte. I don't know that side of me – at least, I am unsure about it. That's why you have to do it.'

Charlotte sighed and pressed her cigarette into the ashtray. 'Oh, all right, Eloise, if you really have to.' She glanced again at the two boys. 'But we can't do it here. We will have to go back to your house or mine.' She drank the last of her coffee. 'Let's finish our shopping first.'

Eloise rose from the table. 'My house will be best,' she said. 'It's closer.'

A little while later, with their shopping concluded, and following a brief rehearsal, Eloise stood to a taut attention in her bedroom. She was ready for the commencement of her experiment. Her lips were pursed, and, adhering to strict scientific protocol, she held her eyes tight shut lest the apparition of a female face should prejudice its outcome. She nodded her head to signal her readiness for the experiment to begin. 'Now remember, Charlie,' she reminded, 'like a boy would do it: be purposeful and self-assured… And hold me like they do.'

'All right,' Charlotte said, attempting to deepen her voice. 'Just imagine that I'm Billy Fury.' She clutched Eloise's shoulders. 'Hi, chick–'

Eloise started laughing.

'What's the matter?' Charlotte asked indignantly. 'Don't you fancy me then? I'm a famous singer, you know.'

Eloise stopped laughing. Charlie wasn't taking this seriously, wasn't getting into the spirit of the research. And it was important: Eloise could learn a lot from this. In fact, her future happiness could depend on its outcome. 'Please don't overact, Charlotte,' she said. She adopted a sombre mien. 'Remember this is a bona fide scientific experiment.'

'I'm just getting into the character,' Charlotte said, grinning. 'It's called method acting – you know, like Marlon Brando.' She took her friend in a firm grip, hugged her close and pressed their lips together, only to pull away moments later giggling.

Eloise huffed. 'You have to give it a chance, Charlotte.'

'It's not that.' She shook her head. 'It's just that our chests feel… you know, sort of squidgy together.'

Eloise nodded her agreement, she too having noted the feminine impediment that threatened the legitimacy of her research. She glanced around the bedroom. There had to be something here to solve the problem, something they could utilise… Yes, A.L. would suffice. She lifted the teddy bear from her bedside table. 'I'll hold Alan between us,' she said, weighing him in her hands. 'You will have to imagine that he is your masculine chest.' She paused, thinking… No, A.L. wouldn't do: he was too closely associated with Paul. They needed something neutral, harder too, otherwise the experiment would be flawed, its outcome biased. She glanced around the room. Yes, one of those books would do. She selected a hardback from the pile on her dressing table. 'This will be better,' she said, nodding. I'll have to hold it between us, because you will require both your hands for the embrace.' She checked her watch. 'Now, let us try again, shall we?'

Charlotte, who had remained patiently silent throughout the changing of props, now took hold of Eloise – who held the book squarely between their feminine tops – and pressed her lips firmly against her friend's.

Behind hooded eyelids, Eloise considered her response: lips too soft, not enough pressure either; skin too smooth, lacking that abrasive coarseness of a shaved cheek, even of a freshly shaved one – not being held quite right… But it was more than that though, more than any one of those things, more even than the sum of their total. Something else was missing; something more subjective. It was something like one being… Feeling vulnerable? Yes, though not quite that. Something more like the feeling of being sexually available… Yes… And the awareness that the person kissing you had the right anatomy to make love to you. Yes, that was nearer to it. But just suppose, then, that Charlie did have the physical wherewithal? And at that point in her deliberations, her fellow researcher broke the embrace – thus ending any further analysis.

Charlotte stared expectantly at her friend. 'Well?'

Trying to give the impression that she was sizing up her friend's ability to receive especially bad news, Eloise returned the stare, nodding thoughtfully as she did so. She would give Charlie a bit of a fright – her friend was so fond of playing the jester, always so cocksure of herself. Now Eloise would get her own back. She took a deep breath, then, casting the hardback book with theatrical disdain onto her bed, she began huskily: 'Oh, Charles, that was everything I hoped that it would be. The story of my ambiguous sexuality was just a charade, a trick to get you to kiss me passionately.' She took a measured pace towards Charlotte, who had moved back after ending the embrace, the better to judge Eloise's reaction to it. 'Forget masculine kissing; forget boys; forget men. I've thought for some time that I might be, that I might be… you know… lesbian. Well, now I know for sure.' She paused and took another step forward, fluttering her eyelashes as fast as she possibly could. 'Oh, Charles… I… I love you.'

Charlotte continued to gaze at Eloise, her eyes still posing the question that she had asked earlier.

Eloise snatched Charlotte's hands and tried to emulate the embrace that Paul had performed on her after the dinner party. 'I mean it, Charles. My only desire is that I surrender myself to you.' She heaved her bosom, as she struggled to overcome her friend's resistance. 'Kiss me again. Go on… Please.'

Charlotte smiled and reversed the embrace, so that it was she who now held the dominant posture. 'Then so I shall, my lady of Lesbos, for my mistress Staidler has taught me well the delights of that fair isle.'

'Oh.' Eloise freed herself from her friend's grasp and plumped herself down onto the bed. 'I didn't fool you, then?'

Charlotte sat down too. 'Of course not. Your ham acting would fool nobody. She lit a cigarette. 'Anyhow, great scientist,' she said, 'what is the conclusion of your experiment?'

Eloise thought for a while. 'I have a theory,' she said at length, 'a relative theory that, I shall argue, will hold true for all female-male relationships.' She stood up and, attempting to emulate the air of a time-honoured scientist she had seen on television, adjusted the rake of her spectacles. Then, taking a lipstick from her handbag, she walked solemnly across the room to her dressing-table mirror. She paused for effect, surveying her audience of one, then, uttering the words aloud as she did so, wrote on the glass: "$E = MC^2$".

She turned from the mirror. 'That is, where: "E" equals Ecstasy. "M" stands for Male of the species. And "C" is for Closeness to the subject.' She grinned. 'In short – and to put it in laymen's language – the closer one gets to a man when snogging him, the better it is.'

'I told you you were normal, didn't I?' Charlotte said.

Chapter Sixteen

Eloise drew to a halt on the impossibly steep incline, then turned around to look back towards the car park, now some way below her, to where they had parked the Morris Minor. She gave it a little wave. 'If this was a proper road, Paul, do you think I could drive the car up here?' she asked, sweeping her hand in an arc from the car park to the cliff top. 'After all, I am quite a whiz on hills, as you know.'

'No doubt you would like to try,' he said. 'But you certainly wouldn't persuade me to stand behind you and push.' He paused to catch his breath, gazing up the pathway to the still-distant cliff top. 'This is probably twice as steep as the hill at Lyme Regis.'

Eloise kissed him on the cheek. 'I could do it,' she said, playfully. She skipped ahead several paces, turning to watch him lumbering up the gradient. 'I am not so certain about that old car of yours though.'

Paul started to chase after her. 'Neither am I,' he said. He clutched at his heart and rolled his eyes in mock distress, sinking his knees in emphasis. 'I'm not even sure that I can make it myself.'

It was the middle of March. Paul and Eloise had driven to Branscombe, a seaside village between Sidmouth and Seaton. They planned to walk the coastal path to Sidmouth, have lunch there, and then return via the same route in the afternoon. Their initial plan had been to renew the search for

"The Primrose Path", Paul having lately been acquainted with the annual quest. However, then realising that it was still too early in the season for the spring flowers, they had decided on the drive to Branscombe instead.

'You can rely on Sherpa James,' Eloise said. 'If the going gets too steep for you, she will throw you down a rope.'

Paul stopped for another breather, turning so that he could survey their progress so far. 'I think we should have taken the south col,' he said, starting after his companion once more.

'Too easy,' Eloise said, over her shoulder. 'Give me my crampons and I'll take the northern route every time.'

Paul halted again. 'Why, Sherpa James?' he asked, plaintively. 'Why does it have to be climbed?'

Eloise went back to where Paul was standing, panting theatrically and gazing up the steep path. She knew that his acting was only part put on, that it was a stratagem to disguise his need for frequent rests. Despite his slim physique, he wasn't as fit as he could be. She took his hand. 'Because it's here, Hilary,' she said, coaxing him forward. 'Simply because it is here.'

'I think that I may need an oxygen mask,' Paul said, allowing himself to be drawn forward once more.

'We are nearly there,' Eloise said, pretending to cover Paul's eyes with her hand. 'An ice floe, a crevasse or two, a glacier – and that's it.'

'No icebergs?' Paul said disappointedly.

In a little while, and not a little fatigued, the jesting couple bettered the ascent; and, just off the path on a level grassy patch behind the cliff-face, sat down for what Paul described as a well-earned drink. Eloise fetched their thermos flask from her bag and started to unscrew the cap, gazing out to sea as she did so. 'I can't see the causeway at Portland,' she said, passing Paul a cup of tea. 'Is that because it's a bit misty on the horizon?'

Eloise had recently bought a telephoto lens for her camera and planned to take some long-distance photographs at various spots along the coast. Today she was hoping to get some of Portland Bill, some thirty miles to the east.

'We are just about at the innermost point of the bay here,' Paul said. 'Farther along towards Sidmouth, the cliffs jut out a little more into the channel. From there, we will be able to see it quite easily.'

She leaned across and kissed him. 'Cool. And we shall take some frightfully good pictures and one day, when we are old and grey, we will show them off to our grandchildren and tell them of the day we conquered the towering cliffs of Branscombe.'

Paul returned the kiss. 'C'mon,' he said, handing her his empty cup. 'If we want to get to Sidmouth in time for lunch, we had best get moving.'

Eloise packed away the thermos and scrambled to her feet. 'I'm coming, Hilary,' she said, brushing down her frock and chasing after Paul, who had already resumed the trek along the cliff top.

However, she had no sooner caught up with him than the morning that had begun bright and sunny darkened on their seaward side. Feeling the stirring of a breeze, she cast a glance across the sea… to where a regiment of black-clad foot soldiers appeared to be tramping towards them – at least, that was how she described the inky-black cloud to Paul.

'It will only be a squall,' he said. 'Nevertheless, it would have been prudent to bring mackintoshes with us.'

Eloise held her spectacles and gazed at the approaching storm. 'Yes,' she agreed thoughtfully. She turned to Paul. 'Do you think we should go back to the car? I mean, it is awfully exposed up here – and if it does rain, then we are going to get drenched.'

Paul too gazed out to sea. 'That's probably our best course of action. On second thoughts, I reckon there's a lot of precipitation in those clouds.' He took her hand in his. 'C'mon. If I remember correctly, there's a path along here that leads straight back to the village. It's an old smugglers' route.'

'A smugglers' route,' Eloise said excitedly. '*Jamaica Inn*. Ships lured on to rocks… Exotic contraband…' She fell silent. 'Maidens ravished by rascally pirates…' Her expression became mock startled, and she added: 'Now I know why you brought me here, Mr Bridgestock.'

Paul laughed. 'You are letting your imagination run away with you, Miss James. For I am no Bluebeard.' He paused, glancing at the storm. 'Anyway, it's going to rain for sure, so let's get going. The path will be a shortcut.'

But Eloise recalled then the purpose of their trip and held Paul back. She stared defiantly at the storm clouds. 'I don't mind getting a bit damp really,' she said. 'After all, we have come quite a long way just to…' And at that moment the leading edge of the approaching weather cut across the sun, bringing an instant gloom to the surroundings, and the temperature instantly dropped several degrees. 'All right,' she said, propelling Paul in the direction of his suggested shortcut.

Paul squeezed her hand. 'This way, Sherpa James,' he said, drawing her alongside him.

Eloise saw that the route Paul had mentioned was no

more than a rough-hewn pathway that curled down between a sweep of winter-worn trees and bracken towards the village. It didn't look as if it had been used recently… it was really no more than a channel cut out by rain water. Never mind though; leaving aside the tricky going, it was clearly a better prospect than getting drenched. And so, claiming the vanguard, she began their descent from the cliff top.

'C'mon, Hilary,' she cried over her shoulder. 'The flag is planted. Now let's get back to base camp before the storm hits us.'

'I'm right behind you, Sherpa James,' Paul said, laughing.

Leading the way down the path, Eloise pointed to the branches of the trees. 'See how they grow mainly in one direction, away from the sea,' she said. 'It's almost as if they've been pruned by a one-armed topiarist.' She paused as she negotiated a weather-exposed tree root. 'Though it is a good example of how living things adapt to their environment.'

'I don't think it has much to do with adaptation,' Paul said. 'Rather that the chill of the prevailing wind stunts growth on the exposed side but leaves the sheltered side largely unaffected.' He glanced over his shoulder at the pursuing storm. 'And it is having a similar effect on us, too.'

Eloise also glanced over her shoulder, almost tripping over another exposed tree root as she did so. 'I don't think we can outrun it,' she said, focusing her attention on their descent once more. 'It's travelling faster than us.'

But presently the path led them out from beneath the trees, over a rickety fence, and into an open meadow. Here they paused to survey their surroundings. Eloise gazed down the hillside to the village of Branscombe, still some way distant, at least in the sense of immediate dry shelter.

'We might get a little wet, I'm afraid,' Paul said, reading Eloise's expression. 'I think you are right: we can't outrun it.'

As if to affirm his opinion, at that moment a single fat raindrop hit Eloise on her nose, prompting her to cast a rueful glance at the rain clouds, which she saw were now almost overhead. 'There is not much doubt about that,' she said, shivering, for the temperature had dropped further, and the cotton fabric of her dress offered scant protection against the changed circumstances.

And then, before the pair had opportunity to decide their best course of action, more fat raindrops began to fall, each exploding in a little powdery cascade on the dry earth of the meadow beside the fence. Eloise smiled at Paul. They were going to get wet, of that there was no doubt. Well, so what... It would be the reason they would give to their grandchildren to account for why they had no pictures to record the day they had conquered the mighty cliffs of Branscombe.

'C'mon, Eloise.' Paul's sudden cry roused her from her reverie and she came back to the present, to feel him tugging at her arm. 'There's shelter over there.' He threw his jacket over her shoulders and pointed across the field. 'That barn.' And with that, he started towards it. Eloise followed, holding her companion's coat around her as she negotiated what she judged to be some pretty nasty thistles.

The barn turned out to be a pretty rudimentary affair, its galvanised metal roof being supported solely by a single wooden pole at each corner. Eloise pulled Paul's jacket tighter around her shoulders. Obviously it was just a place for the temporary storage of hay, or some other kind of animal feed. Nevertheless, it would keep them dry for as long as the storm lasted, and then they could continue their walk to Sidmouth. She guessed the downpour would soon drain away on the hilly coastal path. And if the rain didn't last too long, there might even be time left for some photographs of Portland Bill – after all, it would be a shame to come all this way for nothing.

They stood in the centre of the building, backs to the wind, which now gusted cold from the cliff tops above, and inspected their refuge. The floor was bare earth and levelled into the hillside. Stacked at the farther end of the dry rectangle were a dozen or so bales of hay, with an old wooden ladder lying across the top. Eloise turned her gaze towards the village of Branscombe, now barely visible through the torrent. 'We were fortunate to find this,' she said. She pointed to a spot about halfway between the barn and the village. 'If we hadn't, we would have been about there now, and soaked through.'

'Yes, we were lucky,' Paul said. 'But we can make it even better though.' Then, without further ado, he proceeded to fashion several straw bales into a crescent-shaped windbreak. Another bale to use for seating, and the job was done. 'There,' he said, dusting his hands and grinning, 'see what a handy husband I will make. Five minutes' labour, and I have built accommodation fit for a queen.'

Eloise sat in their shelter and drew him to her, snuggling against the warmth of his shoulder. 'You will be a fine husband,' she said. 'The finest husband any wife could wish for.'

They had of course discussed marriage but – as she had indicated to Charlotte – the discussion always ended the same way, with Paul persuading her of the practical benefit of waiting until after she had taken her degree. Although, to be honest, she didn't actually mind waiting a while before they married. That was not the problem. It was waiting for what went with it that was causing her a headache. Three months on from the Christmas dinner party and she had still not learned how to quell her body's longings. On the contrary, they had increased, had become more insistent – especially when they kissed… There was something about doing that that really excited her; it seemed to her that it should be the prelude to making love, not the finale. It was frustrating. And to make matters worse, there was no one she could talk to, nobody she could go to for advice – at least nobody who would see her point of view, who would agree with her. Her mother certainly wouldn't… And Charlotte was just as bad.

The intensity of the rain had increased and was now drumming on the metal roof of the barn like a military tattoo. All that could now be seen of the village below were one or two cottage windows showing a light against the storm-cast gloom. Eloise wandered across to the front of the barn, the better to gauge how fortunate they had been in finding shelter. She stuck a hand out into the downpour and, at that moment, right on cue, an arc of lightening charged the sky a brilliant electric blue, throwing long shadows of the barn momentarily down the hillside. She turned on her heel and scooted back to Paul's side. Seconds later a rumble of thunder rolled over the cliff top and tumbled past them, heading in the direction of the village.

Eloise snuggled against Paul once more, instinctively shrinking from the violence of the storm. 'Do you think we are quite safe from the lightening in here?' she said. 'I mean, this barn has a tin roof.'

Paul gazed around their temporary accommodation. After a little while, he said authoritatively: 'It's partially insulated by its wooden supports.' He indicated down the hill towards Branscombe. 'There are better, more conductive, objects around here for a random bolt of lightening to strike than this barn.'

'Are you sure?'

He laughed. 'No. But don't worry; this thing has been here for, oh... Probably fifty years, if not longer. It will have seen off worse electrical storms than this in that time.' He paused and placed an arm around her shoulders. 'And it will no doubt see off worse again in the next fifty.'

'Kiss me,' Eloise said.

In a little while, emboldened by the kiss and not a little brazened by the electric atmosphere of the storm, she began to unbutton him.

Paul stopped kissing her. 'Eloise,' he began, 'I thought–'

'Shush,' she responded. 'It's only petting, and there's nothing wrong in that.' She finished unbuttoning him, then, fearing that he might stop her, paused to flash him a glance of encouragement. But he didn't stop her, and she slid her hand into the open fly, and began to feel around. It took a little time, the architecture of male underwear being unfamiliar to her, but eventually she succeeded in pulling him out. He had still not made any attempt to stop her, and her plan now was to bring him along a little, then perhaps he might make love to her. Charlotte had told her – it was meant as a warning really – that once a man was started it was difficult to stop him. But of course, that wouldn't be her concern. She glanced round the barn. It wasn't an ideal place for making love, though – not comfortable.

She noticed then that Paul was looking down at himself, his expression blank, preoccupied, seemingly unsure of what he should do next. She held on to him, squeezing tentatively, tugging too, trying to make up his mind for him. But should she really go through with it? After all, Paul had said that they should wait, and she had agreed.

But she could hardly believe what she had done, could not believe her daring, her audacity. He was actually in her hand. She had probably been too forward though. But she so wanted him to make love to her, to have that intimate contact. The other thing… pleasuring herself was all right, but it seemed dirty and made her feel ashamed. She'd once been in the bath, dreaming of Paul, and must have made a noise for her mother had tapped on the door and asked if she was all right. She felt herself blushing… But this was the first time that she'd actually seen one – let alone touch one. In biology classes she had seen a picture – a sketch really – but that had been a quite different circumstance to this one of course: clinical as opposed to carnal. A little thrill wriggled through her body at the thought. And anyway, then, Charlotte had giggled so much and made so many distracting remarks that serious study had been ruined. Actually though, to be honest, in the wake of so much expectation, it was a bit of a disappointment, a bit of a let down. It felt like a sausage skin… Before you put the meat in.

She glanced up at Paul again, to see that he was sitting upright, drawn stiffly back away from her, as if he fancied her a surgeon about to operate without having first anaesthetised him. He was letting her go on though; he hadn't stopped her. But yes, she had been too forward, too impetuous – and now she neither knew what to say nor what to do. She could put it back, return it from whence it came, button him up again, pretend that nothing had happened… Then she felt it move.

She released it and sat upright, leaning against Paul's shoulder, but keeping her gaze fixed rigidly on the object of her interest. She still could not think of anything to say, nothing sensible anyway. And Paul appeared to have been struck dumb… Paralysed, too. She watched then as tumescence occurred. It was a much slower, a much more protracted process than she had assumed that it would be: a series of little pulses, each one inflating it a bit more than the previous one… It was a bit like blowing up a balloon, where you pause to inhale between each puff. She had always thought that they just… Well, sort of changed, altered their state. A girl at school, she could not recall who it was – not Charlotte anyway – had argued that men had an extra bone down there (like women have an extra rib) that hinged into place at the appropriate moment. But none of the class had really believed it. Then biology classes had scotched that theory.

It seemed to Eloise, observing it thus for the first time, that it looked better this way, not so nondescript, not so down-at-heel as it had previously looked, when it was little. It appeared now more regal – aristocratic, cavalier… *The Laughing Cavalier.* Plucking a piece of straw from a bale, she twirled it round her finger to form a spiral crown… a coronation crown. She glanced up at Paul, smiling wickedly, mentally challenging him to stop her. Then, still smiling, she settled it on him, muttering the words: 'And now, my Liege, my Prince, my Consort, by the power invested in me by divine Covenant, I crown you King… King Paulus I of Branscombe, Sovereign in perpetuity of all these lands and Master of the peoples living hereon.'

Paul's eyes found the roof of the barn. 'The rain is easing now,' he said. His gaze fell back to earth and he removed his makeshift crown. 'We shall be able to leave soon.'

She dropped her gaze too, to where his stare rested. Yes,

maybe you could argue that she had been too forward. Perhaps, then, she should… On the other hand, he had made no attempt to prevent her so far. Eloise nodded a mental affirmation. Her plan was on again. 'You aren't ready to leave yet,' she said, addressing his part. And even if her plan failed, if she couldn't have what she wanted, then she would at least see if biology classes had been accurate.

Paul made as if to move then but before he could do so, Eloise captured him once more. 'You are a wilful boy…' She patted him playfully with her other hand, '…a very naughty boy.' She moved her hand in a special way. 'A reprimand may not be sufficient for you.' Then she moved her hand some more.

'Eloise, what if someone comes along?'

Eloise's hand came to a taut rest. 'Then I shall tell them that you lured me here under false pretences, by deception, that you cruelly overpowered me, and then forced me to pander to your lewd masculine lusts.'

'They won't believe you,' he said, leaning back against the bales of hay.

'Oh, yes they will.' She moved into a more comfortable position. 'I shall inform them that I am a chaste young woman, unused to the ways of the stronger sex.' She glanced up from the object of her physical attention. 'I shall cover my eyes and beseech them to rescue me lest I am struck blind by the heinous vision of my exposed kidnapper.'

Paul ground his hands together. 'Eloise, you are nothing less than a mischievous scamp.'

Eloise returned to her mission, moving her partially opened thigh against his leg as she continued the other movements. While decorum was obviously essential from her point of view, she would nonetheless give him all the stimulation she reasonably could… Although, her efforts so far did not appear to be having the desired effect, were not bearing fruit. Maybe she wasn't doing it correctly. Ensuring that at least one nipple was pressing into him, she turned her upper body so that her breasts made contact with his shoulder… and kept going. Even though Charlotte was opposed to this sort of thing, Eloise just knew that her friend would have been better at it than she was. Still, at least she was trying and continuing to do so. However, despite appearing to be sufficiently contented, he still didn't appear to be responding as she wished him to. His arms seemed paralysed. Her plan wasn't going to work. But at least she had her second option. Or did she? For it crossed her mind then that he might still decide to stop her, that he might prevent her from taking him all the way – and that she would not then be able to gauge the veracity of Miss Staidler's lecture, which had mentioned the explosive force of the ejaculation. The headmistress had been most meticulous in her description of that. But Eloise could now see the reason for it. After all, it made sense that the spermatozoa be deposited as near to their goal as possible. She hoped that Paul wouldn't stop her. But he now seemed acquiescent, even obliging, and she went on uninterrupted, her administrations now eliciting no more that the occasional sigh.

In a moment or two, albeit now acknowledging failure in her main purpose, but knowing somehow that her consolation prize was nearing its climax, she quit her post and fetched a napkin from her bag. As if accepting the *fait accompli* played upon him, Paul shifted his weight uneasily on the bale of hay, at the same time following her movements with eyes that appeared to widen with increasing recognition of her purpose. 'Eloise, what are you doing?'

'Don't you know?' Eloise said coyly. She silently unfolded the napkin and, following a speculative appraisal, placed it carefully in her chosen position.

Paul looked down at himself, shook his head and drew the napkin up an inch or two.

Miss Staidler had not exaggerated. Nevertheless, no little impressed with the ingenuity of evolution, Eloise glanced up at Paul with raised eyebrows.

He nodded.

Afterwards, although the storm had abated, it was too late for them to resume their walk to Sidmouth for lunch. Instead, they returned to Branscombe and found a hotel there that catered for non-residents. A walk later along the pebble beach completed their excursion – then they started the journey back to Eloise's home, where Paul had been invited for afternoon tea.

On their arrival there, however, instead of finding the normal situation of her father in the living room with one of his technical journals and her mother busy in the kitchen, they found the house empty. Given that Paul had been invited for tea, it was not what Eloise had expected – and it was now past four o'clock. But there would be a reason for her parents' absence; maybe her mother had forgotten something, and her father had driven her into town to get it. Her assumption appeared to be correct when she noticed a folded piece of notepaper on the kitchen table.

'It's all right, Paul,' she said. 'There is a note left here on the table. I expect they will be home presently.'

But just moments later, she swung round to Paul. 'It's mother,' she said, taking hold of his arm. 'She's had another stroke.'

Paul took the note from her and started to read it, his hand beginning to shake as his mind absorbed the words.

Eloise stared at him, watched as his eyes scanned the message line by line, her mind in a whirl, her body riveted by the event. Her mother had made a complete recovery from the previous stroke: no one had thought or expected another one. She had been so well recently – it had not crossed anyone's mind that another stroke was likely.

'C'mon,' Paul said, folding the note and putting it in his trousers pocket. 'Your father wants us to go to the hospital.' He grasped her hand. 'Everything will be all right – you'll see.'

The hospital where her mother had been taken was located just around the corner from the family home, and, throughout the short journey, Eloise's hopes for good news remained buoyant. With medical facilities being so close at hand, her mother would have received prompt treatment like the last time. If they had lived out in the country, or even on the other side of the city, then there would have been a delay in getting her mother into hospital. And she knew from the medical insight she had gained from the time of her mother's first stroke, that getting immediate medication to the patient was vital – it could mean the difference between life and death. So it would be all right.

They were taken to a room on the third floor of the hospital, where they found Percy James sitting by his wife's bedside. Eloise saw that her father's face was drawn, lined with anxiety, his hands held prayer-like and clasped so tightly that the knuckles appeared opaque beneath the taut skin. A nurse was busy attending to some complex medical equipment that was attached to her mother, and did not appear to notice their entry into the room. But at least her mother was receiving the very latest treatment, the newest, the best.

She stood behind her seated father, her hands resting on his shoulders. She noted the mottled blue of her mother's face, the sallow cheeks, the thin bloodless lips. It was as if she had aged ten years since this morning. But she was going to be all right, wasn't she? After all, they only lived just around the corner. The ambulance would have been there in no time at all. She would be fine. Her mother's eyelids were partly unclosed. Eloise could see that the pupils were dilated and rolled upwards. She had perhaps been sedated. Yes, that was it – it would be part of the initial treatment. But she was going to be all right; although she would probably need a lot of nursing at home when she came out of here. But that was no problem. Rest, convalescence… Then she would soon get well. But she looked so ill; so terribly ill.

She glanced then at the silent nurse, her eyes pleading for good news – but the nurse still seemed too preoccupied, too engrossed in her routine to acknowledge her. But her mother would be all right, wouldn't she? Yes, of course she would; she would pull through, just like the first time. Her mother wasn't old – forty-eight. Healthy people didn't die at that age. Then, after what seemed like an age of waiting, finally she caught the nurse's gaze. The returning look told her the thing that she did not want to know.

Then she saw again the spring-green meadow, the meandering brook at the bottom of the slope, and the primrose path descending the primrose meadow to the bank of yellow primroses.

She stood outside the vision, watching them both skipping down the path, hand in hand, smile for smile, laugh for laugh. Her mother was young, youthful, full of life and everything we should all have for always. Her blonde hair was flowing in the wake of their happiness. And they were skipping and singing, skipping and singing, and calling to each other down the primrose path – and all the time the bank of primroses wavering golden yellow in the sunshine.

She let go of her father's shoulders. 'Fucking time!' she cried, stamping her foot in despair. 'Why does it always do this?' Then, shaking off Paul's consoling embrace, she turned and ran from the room.

Later that evening, her mother died.

Chapter Seventeen

One afternoon about a month after the death of her mother, Eloise was busy in the kitchen preparing the evening's meal when the doorbell rang. She answered it and was informed by the middle-aged man standing on the doorstep that he was a workmate of her father's, and could he come in and have a word with her?

'Has father had an accident?' she asked, suddenly alarmed. Her father worked with machinery – and so it was possible that he had been injured.

The man shook his head. 'No, Miss James, it's nothing like that… really. I just wanted to… May I come inside, please?'

Behind thick, horn-rimmed spectacles the man's watery blue eyes were kindly cast, and Eloise at once showed him in to the living room.

The man introduced himself as Donald Sanders. Eloise remembered her father once mentioning the name but could not now recall the circumstances. Maybe the visit was about the workers' union… No, he would not consult her on that. He seemed oddly reticent though, as if he didn't know how to begin. Perhaps he was from the management. If that were so, then possibly there had been a complaint about the amount of time Percy had taken off work since the loss of his wife. Her father had told her of the company's selfish stance on bereavement leave, and had worried about his own record on that score.

'Yes, Mr Sanders?' she said, now fearing unwanted intrusion into their lives. 'How may I help you?'

Donald Sanders leaned forward in the armchair. 'It's about Percy.' The use of her father's Christian name immediately quelled Eloise's concerns. However, the relief was short-lived, for her visitor went on: 'I'm... Several of us are worried about him.' He paused to glance down at his hands, before returning his gaze once more to Eloise. 'He gets upset at work. He is still going into the lavatory and crying.'

Going into the lavatory? Crying? Eloise stared at Donald Sanders, shocked, dumbfounded. He had said that her father was crying at work, in front of his colleagues. Still crying, he had said. No, it couldn't be. Try as she might, she could not equate the image the caller's words had brought to her mind with the picture of stoicism she had of her father. She swallowed the lump in her throat. 'You said still crying. Then obviously–'

'Look, Miss James,' Donald Sanders broke in, 'Percy has recently lost his wife... Your mother. It's natural that he should grieve; natural as well that at times he should want to be by himself, to let his grief out.' He stared straight at her. 'But it's getting worse. Sometimes he's in there for ages... And when he comes out... Well, he looks dreadful.'

Eloise had noticed that her father had lost weight since her mother's death. Always a thin, wiry man, that had become apparent early on. She had tried to get him to eat more, but his appetite had seemed depressed. He had become withdrawn too, quieter, introspective. But to be breaking down at work like this... And it was increasing. She should have realised that he was not recovering as he should have been – although, it was still only a month. The problem was that he wouldn't talk to her about it. She knew the loss had affected him deeply. The fact that he had not discussed it with her indicated this more effectively than would have done the shedding of a cataract of tears. But he was a proud man and would never show what he saw as emotional weakness in the presence of a woman, especially when that woman was his own daughter. Clearly he was suppressing his feelings at home, but then going into work and letting them out there.

Eloise took a thoughtful breath. 'Thank you for calling, Mr Sanders,' she said. 'Now that I know about dad, I shall…' What would she do? It would be difficult enough just to broach the subject with her father. '…I shall talk to my fiancé; he is a teacher.'

'It's not for me to say, Miss,' Donald Sanders said, glancing down at his hands again, 'but I think that perhaps you should get your father to see his doctor.'

Eloise nodded. 'Yes, of course,' she replied. 'That's what I'll do. I shall inform my fiancé of what you have told me, and we will ensure that dad visits his GP.'

When Paul dropped by later that afternoon on his way home from school, he was shocked to hear the news about Percy. He too, like Eloise, had thought that her father was coping reasonably well with his bereavement, and to be informed of Percy's emotional breakdowns at work came as a surprise. 'I think it a good idea that he visits his doctor,' he said. 'Judging from what Mr Sanders has told you, Percy is clearly stressed and feeling vulnerable.'

'I blame myself for not noticing that anything was amiss with dad,' Eloise said. She listed the changes she had noticed in her father's health and behaviour, ending: 'I should have had enough sense to realise that he wasn't recovering. I shouldn't have needed somebody else to point that out for me. I should have seen it and called in Dr Shepherd myself.'

Paul put his arm round her shoulders. 'You aren't to blame, Eloise. It's your loss too, and you have had to cope.' He took a handkerchief from his pocket and wiped her cheeks, for she had begun to cry.

She sniffed. 'But I have had you for support.' She snuggled against him on the sofa. 'Besides, it's easier for women. We are expected to be emotional, and that helps to ease the hurt. I cried all through the funeral.' She did not mention the times before or since. 'But did you notice dad? He was stoical throughout. Any show of emotion, especially in public, is alien to him... That's why I am so concerned now.'

Paul stroked her hair. 'Grieving is a natural process, Eloise. It's nature's way of helping us to recover from the loss of a dear one.' He held her face in his hands and kissed her on the nose. 'But people react differently to loss: some take longer than others to get over it. Unfortunately, those who cannot – or will not – release their emotional responses, take the longest.'

'So you think that dad needs medical help?'

'I think we should be guided by Mr Sanders, Eloise – and, remember, he has first-hand experience of seeing how Percy is at work.' He paused. 'Yes, I think your father would be helped by seeing his doctor.'

Eloise sighed. 'I will talk to dad tonight.'

'Would you like me to be with you?'

'No,' she said, shaking her head. 'It will be best if I talk to dad alone.' She noted his look of disappointment. 'I would prefer that you were here, of course, but in those circumstances dad would never admit that anything was wrong, let alone agree to visit the doctor.' She paused, gazing into his concerned eyes. 'I know dad, he is a proud man, and believe me – tonight is not going to be easy.'

Her assumption turned out to be correct. For that evening, in spite of a carefully planned preamble, a fastidious preparation of the ground, during which she outlined the benefits of loss counselling – which had just started at their local surgery – she failed to achieve her aim. Hopelessly. Her father was indeed a proud man, and appeared to interpret her appeal for him to consult his doctor as a slur on his manliness and rejected it outright.

Defeated, Eloise retreated to her bedroom, there to consider the best way forward. She sat in her wicker chair and gazed out at the garden, which she noted was already showing signs of neglect, with couch grass encroaching onto the once well-tended vegetable plot. If her father didn't yet feel able to manage the garden, then perhaps she should ask Paul for help. He wouldn't mind lending a hand. Her father would appreciate that, and when he saw that everyone was rallying round, it should assist his recovery. Pleased with her idea, she drew her feet up onto the chair and encircled her knees with her arms, thinking, trying to come up with other ways that might also aid Percy's recovery.

But her father's disposition had changed a lot since her mother's death. At work, if Mr Sanders's account was correct, he was showing signs of despondency, vulnerability, while at home – she now realised – his mood swings were becoming more and more unpredictable. One day he would be engulfed in a stony silence, the next in an animated ill humour. That was not her normal daddy. It was going to take longer than she had previously thought, even as recently as this afternoon, for her father's grief to be healed and for him to be restored to the daddy she knew and loved.

She got up from the chair and stood by the window. But this was all her fault. She was to blame, solely to blame. She was responsible for it all. If she hadn't done that filthy thing with Paul that day in the barn, none of this would have happened. It was God's way of punishing her, His way of showing her that it was wrong – a sin. Paul had been right all along: sex was for after they were married. If only they hadn't gone to Branscombe, had gone looking for the primrose path instead. They wouldn't have found it... But neither would this terrible time have found them either. And her mother would still be alive.

Realising then that she had unconsciously coiled herself in the bedroom curtain and could no longer look out over the garden, she cast off the drape and went and sat on her bed.

But that way of thinking was ridiculous: nothing she had done was to blame. It was arrogant to suppose that God would single her out, especially when to do so meant making innocent people suffer too. Besides, she didn't really believe in God. So how could she hold something she didn't believe in responsible for what had happened? That was stupid – didn't make sense. But people did that sort of thing all the time – blamed God for life's ills, their misfortunes. Religion was so deep-seated in the subconscious mind. And of course, there was the human desire to seek an explanation for every unexplained occurrence – and if you couldn't find one, the temptation was to fall back on the old scapegoat.

Her mother had once warned her that being a sceptic did not grant you *carte blanche* to commit sin, that it did not exempt you from His punishment, if your views turned out to be wrong – which was all pretty obvious. But being an atheist didn't necessarily mean you were evil, did it? Morality wasn't dependent on Christianity. You didn't have to be a Christian to lead a good life.

Eloise drew her legs up onto the bed, and focused her stare on the rosette overhead. She should stop this constant blaming herself for what had happened, as she had been doing ever since that terrible day. Nobody was to blame: it was simply a medical condition. Her mother had had one stroke and, although no one had suspected it, another one had always been a possibility – the nurse had indicated as much. And now her mother was gone. But, oh, if only she had known – had had the chance to say goodbye.

The following day Paul called on Eloise in the afternoon to take her into Exeter. It was a Saturday and they planned to visit the Moka Café before doing the weekly shopping. Since her mother's death, Paul's car had proved a boon to her routine; for it saved her from having to lug bags of groceries on and off buses, buses that, moreover, seemed poorly designed for the task.

Eloise put on a cardigan and went to her father, who was sitting at the dining-room table, immobile, staring blankly at his newspaper, which she now noticed was upside-down. He had been like this for the past hour, ever since Paul's arrival at the house. She righted the newspaper, then placed her hand on her father's shoulder, kissed his cheek. 'We are going in to town to do the shopping, daddy,' she said, picking up her spectacle case from the table. 'Is there anything we can fetch you from there?'

Percy James had barely acknowledged Paul's presence.

But now, ignoring his daughter's question, he turned to face the younger man. 'Taking her away from me again, are you?' he said, indicating to Eloise with the stem of his pipe. 'And I don't suppose it'll be long before you take her away for good.'

Eloise drew back from her father. 'Daddy, I said–' But Paul hushed her with a gesture of his hand. Then, addressing himself to Percy, he said:

'I have no intention of taking your daughter from you, sir. That I would never do.' He joined Eloise at the table, beside the older man. 'Our long-term plans are still to be finalised, but for the present my only concern is that I assist you both in coping with your shared loss.'

However, despite Paul's words, Percy James merely grunted in reply, then turned his attention to the lighting of his pipe.

Later as they drove in to town, Eloise informed Paul of the previous evening's failed attempt to persuade her father to call Dr Shepherd, concluding: 'Oh, I don't know, maybe if I had been more direct, had mentioned what Mr Sanders said instead of trying to be tactful, then perhaps dad would have agreed.'

Paul glanced across the car. 'No, I think you were wise in not involving Mr Sanders: it might have made things difficult at work.' He paused. 'But I was afraid that that would be Percy's attitude. However, he is clearly depressed and looks to be increasingly so, and although I think that you and I can help him, I also think that he needs professional help as well.'

'Wouldn't our care be sufficient in the end?' Eloise asked. Even though she accepted that her father was not recovering as he should have been, now, following the previous evening's conflict, she was reluctant to pursue something that she feared might ultimately alienate him further.

'That's very important. However, in the short term, Dr Shepherd may be able to prescribe something that will lift his spirits and thus bring about a swifter recovery.'

Eloise swivelled in the seat to face Paul. 'Do you really think that dad will have to take medication in order to recover?' she asked.

'That may not be necessary. Though possibly a tonic now to lift the depression… But, and I am no medical man, it may be that a chat with someone who is familiar with this sort of thing would suffice.'

'But dad is adamant that he doesn't need a doctor,' Eloise said.

'And we must not attempt to dissuade him from that view – for doing so would only make him more stubborn.' Paul paused as he swung the car round the tight bend that led into the Southernhay car park. He found a parking place, switched off the engine and put on the hand brake. 'However,' he continued, turning to Eloise, 'there may be a way in which we can help Percy.' He then went on to outline a plan whereby the doctor would call, ostensibly to see Eloise, but, having done so, would then request a private interview with her father, which he would use to assess Percy's state of mind. 'It is undoubtedly a little surreptitious,' he added, 'and we would of course have to arrange it with Dr Shepherd beforehand; nevertheless, taking into account the urgent circumstances, then I think the potential benefit outweighs the method.'

'It might work,' Eloise said thoughtfully.

'At the very least, we will have gained a professional opinion,' Paul said.

Eloise nodded. 'I will telephone Dr Shepherd on Monday morning to arrange it,' she said.

Dr Shepherd agreed to the proposal and, under the pretext of visiting Eloise, called at the James' family home that evening. However, in line with his brief, following a cursory chat with Eloise, during which she acquainted him further with her father's condition, he requested that her father join him in the living room of the house. He was there now.

While Eloise was on the landing at the top of the stairs – waiting.

She had been on tenterhooks all day, fearing that her father would be diagnosed as requiring hospitalisation, fearing that her intervention would condemn her father to a hospital ward. She had borrowed a medical book from the library and had read the pages dealing with the treatment of depression. She had read of the use of soporific drugs where patients were reduced to near-comatose states – the theory being that patients so removed from everyday stresses would be mentally better able to begin the process towards overcoming the causes of their depression. She had also read of electroconvulsive therapy where electrodes were placed on the patients' temples and an electric current passed through their brains. The book had said that it was often successful – although no one really understood why. Such treatments, she realised, were far removed from Paul's suggestion of a tonic, a pick-me-up. But, even so, once begun, who could predict where even minor remedies may lead? Perhaps it hadn't been such a good idea to call in Dr Shepherd after all.

Eloise stood in position, nervous, fidgeting with the banister, listening for the living-room door to unclose. Once or twice, she had heard the doctor's voice, then her father's, and sometimes both voices overlapping, which, she feared, might mean that her father was telling the doctor what was what, as indeed he had done with her. On the other hand, she had not heard raised voices or the banging of fists on tables. She glanced at her watch – and Dr Shepherd had been in there now for fifteen minutes. Then she heard the door below open.

In the time it took Dr Shepherd to emerge from the living room, Eloise had descended the stairs and taken up her position in the hallway. 'How is he, doctor?' she asked, clutching her hands together in anxiety.

'Your father seems fine, young lady,' Dr Shepherd said, smiling encouragingly, 'particularly so when one considers all he has been through of late. Granted he has lost a little weight, but given time that will return.' He paused, smiling further encouragement. 'And his pulse and blood pressure are excellent.'

Eloise tried to look reassured but failed, her stare becoming questioning as the gist of the doctor's report unravelled in her mind. There was nothing wrong with her father, he had said. It could not be like that. Percy was ill, anxious, depressed; needed medical help. She stared at the gaunt head of the doctor, her mind unable to come to terms with what the man had told her. Had Percy put on a show of bravado for the doctor's sake, had he played the manly stoic? Had he deliberately misled Dr Shepherd? He surely must have done so.

Dr Shepherd appeared to read her thoughts for, nodding to himself, he said: 'Your father has admitted to feeling a little weepy on occasion. But that is quite natural – after all, it is scarcely a month since the loss of his wife.' He patted her shoulder. 'Your father's general health is robust – always has been. Time and the love of his daughter are the medicines that I prescribe.' He smiled down at her, squeezed her hand, then made as if to pass by.

But Eloise stood her ground, barring the doctor's way to the front door. 'But the people at his company, they said that…'

Dr Shepherd placed his hands on her upper arms and circled round her, taking her with him, so that their positions were reversed, and he was nearest to the door. 'You mark my words, young lady,' he said, smiling, 'your daddy is going to be fine.' And with that he let himself out of the house and was gone, leaving a bemused Eloise standing alone in the hallway.

Surely Dr Shepherd could see that her father wasn't recovering as he should have been. In spite of her earlier reservations about seeking medical aid for Percy without his consent, now, having done so, she agreed with Paul's assessment that a mild pick-me-up would help. But why couldn't Dr Shepherd see that too? Why couldn't he see that Percy wasn't well, that he was depressed and finding it difficult to cope with workday life? If he couldn't, then he should have been able to – after all, he had been their family doctor since before she was born.

A little while later, still bemused by Dr Shepherd's diagnosis, she went to join Percy in the living room. But she had no sooner entered the room when her father turned on her.

'And I suppose it was that boyfriend of yours who put you up to it,' he accused, standing in the middle of the room, and staring her down. 'Getting Dr Shepherd round here – trying to make out that I am ill.'

Had Dr Shepherd revealed their part in his visit? Eloise presumed that he must have done so, unless her father had guessed. But either way it didn't matter. She'd been prepared for that outcome; she had planned to tell her father what they had done, anyway. After all, they had acted only out of concern for him. But it would have been better coming from her. 'Daddy,' she began, 'I love you and I have been worried about you. Paul has too. And after our conversation the other evening, it was… It seemed the best way that we could help. You wouldn't–'

'I know what he wants,' her father interrupted. 'He wants me out of here – out of the way. He wants to have me certified. He wants to have me put in the loony bin.' He paused for breath, his hands shaking in temper. 'Then he'll be moving in here with you.'

Eloise had never seen her father so angry. There had been days since her mother's death when he'd been cantankerous, ill humoured – but nothing like this. It was as if he was winding himself up, feeding his fury – the longer he went on, the more enraged he became. And she could see that behind his temper there was an irrational worry… He was inventing scenarios. He'd already accused Paul of wanting to take her away, but this was ridiculous. Paul didn't want him hospitalised – he didn't want to move in here. They weren't even engaged, let alone married. And surely Percy didn't think… She moved nearer to him. 'Daddy I–'

But Percy merely pushed her away from him. 'I don't want you near me,' he said. 'I don't want to hear your excuses – your lies.'

Her father's push had sent her towards the sofa, and she sat down. 'Daddy,' she began again, 'whatever makes you think that Paul wants to move in here? Paul wants to help.

You haven't seemed to be getting over mum's death.' She stared right back at him. We tried to help… that's all. We—'

'We, we, we,' her father interrupted, his face flushed, 'that's all I hear around here nowadays. Well it's about time you thought about me for a change.' He marched across the room to his armchair and picked up one of his technical journals. 'Besides you, this is all that I've got now,' he said waving it at her. 'Do you realise that – do you think about that? No! All you think about is "we". You've turned against me, gone into league with that wheedling boyfriend of yours.'

Eloise stared across the room at her father… But it wasn't her father; not the father she knew and loved. She knew next to nothing about mental illness, but she realised that that could be the only explanation for his behaviour. She wanted to go and hug him, to reassure him of her love, but she felt that if she did so, then he would surely hit her. A month ago he would have died sooner than have done that, but now she wasn't so sure. Then she started to cry.

Her father looked at her. It was a look she had never seen before, one bordering on contempt. It wasn't fair. 'That's right.' He almost spat the words. 'Try it on. Use the oldest female trick in the book to get your own way.'

Eloise wiped her eyes, and then stood up. Her daddy might be ill, and perhaps it had been wrong to go to the doctor behind his back, but that was no excuse for his selfishness. He wasn't insane. He could think; he could reason. She turned to her father. 'I'm sorry if my trying to help has offended you, daddy.' She turned her body towards the door, but kept her eyes on his. 'You may have lost your wife,' she said unblinkingly. 'But I've lost my mother.' And then, crying once more, she fled from the room.

Chapter Eighteen

On that cheerless June day Eloise stood on the doorstep, her face instantly blanched by the scene before her. It was a scene that she would never forget, a spectacle that would sear itself in her mind for all time. Standing before her was Donald Sanders and another man. Draped between them, unable to stand unaided, was her father. His eyes were inflamed from the hostility of his crying, and a trail of snot ran from each nostril down to his mouth, from which, every second or so, a tongue flicked out lizard-like to clear away the excess mucus.

A month had passed since Dr Shepherd's visit. It had been a month in which Percy James' mental stability had lost further ground. He had become more irritable, more cantankerous, harder to please, seemingly alert for every opportunity to find fault. A favourite target of his ill humour was his daughter's cooking, to the extent that he would often throw his meal into the waste bin and demand that she cook him another one. On one occasion she had actually cooked him three different meals before she had been able to get him to finish one. And any attempt to reason with him was sure to exacerbate the situation. But now, standing in the open doorway – stark to the scene confronting her – and torn of heart at her father's condition, she resolved to contact Dr Shepherd herself. The doctor would have to do something now.

Eloise ushered the men into the house and led them through to the living room, where they lowered her father into an armchair. She took a handkerchief and wiped her father's nose. She saw that his lips were moving soundlessly, as though he were an automaton whose speech process had been disconnected. Perhaps, then, he wasn't suffering; all this was passing him by as if by rote, on the other side of the road. Perhaps something in his mind had shutdown so that his feelings were no longer his own. As if shocked into inertia, she stared at her father, motionless. But no, this was suffering – this was what it was all about. She wiped his nose again, resting her other hand on his shoulder, as though he were a child. 'It's going to be all right, daddy,' she reassured him. 'You're home now.'

'You had best call his doctor, Miss James.' Donald Sanders' words cut across her thoughts. 'We will stay with you until he comes.'

Eloise turned from her father. 'Yes,' she said, simply. She fetched a cardigan and shrugged it around her shoulders. 'Yes,' she repeated. Then, with a nod to Donald Sanders, she ran to the telephone box at the end of the road and made the call. Thirty minutes later Dr Shepherd arrived.

Between them, they put her father to bed, and Eloise went downstairs to see Percy's colleagues out and to allow the doctor time to carry out his examination in private. But this was the doctor's fault: if he had listened to her the first time, if he had prescribed something then – a tonic, as Paul had suggested to her – then this wouldn't have happened, and her father's suffering could have been avoided. He was worse now than he'd been a month ago – and all because of the doctor's dithering. Dr Shepherd had better give him something this time.

After a little while, hearing Dr Shepherd's footfalls on the stairs, she scurried down the hallway, eager to hear his verdict. 'How is my daddy?' she asked, staring down at the doctor's black bag, from which she hoped a magical cure-all had been administered. She clenched and unclenched her fists. She could blacken the man's eye. 'Have you given him anything?'

Dr Shepherd placed his bag on the floor. 'Yes,' he said. Eloise's anger started to dissipate. 'I have given your father a sedative.' He glanced at his watch. 'It is almost five o'clock now and he should be all right through the night. But you should check on him every once in a while, just to make sure that he is comfortable.' He paused to hand her a slip of paper. 'Here is a prescription for further medication.'

Eloise stared at the indecipherable handwriting. How could the chemist be sure of what to make up from this? She nudged her glasses higher on the bridge of her nose, then stared at the prescription again. 'Is my father going to be all right?' she said, glancing up at the doctor.

'Certainly he is, Eloise.' He looked her up and down, his eyes at length coming to rest on hers. 'He has suffered a mental breakdown, but–'

'A mental breakdown,' Eloise interrupted. 'But that's serious. Surely–'

Dr Shepherd took her by the arm. 'There is a general misconception about these things,' he began. 'A breakdown does not mean that your father has gone insane or, indeed, is incapable of rational thought. On the contrary, in his case, all it means is that he has found it difficult to cope with the stresses of life since the death of his wife. The consequence of which is that his resolve has given way and he has suffered a minor emotional collapse.' He withdrew his hand from her arm. 'The medicine that I have prescribed will calm him and allow the healing process to begin… Although, Eloise, I should warn you that your father's recovery is likely to take longer than we all initially thought. However, for the present, ensure that he follows the whole course of treatment.' He paused, assessing her. Then, after a while, apparently reaching a conclusion, he added: 'And please do not allow him to fatigue himself – see to it that he has lots of rest. Be a loving daughter and care for your daddy accordingly.'

Judging from his patronising tone, Eloise was convinced that he was criticising her efforts to date, when, if criticism were due, he was the one who should receive it. She should remind him of what she had said a month ago – she should remind him of his negligence. She looked up at the doctor. 'I shall ensure that dad gets plenty of rest,' she said tonelessly.

'Good, good.' Dr Shepherd wrung his hands together. 'Now, have you anyone who is able to assist?'

'My friend Charlotte will help me,' she said. 'And her father *is* a surgeon. But anyway, I am sure that I can manage alone if necessary.'

'That's what I wanted to hear. You are a practical thinking girl, would have made a splendid nurse.' He smiled down at her. 'Now, your daddy may require assistance with his ablutions in the morning. But you will find that by the afternoon, he will be well enough to venture downstairs, to read or to watch television… To move around a little.'

Eloise stared at the doctor. Her father could get up; he could come downstairs tomorrow. That was good news: he wasn't confined to bed. Whatever Dr Shepherd had given him, must already be working. Or had she misunderstood his instructions? She continued to stare at the doctor. 'Daddy doesn't have to stay in bed?' she queried. 'He will be able to come downstairs?'

Dr Shepherd nodded. 'Indeed,' he began. 'He is physically sound. It won't do him any good to lie in bed moping. Far better that he gets into a routine – gentle, mind you. Don't let him over-extend himself: walking around the house will be sufficient for the time being.' He glanced at his watch. 'If you require anything, give my secretary a ring.' And with that, he picked up his bag and let himself out of the door.

The next day, following both breakfast and lunch taken in his room, Percy was indeed able to come downstairs to watch television. Not only that but, as Eloise discovered, his recuperation was sufficient to keep her occupied with the carrying out of essential chores, from providing cups of tea and biscuits to reading to him from his newspaper. She had even received – and mastered – her first lesson in the technicalities of lighting his pipe. She may never turn out to be a Florence Nightingale… Although it was still early days.

Paul had already indicated his willingness to assist further in whatever role he could and, with Percy's constitution clearly improved, and with her thought that the doctor's prescription had already started to work reinforced, Eloise decided to broach the subject with her father. She was optimistic of obtaining a favourable result. Percy's appetite was good, as too was his mood. He had even managed to smile as, puffing on his pipe to get it started, she had drawn in too much smoke and had fallen into a coughing fit. Acknowledging now these signals with rising cheer, she voiced her question. However, in spite of her optimism, her words appeared to null and void her father's good humour; for at the mention of Paul's name, his brows lowered and his mouth became a taut line of displeasure.

'No, I won't have it,' he said, shaking his head. 'I will not allow any more outside interference in family matters. I will not have interlopers coming around here and meddling in our affairs.' He snatched his pipe from his daughter's hand. 'I know his game,' he went on. 'He wants to take you away from me.'

Despite fearing a repetition of the haranguing that she'd received following Dr Shepherd's first visit, Eloise decided to press on – to try and convince her father of the benefit of having Paul's assistance. 'But daddy, that is ridiculous and Paul would be a great help with the gardening until you feel up to doing it again.' She paused to pour her father another cup of tea. 'And he would be happy to take us out for drives, to the country, to the seaside... The fresh air would be good for your health.'

But Percy James fixed his daughter with a cold stare. 'I know what's good for my health,' he said. 'And I also know what that boy's after.' His eyes narrowed. 'I don't want him calling on you again.'

'But daddy-' Eloise began. However, before she had chance to say anything else, her father said:

'You heard what I said, girl. He is barred from this house. And I don't want you sneaking out behind my back to see him either.' He handed his pipe back to Eloise. 'There are more important things in your life at the moment than gadding around with boys.'

Suddenly dumbfounded, Eloise plumped herself down at the table. Before her mother's death, he would never have accused her of "gadding around with boys". And as for addressing her as "girl"... not in a million years. She stole a glance at her father. But if she wasn't careful, if she mentioned Paul's name again, she was going to provoke him into a rage, and that would do his recovery no good. Yet he had seemed so much better today – after starting the medication. But her question had sharply reversed that situation. She wouldn't make that mistake again. She got his pipe glowing once more. 'You're right, daddy,' she said brightly, handing it to him. 'We don't need anyone else.'

She started to clear the table, placing their cups and saucers and the biscuit tin on a tray. She noted her father's expression, now relaxed again following his earlier tantrum. She watched the smoke curling in little whorls from his pipe, saw his eyes tense – unlike his expression – and she realised how fearful he was of losing her, that she was the only person in the world he had to rely on. She bent and kissed his cheek. He was ill – but he would get well again. She would look after him, nurse him. And he was under Dr Shepherd's care as well. Together they would restore his health – his confidence. Then he would accept Paul back into the family. Life would never be quite the same again, as it had been before her mother's death, she realised that. Nevertheless, it would improve; it would steadily get better.

Yet for all her optimistic thoughts, later that evening, after her father had gone to bed, she sat on the sofa in the living room and stared at the empty television screen. She missed her mother, her always being here for her, their shared interests. She missed their girlie conversations, conversations that invariably ended in fits of giggles, hilarity that her father had scoffed at and declared to be "nothing but silly female antics". She missed Paul's visits; for although Percy had only just banned those, the atmosphere between her father and Paul had become so strained over the past weeks that Paul had already become a less frequent visitor. And now she had even been barred from going out to see him. She had of course yet to inform Paul of that, but she knew that he would accept it; he would argue against their doing anything that would upset her father. Paul was bound to try to assure her that it was only temporary, and that everything would eventually turn out all right, "when Percy is restored to health". Indeed, she could almost hear him saying the words now. But she didn't want it to be temporary; she did not want to have to wait until "Percy is restored to health".

She switched on the television, saw the image of a packet of Bisto appear on the screen. Why was it that every time you turned on the TV it was the adverts? She could try the other channel… But it was only the news – same old doom and gloom. She had enough of those in her own life, without sharing someone else's. She switched the set off again. What she needed was someone to talk to, someone who would listen, someone who would sympathise. Even though that sounded selfish, that was the thing she needed most. Making up her mind, she went upstairs and checked on her father. He had taken his medication and was sleeping soundly. Eloise had to talk to someone. She collected her bag, double-checked on Percy, then went out and telephoned Charlotte, and informed her friend of Percy's ultimatum, concluding tearfully: 'He is determined to prevent my seeing Paul again.' Ten minutes later a taxi drew up outside and Charlotte came marching up the path.

Charlotte filled two wine glasses, then fetched them from the sideboard to the dining table, where Eloise was sitting, glumly staring at their two placemats. She set the glasses down, spilling a little liquid from each one, then sat down beside her friend. 'Right then,' she said, 'what are you going to do about it?'

'I don't know, Charlie.' Eloise shook her head. 'I really don't. The last thing I want to do is disobey dad but, on the other hand, I don't want to stop seeing Paul either.' She gulped a mouthful of wine. 'I love him and, regardless of how dad feels, I want us to be together.'

'And so you should be,' Charlotte said defiantly. 'Percy is hardly on his deathbed and, let's face it, now that he has you exclusively to himself, he appears to have made a remarkable recovery.'

'That's a little unfair,' Eloise said. 'You should have seen him when they brought him home... And the medicine that Dr Shepherd prescribed has helped.' She paused, thinking, twirling the stem of her wine glass. 'You know – and I realise that it's only been a day – but I think that being away from the stresses of work, knowing that he doesn't have to go back there for a while, is the thing that has brought about the biggest improvement in him.' She shook her head. 'He looked simply awful when they brought him home from there.'

'Eloise, I am not suggesting that Percy is malingering. As you say, he is not well. But his behaviour isn't fair on you. It's indefensible. He is being utterly selfish – and he cannot expect you to become a twenty-four-hour-a-day nursemaid, especially when that is not what is required.'

Charlotte lit a cigarette, then offered the packet to her friend. Eloise shook her head. 'Go on, Ellie,' Charlotte encouraged. 'It will do you good, it will calm your nerves.'

Eloise stared at the open packet of cigarettes, started to shake her head again, but then changed her mind and took one.

Charlotte lit it for her. 'Look, Ellie,' she said, 'there is absolutely no reason for you to stop seeing Paul. Continuing to see him will do Percy no harm; it will be good for you – and what's best for you, will also be best for your father.'

Eloise contemplated the cigarette, her expression thoughtful. Charlie was right: it had to be a two-way thing. She couldn't be a nursemaid and care properly for her father if her own needs were neglected. But it hadn't been long, and there already appeared to be measurable progress in her father's condition, so maybe she was being too glum, too pessimistic. Maybe in another week she might be able to persuade him to allow Paul to start calling round again… just to help out with the heavier chores, drive her in to town for the shopping… And then they could pop into the Moka for coffee…

'And you know what Percy's next target will be, if you give in to his demands over Paul, don't you?' Charlotte went on. 'University. He will try to stop you going there.'

Eloise came back to earth with a thump. She shook her head. 'Dad wouldn't try to stop that. He knows how much that means to me.'

'And he doesn't know how much Paul means to you?'

'They are not the same things.' Eloise paused, lifting the bridge of her spectacles between her thumb and forefinger. 'You know, as ridiculous as it sounds, I honestly believe dad thinks Paul intends to take me away from him – for good.' She held her friend's gaze. 'He has even accused me of conspiring with Paul to get him out of the way so that Paul can move in here – with me.' She sipped her drink, then, placing the glass back on the table, added: 'But, even so, I don't think he sees my going up to university in the same way.'

Charlotte drew on her cigarette, then released the smoke in an extended exhale. 'If Percy actually believes any of those things, Eloise, then he is no longer the person I know. He must be ill – really ill.'

'He is,' Eloise said. 'His whole personality has altered. He is suspicious of every one and anyone who calls. He questions my every move: whenever I go anywhere outside the house, even shopping – and shopping is just about my only reason for going out nowadays.' She wiped away a tear that was threatening to run down her cheek. 'He is ill, Charlotte. He is ill and I have to help him in any way that I can…' She sighed and shook her head. 'But, all the same, I just cannot bear the thought of not seeing Paul anymore.'

'Look, Ellie,' Charlotte paused to give her friend a hug, 'do all you can for Percy: nurse him, show him that you care, that you love him, try to make him feel less vulnerable. I will help you – and he won't mind that. After all, we are not Miss Staidler and Miss Marshall, are we?'

Eloise snubbed out her unfinished cigarette. She smiled wanly, and wiped away another tear. 'No, we aren't,' she replied.

'Well, there you are then,' Charlotte said, confidently. 'Do your duty by your father. Monitor his recovery, play it by ear.' She paused, nodding to herself. 'It is still only June. Given time, everything will come out right – certainly by the start of the university term in September.'

'And what about Paul?'

'Meet him less frequently. You go into the city shopping at weekends. That's not going to stop, is it? So arrange your times so that you can meet him then.' She paused. 'OK, I know it's only one day a week, but at least you'll see him and keep in touch. And it will give you something to look forward to.'

'Oh, Charlie, I don't know. What you're suggesting sounds so… so underhand. I love Paul very much but…' Eloise faltered as her words caused her voice to break – and it wasn't until some moments later, following another hug from her friend, that she was able to finish her sentiment. 'I would feel disloyal, deceitful, if I did anything like that behind father's back.'

'Eloise, look. He is being unreasonable, selfish. Besides, what he doesn't know isn't going to hurt him, is it? And if you give in to him now, you will come to resent him for it. He will control you. You will be stuck in the house – a virtual prisoner – and will come to see yourself as a skivvy; a skivvy at his beck and call. But, and as if that wasn't bad enough, you will also be deprived of Paul's company and support.' Charlotte paused to catch her breath. 'You will become bitter – or worse – towards him. And what good will that do either of you?'

'You're exaggerating, Charlie.'

'Am I?' Charlotte said. 'The best way to be fair to Percy, Eloise, is to be fair to yourself too.'

Eloise finished her drink. 'I suppose that once a week during shopping isn't going to harm anyone.'

'Certainly it isn't.' Charlotte paused, her expression thoughtful. 'By the way, when are you next seeing Paul?'

Eloise's face brightened. 'Tomorrow, when I go shopping. We always go to the Moka for coffee on Saturday afternoons.' Her expression lapsed into gloom. 'But this time was only to tell him that I cannot meet him anymore.' She sniffed. 'I have to let him know that.'

'Well, now it's to tell him that you will continue to meet him on Saturdays, as usual,' Charlotte said, defiantly.

Eloise blew her nose. 'If Paul will agree to it,' she said, gazing at her friend with tear-filled eyes.

Eloise glanced out the window to the Cathedral Green, then back to Paul. 'And that is what Percy has told me,' she said, shaking her head sadly. 'He has forbidden me from seeing you; he has also forbidden you from coming to the house.' She held Paul's gaze, her eyes pleading for him to tell her they could continue to meet, somehow, someway, behind her father's back, anywhere… anyhow. She looked down at her clasped hands. 'That's his ultimatum,' she concluded tearfully.

Paul reached across the table and took her hands in his. 'And we must respect it, Eloise. We must do so until Percy is well enough to rescind his order.'

Even though she had expected them, they were not the words she wanted to hear. After Charlotte had gone home the previous evening, left to her own thoughts, she had come to see the truth of her friend's reasoning. She agreed that, were she kept at home, barred from having any contact with Paul – prevented from seeing the man she loved – then she would eventually come to hate her father, would despise him for what he was doing to her. She had resolved that it would not happen. Going against her father's order would torment her heart, but losing Paul would break it. 'And what if he never relents?' she said.

'What you are suggesting, Eloise, is that your father will not recover – and that is incorrect. Everyone gets over his bereavement sooner or later. We must be patient and give him time.'

She looked around the café, at the other couples, chatting, smiling at one another, laughing; having a good time. But why did this have to happen to them? They had done nothing wrong; they didn't deserve this. Everything was spoiled: their relationship, going up to university… her whole life. It wasn't fair, it really wasn't. And now she was feeling sorry for herself. She sipped her coffee, then gave herself a mental kick. There was nothing to be gained from self-pity. 'I just want us to be how we were,' she said.

Paul squeezed her hands. 'And we shall be, I promise. Percy will get well again. His underlying health is good, as Dr Shepherd indicated. All we – you in particular – have to do is assist his healing in any way that we can.'

Eloise nodded, accepting his long-term prognosis, but at the same time searching for a compromise – an arrangement that would go some way towards fulfilling her own needs, but which would also adhere to the principle of her father's ultimatum. 'But would there…' she began hesitantly, '…Would there be any harm, if, when I come in to town on Saturdays, we had coffee together? In any case, I have to keep you informed of Percy's health.' Her eyes became imploring. 'And you know that it would help me, and that would help father.'

She watched Paul considering her question, watched his expression remaining serious as he did so. She studied his seriousness. He was taking a long time to make up his mind. But he was so honourable, so principled, so fair-minded. He would do nothing to compromise his moral standards. But it was such a small thing to ask. Unable to wait any longer, she said:

'It would be just like a chance meeting, really. And just half an hour… Just long enough to tell each other what we've being doing… How we are…'

Paul's expression relaxed. 'No,' he said. 'No, I shouldn't think there would be any harm in a *chance* meeting like that.' He paused, his expression breaking into a smile. 'As long as you promise not to bring Percy's pipe with you.'

Eloise had informed him of that, of how one of her duties was the lighting of her father's pipe. When she had told him, despite the sadness of the occasion, Paul had been unable to resist making a joke. 'I bet you look like George

Sand,' he had said. 'Or like one of those little male impersonators.' Now, sitting in the café, she gazed at him. 'Actually,' she said, grinning, 'I'm thinking of buying my own – otherwise we may start fighting over that, too.'

The mood in the car as they drove back to St Leonard's, while not being a joyful one, was nonetheless far from being downbeat. Eloise had gone to the Moka fearing that Paul would, because of his principles and his respect for her father, insist they honour Percy's command, that they stop seeing one another until Percy was well again – the timing of which she had no idea. But her fears had proved groundless; for in the event, Paul had agreed to their meeting weekly. She saw them having coffee, lunch, then, as her father's health improved, the better part of the afternoon together. Indeed, things hadn't worked out too badly after all. But most important of all, Paul was right: Percy's underlying health was good; he would get better – he *would*.

The bereaved always got over their loss, eventually. There were surely very few cases of couples actually dying together, except in accidents. And how many people left alone died of broken hearts or took their own lives? Not many, she thought. Even Charlotte's aunt had eventually recovered – had actually found somebody else and remarried – and she had been devoted to her husband. No, Percy would be all right. They just had to be patient.

In a little while, Paul drew up outside of Eloise's home. 'I'll help you carry the bags to the front door,' he said, turning off the car's engine.

She dearly wished that he could come inside the house but knew that such a step would be to invite the wrath of her father – and she didn't want to do that. She didn't want to do anything that might upset Percy, that might retard his recovery. 'Thank you,' she said.

They walked up the path to the front door, the same door that Paul had passed through so many times but which was now barred to him. And behind it the hallway where *he* had first kissed her, the light shade where she had hung the mistletoe, the living room where they had toasted her success and future happiness – her father so proud. Memories – good times – and not so long ago. But they would come around again. It was only a matter of time.

Paul handed her a shopping bag, and she placed it on the doorstep. He then circled around her and placed another bag beside the first, moving back immediately, as if he thought that by coming too close he would violate Percy's ultimatum.

'Thank you, Paul,' she said.

She noted then that the lawn looked already unkempt, and it seemed just days since she had mown it... Or perhaps it was longer. She would do it in the morning, if it didn't rain tonight. She looked up at Paul, sensing that he was following her thoughts. But never mind the chores. If only he could come inside, stay with her for an hour, an hour longer before they parted, parted for a whole week. 'I will meet you in the Moka next Saturday,' she said, instantly feeling like a schoolgirl confirming the arrangement of an unblessed liaison.

He gripped her upper arms. 'Is that a promise?' he said, squeezing her flesh gently.

She held his stare. 'Yes,' she said nodding. 'I'll be there'

He kissed her but, just as she wanted it to go on for longer, he pulled away again. She sensed that he wanted to say something, to convey some meaning; something that he clearly considered to be important.

She watched as his eyes became suddenly sombre, the brows lowering as he held her stare, the effect changing his expression like a stray cloud can shadow the aspect of a sunny day. Had he changed his mind, decided they should not meet – not meet clandestinely? She watched his lips moving, watched his mouth forming the words. Then she heard him say:

'I will always love you.' Moments later – although it must have been longer – she heard the car start, and he was gone. She was alone.

She stood outside the house, unwilling to go immediately inside, fearing that if she did it would somehow be the end of everything, that her world would fall apart, broken up like the pieces of a dismantled jigsaw puzzle – a jigsaw that she would not be able to put together again. She blinked away a tear. But why say goodbye like that? "I will *always* love you". Why not "I love you"? Or simply "Goodbye, darling... See you on Saturday". It was a strange way of saying goodbye to someone you would see again next week. "I will always love you".

In the distance, in the unruffled June air, she heard the drone of the Morris Minor's engine as it joined the Heavitree Road and accelerated towards the city. "I will always love you". It sounded so final, terminal, like a curtain closing at the end of a play. Final. It was as if he thought that he would not see her again, that they would never meet again. "I will always love you". She bit her lip as tears welled in her eyes again. She would be in the Moka next Saturday. She would be there. She would be there, come what may... *Whatever it took.*

Eloise turned then, intending to go into the house. But as she did so, she noticed the curtain behind the downstairs bay window settle back into place, and then she saw a figure scurrying away into the shadows of the room. She saw that the window was open: her father had been watching them, listening to their conversation. But it didn't matter. He couldn't prevent her going into town next Saturday. She would have to do the shopping. And anyway he wasn't so helpless that he couldn't be left alone for an hour.

Chapter Nineteen

Eloise opened the door to find Charlotte and Miss Staidler standing on the doorstep. The couple looked so much at one, so close, that, just for the briefest of moments, she thought that her friend had usurped that place in Miss Staidler's heart previously occupied by Miss Marshall. Then her brain caught up with the event, and she saw that Charlotte had been crying.

It was Sunday morning, the Sunday morning following her failure to meet Paul at the Moka Café. Despite her heartfelt resolution, a sudden relapse in Percy's health yesterday had forbidden her from leaving his bedside; had prevented her from keeping the date. She had been initially concerned about her father, but an unexpected lifting of his spirits – after she had not gone out to meet Paul – although alleviating one anxiety, had turned her thoughts to her broken date. Had Paul worried about her? Had he waited for her, becoming more and more anxious as the afternoon had worn on without her arrival? Or had he – as his final words had intimated – not expected her to turn up? They were unanswerable questions – and then the long night of fretful sleep, as she had tried to suppress thoughts of having let Paul down.

Her gaze swayed between the two women, the one upset, the other dour, but both with faces raised to hers, waiting, or so it seemed to Eloise, for her to speak – for her to be the one to break the silence. But she could not; for it came suddenly to her then that she should hold this tableau longer, that this moment was all she had left of her life. Then, almost as if he had walked around the corner of the house, yet surreally, Paul appeared behind her two visitors, standing on the path, where he had stood last week, and although he did not speak, she heard him say again: "I will always love you". She started to call his name but before any sound came out, as quickly as it had appeared, the apparition faded, and she knew the thing they had come to tell her.

And she never got to say goodbye.

'May we come inside, Eloise?' Miss Staidler's words crowded into her mind. 'We have something that we must tell you.'

Eloise continued to look from one woman to the other, her gaze finally resting on her friend. How awful to be the bearer of such news, to have to tell someone you loved that her boyfriend was dead. If positions were reversed, she knew she wouldn't be able to do it.

Charlotte started to speak then but her voice sounded hoarse, enfeebled, and she fell silent, unable to continue.

Eloise smiled and held out her hand and helped her friend into the house. She had felt something like this was going to happen, ever since last Saturday, when Paul had told her that he would always love her. She had felt then that she would not see him again. A numbing sensation had started to creep into her heart then, had increased until now she was inured to the full impact of the news. She looked at her friend, who was standing in the corner by the door, seemingly paralysed and unsure of what to say or do. She herself was OK though. This thing was a bit like shock. It was almost like the time she had been knocked unconscious by the motorcyclists, and couldn't initially remember anything about it: the memory had only slowly returned – the body's protective mechanism. Only this time her body had seemingly prepared her beforehand, had lowered her ability to feel the hurt, had anaesthetized her emotions, so that now everything around her was a stage play and she merely an onlooker. She held the door open so that Miss Staidler could follow Charlotte into the house, then she closed the door behind them.

Eloise turned to her friend, held the tearful expression, heard Charlotte mumble the word accident. It was as if Charlotte's whole world had collapsed. Oh, Charlie, you were always the strong one, so assured, never ruffled, so protective… Concerned for her… Eloise… Then she had it, and they were in each other's arms, and Charlie was crying as if she were going to die.

In a little while Eloise led Charlotte and Miss Staidler into the living room. She directed the teacher to the chair by the fireplace, and then joined her friend on the sofa, felt the immediate consoling embrace encircle her. It might be selfish, even heartless, but all she wished for now was for the visit to be over, to be spared hearing the words; all she really wanted was to be left alone, left alone with Paul. Perhaps if she went outside to the pathway…

Miss Staidler coughed. It was the cough she had always used at school, when she had wanted to gain the attention of her class. 'Paul has had an accident…' She paused, holding Eloise's gaze with her teacher's stare. '…I am afraid that he is dead, Eloise.'

At the words, Charlotte let out a sob and dropped her head.

Eloise turned away from Miss Staidler. Her gaze fell on

the open doorway, to be drawn up the stairs to the landing, there to alight upon her father, who had issued from his bedroom to see what was going on. She thought that he had not heard Miss Staidler's words, had not heard the teacher say that Paul was dead, for his expression was genial, serene – an aura of contentment. He must have slept well last night. Placing her arm round Charlotte's shoulders, she tuned back to Miss Staidler, who was now saying:

'Paul was in the front passenger seat...' *How could her father have thought she would abandon him?* '...Another car emerged from a side road into their path...' *How could he have thought that she would turn her back on him and walk away to a new life?* '...Paul was thrown forward by the force of the impact into the car's windscreen...' *His confidence had evaporated since the loss of her mother, which had left his mind vulnerable to morbid thoughts.* '...He was taken immediately to hospital but was pronounced dead on arrival...' *How paranoid her father had become. But it wasn't his fault. He was ill.* '...The other occupants of the car were also taken to hospital although only the driver had serious injuries but is expected to make a full recovery...' *But she would look after her father, care for him, nurse him back to health.* '...The driver of the other car was unhurt but is certain to face charges of causing death by dangerous driving.' *She would not desert her father. She would do her duty.*

Miss Staidler rose from her chair then. Eloise watched her coming across the room, and stood up to meet her. The teacher's job was done; she had delivered her message and was now going to leave. 'I have telephoned Mr and Mrs Bridgestock, Eloise...' Eloise realised then that she had never met Paul's parents. The first time she would do so would be at their son's funeral. She pushed her glasses higher onto her nose, staring stupidly at Miss Staidler, who was now saying: 'We will arrange everything between us, so please don't worry about a thing… and Charlotte will stay with you for a while longer.' She paused, taking Eloise's hand. 'I am so sorry that this has happened, my dear. It's shocking to lose the one you love, I know… And you are so young. I am truly sorry.'

Eloise continued to stare at the teacher. In seven years, it was the kindest words she had ever heard her utter. She squeezed the teacher's hand. 'Thank you,' she said, smiling. 'Thank you very much… For everything.' Then she showed Miss Staidler to the door.

Before returning to the living room to join Charlotte, Eloise decide first to pop upstairs to check on her father. She found that he had returned to bed and was apparently fast asleep, which struck her as being odd as his earlier radiance had made her think that he had slept well. She listened to the contented snore, rhythmic in his throat. Best not to disturb him. She would call him down later when lunch was ready. Then she went to her bedroom, collected her teddy bear, and went back downstairs.

She found her friend sitting on the sofa contemplating an unlit cigarette. Eloise took it from her, lit it, and then inhaled. Actually, Charlotte might have something: smoking was quite pleasant – once you got used to it. She passed the glowing cigarette along the sofa. 'What with Percy's pipe, I'm getting quite good at this sort of thing,' she said, sitting down beside her friend. Thoughtfully, she settled A.L. in her lap. 'I'm going to change his name,' she said, fluffing up his ears. 'From now on, I'm going to call him P.B.'

Charlotte smiled wanly. 'Why don't you put Paul's initial in front of his name, then you'll have Pal?' She drew on her cigarette, then turned to Eloise. 'Why did this have to happen, Ellie?' she asked, dejectedly. 'Goodness, it's only three months since your mum–'

'Don't, Charlie,' Eloise broke in. 'It will do no good. It's happened. I'm hurting; you're hurting. But it's too soon to question.'

But Eloise knew why her latest tragedy had happened. If her father hadn't turned against Paul… If he hadn't prevented her from meeting Paul last week… If he… Then it came to her. With a sudden jolt, like a shock of fusing synapses in her brain, she realised that Percy had made it up. All that fuss about not feeling well. That had been a sham. She could see that now. Percy had put that on so that she couldn't leave him alone, so that she couldn't go out to meet Paul. She thought back to the time when Paul had brought her home from the café, when Paul had brought the shopping to the door… When she had seen her father scuttling away from the window – the open window. He had overheard them arranging to meet, and had made his plans there and then. And she knew, common sense told her – her heart told her – that if she had been allowed to keep her date, Paul would still be alive today.

'Oh, I'm sorry, Ellie,' Charlotte apologised, clasping her friend's hand in hers. 'I'm sorry… I'm supposed to be helping, but I'm making it worse.'

'It's OK,' Eloise began steadily. 'I'm going to be strong. I'll get over this… just as I did with mother's death. It was awful then, at first…' She fell silent, remembering the sleepless nights, her pillow wet from her constant weeping – and the days when she'd been strong for Percy. She bit her lip – the irony of that. 'I'll be all right,' she concluded.

Charlotte put her arm around Eloise and hugged her

closer. 'I know you will, Ellie,' she reassured. 'You're more resilient than I am. I wish I were as strong as you.'

Eloise laid her head on her friend's shoulder. 'I always thought you were the stronger one,' she said, closing her eyes.

'On things that don't matter an awful lot to me, perhaps,' Charlotte replied, catching Eloise's hand in hers.

'Remember when we used to do this as kids?' Charlotte asked, after they had been sitting there for a while. 'Snuggled up like this, and taking it in turns to play the boy.'

Eloise smiled. 'I wish we were twelve again,' she replied wistfully. 'Everything was so much simpler then.' Then she felt Charlotte move, felt her friend's lips briefly touch her own.

'I'll always be here for you, Ellie,' Charlotte said.

'Please don't say that, Charlie.' Eloise was sad. 'I've just lost the two people that mean most to me… And bad things are supposed to go in threes.' She paused, idly stroking her teddy bear. 'If anything should happen to you, I don't know what I'd do.'

'That's only a superstition,' Charlotte replied. 'Nothing's going to happen to me. I'll always be here.'

Eloise kept her eyes closed. She had hardly slept last night, and was now feeling tired… Really sleepy. It was good sitting here with Charlie like this, dreaming. Then she felt Charlotte's lips brush hers again, heard her friend's reassuring voice tell her that everything would be all right, that it would take more than a nasty old superstition to do for her. But it was all right for Charlie to talk like that, but there was usually something behind these superstitions, something had inspired them. It didn't do to tempt fate. Then she experienced Charlotte kiss her again. Holding on to Pal, she twisted her head towards her friend's kiss, relaxing… It was

252

nice like this, drifting… Being looked after. Round and round the garden, like a teddy bear, one step, two steps… Tickle you under there. Eloise smiled inwardly. Charlie's idea to rename her bear was a good one.

In a little while, Eloise came slowly back to herself. She stretched her legs out straight and smoothed her skirt. 'I had better start preparing lunch,' she said, giving her spectacles a nudge. 'I expect Percy will be hungry by now.'

Charlotte yawned. 'I'll help you,' she replied. 'What are we having?'

Eloise stood up, then turned and helped her friend up too. 'Oh, the usual roast beef and Yorkshire pudding… Father insists on having that on Sundays.'

As they went out into the hallway they met Percy coming down the stairs. Eloise saw that he was still wearing his pyjamas and dressing gown. His earlier serenity had faded a little. Perhaps he hadn't slept quite so well after all – he still looked pretty contented though. The medication was obviously working, lifting his depression, keeping him cheerful.

'Good morning, Mr James.' Charlotte was the first to speak. 'You look well.'

Eloise watched as her father stopped on the staircase. He looked surprised. She knew that he had seen Charlotte and Miss Staidler arrive earlier… Perhaps he had expected Charlotte to have gone home by now. He wasn't going to create a fuss, was he? There was no reason for him to do so. After all, Charlie wasn't a man – there was little danger of her upsetting her father's status quo. Then she saw his lips spread into a smile, an almost comical smile – a smirk that made him look like nothing so much as a boy caught with his hand in the sweetie jar.

'Hello, Charlotte... How are you keeping? How are your parents? It's nice to see you… Come over to lend Eloise a hand I expect, haven't you? Well, she's doing very well, but an extra pair of hands will be–'

'I am fine, thank you,' Charlotte broke in evenly. 'And mum and dad are fine, too. Father said to tell you that he would visit you soon. And yes, I have come over to assist…'

Eloise listened to the exchange, her eyes flitting from one party to the other. Her father's words had come out in a stream, flowing, the sentences spilling out one after the other – automatic. It was almost as if he had been spoiling for time. Of course, she hadn't told him about Paul yet. She would have to do so. She wondered how he would receive the news. It would be a shock. The two men hadn't seen eye to eye recently – but it would still be a shock to him. He had once got on well with Paul. Paul had helped him solve that technical problem. His company had awarded him a handsome bonus for that. Yes, she would need to be extremely careful how she broke the news. She didn't want to upset him, make his condition worse.

'Good, I'm glad you are able to help,' Percy was saying to Charlotte. 'Eloise has never been that practical, as you know… And now with Paul dead–'

Eloise's gaze instantly settled on her father. She saw his mouth agape, as if he had been instantly petrified by a sudden and overwhelming catastrophe. He already knew that Paul was dead. But how could he have known that? She hadn't told him, and she knew that Charlotte hadn't either. Neither of them had. But he had known. Then in her mind's eye she saw him standing at the top of the stairs… She saw his earlier expression again, the one she had seen from her place in the living room. She saw once more her father standing in his "aura of contentment"… The look that she now realised had reflected his relief on hearing Miss Staidler deliver the news of Paul's death.

As if recoiling from something foul, she took a pace backwards down the hallway, her hand clasped across her mouth, her stare transfixed on her father – her own flesh and blood. Oh daddy, you bastard, how could you?

Chapter Twenty

Eloise sat in the front pew next to the central aisle in the parish church of St Leonard's waiting for the service to begin. She was wearing the black organza silk dress that Charlotte had picked out for her, but she did not really like it – and she wasn't a hat person either. Beside her, Charlotte fidgeted with a prayer book. Every once in a while, she noticed Charlotte's nervous glance in her direction. It was as if her friend were awaiting the signal to supply the first handkerchief. Next along the pew were Charlotte's parents and brother. Across the aisle, Mr and Mrs Bridgestock, who had travelled down from the Isle of Man for the service, gazed stiffly at the vicar. They had agreed to Eloise's wish that Paul be buried locally. At Eloise's feet, a dusty prayer mat lay unused. She didn't believe in God. But in these moments she really hoped that He existed and was watching her. Because if He expected her to get down on her knees and pray after the terrible thing He had done to her, then He had another think coming.

It was Friday the 6th of July. Almost a week had passed since the car crash – a week of sleepless nights, a week of dawning reflection of what had been taken from her, a week of awakening realisation of her new circumstances. But despite all that she had not yet truly acknowledged the finality of Paul's death – she had not yet been able to weep. She had cried a bit with Charlotte. She had experienced grief, was grieving now – but it was not the same as when her mother had died. Her tears had been frequent and copious then – and those times had helped. She had been occupied helping Paul's parents and Miss Staidler organise the arrangements for the funeral, and she had been busy caring for her father, attending to his needs, but none of those things should account for why this numbness was still with her. She had determined that she would be strong. But it was more than that… It was as if her brain had permanently numbed her heart, had tranquillised her feelings so that now she was unable to fully acknowledge her loss.

Then the church organ started up and the vicar invited them to stand and sing the hymn *Be Still My Soul*. A bar behind the other mourners, Eloise got to her feet, fixing her eyes on the stained glass window behind the altar, as the surrounding voices rose and fell to the tune of the familiar hymn. She felt her friend's arm link with hers, and then the gentle tug as Charlotte pulled her closer. She glanced at Charlotte, and saw that she had begun to cry again. The sentimental hymn had no doubt prompted that reaction. She reached into her bag, took out a handkerchief and passed it to her friend. Charlotte took it and sniffed. Charlotte's mother nodded to Eloise and smiled. Eloise acknowledged the smile, and then returned her gaze to the stained glass window behind the altar.

Presently the hymn was over and they were seated again. The vicar was saying something about a great setback for the school. Charlotte was fidgeting with her prayer book once more but had stopped crying. Mrs Bridgestock looked across the aisle and nodded to Eloise. Someone near the back of the church coughed. Eloise thought that it sounded like Miss Staidler, although it might have been Mr Barnes. Outside the church, Eloise knew that the sun shone and motorcars passed along the road just like on any other weekday morning.

For the first time since they had entered the church, Eloise allowed her gaze to wander to the top of the central aisle, adjacent to the chancel steps – to the place where Paul's coffin rested on a cloth-covered stand. Even though it was fundamental to the Christian funeral service, the tradition of placing the coffin of the deceased there was one that she did not particularly care for. It was tantamount to inviting distress. At the funeral of Charlotte's uncle, who had died quite young from lung cancer, the bereaved spouse had quite literally collapsed in a grief stricken paroxysm when confronted with the box that held the body of her dead husband. Of course, they couldn't hide the coffin away, in some side room – that would be even worse. But it didn't seem right, having it there, as if on show.

She hadn't gone to see Paul in the chapel of rest. Charlotte had gone, had tried to persuade her to go too, to say "goodbye". Obviously Paul's parents had gone, and the teachers from the school… some of his pupils as well. None of them had been able to understand her decision: of all the people who had gone, she should have been one of them. But she hadn't wanted to see him like that; she hadn't wanted her last view of him to be a waxy corpse, a lifeless cadaver. She wanted to remember him alive, the fun moments, the caring moments, the look on his face as he came back to her after winning Pal at the funfair, his touch, his expression when she was sad, but most of all that look on his face when she had driven the car up the hill at Lyme Regis. She glanced down at the prayer mat, brought her foot back, aimed, and then kicked it with every ounce of strength she had in her.

Placed along the top of Paul's coffin were the wreaths given by the mourners. She could see hers: a simple hoop of Madonna lilies. Primroses would have been better, but they were out of season now... Yet someone had got some from somewhere; she could smell their delicate scent. She glanced around the church, at the altar, the chancel, the lectern, the nave, along the pews, every place where the primroses might be, but she was unable to locate them. Defeated, her gaze fell back to the coffin... And then, as if in a dream, that part of the church behind the coffin faded in her vision and she saw again the primrose meadow of her childhood... And the primrose path leading down to the stream and the bank of primroses at the bottom of the meadow.

And she was running, skipping, singing down the primrose path to the primroses, to the bank of golden yellow primroses at the bottom of the meadow. And Paul was beside her, running apace and pointing to the shimmering yellow bank below them. And they were singing, calling incomprehensible words at the tops of their voices into the rushing air as they ran and skipped towards the primroses.

And they had found the primrose meadow. Oh, thank you, mummy. And down the primrose path were the primroses, the bank of wavering golden yellow primroses. Oh, thank you, mummy. And they ran and they skipped and they called and they sang down the primrose path to the primroses.

And they were at the bottom of the primrose path, beside the primroses. They would gather bunches of the flowers – bunches and bunches of primroses. She turned joyously to Paul... But he was no longer beside her. Her gaze reeled this way and that as she attempted to find him, back up the meadow, at the primrose bank, then back up the meadow once more. But he had gone.

All at once she saw her mother on the other side of the stream, in the meadow over there. Her mother was smiling, young and full of everything we should all have for always. Her mother waved. Eloise waved back, called out, started to scramble up the primrose bank. It looked nice over there. Perhaps Paul was there, too. All she had to do was cross the stream.

Then suddenly, she saw the coffin. It had been placed on the bank of primroses. She saw that the flowers on the bank were still and wilted. And she was returned to the bottom of the bank again, and could not see across the stream. But she had to climb the bank and cross the stream, because Paul and her mother were over there. She started to climb towards the coffin, but the flower petals were mildewed and falling away to dust beneath her feet, and she kept slipping back. She would never make it now. It was not possible, for the primrose bank was growing steeper, growing higher.

She stood still, no longer trying to climb the bank, for it was not to be done. It was cold, and she wrapped her arms about herself and stared at the coffin. Then she heard Paul calling her name, but she could not gauge the direction from which the calls came, for the wind was swirling the dry primrose petals into rasping lakes of autumn leaves, and she gazed about herself as though she were in the grip of a befuddling fog.

The calls were becoming fainter... Because Paul was going away. And she heard him say that he would always love her, though his voice was now only part of the wind. And she turned her gaze back to the coffin. The primroses were growing over it, their spindly stems engulfing it, entwining it in a runaway embrace, until all were one – only the primrose bank. Then, as it had come to her, the vision faded and she was returned to the church, to the mourners – and to the coffin. The primrose meadow was gone... Paul was gone.

She was sitting in the pew. Charlotte had both arms around her. Charlotte was crying again. 'Please don't cry, Charlie,' she said. 'We had good times.' She sniffed and smiled through her tears. 'We really did.'

Chapter Twenty One

Eloise adjusted her spectacles and peered around the Moka Café. Time travel, coming back in time, was OK, but this was a different matter. Paul should have been here by now. She glanced at the clock again. He was late. They had always met here at two o'clock on Saturdays and he had never been late. She took the newspaper from her bag and stared at the date. So he wasn't coming; he wasn't going to turn up. Perhaps, then, his words that had – back then – seemed to her so final really had been final. "I will always love you." Perhaps they had been his way of saying goodbye, of telling her their romance was over. After all, her father's orders barring him from coming to the house, prohibiting their meeting, must have seemed insurmountable, and there had been no indication of when her father might recover. But Paul would surely never have let her down. They were in love, truly in love, planned to marry. He wouldn't... Unless – thinking of her best interests, of saving her from continuing hurt – he had intended to make a clean break of it, had intended to give her the chance to find somebody else.

She pushed her chair away from the table. It was smoky in here now. It would be nice to get some fresh air, to walk up through the city centre in the sunshine, see the old ABC Cinema – and The Theatre Royal. She rose from her chair; however, in the process of doing so, her gaze took in the scene outside the window – where she saw Paul walking up the Cathedral Green, striding towards the café, coming here. She sat down again.

Presently she heard the customer bell ring downstairs, as the door was opened and closed – the footfalls on the stairs that led to this floor; the knowing that he was here, here in this room; the wait as she sensed him ordering coffee; his footsteps as he crossed the wooden floor. He was coming to this table – but she had known that he would.

'Is anyone sitting here?'

She turned and looked up at him, and their eyes met. Eloise had dreamed of this moment so many times down the years, wished for it… and now it was here. She knew if she tried to speak her voice would come out a nervous falsetto – or an equally nervous croak. His approach had been too sudden, too abrupt. If she had been facing into the room, watched him enter, watched him buy the coffee, watched him walk over here, then she would have had time to prepare herself, would have had time to control her emotions. Experiencing a quickening of her pulse, Eloise smiled and shook her head.

She watched him place his cup on the table, pull back the chair and sit down…To direct his gaze away from her, out the window to the Cathedral Green. Good: more time to compose herself. She needed to remain cool, detached – at least for a while, until she recovered her emotional equilibrium. Then, with her nerves under control, she would be in a better position to manipulate an opening, to reveal herself to him. But until then, it would be best to "play it by ear".

Eloise focused her attention on Paul, whose scanning observation of the Cathedral Green negated any need for her to conceal her curiosity. He was wearing the tweed jacket with the leather patches at the elbows, grey cotton slacks and a maroon casual shirt. She had a photograph of him wearing this very outfit, leaning against his car on the seafront at Sidmouth. Eloise smiled to herself. She remembered teasing him about that picture. She hadn't noticed at the time, but when the photograph was developed, it had shown him ogling a busty blonde who happened to walk into shot just as Eloise had pressed the shutter-release button. Of course, he had pleaded his innocence – but she recalled him blushing all the same. But now, watching him as he gazed out the window of the Moka Café, she noted the unruly lock of hair, loose across his brow as he bent slightly forward the better to expand his view. Eloise wanted to reach across the table and brush it back from his eyes, back from the eyes that were fixed with magnetic force on the bustling scene outside.

'Are you expecting someone?' The question surprised Eloise: for although she had asked it, its spontaneity and familiarity in such a situation had defeated her rehearsed caution.

Paul turned from the window, clearly startled from his search. 'No,' he said. He glanced at his watch. 'No, not now.'

Eloise stared at him, emotion welling in her breast. She wanted to explain that her father's illness had prevented her younger self from coming here, from keeping their date, that Percy's relapse had forbidden her from leaving him alone. Instead, she held his gaze and, with everything she had, tried to will the message to him – tried to let him know. 'Perhaps she'll be along in a minute,' she said, automatically, searching blindly for an opening. 'Perhaps something has delayed her.' Now she wanted to tell him that she was already here, to throw her arms around his neck, and to kiss him exactly as she had kissed him on the hill at Lyme Regis. But she could not do so. And it had nothing to do with the anachronistic circumstance of their meeting. It was a far more difficult obstacle to overcome than that. For she was no longer an overexcited girl who had just driven a motorcar up a hill at the seaside, she was now a staid middle-aged woman engaged in a conversation with a young man in a coffee shop – and she had no desire to be thrown out of here for sexual harassment.

Paul grinned. 'Why do you assume that it's a "she"? I might be waiting for a male colleague, or my father...' He paused and grinned again. 'Or a mate from the cricket team that I play for.'

Eloise experienced the warmth of colour suffusing her cheeks. He was teasing her, of course. But it was a difficult situation to be in. All the years of dreaming, of imagining such a scenario as this, had not prepared her one iota for the real thing. It was not easy holding a conversation with someone you had known well, loved, yet nevertheless had now to treat as a stranger. And it was an even more difficult thing having him treat you as a stranger, as if everything you had shared together, everything that had gone before, had never been. In her dreams it had all been so simple: they had just known, like in the films. She concentrated her mind on the present, the now. 'Just a natural assumption I suppose.' Eloise paused to glance around the room. 'But it's this place: the ambience here always seems to speak of lovers' tryst... Liaisons...' She paused again, silenced by Paul's amused smiled. 'I'm sorry,' she said at length. 'I have been indiscreet.'

Paul continued to smile, his gaze now roaming her face with the intensity of someone trying to recognise a person from an old photograph.

Under the examination, Eloise felt herself blushing again. She wasn't handling this very well. He had always teased her about her romantic notions concerning the Moka. She lowered her gaze to her cup and, picking up a spoon, stirred her coffee thoughtfully. Then she pinched her arm.

'Why did you do that?' Paul asked, becoming serious.

'I was trying to wake myself up,' she said brightly, nudging her spectacles nervously. 'I used to come in here years ago with someone who looked like you and for a moment I thought that I'd been magically whisked back in time.' She took her makeup compact from her bag and looked at herself in the mirror. 'No,' she added, shaking her head sadly. 'It's the same old me.'

Paul laughed at her joke. 'Funnily enough, I thought just now that I recognised you... But it couldn't be.' He paused to re-examine her face. 'But you do bear an uncanny likeness to someone I used to know, except that your hair is shorter and darker.'

Was this her chance to reveal herself, or at least to start the process off? 'Is it the one you were looking for earlier?' Eloise indicated to the window. 'Out there.'

'Where? Oh no.' His face became grave. 'No. The person you reminded me of died earlier this year.'

Eloise stared at him stupidly. Who did he know who died this year? Then her brain caught up: her mother. She felt flattered: Mary had been considered pretty in middle age. 'I'm very much alive,' she said, smiling happily.

But Paul did not appear to pick up on her mood. 'I wish the other one was,' he said, dropping his gaze to his hands, which were resting on the tabletop.

Eloise waited for him to continue, but he did not seem immediately able to do so, and his gaze remained directed at his hands. Her mother's death had been the start of his troubles, their troubles, and she knew what he was thinking. But if she were to encourage him to talk about it, then surely that would ease his hurt, would cheer him up. Not only that, but it might even open the door for her to help him in another way. Knowing full well what his answer would be, she said: 'Would it have made a difference to your date today if she was?'

But once again, he did not respond, and for a moment she thought that he had not heard her question. But then he lifted his eyes to hers. 'Yes,' he said, nodding. 'Yes, it would have made all the difference.'

Eloise felt that she might cry, experienced tears welling in her eyes. However, suddenly realising that her hand was inching involuntarily across the table towards his hand, she arrested the movement and drew her hand back. She took a deep breath, and gave herself a mental ticking off. No, she really did not wish to be ejected from the Moka for sexual impropriety. 'Is the person you planned to meet this afternoon, the daughter of the person who died?' she asked, clasping her hands firmly in her lap.

'Yes.' His eyes held hers, and she knew that if this conversation were to continue then she would surely go around the table and hug him – regardless of convention, regardless of the fear of being thrown out on to the street. 'Yes, she is.' He smiled, wryly. 'You woman are so intuitive: I don't think that I would have made the connection myself.'

Eloise suddenly felt herself a fraud – a cheat. Although, in her defence, she had been trying to help; nevertheless, she had led him along while knowing the answers. But she felt certain that she would have made the connection anyway, irrespective of the circumstances, irrespective of her position. 'Would you like to talk about it?' she asked.

For what seemed like a long time, he gazed into her eyes, assessing, she knew, whether he should confide in this stranger. He was not the sort of person to reveal his troubles to anyone, especially to someone he had only just met, and she did not think that he would accept her offer. Eventually, though, his expression relaxed and he nodded silently.

Over the following half hour, Paul recounted the story of his interrupted romance. He even, in order to emphasise a point concerning his girlfriend's power of persuasion, gave her an abridged account of her illegal drive up the hill at Lyme Regis. However, much to her dismay, he did not include the episode of when she had kissed him – although she had known beforehand that he would not mention anything of that nature. Nevertheless, as his story had unfolded, his speech had become more candid, more revealing, and he had been able to talk about his fears regarding the effect that her father's illness might have on their romance. He had been especially pessimistic concerning the length of time he thought that it would take for Percy to recover – the length of time that it would be before they could start dating again. It was of course a different opinion to the one that he had once given to her younger self, when he had tried to reassure her that Percy's illness was only transitory and that their romance would soon be returned to normal.

Paul leaned back from the table. 'You know,' he began, 'I think this has helped. Talking to someone older has–' He halted abruptly, clearly abashed by the sudden frown that had appeared on his listener's face. 'I've been selfish. I've bored you with my troubles. I apologise.'

Eloise shook her head and smiled. 'There is no need to apologise,' she said. 'And I am certainly not bored.' She held his gaze with everything she had. 'She is a lucky person to know you and…' Eloise wanted to say love but knew that if she attempted to pronounce the word, her voice would break. Instead, she concluded: 'I hope that everything comes out OK.'

Paul nodded and smiled abstractedly, his mind, as Eloise knew, pondering once more the reason for her absence here this afternoon.

'Something unforeseen must have cropped up to prevent her meeting you,' she said. 'Possibly a deterioration in her father's health.' If she did nothing else today, she had at least given him the reason for her missed date.

'Yes, I expect that's it. Eloise would never let anyone down without very good reason.' He finished his coffee, then glanced out the window, and in doing so missed seeing Eloise dig her nails into her arm. 'Whatever happens, I hope she does go on to university at some point,' he said to himself.

Eloise flinched from the pain. 'She did,' she said quietly.

Her father's health had improved that summer following the car crash, and she had been able to go up to St Hilda's with Charlotte. But his recovery had only been a temporary one. He never fully recovered from the loss of his wife and, within a year, a mild case of influenza developed into pneumonia, an illness from which sadly he would not recover. Even though the doctor had written pneumonia as being the cause of death on the death certificate, Eloise had thought that a more precise diagnosis might have mentioned a broken heart. Her father had never been a demonstrative man. She could count the times on the fingers of one hand that she had seen him kiss her mother. He had always seemed to be more involved with his technical books than with shows of affection. But a deep love for her mother must always have been there, hidden beneath his reserved exterior, for the loss of his wife was surely the thing that had killed him.

It had taken Eloise a long time to forgive her father – if she ever truly forgave him. Of course, she had come down from Oxford regularly during his final months – and she had been at his bedside when he died. But she had been young then, and her recent loss had weighed heavily on her youthful shoulders, and it is not so easy to forgive when you are nineteen years old and you see your life ruined by a gross act of unnecessary selfishness. But the years had passed, she had got a job, had partners, and life had taught her that, despite the occasional show of altruism, people generally are motivated by self interest. Her father certainly hadn't been an exception to the rule.

Eloise rubbed her arm. If she stayed here with Paul for much longer, she would have to trim her nails.

Paul suddenly swung round to face her, knocking the table and rattling his cup in his animation, and for a moment she thought that he had heard her remark. But he clearly had not, for, with an eager smile, he said: 'Say, if you've nothing planned for the remainder of the afternoon, would you like to come for a drive round the city in my car?' However, before she had chance to respond to his invitation, his expression fell, and he added: 'I am not making a pass or anything like that, but it's just that I have enjoyed your company so much that I thought that perhaps... Well... I could drop you off somewhere.'

She hadn't kept the date, nevertheless it hadn't taken him long to make another one, another one with someone else. Eloise rubbed her arm again. She had never thought of him as the two-timing kind – although of course it wasn't really like that, not in the accepted sense… Wasn't it? He was asking another women out. Yes, but only for a short tour round the city – that was innocent enough. Thinking quickly, she said: 'I have a train to catch later, but not at any particular time so–'

'That's settled then,' he interrupted. 'A spin round the town, and afterwards I'll drop you off at the station. Now, which one? Central or St David's?'

'I don't think it really matters,' she said thoughtfully, 'but the Central will be most convenient… I think.' Well, at least it was the one nearest to where she lived. But she had no idea who would be in residence there now. Oh well, she would worry about that when the time came – if it came. But if push came to shove, there was always the police station.

Paul rose from his chair. 'C'mon, I am parked just round the corner.'

In her mind's eye Eloise pictured the car park and the little Morris Minor car with the phobia of hills now parked there. No need to worry though, for it was level ground over there. 'Cool,' she said.

Paul stood back and waited while she got up from the table. 'You have a nice way of saying that,' he replied.

Chapter Twenty Two

From the Moka Café, they walked the short distance up to Bedford Street. Eloise had hoped that Paul would hold her hand, as he used to do – she had almost taken his, as they had left the coffee house, out of habit, or on impulse. Now that they were out in the open air, she was feeling a touch more daring in that respect… But Paul was so proper, so old-fashioned – such a fuddy-duddy… Although, back there in the café, he had seemed pretty keen on taking her out. But he hadn't held her hand. To be honest, in view of his uncharacteristic presumption, she had been a bit disappointed when he hadn't done so… Or at least taken her by the arm as they'd walked along. That would have been really nice, like old times; she had always felt good, secure, when walking along with him like that.

Now as they walked along, side by side, she glanced across the street to the Princesshay Shopping Precinct, to the plaque which proclaimed its opening in 1949 by the then Princess Elizabeth. All this area, together with the upper end of the High Street, had suffered terrible bombing by the Luftwaffe in 1942. Bedford Circus, whose terrace of Georgian town houses was said to rival those of the Grand Crescent at Bath, had been entirely razed to the ground. Eloise glanced again at its replacement. It was not aesthetic, had no character, and was, it seemed to her, an amalgam of right angles and rectangles and squares – concrete and functional. It was the first of its type to be built after the war – a product of post-war austerity. Although, after the bombing and the deprivation of wartime, she guessed that it must have seemed pretty nice all the same.

'There's the post office,' Paul said. 'Do you require any stamps, or a letter to post perhaps, before you go home?'

Eloise smiled to herself. It was a question he might once have asked her on such a stroll along here – a question that typified the relationship of a couple "walking out together"… almost an intimate question. Or was she merely being romantic, getting carried away with the ambience of it all? She was quite enjoying all this. Her gaze wandered over the concrete and glass construction that was the post office. 'I don't think so,' she said.

Just beyond the post office, they arrived at the junction with Southernhay. Eloise surveyed the scene. They were still only a stone's throw from the city centre, with its stores of bustling shoppers, but here was a more tranquil side of Exeter, classical Georgian architecture and Capability Brown gardens. The Luftwaffe's bombs had missed this part of Exeter. As there was no industry to speak of in Exeter, it was thought that the pilots had been merely jettisoning the bombs they hadn't managed to drop on the navy dockyards in Plymouth. Eloise continued to scan the Palladian lineaments of the Southernhay terraces. It was nice that something from a grander age had survived. Turning away, and once more resisting the desire to take his hand in hers, she walked with Paul along the street to the open-air car park.

Paul led the way between the rows of neatly parked cars. 'Just along here,' he said, glancing over his shoulder.

Eloise followed, noting the preponderance of the colour

black, and the car with running boards like the one her father had had. Those running board things had been useful though for getting in and out of the car, especially when you were wearing a long dress. They should– 'There it is,' she said, pointing excitedly to the next row along, where Paul's car was parked. 'Over there by...'

Paul stopped and turned around to face her. 'That's right...' His stare became quizzical. 'But how did you know which one was mine?'

It was hot in the car park, with no breeze, the sun's rays seemingly reflected at her from every window and every windscreen of every car. She returned Paul's stare. Was this her opportunity? But he would never believe her... There was bound to be a better chance. 'I didn't.' She paused, her gaze flitting between him and his car. 'But you mentioned earlier that you were a teacher and that one stands out from the rest as being a teachers' car.' She paused again, thinking. 'I'm quite good at guessing a person's profession from the car he drives... It works the other way round too.'

'Obviously.' Paul smiled generously and pointed to a two-tone Hillman Minx that was parked next to his car. 'And what profession would you ascribe to the owner of that one?'

It wasn't a test, not a serious one – not like that. Her wandering gaze then alighted on a bowler-hatted motorcar salesman, who was standing in the forecourt of a nearby garage. The car might suit him.

'Defeated?' Paul's question woke her from her reverie.

'It is a solid, dependable motorcar,' she said, returning her gaze to Paul. 'Perhaps a little too ostentatious for a business gentleman, though perhaps a solicitor... Certainly not a doctor...' She paused for effect. 'My guess would be that it belongs to a salesman, one who requires a respectable image but who at the same time needs to appear in the vanguard of motorcar fashions... Therefore... Possibly a motorcar salesman.'

Paul laughed. 'Very well thought through, Emily' he said, 'and your conclusion may be correct. You have a logical way of thinking.' His eyes became examining. 'Eloise is like that too.' He nodded thoughtfully. 'You two would get on well together.'

Eloise turned away. She had told him earlier that her name was Emily. In the light of his observations, it now seemed too close to her real one for comfort. She now wished that she'd said it was Caroline or Rosemary or Heather – anything long and not beginning with E would have been better.

'I'm sorry, it's a little basic, not very luxurious.' Paul said. 'But it gets me around all the same.'

Eloise nudged her spectacles and gazed at the Morris Minor, at its sleek pointed bonnet, at its chromium bumper, its running boards. 'It's cool,' she said. She swung her arm round in a full circle, encompassing the whole car park. 'It's the coolest car of them all.'

'I don't know about that,' Paul said, grinning as he held the passenger door open for her. 'You may change your mind once we have encountered a pothole or two.' Eloise frowned in disbelief: surely they were a modern invention.

She lowered herself into the seat, briefly smiling up at Paul – who was still holding the door open – before swinging her legs in behind her. She dropped her bag in the space beside her feet. 'Cool.'

As Paul went around to the other side of the car, she wound the window down, then turned to examine her surroundings. She glanced across at Paul, who had just taken his place in the driver's seat. Almost unable to control her glee, she said: 'I won't ask to drive.'

Paul laughed. 'Eloise would have,' he said.

He started the car, and they drove out on to Paris Street, heading for the junction with Sidwell Street and the High Street. Eloise turned to look at the new Wimpy Bar, which was on the left hand side of the street. Plastic and metal, Formica and glass, fluorescent lighting and those... Tastee Freeze milk shake things. How could the Moka have lost out to that – and its ilk? Perhaps she should get Paul to stop so that they could go in, see if Charlotte was in there. If she was, Eloise would give her a right dressing down, then when – if – Eloise returned to the present, she could phone Charlie and ask her if she remembered once being harassed by a middle-aged woman in the Wimpy Bar. Eloise grinned. That would be fun... If she did get back to her own time.

At the top of Paris Street, Paul had to wait for a coal lorry that was edging across the junction towards the High Street, giving Eloise the opportunity to look around. There was the ABC Cinema, where the music gigs were held, where they'd seen Billy Fury – and he had come onto the stage from the darkness of the wings, in the fabled Billy Fury style, looking mean and moody and oh so sexy, and had sung *Halfway to Paradise*. Charlotte had screamed; and some girls in the front had rushed the stage, had tried to climb onto it. Knowing Charlie's record, it was fortunate that they'd been sitting upstairs. But it had been pure pandemonium. And Billy Fury – completely unruffled – still singing *Halfway to Paradise*. Cool. She turned to Paul.

'Is it possible to stop over there?' She indicated across the junction to the large art deco building. 'Over there by the cinema.'

Paul drove over the crossroads, then swung the car in against the kerb, adjacent to the cinema. 'Is this near enough for you?'

'This is just fine,' Eloise said. She turned her gaze to the ABC Cinema, whose depth stretched for several hundred feet along the street. '*Brief Encounter*,' she started to read the billboard aloud, 'Starring Trevor Howard and Celia Johnson.' She glanced at Paul. 'That's an old movie,' she said.

Paul studied her for a while, his gaze more than a little curious, slightly bemused. She smiled at him, wanting to brush the lock of hair back from his eyes – Alan Ladd hadn't been in *Brief Encounter*. Finally he nodded his agreement. 'Yes, it's summer,' he said. 'They tend to put the older films on now, don't they? You may recall that H.G. Wells' *The Time Machine* was on last week.'

'Was it?' Eloise returned his stare, her eyes shadowed. 'I missed it – and I really like that one, too.'

'Shall I drive on now?' Paul asked, turning back to the car's controls, away from Eloise, who was once more studying the cinema's offerings. 'We are sort of in the way parked here.' But Eloise was still engrossed in her study and did not answer. Paul waited for several moments longer, but when he still did not receive a reply from his passenger, he engaged first gear, and set them in motion again, down the New North Road.

As they moved off, Eloise glanced across the car to the other side of the road, to the new Debenhams departmental store… and then, as the car gathered speed, to the empty shell of the derelict Theatre Royal. Her eyes momentarily absorbed its faded nineteenth-century frontage, the fan-lighted entrance, the wrought iron pillars and railings; and the tattered advertisement slogan that announced its closure. 'Yes,' she said. 'Yes, please drive on.'

A quarter hour later found the pair driving down the Fore Street towards the Exe Bridge. Since their departure from the cinema, Eloise had chatted merrily, pointing out places and premises long-lost to her modern-day eyes: The Clock Tower Restaurant, Timothy White's Household Stores, Brock's Quality Furnishings, and the tram traction poles which, although long defunct, she noted were now enjoying another lease of life as electric lighting stands. Funnily enough, she could not recall their being utilised like that. And look at the lady over there now, pushing one of those old larger-than-necessary perambulators, the ones with the folding canvas hoods and tiny wheels, up the steep street from the Exe Bridge. It occurred to Eloise then that if she really did get stuck here and couldn't return to the present, there was a fortune to be made in inventions, in introducing a few modernisations.

Soon they were approaching the river, a place she knew well for its summer walks, but she barely had chance to acknowledge the Riverside Cafe and Hotel, let alone the old Exe Bridge, before Paul rounded the junction and swung in to Bonhay Road. It was all going too fast. She wished Paul would stop the car again, so that she could savour more of it.

And just then, as if reading her thoughts, and much to her delight, Paul pulled the car off the road on to the grass verge that overlooked the river, parking so that they had a good view in both directions. Eloise almost clapped her hands in glee at the old-time parking ease. Paul put on the hand brake, turned off the motor, and leaned back in the seat.

After a moment's pause, gesturing to the riverside path, he said: 'Eloise and I used to come for walks along here.'

Eloise followed his indication to the well-trodden pathway, baked now a dusty brown by the summer sun. "*Used* to come for walks along here". Her younger self had only missed one date, yet he had used past tense. She considered his use of them. Perhaps he really had thought that her father would succeed in breaking up their relationship, and that they would not come this way again. He had been pessimistic in the café earlier regarding the length of time he thought that it might take for Percy to recover. 'Yes, all the way out to Cowley Bridge,' she said wistfully, still absorbed in her negative thoughts.

At her words, Paul swivelled round in the driver's seat, his expression puzzled. 'How did you know that?'

A little way down the road from the parked car, a train laboured across the inclined bridge, heading for the tunnel that led to the Central Station – streamers of working smoke billowed in the vortex of its wake. How did she know? It was one of those things that only she would be aware of. Perhaps, then, it was time to implement her plan, to reveal herself. Eloise turned to him to see that his stare was intent, his eyes challenging. He was waiting for an answer. But it wasn't exclusive knowledge: someone could have told her about it. It wasn't the time then. Or was she being a coward, afraid of trying to explain... Afraid of his rejection? No, there would be a better opportunity, one in which her word would be irrefutable. Playing for time, Eloise focused her mind on the scene. 'Look at the train,' she said absently. 'Isn't it amazing how they climb such a steep slope?' But Paul did not answer and, after a little while, having received no reply, she returned her gaze to him and his questioning stare. She laughed nervously and shrugged her shoulders. 'You must have mentioned it in the café,' she said.

'I don't recall doing so.'

She wound the car window right down and looked out across the river, to where the current meandered towards the sea. Two swans drifted downstream in the languid afternoon air. One embarked on a single paddle to catch up with its mate. 'You may not have,' she said. 'Years ago my boyfriend and I used to do the same thing.' She paused and turned back to face him. 'So it probably just seemed the natural thing for you to do too.'

Paul held her gaze, and his eyes became intense. 'You are not a representative of the school's board of governors, are you?' he said at length. 'I mean, I haven't been in teaching for very long: St Leonard's is my first school.' He paused, frowning. 'You are not checking up on me by any chance?'

Eloise relaxed. 'May I remind you that it was *you* who picked me up,' she said, artfully.

Paul blushed.

She watched his embarrassment, recalling how some of the girls in class had set out deliberately to aggravate his initial diffidence. But perhaps... 'Do you believe in time travel?' she said, catching his stare.

Paul laughed. 'You mean like journeying into the future... in the sense of that film that was showing at the ABC last week – *The Time Machine*?'

'Yes, something like that.'

'That is just a story, a piece of fiction,' he said. 'But how can one travel forward to something that has yet to happen?'

'Then how about going the other way, travelling back in time,' she said, 'would that be more likely, do you think?'

Paul considered her question for a while. 'My guess is

that that would be equally impossible.' He fell silent, his gaze following the progress of the two swans as they drifted with the current towards a sweep in the river, there to disappear from his view. 'Once an event has occurred, concluded,' he went on, 'it is over – past. Recollection or reconstruction of it by those present at its time of happening is of course possible. Nevertheless, the event itself is gone for ever – into history – and could therefore not be re-visited.'

She watched a train drift down the embankment from the Central Station, only the metallic clanking of its connecting rods audible inside the car. Paul was so logically minded, reasoned, his thinking clear-cut; there were no shades of grey; there were no fuzzy edges. And of course theories that saw time as a continuum, where travelling along it was theoretically possible, were yet to be proposed. 'Yes,' she said. 'Yes, that's my view too.'

He looked straight at her, held her gaze, and his eyes became searching. 'But why did you ask the question?'

Eloise returned his stare, her gaze flitting from one blue eye to the other. After a little while, she said: 'No particular reason. It's just that this scene seems so ageless. It just occurred to me that, if you didn't know otherwise, it could be the 1950s, the 1960s – any era really. I bet nothing has changed here since the nineteen-fifties.'

Paul laughed and glanced around the interior of the car. 'If it were the 1950s,' he said, 'this old jalopy of mine would be a bit newer.'

Eloise touched the dashboard. 'He looks well cared for,' she said. She shot him an amused, confident look. 'But will he make it up St David's Hill later, when you drive me to the Central Station?'

Paul grinned; it was a grin that she had seen before,

when they'd been together, buddies… In the old days. 'Oh, he will manage it all right,' he said. 'But if he doesn't, then you can drive.'

Eloise laughed. 'I'd be no good,' she said. 'The person we really want is Eloise. If she can do Lyme Regis, then…' She fell silent, her light-hearted banter muted by the suddenly changed expression that had appeared on Paul's face. Ever since their time in the Moka, when he had told her his story, she had been trying to cheer him up, and now she had reminded him of his missing date and his troubles. But he had reminisced… Yes, but it was all right for him to talk, to confide – perhaps even to feel sorry for himself – but to him, she was an outsider, someone who had played no part in any of it. And, of course, it was all so fresh for him, when for her it was history. But then another thought occurred to her: Or was his sudden change of mood because Eloise – during their chatting – had temporarily slipped his mind and that his thoughts had become focused on Emily? She glanced at the river. Where the swans had been, several ducks were now squabbling over a titbit that a passer-by had thrown to them. No, it couldn't be that, life had made her cynical: it was the abrupt reminder of his woes, that was all. 'I'm sorry,' she said.

'There's no need to apologise,' Paul replied. 'I should be the one to do that, for I have burdened you with my problems. Therefore, I do apologise.' He paused, his expression becoming thoughtful. 'And to show that I am sincere, I will drive you to the station straightaway.'

But now it was Eloise's turn to have her mood dampened. Paul's words had reminded her that time was running out. She had thought they had a little longer together; that perhaps they would drive out to Cowley Bridge, and she would see the café where the fracas with the motorcyclists had occurred.

She would love to see that again. But he was going to drive her to the station now. If that were the case, she needed to be honest, to come clean, to reveal herself – quickly. But she also sensed that now was not the moment to do so. Something was holding her back. Was it cowardice, fear of breaking the spell, fear of attempting an explanation… or fear of his rejection? She couldn't say which, even if any one of those things was the reason. Oh, if only it were as easy as in films, in books… 'All right,' she said, raising her eyes to gaze out the car's windscreen, 'the station it is then.'

'By way of St David's Hill… if my car will make it,' he joked, looking her up and down.

She glanced towards him, watched him reaching for the car's ignition. Soon they would part. It would not be like the last time, when he had held her, kissed her, and told her that he would always love her. This time he would drop her off, say something trivial, as casual acquaintances do when saying goodbye, smile, wave, and drive away – for ever. Knowing with certainty what was to follow would make this time worse – much worse. It would be… And with that half-thought tears clouded her vision, threatened in an instant to overflow her eyelids. She started to turn away – but not quick enough to conceal her sudden emotion.

'Are you all right, Emily?' Paul asked, following her movement, his gazed fixed on her expression.

She laughed nervously. 'Yes.' A tear toppled over her eyelid and ran down her cheek. She brushed it away with the back of her hand and laughed again. 'I was just thinking about an old boyfriend, that's all.'

'That's not all,' he said, moving his body towards hers. 'Do you wish to talk about it?' He shuffled farther across the seat. 'I'm a good listener.' He paused, his hand hovering over her arm. 'After all, you listened to my cares, now it's my turn to be counsellor.' And with that, he placed his hand on her arm.

Except for brushing against one another earlier – when they had come out of the Moka, when she had got into the car – it was the first time that he had touched her, and her body responded with an involuntary tremor of passion. She could feel his breath on her neck, the magnetism of his body. She wanted to turn around, to let that magnetism draw their bodies together, to have him kiss her in that special way. She had dreamed of this moment a thousand times, she had imagined it many more times than that. But what would he think – how would he react – if this middle-aged pickup threw herself at him like that? Her answer came in a mental picture, an image that showed him recoiling from her, his body taut, his face aghast. She turned farther towards the window, almost sticking her head through it, and pressed her chest against the ledge, bearing down, bearing down hard – until the physical hurt cancelled out the emotional pain. Moments later, when she turned back into the car, she had regained her self-control. She took a handkerchief from her bag and dabbed her cheeks. 'No,' she said. 'No, it was a very long time ago.'

Paul let go of her arm and pulled back to his side of the car, turning to gaze through the windscreen as he did so. Eloise shot him a nervous glance. The moment had passed. She breathed a sigh of relief, feeling the pounding in her chest ease. She had herself under control. Sometimes, although being mostly a disadvantage – especially in a social sense – the condition she had and which, she knew, gave her her routines, her rituals, and her analytical mind, came in useful. Over the years she had been called cynical, calculating, frigid – especially that – but, as the saying went, every cloud had a silver lining.

After a while, Paul coughed and glanced across the car.

'Look,' he began, 'I realise that what I am going to propose is not the done thing, we having only just met...' He paused. 'Probably forward of me as well – but if you are not in a hurry to be off home, would you considered coming to my rooms for afternoon tea?' He paused again, studying her face, clearly gauging her reaction to his invitation. 'I do hope you will feel able to accept,' he added.

Eloise smiled at the old-fashioned reference to his flat as "my rooms" – and the formal "afternoon tea". Emily had received an invitation – and yes, she would like to accept it, on behalf of Eloise. But wasn't this supposed to be the age of modesty? Denying herself the almost overwhelming desire to accept him with a prompt "Oh, yes, please", she remained silent, nodding her head thoughtfully as she pretended to consider his offer.

Paul's eager expression vanished. 'No, no,' he continued, at length, still studying her face. 'I should not have asked.' He paused, shaking his head. 'Please forgive my presumption.'

Eloise continued with her pretence, pursing her lips as she looked him up and down. Finally though, allowing that he had suffered enough, with a smile, she said: 'There is nothing to forgive. I would very much like to; for I am sure that you are a gentleman and that my *reputation* will be quite safe.' She had almost said *honour* but felt that that would have been a tease too far.

Paul shifted uneasily in his seat. 'C'mon, then,' he said, restarting the car. 'It's not far: just past the station, near the university.'

Eloise already knew that but managed to stop herself from telling him so. 'Cool,' she said, smiling coyly.

He turned to her, grinning. 'I really like the way you say that, Emily.'

Chapter Twenty Three

Paul's flat was on the ground floor of a converted Victorian town house. The road that it stood in ran adjacent to the southern boundary of the university campus and – following the arrival of higher education and its accompanying influx of students to Exeter in the nineteen-fifties – many more of its other houses had also been converted into flats. Eloise remembered the flat as being a little bit drab, a little bit dreary – student accommodation in all but name – but that, from the sitting-room window, it gave good views across the nearby railway marshalling yard and river to the village of Exwick. If you had nothing better to do, you could always sit in that window and watch the world go by.

Paul unlocked the door and they passed through to the communal hallway. Eloise turned on her heel, remembering, recalling the layout. The area was painted in the Great Western Railway colours of chocolate and cream, and had always reminded her of a railway carriage, her feeling being reinforced by the railway prints that were hung along its walls. At the far right-hand end of the elongated lobby, a flight of stairs climbed to a landing and the flat above. To the left, across the pseudo railway coach, another door gave access to Paul's flat.

'It's this one,' Paul said, opening the inner door. 'I have to admit that it's a little small.' He let out a nervous chuckle and held the door ajar for her. 'Teacher's salary,' he added, as though giving her an explanation.

Eloise smiled. 'Don't I know it,' she said, following him into the inner hallway. 'And I bet it never gets any better either.' She fell silent, still smiling, gazing around, taking in the atmosphere, taking pleasure at being in Paul's "rooms". But then, of a sudden, she noticed his cricket equipment – and her smile faded. She stared at his bat and pads, his boots – and a holdall, which would obviously contain his "whites". It was all stacked against the wall, by the door – ready for the match this evening. Holding the frame of her spectacles in both hands, she continued to stare at it. It would not be used this evening. It would not be used again… Ever. If only she could snap her fingers and make it disappear, make it vanish like a prop in a magic trick, for then he would be unable to go to the match. Yes… She couldn't do that, but just suppose she could hide it, get a moment to herself, then sneak out here and move it, move it somewhere where he wouldn't find it… But where…

'The kitchen and dining room are along here,' Paul said, starting off down the hallway.

Jolted from her planning, Eloise followed him, pausing briefly to steal a glance in at the open door of the little box-room on the left, which she knew he used as a study. She saw that a number of books were piled on his desk and, even though it was now the school summer holiday, several exercise papers lay as if awaiting his attention. She recalled her first term with him… When somebody had put her piece on *Lady Chatterly* in to his review pile. She never found out who did that. Probably that big bully… Pamela… Pamela… What was her name? Eloise couldn't remember it. But clearly, Paul was preparing for next term, fresh pupils, new girls – but he wouldn't be there for them. Eloise turned away and skipped forward to catch up with him.

The combined kitchen dining room she recalled as being more practical than decorative, a memory that was now confirmed as an array of Formica worktops and cupboards greeted their arrival into the room. She inspected her surroundings. Sink to the right of the door, by the window, overlooking the rear garden – kitchen cabinet next to it; shelves on that wall... Golly!

Eloise crossed to the shelves. On one of them, propped against several books, was a photograph of herself, the one he had taken on the Cobb at Lyme Regis. She had forgotten that it was here. She felt the lump in her throat as fresh memories of that day came flooding back. That was the day when they'd found the fossil, and she'd driven the car up the hill... The day of their first kiss...

'That's Eloise.' Paul's words broke into her reverie. 'She's the girl I am going to marry.'

Eloise snatched the photograph from the shelf and held it up before her, her back to Paul, and all the time nodding her head like a crazed chicken, doing so in order to avoid having to turn around. It had been a mistake to come here. The day had been lovely, truly lovely: the Moka Café, the tour of the city, their time by the river, recollections, reminiscences. She should have left it at that, let him drop her at the station, said goodbye and... It could only go downhill from here. She continued to nod her head at the picture of Paul's young bride-to-be that she held in her hands.

'Please... please sit down,' Paul's words again interrupted her thoughts and, beginning to rein in her emotions, she slowly and deliberately re-placed the photograph, moving it imperceptibly to ensure its alignment to the front of the shelf. Several more seconds passed before she at last felt able to face him. But at length, breathing evenly, she turned back in to the room. He was gesturing to the small metal-framed table in the centre of the dining area, inviting her to sit there. There really was a striking resemblance to Alan Ladd. A sudden thought struck her then. Perhaps she could persuade him to let her go with him this evening, go with him in the car? Perhaps she could prevent the accident, save him? Or would she be killed too... Both of them die together? Yes; that was how it should be. She hadn't found a way to tell him who she was, but in doing that she wouldn't need to. Die together. A thrill tingled through her body at the thought.

She started towards him, her mind suddenly made up, her idea already crystallised in her mind. 'No, no,' she said. 'Let me help you.'

'All right,' he said, turning towards the food cabinet. 'I always eat simply myself, so I'm afraid that tea will not be an elaborate affair.' He paused and swung around to face her, running his eyes over her figure as he did so. 'And I imagine that you do the same, Emily.'

The suddenness of his turn caused her to stop dead in her tracks; and, under his scrutiny, she instinctively moved to draw her cardigan across her chest, only to remember that she wasn't wearing one.

'Yes,' she said, slightly off-balance. 'Yes, I always try to keep to a healthy diet.'

With another glance at her figure, smiling, Paul turned back to the food cabinet and pulled open the doors. Also smiling, Eloise reached past him and lowered the flap that acted as a temporary worktop – she hadn't used one of these in years. Her smile widened. Gosh, he really had looked her over though, had taken in every salient feature of her body.

She pulled open another drawer and scooped out a handful of cutlery. If she hadn't known him better, she would have thought that he was about to make a pass at her.

They had chatted casually throughout the meal, and Paul had spoken of his interest in photography. On this subject, having visited Hinton Lake's photographic shop earlier in the day, Eloise had been able to discuss the "latest" cameras and lenses with some authority – although at one point in the discussion, she had only just managed to stop herself from mentioning digital cameras. It was so easy to relax and talk with him, and that made it all the more difficult to edit out things that she knew he would know nothing about. But it had been a lovely conversation all the same; just like old times. In fact, her whole experience in his "rooms" had been perfect. But now, as between them they shared the clearing up, she could see from his expression that he had something on his mind. He had mentioned the school board of governors again, albeit in a light-hearted way, and now she thought that perhaps he still connected her with them.

Paul placed a cup on the draining board and turned his head towards her. 'Do you mind awfully if I ask you a personal question, Emily?'

Eloise experienced her pulse respond to the butterfly feeling that the question had evoked. Obviously she had no idea what he wanted to ask her, other than that it was a personal question – and that could mean almost anything – but she sensed that it was not going to be an easy question to deflect. She had noticed him glance at her figure again, several times. But to be fair to him, on that score, that was quite a natural process; most men did it. All the same, Eloise prepared herself for a proposition. But what would she do if she received one… A sexual one? She smiled inwardly. Now, Miss James, that was a daft question. She picked up the cup and started to dry it, instinctively moving towards the table, where she had placed other items of crockery. 'I'm not telling you my age,' she said. She laughed nervously and glanced towards him, trying to smile. 'All right then, fire away.'

For a moment he seemed confused – possibly it was the trite joke about her age or, perhaps, her expression "fire away" that had caused his puzzled look. But whatever it was, he remained silent, his eyes studying hers.

She laughed again. 'No, I don't mind,' she said.

Another second of thought passed, before he lowered his gaze to the cup, still clasped in her hand. 'It's nothing really,' he began, thoughtfully. Eloise's hopes nosedived. 'But I have been wondering if you… oh, I don't know… have been away from Exeter for some time.' He paused to fish some cutlery from the washing up bowl. 'It's just that when we were driving around the city, you appeared like someone witnessing the sights… oh, not for the first time, and not even like someone seeing them after a long absence…' He paused again. 'At times, you were extremely sentimental.' He placed each piece of cutlery singly on the draining board. 'It was almost as if you were seeing them as they used to be after having seen them changed to something else.'

He had always been astute, perceptive, had that knack of "knowing", and he had always been able to read even the slightest change in her mood. And, while some people hear what they want to hear – or expect to hear – he had always been attentive to what was said. Clutching the tea towel to her chest, Eloise turned from the draining board and caught his gaze. This was her chance: she wouldn't get a better one.

'Your guess is correct,' she replied: 'I have been *away* for a long time.' She felt herself sway as his eyes held hers. 'But *nothing* I've seen today has changed since my childhood.'

For a long moment he gazed at her, and then his brow furrowed ever so slightly. 'I'm not sure what you mean... some things must have...' And at that moment a clock in another room commenced to strike the hour – and he fell silent, listening as the clock chimed four times.

Suddenly nervous, suddenly scared, Eloise's resolve failed her. 'It's been a lovely afternoon,' she said, seizing the opportunity given her by the timepiece, 'and I don't wish to appear rude, but I should be going home.'

'And I have a cricket match to prepare for this evening,' he said, smiling.

She smiled back at him, relaxing as the throbbing of her pulse faded in her ears – coward... But hadn't she always been? She had never taken her opportunities – and now this one was gone. If this had been Charlotte, she wouldn't have hesitated. Her dearest wish had come true and she'd thrown it away.

Yet somehow – possibly in the intimacy of their conversation – they had come closer together. There was now no distance between them – and their eyes seemed even closer still, as if... Suddenly, she knew what to do; at least she knew what she wanted to do. Then, just like she had done all those years ago on the hill at Lyme Regis, she reached up and put her arms around his neck and kissed him, rising on to tiptoes as she brought herself to him, and all the time thinking nothing other than what a great guy he was and what great times they had together. The feeling was delicious and she let the kiss go on and on, thrilling to the feel of his lips moving on hers as he responded to her passion.

Unlike that first time, when he had broken the embrace, this time it was Eloise who eventually released him, fearful that any delayed opening of her eyes would cause him to vanish like some spectral fairy-tale prince, and she would be left kissing her pillow.

But he had not vanished, and she tilted her face to him again, waiting for him to kiss her, waiting... But he appeared spellbound, like an image frozen in an instant of time, still shaking from the click of the camera, unable to respond with anything other than his stare. Then she saw that stare widen, saw his lips move silently, as if he were trying to form a question, yet at the same time being unaware of what that question should be.

'Don't say anything... Please, not yet,' she said. She had in truth been here before, in a dream, but never further. This time seemed much different, but it did not stop her from being terrified lest a word should break the spell and smash the image and, with it, her heart to smithereens.

He caught her hands in his, his fingers entwining with hers, and held them at her sides. She tilted her head towards him again, waiting and wanting to be kissed. A long time ago, a lifetime ago... Last Saturday, she had told him that she would be here, *whatever it took*. Well, she was here. Then *he* kissed her.

Eloise entwined her arms round his neck, pressed her body against his, drowning in the whirlpool of his mouth on hers. Finally she knew why she was here. Then she felt him lift her and carry her through to the bedroom.

In her mind's eye, Eloise stood on the rug in Miss Staidler's study, tentative, nervous, but nonetheless kissing him back as she felt him reach down and start to unfasten her gymslip.

There could really be no going back now: the commitment had been made; the contract had been sealed. As Charlotte had written in her essay on Mrs Simpson, "She had passed the Rubicon". Eloise was going to lose her virginity – and good riddance to it. It was overrated: an unnecessary encumbrance to a loving relationship, a barrier to the expression of one's feelings. Hanging onto it… keeping it for the marriage bed was a religious con trick – no better or worse than a nun keeping herself pure for Jesus. Eloise smiled and closed her eyes. "Farewell and ado to you fair English maiden, farewell and ado to your fair maidenhead. For I am entranced by my dear Mr Bridgestock, and in less than a trice we will both be abed". Unclosing her eyes, she caught a sidelong glimpse of her blazer slung over the back of the chaise longue, the school badge and crest having creased in falling so that the eagle's eye appeared fixed in a permanent frown of disapproval at her youthful audacity.

But what would the other girls in class say if they could see her now, about to do it with Sir? She could guess what Pamela Palmer would say. "The apple worked then, Eloise". Childish girl. Somebody like Charlie would have introduced a cherry into the metaphor. But it would certainly give them something to talk about – gossip. They didn't even know that they were going out together, not in this sense anyway – merely as members of the camera club. Charlotte did of course. But even she would not have guessed at this.

He finished unfastening her gymslip, then pulled the garment up and over her head, and dropped it on top of her blazer. There, that had blinded that silly old eagle, had stopped it from seeing what was going on. She started to unbutton his shirt. But even if Charlotte and the other girls guessed this much, they would never believe her daring, her forwardness, would never believe that she had taken an equal part in "going all the way". But of course she had; she had kissed him first. Even though it had been a spur-of-the-moment thing, spontaneous, she had taken the lead. And now – right now, this minute – she was helping him to take his clothes off. She wondered then if there had ever been a time when Mary had undressed Percy. Such a thing did not seem likely.

He loosened her tie and unbuttoned her blouse, placing that on the back of the chaise longue too. All that was left to come off now was her underwear. They all thought that butter wouldn't melt in her mouth, that she was little Miss Innocent. They would all say that Mr Bridgestock had abused his position, that he had taken advantage of her – that he had seduced her. But if it did come out, she would have to set the record straight: she wouldn't let him take all the blame. Yes, but she was under-age. She puffed up her chest. Below the legal age of consent – his fate would be sealed… And he had such a fine physique; delineated muscles and none of that horrid hirsuteness that a lot of men were said to have.

He started to take off her suspender belt, not realising that her knickers had to come off first – although he succeeded in sorting out the order of things in the end. Silly boy. How did he think she used the lavatory? If she had to undo her suspenders every time, it would take for ever. Silly-billy. And now she had to help him with the clasp of her brazier. Of course, things would be different in class from now on, but she must never show it though, must never give any hint to anyone of the altered state of affairs. She started to unbutton the fly of his trousers. If girls could wee-wee like boys, there would be no problem.

He was careful with her stockings, rolling them down her legs so as to avoid causing ladders. She had never been naked in front of a man before – except for Dr Shepherd, but that was different of course. And, anyway, he hadn't undressed her – as Paul was doing now. There was a lot of fun to be had in that; he was doing it with purpose, concentrating, being methodical… Working his way towards the endgame. And she knew that once he had finished, he would be ready to begin, ready to begin making love to her.

She had once seen her parents making love, by accident – that was, it was an accident that she had seen them making love, not that they were making love by accident. Although, it might have been an accident, for Miss Staidler had once told them that most accidents occurred in the bedroom. But that was a bit arcane, left too much for their imaginations. None of them had really understood what she had meant – and none of them had had the courage to ask – even Charlotte. Her parents' bedroom door had been ajar and she'd heard noises and peeped in. At first she hadn't realised what they were doing. You never imagine that your own parents do it – although of course they must have done. Your friends' parents, yes, but not your own. She hadn't seen much anyway, because the bedclothes had been in the way. But her father was supporting himself on his hands, his arms straight and rigid so that he was a long way above her mother, distanced from her. But his face had been expressionless, blank, like he wasn't really there, as though he were an automaton performing a perfunctory task – and only the bedclothes moving above where his bottom was giving any hint of what was going on.

Paul still had his underpants on, but it would be best if he removed those himself. She didn't wish to appear forward. There might be a time and place for that – but she didn't think this was it. Restraint and decorum were required now, otherwise he might think her coarse. Eloise had told Charlotte what she had seen, and Charlotte being Charlotte had picked up on the funny side of it and made asides about Percy poker face and passionless Percy. They really were childish jokes, but they had both laughed till their sides hurt all the same.

She could feel him against her now, and they were kissing again. If truth were known, the other girls in class would be jealous, would envy her adultness, her maturity… Her sophistication. Even Charlotte would be piqued, for her friend was always the one who found things out first, who was the precocious one. That may be true. But even so, Eloise had always found herself more confident, more adventurous, with Paul. She could do things with him that would be impossible with anyone else. That was person-specific precocity – and that was almost as good. Thinking about what they were doing now, it was better.

She felt him place his hands over her breasts, pressing them so that her flesh ballooned on either side of his palms. If he wasn't careful, he would push her over. Then she felt him spread his fingers, stretching her aureoles so that her teats rose above his knuckles, like mountain-tops peeping above clouds. And then he lowered his head, and then… And then… And then he began to lollipop them. Mummy… She screwed her eyes tight shut. Her legs felt unsteady, and if he didn't stop what he was doing she was going to fall down. Making love was even better than she had thought that it would be. He was probably disappointed with her size though. After all, Charlotte's brother had said that big was best. But Peter was just a boy, a year younger than Charlie, and most likely had only repeated what he had heard someone older say. Young boys were like that. And then she experienced his hands descend in a taut embrace across her waist and on to the swell of her hips.

He reached behind her and cupped her orbs in his hands, lifted them, drew them up, holding them there, causing a tugging somewhere else. Eloise stifled a giggle. Charlotte had started that off: referring to her bottom cheeks as orbs – ever since that night at Exmouth when they'd gone swimming in the nude. Too silly. Then he released them suddenly, letting them fall, so that they whirly-gigged as the flesh settled, and all the time the tugging somewhere else… Until her bottom stilled. It would be better if it was not quite so wobbly. She had trouble getting dresses that fitted – separates were all right of course. And she was always being teased about it. Then he lifted her orbs again, pulled them right up, so that the tugging sensation was quite taut – held them there while he kissed her. And it was like something was feeling to happen, like she wouldn't be able to stop whatever it was that was going to happen if he didn't stop lifting her bottom like this. But he didn't stop. He lifted her orbs even higher, so that she rose on to tiptoes. She was going to wee-wee. Then he dropped them again, and the whirly-gigging, and the tug, tug, tug, tug. It was nice. She liked it. And it made her want to go on.

Eloise allowed herself to be guided to the chaise longue and lowered onto the seat, lifting her head as he placed a cushion beneath her. Should she open her legs, or would he do that for her? The last thing she wanted was to appear too eager. She decided to wait and see what he did. Decorum would remain her watchword. But any moment now, she was going to lose her virginity. She supposed then perhaps they really should have waited until after they were married. Her mother had said that virginity was precious and should not be given up lightly; that throughout all known history and all known cultures, unchaste girls had suffered nightmares of misery on their wedding night because they knew they had let their husbands down. But Eloise had guessed that all the husbands would have already done it. And anyway she loved him; and he loved her – and that was really all that mattered. Besides, she was almost an adult, would be off to university soon. Plenty of her contemporaries there would have done it.

He lay beside her on the chaise longue, and she watched as he placed one of those things on himself, like the ones that Charlotte had brought into school from home; they had tried to figure out how they worked. The basic principle had been straightforward enough, but none of them had been able to fathom how they stayed on. Charlotte had thought that an elastic band or a piece of string might have been the answer; and Betty Parkinson had suggested glue. But both ideas had seemed a bit fussy, a bit Heath Robinson. Of course none of them had been able to ask their mothers for fear of being suspected of doing it – or, at least, of thinking about doing it. But from what Eloise could see now, it appeared that they just stayed on, rested in place… It would be horrible if it fell… He kissed her again, and then placed the heel of his hand on her pubis, moving it in little circular orbits, so that she wanted to cry out but couldn't because he was kissing her. Oh, she mustn't wee-wee on his hand. He swung his leg over… And it was ever so funny, because he reminded her of a great big bird of prey as he settled on her… Or perhaps it was more like Count Dracula in one of those horror films, when he folds his cloak around his victim. It was nothing like when she and Charlotte played their games. Then he told her to suck his finger, and then she felt him reach down... He was ever so gentle. And a last inquisitive peek down between them was all that she needed.

And now they were doing it. And it hadn't hurt like Charlotte had said that it would... only the surprise – nothing more than that. But, then, Charlie was given to exaggeration. And he loved her, was loving her, and would always love her. And how would Charlotte know, anyway? And she loved him, was loving him, and would always love him. Charlotte had never done it. And Eloise was so grown up. And they were loving each other. Loving each other together. And he would always love her. They would be married, would have children... And he told her that he loved her. And... Oh... And...

And they were swooping down the hillside, down the hillside with the primroses, raiders on angels' wings. Sailing down the hillside with the primroses. Everywhere primroses. Heaps-full. Hands-full. Mountains-full. Golden yellow. Golden yellow primroses. Torrents of golden yellow primroses washing down the hillside, washing over her, engulfing her in their joy – a deluge of dazzlingly colourfully fragrant sparkling flooding primroses. Oh thank you mummy. Thank you mummy! Golden yellow primroses merging into golden heaven. Topsy-turvy golden yellow primrose wonderment, raining down on them from a sky of golden primrose yellow – down the primrose path.

Primrose (-z) *n:* Plant of genus *Primula* (esp. *Primrose Vulgaris*).

I shall the effect of this good lesson keep
As watchman to my heart. But, good my brother,
Do not, as some ungracious pastors do,
Show me the steep and thorny way to heaven

Whiles like a puffed and reckless libertine
Himself the primrose path of dalliance treads
And recks not his own rede.

1.

Eloise watched Paul carefully peel the sheath from his penis. But what if her mother found out? She wouldn't though. But suppose that she did. But she wouldn't. She might. But how could she? Yes, but just suppose that she *did* find out… Just suppose. Eloise saw that the little pod at the end of the sheath was filled with seminal fluid. There would be a scandal. She would be taken out of school. Paul would be dismissed from his post, his first teaching post, his career in ruins; for they would all blame him, say that he had seduced her. Eloise watched Paul walk across the study, open the door and disappear into Miss Staidler's lavatory. But her mother would not find out. No, she wouldn't. But just suppose that somehow – like mothers do – that she just knew. That reading between the lines of an unguarded remark, or a telltale look, told her what had gone on. Eloise heard the lavatory flush. She would be sent away to some distant relative – would miss out on university. She would be disgraced, a disappointment to her mother, a disappointment to her father. Eloise watched Paul came back into the study. Her mother mustn't find out… her mother must not find out.

Afterwards, they dressed and went back to the dining room. Paul made them another pot of tea, although time until they would have to leave was running short. But the ambience of the afternoon seemed now so leisured, so relaxed. It was as though time were being drawn into one of those dark places

[1.] Ophelia, Hamlet I. iii. 50

of the universe, decelerating, and so making everything run in slow motion. Eloise glanced at the clock on the mantle. If only its hands would come to a complete standstill, and they could stay here, together, for ever and ever – for always.

She gazed across the table at Paul. In the wake of what had gone before, he now seemed pensive, subdued, preoccupied with his own thoughts. She had been certain, when she had kissed him earlier, that he had known who she was – although that idea now seemed ridiculous. But it had been an odd moment. His expression… It was probably the shock of being kissed. She was back to where she'd been before they'd made love. But perhaps he regretted having made love to a woman that much older than himself. Although that wasn't how she had seen their lovemaking. Incredibly, during that time, she had become his Eloise. She thought for a moment. But, in a way, it wasn't really so unusual: it was little more than what had happened with some of her other partners, when, for her, they had become Paul. She stole another peep across the table. But he was certainly musing on something, weighing some concern in his mind. His silence was making her feel embarrassed, as if she had done something wrong. She noted his downcast stare, his eyes avoiding her own. Was he feeling guilty about having made love to someone he had met only for the first time this afternoon? Thinking about it now, she was surprised, shocked, that he had so easily done that… Sex with a stranger… A casual pick-up…

'I am afraid that we must hurry.' The sound of his voice startled her from her reverie. 'You have a train to catch, and I have a cricket match to go to.' He glanced at his watch. 'Robert is picking me up at six.'

She could ask to go with him, as she had earlier thought

about doing. She wanted still to do that. For despite what had happened, their lovemaking, the absence of which had plagued her all her life, she was still here: surely then there was something more for her... something more that was required of her. If she went with him, was there perhaps a way that she could prevent the car crash? Eloise raised her eyes to meet his. 'I was wondering if... wondering if perhaps...' She fell silent, her gaze glued to the image of the man she had never expected to see again.

'Yes?'

She continued to gaze into his eyes, willing something – she did not know what – to take control, to bring everything to a satisfying conclusion, so that *they* could live happily ever after. Eloise took a deep breath. 'I was just wondering if I could come to the match with you?' There, she had said it. She shrugged nervously. 'I've nothing planned this evening... And... And it would be fun.'

Paul stared at her, his expression wide-eyed, as if her request had caught him off guard... Rather as if it were a superfluous question, an unnecessary question, the answering of which would do no more than delay his preparations for going to the match. 'There won't be room in the car,' he said brusquely, rising from the table. 'Besides, as soon as the match is over, I want to see if I can find out what's happened to Eloise.' He paused, eying her piteously, as if she were a simpleton, a simpleton who lacked even the basic grasp of etiquette, of common sense. 'She is my fiancée, you know.'

Eloise felt a pang sting her heart – and just for a moment, she actually was Emily. 'Ah,' she said, 'I want to–'

Then the doorbell rang.

'That will be Robert,' Paul said. He glanced at his watch again. 'For once, he's on time.'

He gazed around the room, impatiently, then started to gather together several items; some loose change from the cabinet, a comb, and his jacket. Then, taking her by the arm, he led her out of the dining room and into the corridor. Eloise glanced over her shoulder, held back, tried to get a final glimpse of the room through the open doorway – but it was too late. It was all going too fast. Paul was in a hurry – and she was being dismissed. And she hardly had time to register her humiliation as she felt him begin to usher her along the passageway, past the box room on the right, towards the front door, towards where Robert waited with the car in the road outside.

They arrived at the end of the corridor. Eloise gazed forlornly at Paul's cricket equipment. She hadn't found an opportunity to hide it. It was too late now. But then, abruptly, she felt Paul draw up, release her arm, and start off back down the corridor again.

'Won't be a moment,' he said, over his shoulder.

Eloise stared after him, watched him disappear into the dining room. Had he changed his mind, decided not to go to the match? But why would he do that? There was no reason why he should. She was just being optimistic – hoping for a miracle. He had probably just forgotten something, that was all. She swung back to his sports gear. But where could she hide these? She would have to be quick: whatever he had gone back to fetch, wasn't likely to take him long to collect. Her eyes started to scan the area.

Then the doorbell rang again.

'Let Robert in for me, Emily.' Paul's voice came to her down the corridor.

Eloise ignored the request. There might be somewhere in the room at the front of the flat. Failing that, she could always throw it out the window, into the bushes. But Robert was out there…

She glanced across the hallway, to the door that let into the front room. There wasn't much time. She reached down and gripped the holdall, started to lift it… And at that moment, Paul came down the corridor. She placed the holdall back on to the floor.

'Here you are, Emily,' he said, holding aloft her shoulder bag. 'Mustn't let you go without this.'

Eloise took the bag, then watched as Paul picked up his cricket items. She started to open the door to allow Paul through. It was a doomed idea anyway: someone in his team was bound to have had some spare equipment.

Chapter Twenty Four

Paul held the front passenger door of the car open. 'C'mon, Emily, hop in,' he said, brightly. 'We'll drop you off at the station.'

But Eloise hung back, her eyes fixed on the Ford Consol. How she hated that car, had hated its memory ever since… Now here it was again, and she was being asked to ride in it – in the front seat. She stared in through the door that was being held open for her, at the speedometer, at the steering wheel… At the clock on which time was being counted down, the minutes ticking inexorably away. But it was almost as if the vehicle were a sentient being, had a life of its own – was in some way human, capable of thought, capable of planning, scheming, capable of destroying other people's lives. She'd even worried, after the crash, that the metal might be reused to build another car, and that the evil would in some way be transferred with it. But of course, that wasn't possible – and it wasn't the car's fault anyway. For how could you blame a machine? That was irrational. She always had though. But if anyone was to blame, it was the driver – he had been driving too fast. Yet he was only partly to blame: it wasn't entirely his fault: the other car had pulled out in front of them.

'C'mon, Emily,' Paul repeated. He glanced at his watch. 'We cannot afford to be late for the match – our supporters are expecting me to bat a captain's innings this evening.'

But still Eloise hesitated, her eyes now fixed on Paul's friend Robert who was sitting in the driver's seat of the vehicle. Until they got to the station, Paul clearly intended to sit in the back, with his other two friends. Then, after they had dropped her off, he would take his place in the front passenger seat.

'Emily!' Paul's voice came again.

Eloise removed her spectacles and pretended to clean them with the lapel of her frock. 'I think I'll walk,' she said. 'It's not far and…' Then she had an idea. If, when they got to the station, when Paul got out of the car to change places with her, she could distract him, could distract him for long enough to get one of his other friends in the rear seat to go into the front, then Paul would have to get into the back… And… 'Sorry,' she said, stepping into the vehicle.

'That's a good girl,' Paul said. 'There's no sense in walking when you have chauffer Bob's limousine at your disposal.' Then, barely giving her time to gather in the skirt of her dress, he slammed the door shut behind her.

Eloise turned to glance over her shoulder, to see Paul, as she had guessed that he would, squeeze into the back of the car, beside his other two friends. Then she heard him say:

'C'mon, Bob. Step on it, we're already late.' And with that, the car lurched forward.

Eloise half turned, instinctively reaching for the seatbelt, but only, a moment later, to return an empty hand to her lap. Somebody in the rear of the car had clearly noticed her futile gesture and had read it as a sign of her anxiety, for she heard him call out:

'Slow down a bit, Bob. Our lady passenger is of a nervous disposition. We can make up the time later.'

It was less than a mile to the station, and as the car

headed up the hill towards the clock tower, Eloise hurriedly prepared her plan. One of the boys in the back, Edward, she knew was studying medicine. Therefore, when she was getting out of the car, if she pretended to slip, made as if she had sprained her ankle, then surely he would get out to help. She would then detain him for as long as possible, at the same time blocking the way into the front passenger seat... Until Paul – impatient to get on with the trip to Exmouth – got back into the rear seat again.

Eloise held onto the dashboard as the car negotiated the junction at the clock tower end of Queen Street. There was the station, just up there, on the left. But yes, the plan might work. She reached again for the missing seatbelt. Yes, it might... But she would have to make her fall look authentic, if she were to fool Edward. She could manage that all right though: she always shone in the school plays. Geoffrey had once likened her to a female Ralph Richardson. Eloise glanced out the rear window at a cyclist who was shaking his fist at them after being all but flung from his bicycle by their breakneck advance along the thoroughfare. But the thing she was planning flew in the face of all morals – all ethics. It was tantamount to murder – murder by proxy. She was sitting here calmly plotting someone's death. If her plan worked, someone other than Paul would be killed. It was all very well to save Paul, but at the expense of another person's life? She was in effect exchanging his death for someone else's.

Then, quashing any second thoughts she might have been entertaining from her mind, the car pulled up in front of the Central Station.

As she had expected, Paul got out and opened the passenger door for her. She glanced down at the pavement.

Robert had stopped the vehicle about a foot from the kerb, so if she stepped out on to the road, turned, and–

'Take my hand, Emily.' Eloise looked up, to see that Paul had extended his arm into the car. No! She didn't want any help – she needed to slip, to fall; she needed for Edward to get out of the car, to make room for Paul in the back. Her plan was in danger of falling apart. Please, please take your arm away.

But Paul didn't, and reluctantly she grasped the extended arm, swung her legs on to the pavement, and allowed him to assist her from the front seat. Fate would not be cheated. But then, just as she was almost upright, Paul relaxed his arm, her trailing foot accidentally caught the edge of the kerb, and she tumbled forward on to her knees. Her plan was resurrected.

'Oh! Oh, my knee… Oh!' Eloise cried, scrambling to her feet and grasping her left knee in both hands. 'Oh!' Even to her, her cries seemed exaggerated. If Geoffrey ever found out about this performance, he would surely downgrade his opinion of her acting prowess.

Nevertheless, what happened next went off like clockwork; for, before Paul barely had chance to react to her distress, Edward had slid from the car and was propping her up. Paul's place in the rear seat had been created. Now all Eloise had to do was ensure that he took it, that Edward sat in the front.

'Are you all right?' Edward asked. 'That looked quite a nasty tumble.' He turned to Paul. 'You nearly dropped her,' he accused. He grinned. 'You had better not field in the Slips this evening.' Then, as a serious-faced Paul took over the job of holding her erect, he bent to examine her knees.

'Sorry. I am sorry,' Eloise said, gripping Paul's arm tighter. As if in some pain, she hobbled round, taking him with her, so that she was placed between Paul and the front passenger seat, blocking his way into it. 'Sorry,' she repeated, wincing pathetically, 'I'm keeping you from your game.'

Paul tightened his arm round her shoulder. 'It's me who should apologise,' he said, glancing briefly at the car, 'for being so clumsy.'

Edward, who had been obliged to pursue Eloise's earlier manoeuvre, straightened from his examination. 'The patella's definitely not broken,' he said. He dusted his hands on his trousers, then glanced at Eloise. 'Looks like you were lucky: not even a bruise or a graze to commemorate your trip.'

Just then there came a prolonged honk on the car's horn. Robert was impatient to get underway. But Eloise stood her ground.

It was time for Paul to get into the rear seat of the vehicle. But even though Eloise had blocked the entrance to the front passenger seat, he seemed stubbornly reluctant to do so. Please go into the back seat. Please... But he wouldn't budge, and kept throwing impatient glances round her to the other seat.

And then, in a slow motion, heart-stopping twist of fate, Eloise saw Edward climb back into the rear seat of the Ford Consol. Her plan hadn't worked. She watched, frozen in despair, as he gave her a brief wave, before turning to direct his gaze up the street.

It hadn't worked.

Paul gave her shoulder a little squeeze, then turned towards the car's open front passenger door. She felt his touch fading, felt his warmth leaving her skin as surely as he was leaving her. Her plan had failed. 'Goodbye,' she said, watching him getting into the filthy fucking car. 'Goodbye,' she said again. But it seemed such a trite expression, such a commonplace farewell. Goodbye. But it said it all.

Then she saw Paul turn to look through the side window of the Ford Consol. He deliberately caught her eye, held her stare. Had he changed his mind? Was he now going to let her go with him? Eloise felt the air rush from her lungs. She took a step towards the car. Then she saw him nod, wink his eye… and mouth the words: 'Thanks, Emily.' And with that, the vehicle lurched forward and accelerated off up the street.

Eloise stood on the pavement, staring after the disappearing car, her mind dazed, trying to interpret Paul's gesture. It didn't seem an appropriate thing to do. What was he thanking her for anyway? Surely not…? Paul wouldn't do that. She took several absent paces along the pavement. Then she saw the car turn left on to the High Street, heading for the Exmouth road. He probably meant nothing by it… Thanking her for her company this afternoon, nothing more.

But Paul was gone. She should have asked again to go to the cricket match with him, when they were all there, in the car together. He might have agreed, said yes, especially if she had been able to get the others on her side. And there had been room for her. The seats weren't individual ones, like those in modern cars: they were the bench type that went all the way across the car, seats without body shaping, body moulding. There was plenty of space for her there… Yes, plenty… But, anyway, he had had something else to do after the match, hadn't he? Eloise persisted on the pavement, alone, staring forlornly up the street. Paul was gone; she had failed him.

In her mind's eye, Eloise saw the car leaving the city, accelerating along the Exmouth road. The boys were laughing, making jokes, looking forward to a good game, a few beers afterwards. She saw Paul demonstrating with a swing of his arms how he intended to hit a six. She saw

Robert take his hands off the steering wheel and emulate his captain's swing. 'Yes, right out of the ground and into the sea.' It all looked so jovial – boys on an evening out.

Eloise stood like a statue, still staring at the street corner, where she had last seen Paul. People passed by; cars passed by. Maybe if she flagged one down… chased after them… got them to pull over… No, it was too late for that now. But she'd been hopeless today, indecisive. Why hadn't she just locked him in somewhere… even told a policeman that he had assaulted her – had him arrested, locked in the cells? It would have been simple. She wouldn't have needed to tell her story, how she had got here, would not have needed to introduce complication. It wouldn't have taken much to get him arrested. 'Yes, Officer, he propositioned me, and when I refused, he assaulted me.' That would have been all that was required; that would have done it. Then later, when the crucial time had past, all she would have had to do was retract her complaint, and Paul would have been released. They would of course have arrested her: wasting police time, making a false allegation… or whatever they called it. But it would have saved his life; and they would have let her go eventually.

But would the timing have affected the outcome? Fate had decreed that Paul would die today… And he would. Eloise glanced down at her sandals, then blinked away a tear. So even if she had succeeded in preventing him from travelling in the car, in all likelihood he would have died in some other way. Fate could not be outwitted. Yes, but she could have at least tried, she should have had a go. The story of her life… Missed chances… Her character, her outlook on life: she was apathetic, a lazybones. She wasn't a doer: she had blundered through life just letting things happen to her.

She kicked at a tiny ball of silver paper on the pavement. But at least she had their afternoon. And then she saw once more the gesture that Paul had made, read the words that he had mouthed through the window as the car had sped away. Did she?

A nearby church clock started to strike out the hour then. She counted the leaden beats: four, five, six, seven. A motorcar accident had just occurred on the Exmouth road.

On the busy thoroughfare in the heart of the city, Eloise began to cry.

'Is anything the matter?' A stranger's voice. Eloise turned to it.

'No,' she said. She forced out a smile, then sniffed. 'No, nothing's the matter: it happened a long time ago.'

The stranger eyed her curiously, then shook his head and walked on.

After a while, she turned and walked the few yards into Rougemont Park. The flower borders still looked splendid. People still strolled the summer pathways, still relaxed on the benches, all enjoying the flower-scented air. She wandered along the path that she had taken this morning – now seeming a lifetime ago – to the little strip of green by the railings.

Just then a train droned into the railway station. Eloise watched the passengers alighting on to the platform, watched them walking towards the exits. She glanced back at the train. It was an old diesel locomotive – a local service connection from Exmouth. Some passengers were still getting off the train. But none of them knew that Paul had just been killed. They would read about it in the local paper tomorrow, but they were unaware of it now.

Suddenly tired, she sat on the grass and rested her head

in her hands. She was still here... Wherever *here* was. She would go to the police station in a minute and tell them her story. At least she would have somewhere to sleep tonight. She closed her eyes against the aurora of the evening sun, still high above the distant horizon of Dartmoor. It would be another fine day tomorrow.

Chapter Twenty Five

Eloise propped herself on her elbows and peered groggily around the room, at the wallpaper, at the curtains, at the chest of drawers – at the familiar surroundings of her bedroom. But... She was fully clothed, and it was daylight... And she still had her spectacles on. She stuck a hand out towards Geoffrey. He wasn't there. She glanced at the digital clock on the bedside cabinet... Sleep's befuddling cocoon fell away and her memory switched itself back on: recall – recollections of yesterday. They all came back – she remembered. But above all, she remembered meeting Paul in the Moka Café, going home with him and making love. Her initial thought was that she had dreamed it all, the whole day. It was incredible. But then, as she tidied her memories in her mind, she knew it had been too real for that. How many times had she pinched herself yesterday, doubted her consciousness? She recalled the overdose and how she had initially ascribed her dated surroundings to an effect of that. But her conclusion was, indeed as it had been yesterday, that she had time travelled.

In a little while, Eloise swung her legs over the side of the bed and sat upright. She had returned to the present to her relief: she hadn't really fancied sleeping in a cell at the police station. But how had she got back here? The last thing she could remember was sitting on that strip of grass, by the railings, where she had lost her watch. Instinctively, she glanced down at her wrist. The watch was there – she hadn't lost it. As if not believing the evidence of her eyes, as if visual evidence alone was insufficient proof to establish that it was actually here, here on her wrist, she grasped the wrist with her other hand. But it was. Like her, it too had returned to the present. She had worried about losing it, especially as Charlotte had bought it for her. But she had been right: she had been wearing it when she'd gone out. She checked the time against the digital clock. And it was still working, the time correct. It hadn't been damaged during its time away. That was interesting: the date was wrong. She checked it again, this time against her diary. It was a day out, one day behind today's date. During its time missing, it had lost one day. Eloise thought about that for a while: a day in limbo. It didn't make sense.

Following a shower and a change of clothes, she went downstairs to the study and switched on her computer, watched as it started to boot-up, waited until the sequence was completed, then tried the Internet connection. "Website found". It was working once more – which was just as well: she couldn't afford a new one. It was the same with the television set too – a multitude of digital stations all waiting to be viewed. But she wouldn't get rid of the old analogue set just yet, just in case – although the signal was going to be switched off soon so it wouldn't be of use for much longer anyway.

She picked up the telephone and dialled Charlotte's number. But it would be the middle of the night over there now. Better wait until–

'Hello.' Charlotte's sleepy voice confirmed her concern.

'Hi, Charlie. It's Eloise… Um… Sorry to…'

'Ellie!' Charlotte was immediately wide-awake. 'We've

been trying to contact you, ever since we lost the link yesterday. We tried all day. And the phone company was unable to help: all they could tell us was that the line was OK. And it was: we tried mother's number, and that worked fine. We've been so worried. Where were you?'

Eloise gripped the telephone tighter. I've been out with Paul. We met up in the Moka, as planned, then we went for a drive around Exeter in his old Morris Minor… And then we went back to his place and made love. She relaxed her grip on the instrument. Eloise knew that she couldn't tell Charlotte about it yet: it was too soon. She needed to get things straight in her mind before she did that. 'After the connection was broken,' she said, 'I went for a walk in the park. It was lovely weather; and I had a wonderful time.' She paused, gazing through the window. She would finish loading that basket with potatoes later, take them down to the refuge. 'Actually, I didn't get home until quite late… Sorry.'

'All day in the park?'

'Well, not all day there. I went to other places too.'

'And you're all right?'

'Yes, of course,' Eloise replied, holding the telephone to her ear and nodding. 'That headache thing yesterday, but tablets soon dispensed with that… Plus, as I said, the walk in the park.'

'And there's nothing wrong; nothing's happened to you?'

'I'm absolutely fine. Really.'

'We were concerned though, Ellie,' Charlotte said. 'It wasn't so much losing the phone connection – that's happened before – it was more the feeling of… you know, when I phoned yesterday.'

'Oh, that: that's your imagination.' Eloise frowned, remembering their row. 'But I got the impression yesterday that you were more concerned with getting Geoffrey and me back together. In fact, you seemed quite determined.'

'Yes, well... Perhaps I did get a bit heated... But, Eloise, it was only said out of concern for you... And sometimes you can be exasperating...' Eloise looked around the room: she would have to give the piano some attention soon, with the exam coming up. She wondered whether, if she placed the phone down quietly on the coffee table, she had time to practise a few scales – probably not. 'And as I said before,' Charlotte was going on, 'you and Geoffrey seemed made for each other. But anyhow, Ellie, if I upset you, I apologise.'

'There's no need to,' Eloise replied. 'You were right... as usual. You were always much smarter than me. You–'

'Oh shut up, Ellie,' Charlotte interrupted. 'You're as smart as anyone I know... when you're not being sentimental. You just need to get your priorities sorted out, decide what you what to do with the rest of your life. And *do* it.'

'You're right,' Eloise conceded happily. Then, suddenly, she had a wild thought, something from long ago that had latterly taken on new significance. 'Charlie,' she went on thoughtfully, 'do you think Paul was gay?'

After a longish silence, Charlotte replied: 'You should know, Ellie. You were going to marry him.'

'Yes, but what do you think?'

Another longish silence ensued, then Charlotte said: 'I never thought that he was... But I don't see what difference it makes now.'

'Do you remember once suggesting that he might be?'

'No.'

'It was that Christmas when I got my "A" level results. We were in the Moka and–'

'Christ, Eloise, that was ages ago.'

'Yes, but do you remember it?'

'No.'

'You don't?'

'I said no… I have no memory of it… But obviously you have.'

'Not really…' Eloise smiled, recalling yesterday. 'It was just that I wanted to assure you that he wasn't.'

'Leave the past alone, Eloise, and get on with your life. Anyhow, you know what time it is over here, and I'm going back to sleep.' Then Eloise heard a click as her friend put the phone down.

Eloise replaced the telephone receiver. No, Paul wasn't gay. She had known that ever since she was a schoolgirl. She realised then that she was feeling quite hungry. She hadn't eaten breakfast yet. In fact, she hadn't eaten anything since having tea with Paul yesterday. Eloise grinned. And who could say how long ago that was? She would… *A day in limbo* – an earlier thought rebounded then, came back and jolted her conscious like a returning boomerang. Eloise glanced at her wristwatch. It had lost a day, yesterday, because it hadn't existed then. She had time travelled to an era before digital technology had been invented. But could that really be it? Well, she had left home wearing it and she had woken up wearing it. It had been missing only at the crucial time – make of that what you will. You couldn't argue with facts. Eloise had convinced herself. She stood up and went through to the kitchen.

Shortly, Eloise sat on a high stool, her bowl of cereal on the worktop in front of her. It was Sunday, so breakfast today was cornflakes. Several decades on from her school-days and her mother's acceptance, and she still had her routines; she was still just as well organised. She glanced around the kitchen: a place for everything, and everything in its place. Like her breakfast cereal cupboard: Monday to Sunday – puffed wheat to cornflakes. And the other meals were similarly regulated too. You knew where you were like that. It took the guesswork out of life, made decision making easy. Geoffrey had found it quite amusing at first, but he had come to see the benefits of routines. Having a menu allocated to a particular day of the week had initially led him to worry about a lack of variety. And so she had challenged him, had listed the week's meals, and he had drawn up a spreadsheet: breakfast, lunch and dinner in one axis against the days of the week in the other. 'Golly,' he had said, staring at the data. 'No two days are anything like the same.' And then, after a moment of thought, he had looked up from the spreadsheet and added: 'And it must make shopping a lot easier too.' Geoffrey was a bright boy: he caught on quickly. But yes, he appreciated her routines now – although, there were some things that he refused to have ordered, to have prescribed for him: like the thing he had wanted to do in her classroom on the final day of term. He advocated spontaneity in that activity. Eloise smiled. But of course, she should have pretended to go along with him that day, called his bluff: that would have sorted him out. On the other hand, what if it hadn't. He would definitely have done it, she knew that, he would have made love to her. But he would have lost the argument: the nays would have had it… No they wouldn't: he would have returned to the argument sooner or later, when it suited him. At some point, he would have accused her of "being chained to the past… like a little puppy dog at the beck and call of a ghost".

She scooped up a spoonful of cereal, glanced out the

window. She would take those potatoes over to the refuge later… Dig some carrots for them, too. Geoffrey could be a little mischievous though… Impulsive… Even devil-may-care at times – like that time at Branscombe, when she had wanted to walk the coastal path to Sidmouth, by the steepest route. She'd done it with Paul once. But Geoffrey was a big man and had cried off, declaring that he wasn't going to "lug eighteen stones up there". And so they had walked to the village of Beer instead, which was closer, and even then he'd insisted on taking the beach route. Actually, she'd thought that he had been more attracted by the name of the place than by anything else. They'd had a nice time there, found a good pub… Had stayed too long though. For on the way back the tide had come in and they hadn't been able to get around the headland. She had suggested they go back to Beer, and then take the coastal path to Branscombe, where the car was. It wasn't so very steep going that way – more of a gentle slope. But he had said that they would wait until the tide had dropped a little, that it was on the turn, and they wouldn't have long to wait. And she hadn't had long to wait either, for he had started messing about, chasing her over the rocks, and getting fruity. Gosh, for a big man, he really had been able to move fast, scuttling around like a mountain goat and cutting off all her avenues of escape. That was because he had wanted something. She'd asked him to stop. But he hadn't and, before she knew it, they had been making love, right there on the beach, on a little strip of sand, tight against the cliffs, just above the high water mark. Obviously, with the tide right in, it was unlikely that anyone would wander by. But anybody walking along the cliffs would have had an auditorium view – funny though, but that thought had added to the thrill of it. But yes, he could be a bit naughty at times.

Eloise made a cup of coffee, and then sat down again. There were several things niggling her about yesterday, concerns that had hovered in the back of her mind ever since she had woken up this morning, but which she hadn't yet found the courage to tackle. They weren't so much about how she'd got there or the mystery of her wristwatch, she accepted those things; her anxieties had more to do with the actual day itself. She'd had a great time, seeing all those things from her childhood, the Moka Café, the old cinema and theatre, other sights... Of course she had settled the other thing: that sex thing that doctors had told her was the origin of her problem, and that Geoffrey had described as "the catalyst for your woes". But the subject that was playing on her mind now was Paul himself. Why for instance, after barely half an hour with him, had he asked her out, invited her to go on a drive around the city with him? Obviously he hadn't known who she was... just someone sitting at the same table, a stranger with whom he had started a conversation. To be fair to him, it was quite likely that his motives had been innocent. They had talked, struck up an accord, discovered shared interests, and he had offered her a lift to the station – a roundabout lift to the station. You couldn't question something that innocent. And Eloise wouldn't have done, had other things not occurred later to give it added significance, to lend it further consequence.

He had made love to her. Why? She had kissed him... Encouraged him... and clearly he must have read that as an invitation. But he had a girlfriend, a nineteen-year-old girlfriend whom he had come to the Moka to meet. Hadn't he thought about her when he had decided to have sex with someone else? Obviously not, because, to put it plainly, when his girlfriend had failed to turn up for the date, he had picked up a middle-aged stranger, taken her back to his flat, and had sex with her. Certainly it was the sort of thing that some men would do. In fact, given the right set of circumstances, you could argue that most men would – men were opportunistic in that way. But she would never have been persuaded that Paul was one of them. But Charlie had always said – when they were teenagers and finding out about boys – that male and female attitudes towards sex were different. She had been right, of course. And science had since proposed why this should be so. Eloise sipped her coffee, thinking, recalling a book she had once read. Its premise had been that, because a woman's opportunities to bear children are limited, in order to pass her genes on to the next generation most effectively, her best interests lie in choosing the best possible mate, in being discerning in her choice of partner. A man, on the other hand, can reproduce at will, and so to pass his genes on to the next generation, his best interests are served in having numerous partners, in promiscuous sex. But, even though the theory may explain the different drives of the sexes, it did not excuse playing around. Morals came into it too.

And this also bothered her. Paul had always been so moral, so respectable, so decent; a gentleman. Gosh, she had been the one wanting sex – but he had always said no. He had persuaded her they should wait until after they were married – and yet here he was taking the first opportunity that came his way. It was puzzling. He hadn't wanted to make love to his girlfriend, but it seemed that anyone else was fair game. Absently, Eloise dipped her spoon into her cereal. Yes, maybe it had been something like that, with wishing to maintain respect for his future wife. But if that were true, then what happened yesterday may have occurred on other occasions too… with other girls. Their time together may have been peppered with such instances. Eloise lifted her spectacles, gazed at the fuzzy scene beyond the window, then set them back down on her nose again. No, Paul wouldn't have done that. Life had made her cynical, that was all it was.

She recalled then the time years ago at Branscombe, when they had been sheltering from the rain, and she had masturbated him. It was the closest they had ever come to having full sex. Apart from that one time, it had been kissing only. She had thought a lot about it down the years. It had been a naïve attempt at seduction, and she had failed. But she had always considered it odd that he had said no, yet had let her do it all the same. He could easily have stopped her, but he hadn't. In fact, he had been quite compliant, even eager towards the end. When his orgasm had begun, assuming that that was the end of it, she had discontinued her ministrations, but he had urged her on, clutching her hand and resuming her movements until he was completely done. She smiled at her teenage innocence.

Eloise finished her coffee. She would pop round to Margaret's later and apologise for not calling in for the cup of tea yesterday. She glanced down at her clasped hands. But the thing that chaffed most in her mind, even more than Paul's willingness to make love to a stranger, was her final image of him winking at her and mouthing the words "Thanks, Emily" through the car window. The gesture was so characteristically masculine. She had felt humiliated by it – tainted by it. It was tantamount to offering her payment for her service. But she supposed that his behaviour had been influenced by the circumstances: he was with his mates, on a night out, he had just pulled, just scored… Maybe he had felt a bit smug… And then another thought occurred. Had he boasted to his friends about his Saturday afternoon conquest?

'Hey, chaps, that bird we just dropped off, well I bonked her… a right little goer.'

'But what about Eloise?'

'Oh, I love her; she's going to be my wife. This makes no difference to that. This was just a pickup… No difference to spanking the monkey really.'

'Didn't get her address did you, mate?'

Eloise slipped down from the kitchen stool. But of course it wouldn't really have been like that, not so coarse, not so flagrant, anyway. Paul would be able to explain, if he were here. She still loved him, she always would, and she was glad they had made love. Eloise would have to fetch those potatoes in, go round to Margaret's. But there was something else to do first.

She went upstairs to her bedroom then and collected Pal from the dressing table. The teddy bear was a bit moth eaten after all these years. She sat on her bed and held him in her lap. He had helped her a lot, had been a comfort through the worst times. Yes, he'd helped her a lot back then.

Then she took him up to the attic, opened the trunk where she kept her childhood keepsakes and, with a final cuddle, placed him inside and closed the lid.

And then she went downstairs and dialled Geoffrey's number.